The
Daughters of Ironbridge

The
Daughters of
Ironbridge

MOLLIE WALTON

ZAFFRE

First published in Great Britain in 2019 by
ZAFFRE
80–81 Wimpole St, London W1G 9RE

Copyright © Mollie Walton, 2019

A CIP catalogue record for this book is
available from the British Library.

PAPERBACK ISBN: 978-1-78576-763-0

Also available as an ebook

1 3 5 7 9 10 8 6 4 2

Typeset by IDSUK (Data Connection) Ltd
Printed and bound in Great Britain by Clays Ltd, Elcograf S.p.A.

Zaffre is an imprint of Bonnier Books UK
www.bonnierbooks.co.uk

*To my lovely Mam, my compass in
fair weather or foul.*

Prologue

The iron bridge glimmered in the moonlight. A woman trudged across it, carrying a precious package. She could barely walk, one foot dragging as she struggled to place it before the other, dry leaves crisping underfoot, her pale face wincing with every step. She peered up at the full moon, took some distant hope from it and looked down at the face of her child, asleep in her arms, wrapped in rags. She tucked the cloth tighter around her tiny baby, trying to protect it as best she could from the autumn chill. She could feel its bones. It was thin, too thin and too quiet. She had given her child every ounce of milk she could but it had dried up. She was too hungry herself to nourish her child. Weak and exhausted, she knew she could not go much further. With all of her will, she reached the centre of the bridge. The centrepiece stated the date it was built: 1779. Fifty-five years ago, just over a half century, since the town itself began to bloom alongside its namesake. Her master had been a boy then, a spoilt boy no doubt; that family always spoiled their children. It was why they all turned out that way, all turned out bad. She looked down at her babe in arms again.

'Not you, little'un,' she whispered, her throat hoarse from thirst. 'You'll be different. You'll be sunlight, not moonlight.'

She kissed her child's head and looked up at the imposing mansion, built on iron money, that loomed above the town, above the bridge, above them all. If only she could keep going. But her legs were now as heavy and immovable as stone. She had come to the limit of her endurance, the final shred of her strength gone. She heard footsteps. She looked up to see a man in a broad hat walking purposefully across the bridge. He was coming towards her and he was talking to her.

'Good woman,' he was saying, 'can I assist 'ee?'

Good woman, she thought. *I was a good girl, once.* Her thighs were shaking. She felt her knees buckle. 'Will you help me, sir?' she croaked. 'Please, hold my baby as I canna stand no longer.'

The man, who she now saw wore the simple, curious clothes of a Quaker, came to her quickly and took the child. The moment the weight of her warm bundle was lifted from her, it was as if her body knew before her mind did that it was time to rest. She felt her legs give way and the bridge came up quickly, the ground smacking her face with a hard, iron slap. She heard her child whimper in the kind man's arms. It was the last sound she heard.

Chapter 1

Fire and smoke, suffocating and infernal, reached up into the sky, staining it red and black for miles around. A traveller approaching Ironbridge and Coalbrookdale would be met with the wonder of it and stop to stare. The blast furnace belched with heat and life all day and all night, the whole year round. Men fed its mouth with fuel, men like John Woodvine, furnace fillers who nourished the monster to try and meet its hunger, but it was never satisfied. Always, the furnace wanted more. They filled the barrows with coke, iron ore and lime-stone, pushed them out along a gangway and tipped the charge into the boiling throat of the furnace. Inside, the heat did its magical work and out came molten iron in the cast-house below. Around them, the fire, smoke and gas billowed and blinded them.

A shift at the furnace was twelve hours of hard labour and in the heat of this summer, it was hard indeed. John Woodvine thought to himself, and not for the first time, *It'll be summat like this in Hell.* John would come home filthy with smut and ash and so exhausted of limb and heart, his wife Rachel and his daughter Anny barely had a word from him before he collapsed on their hard bed. Rachel would wake him to eat before he fell back into a dead sleep again till the birds about their cottage sang and day had come, then he would have to start it all again. Excepting Sundays, his one day of rest, when he could talk to Rachel and watch Anny grow and giggle, sweet child that she was.

'Woodvine!' shouted the foreman. 'Stop your dreaming, mon!'

John shook his head to rid it of his daydreams. A moment of distraction in this awful, dangerous place could be fatal. Men were injured here; blinded, lost fingers, lost arms, received dreadful burns from fire, steam or hot metal, suffocated, bruised and battered, limbs crushed. Some never recovered to work again; some died. You had to have your wits about you. He looked about him, focused his eyes and forced himself to concentrate. But he had a bad feeling that something was amiss.

'Look out, there!' someone shouted and John whipped around, terrified of what terrible thing was coming this time.

∞

Anny looked at her fingers. They were red raw from scrubbing clothes. They had welts from carrying the buckets back from the water pump, a third of a mile away. They were not even her clothes, or her parents' clothes either. Her mother took in washing to make ends meet. Anny did not go to school. She had been working for three years now, since she was nine years old. She looked up at her mother, careworn and sweating in the heat of a hot June day, as she pushed a shirt through the mangle, huffing and puffing.

'Let me do that for you, Mother,' Anny said and went to her, but her mother shook her head.

'I worry about your fingers,' she said, and shooed her daughter away. 'I canna have you losing your fingers.'

'Dunna be daft, I'm turned twelve. I anna got little fingers anymore.'

Her mother looked up at her and smiled. 'You're right. I always think of you as my babby. But you're a young lady now.'

Anny smiled then saw her mother's face fall. What was she thinking about, that made her sad? 'What is it?'

'Just thinking that I wish I could give you more, Anny.'

'But you give me everything. You give me all your love, every day. And you feed me and keep me warm.' She wiped the sweat from her brow. 'Leastways, too warm, sometimes!'

They laughed. But her mother was still frowning. 'And you taught me to read and write when everyone said what's the point of it, for a lass like me? But you did it anyway.'

'Yes, well, maybe they were right. What can you do with your book learning here? I was learnt to do it by my mother. But what could I ever do with mine, in this house, with these piles of washing ever biding for me and never seeming to lessen?'

'It's good we have plenty of washing. Because washing means money and that means we'll be all right.'

Her mother smiled proudly at her. 'Always the sharp one. Oh, but I wish you could be a lady, Anny. A proper lady like that Margaret King. You were born in the same month, in the same year. I wish I coulda given you everything she had.'

Anny wrinkled her nose in disgust. 'Oh, I wouldna want her life. Not all that curtseying and how-do-you-do. I wanna be here with you and Father.'

'Oh, your father! Your father's bait!' cried her mother. 'His slice of pie is there on the side. He forgot it this morning. Run and take it to him. He'll be clemmed without it.'

Anny grabbed the cloth-wrapped slice of fidget pie, his favourite. Her mother lovingly made a portable dinner for her father six days a week. It might be a slab of rabbit or pigeon pie, or if times were hard it would be filled with crow or sparrow. Or it might only be a Dawley doorstep, simply a hunk of bread spread with butter or sometimes cheese. Or if a pig they had shares in had been butchered, it might be his favourite: a thick wedge of the gammon, apple, tatties and onion pie he loved so much.

'You'd best hurry, lass!' cried her mother, but Anny wanted to do one thing before she went. She grabbed a stubby pencil from the stool beside the hearth where she would sit and write stories and poems of an evening. Taking a scrap of paper her parents saved up to purchase for her, she scribbled a quick note: *I love you more than anything, even more than cake!* She slipped the note inside the cloth and sped from the room.

Anny was thrilled to be away from the endless washing and the heat inside their tiny house. She ran across the dusty yard, their home flanked by six other dwellings shoved up against each other. She thought, *It's as if those builders wanted us poor folk to take up as little room in the world as we can.* Some of the neighbourhood wives outside their tiny houses looked up and saw her whisk by. One neighbour, Mary Malone, taking the scraps out for the pig, called to her, 'Lucky littl'un!' ribbing her for escaping work. 'Where are you heading, lass?'

'There and back to see how far it is!' cried Anny, and ran off. It was a bit bold, but folk didn't seem to mind her kind of cheek. They liked her clever replies. And people liked to smile at her. Her father always said she was a laughing lass, a kind one and sweet-natured. She knew she was not overly pretty, but she had an open, friendly face dotted with freckles. Her beauty was all in her thick red hair, as her mother would say, the colour of a fox's coat. She was clever like a fox too, though never sly. Some said that Woodvine girl was too clever for her own good.

Her mother had taught her to read and write. She had some ambition for Anny, but often said she could not see how any of them could escape the narrow confines of their situation as poor ironworkers. Her parents told Anny she was a ray of sunshine in that dark world of iron ore and coal dust and endless toil. Despite the hard work at home, Anny was always cheerful and took her greatest pleasure in anything that used her mind.

'Dear heart,' her mother would call her sometimes. 'One day you'll escape this place for good.' But Anny didn't want to escape it. Despite everything, she loved her life here by the river. As she moved through the trees towards the water, the air buzzed with summer heat and insect life. Butterflies fluttered along the banks of yellow and pink weeds blooming haphazardly along the riverbanks. On the river itself, a variety of craft passed by, barges, trows and wherries carrying people and produce and the odd circular coracle paddled by a fisherman apiece. The shouts of watermen and the clangour of the forges downstream rang along the banks, muffled only slightly in the thicker parts of the wood. The water flowed smugly along, lazy and warm that day. It seemed proud of itself, how it made life here possible for every living thing – water voles, rats, otters, ducks, moorhen, snipe, chub, shad and elvers – as well as the people who needed it to survive. For the mighty River Severn provided folk with water to drink and wash with, also transporting the goods and materials that industry swallowed and vomited out into the world from this leafy, deep-wooded part of Shropshire.

Anny trotted along the river path, enjoying her burst of freedom from the toil of washing. But her fun was short-lived, for the air grew thicker as she approached the furnace, filled with heat and the stink of industry. Soon she saw the blast furnace, set up above the riverbank, belching out cruel fire into the already sticky warmth of the summer afternoon, and the racket of the ironworks was roaring over her.

Anny climbed up the bank to gasp at the furnace. It never ceased to amaze her. She thought it awful, in the true sense of the word: a thing of awe. She was proud her father worked there. His seemed an important job, a vital one, sending iron out into the world to make pots and pans, railings and boot scrapers, hearths and grates, benches and balusters, window frames and sills, eaves and gutters, even bridges and boats. She clutched her father's lunch and stared at the crimson flames, felt the blast of heat in her face, before looking down to scan the figures around and about, searching for her father. But there was a big group of men all bent over something in the yard before the furnace, some shaking their heads, some waving their hands in distress, calling out to others who came running. Something was wrong. Something had happened.

Her pride in her father's work replaced with terror, she ran across to the huddle of ironworkers and tried to peer through the gaps between their backs. Someone was on the ground. She could see a man's legs poking out. They were still, very still.

'Who is it?' she said, but nobody could hear her little, high voice behind them. So there was nothing for it but to thump on the backs of the men closest to her. She simply had to get through this wall of men to see who was on the ground. Her fists pummelled them as she cried out, 'Let me through!' The bodies parted and she heard gruff shouts of 'What's this?' and 'Oi!' but she didn't care. She simply must know. She saw the man's naked chest, slicked with sweat, smut and matted hair and then, with a horrible shock, saw the bloody mess of his arm, burned and crushed. His arm was destroyed. But she had no time to be horrified, no time to feel sick or look away. She peered at his face, turned away from her, covered with black. They often joked that all iron-workers looked the same, their features disguised by filth when they worked. She bent over the man's face and felt her heart leap into her mouth. *Was it him? Was it Father?*

Chapter 2

Slap! Hard and swift, right across Margaret's cheek, catching a tooth against her lip, so she knew it would bleed afterwards.

'You will go to Grandfather's wake, you little wretch. And if you tell Papa I hit you, I will deny it and you know he always believes me over you.'

Margaret dabbed her fingers against her mouth and there it was: blood. She looked at her elder brother Cyril who saw the blood too and smirked proudly. He took pride in his ability to maim and wound, to hurt others in any way he saw fit.

'Now clean yourself up and present yourself down-stairs forthwith. You're an embarrassment to this family.'

Cyril turned on his heel and left the room, leaving the door open, as even door-shutting was beneath him. Margaret stood up from her bed and closed the door, catching a glimpse of a maid, Lucy, who gave her a quick, sad but understanding smile. She wanted to run to Lucy, even though she did not really know the girl. Lucy had a nice face and she felt Lucy would understand her and sympathise with her. Margaret had seen Cyril shout at Lucy, too, so she knew the girl must feel the same. But it was forbidden by her father to converse beyond what was strictly necessary with the servants. As an iron-master, Mr King would not countenance fraternisation between his daughter and that other breed of person, a lowly servant. Even the ironworkers were beneath him. He conducted all his business with them through his estate manager, Mr Brotherton, a chatty man with red cheeks whose booming voice frightened Margaret a lit-tle, though he was friendly. Lots of things frightened her. Margaret knew what a bitter disappointment she was to her father, knew she had caused great harm to the family, killing her mother in childbirth and thus was born cursed. She carried the weight of that daily.

'Now then,' she tried to comfort herself, inspecting her cheek in the dressing table mirror. She could powder it to cover the red mark. The bloody lip would be impos-sible to hide. She'd have to invent another clumsy fall, all too easily believed by her father. Her face powdered, she said aloud, 'That'll have to do.' She talked to herself from time to time, mostly because there was nobody else to talk to.

She left her bedroom and crept down the stairs, the hubbub of her grandfather's wake drifting up to her, filling her with her usual dread of social occasions. She liked gentle people, talking quietly to quiet folk. But her family's gatherings were always noisy, full of loud-mouthed relatives, sharp-faced and unforgiving. She knew she wasn't like them and she knew she was a disappointment. As she approached the door to the drawing room, she steeled herself and turned the handle. As usual, nobody noted her entrance and she was able to slink over to a chair in the corner without incident. The room was populated by a crowd of relatives all dressed in black, holding cups and saucers or tiny plates of cucumber sandwiches and thin slices of fruit cake. Her father – Mr Ralph King – was holding forth about his father – Mr Ralph King senior – who had been buried that morning. Margaret had not loved her grandfather. He was a bullying man. A few months ago he had had a funny turn and since then had been bedbound and wordless, with staring, accusing green eyes that disturbed her. Her father was saying what a great man he was, a pillar of the community. 'Beloved of nobleman and commoner alike,' said Mr King.

'Beloved? Stuff and nonsense. Not even I liked him. And I was his wife!'

An embarrassed silence fell over the room and Margaret stared at her grandmother, Alice King, the matriarch of the family and now its oldest member.

'After all, I only told him yesterday that he was a cold man, an iceberg of a man. He had no feelings. Like stone. Like ice. I told him that. Only yesterday.'

Nobody spoke. Awkward glances were swapped. Her husband had died over a week before. Grandmother could be sharp and cutting. But Margaret admired her for her straight-talking, no-nonsense approach to life. She wished so much that she was more like her. They said that when she married into the King family, she ruled it so imperiously that she earned the nickname Queenie, and it had stayed with her ever since. Margaret was a little afraid of her grandmother's moods, but Queenie was the only member of her family she could talk to. Their conversations were often brief, but at least her grandmother made time for her every now and then. At least Queenie did not seem so very disappointed in her shyness – she did not indulge it – but she seemed content to let Margaret be watchful and quiet, without punishing her for it, as her father and brother did.

'Mother . . .' Mr King began. When he pleaded with his mother, Margaret noticed that her father's voice was high and whining, which made her smile to herself. Only Queenie could bully Ralph King. This gave Margaret pleasure. She liked her grandmother, though she was somewhat odd, it had to be said.

'Mother nothing. He was a nasty old goat. Everybody knew it. Everybody is thinking it, but nobody has the nerve to say it. I'm glad he's dead. And so are you, Ralph. We all are. Good riddance to him. Now then, where are my meringues? I specifically asked Cook for some little hazelnut meringues.'

Queenie's latest rant over, the guests resumed their hushed discussions, now peppered with smirks at the way the great Mr King could never control his mother. Margaret watched them – utterly ignored and content to be so – wondering how people performed this magical feat called conversation. If she could master it, perhaps she could find a friend. But, schooled at home and with only a cruel brother for company, kept closeted away from the world and its ruffians and blackguards – as her father described it – there wasn't much chance of that.

Once the guests had departed, Margaret watched her father standing proudly before the fireplace, his shoulders back, his chest puffed out and his stomach sticking out the furthest before him. He was pleased with himself. The wake had largely been a success. The Mayor of the borough and his wife had attended, as well as a clutch of other local dignitaries. The service had been suitably sombre and the weather had held. She imagined Father would be most pleased that no summer rain had caused his new shoes to become muddied. He glanced over at his mother and his gaze narrowed. He would be annoyed at her, for embarrassing him. Margaret guessed her father had been hoping Queenie would have retired from a fit of fatigue, yet she had chosen to stay – nobody could tell Queenie what to do – but only because there were some hazelnut meringues left. 'She could eat and eat and never get fat,' he would say of his mother, with envy.

Then she saw her father pass his hand over his own rounded stomach and glance at his pretty young wife, Benjamina. This was the woman he had married two years ago, twenty years his junior. She was only nineteen years of age now, only seven years older than Margaret and five years older than Cyril. The Mayor had not been able to take his eyes off her. Her father smiled smugly, then breathed out quite sharply. Margaret wondered if he felt his trousers pinch under his bloated stomach.

Her father turned to look upon his beloved son. *My little prince*, her father would fondly call him. Cyril gazed up at him, awaiting his father's next words. Cyril's blond, unruly curls framed his permanently red, round cheeks. He was short of stature for fourteen, and Father sometimes told him he was 'a bit of a runt'. Cyril was slim and lithe, yet Father once said, 'I shall have to watch your treats. I can't have a fat hog of a son.' But despite his critical remarks from time to time, the boy seemed to fawn over him.

Then her father turned to look straight at her and grimaced. Whenever he noticed her, he made a face like that. She lowered her eyes, staring at her hands in her lap. She knew she was not unpleasant to look at. She could never be as handsome as Benjamina, of course, but she was considered quite pretty. She had the same blonde curls as her brother, yet much larger eyes. But she knew her lack of social graces was a bitter disappointment to her father. He said to her once, 'When you are a bit older, you'll have plenty of suitors. You are rich, after all. But will you be able to speak a word to them? Nobody wants a wife as silent as the grave. A quiet one, yes. That is agreeable. Nobody wants a scold. But not one who couldn't say boo to a goose. What am I going to do with you?'

Sometimes she wondered if he might prefer it if she never married. That way, she could wait upon him and Benjamina as they got older. She would stay in this house for the rest of his life, a useful nursemaid. Best of all, being family, there was no need to pay her a wage. The thought of such a fate sickened her. If only her mother had survived. Her poor mother, who had died bringing her into the world.

Her mother was a shadowy figure in her life, as her father never spoke of her. All she'd heard from him was that she was a 'weak, yellow-haired girl'. What a cruel description for the person who had been the centre of his world, who haunted Margaret with her loss. She thought she might cry then, as she considered her real mother, dying in childbed, lost forever. She wanted to slip away and go to her room, and weep quietly, alone.

But her father was clearing his throat, ready to make a pronouncement. Her grandfather used to stand just there and make those regularly. Now it was her father's turn, and how gratifying it must be for him, to step into his dead father's place and be the man of the family at long last.

'My children,' he began, closing his eyes for a moment to savour their attention. 'There is undoubted sadness at my father's passing, which I am sure you both feel

17

keenly too. But I must say that this is also a new beginning for us all. For myself, it is an opportunity to honour his memory, to prove myself worthy and take his place in society, that of one of the original and most powerful ironmasters in Shropshire.'

'Oh yes, Papa,' said Cyril. 'And I will take your place in years to come. Three proud generations of great and mighty gentlemen.'

'That is the right and true way of things,' simpered Benjamina, a picture in the latest fashions, lolling on the chaise longue. She could always be relied upon to agree with him. Margaret watched her stepmother pet her horrid little dog, a hot-tempered King Charles Spaniel called Chloe. She'd tried so hard to like her stepmother, as Benjamina was the only mother she had ever known. But this child-woman was as much like a doll as any woman who ever lived. She was in love with her lapdog and adored it more than anything else, apart from dresses and ribbons, and little cakes and sweets. Perhaps the worst thing about Benjamina was that she was another voice in the house that echoed Mr King's every whim. Margaret knew that wives must obey their husbands, but Benjamina's simpering ways seemed somehow false. She wondered what really went on in that empty head of hers. They rarely spoke to each other, because they had not a word in common. Margaret despised her. In fact, as she looked about her close family, she realised with a pang how much she hated all of them – excepting

Queenie – and then she felt guilty about such thoughts. But the truth remained: her family was dreadful and it made her ache with loneliness.

'Hmph!' began Queenie. Margaret turned to her with interest, eager to see what her disreputable grandmother would come out with next. 'There was nothing great about him. He was a sneak and a liar. Just ask the baby on the bridge. See what the baby on the bridge would have to say about this 'great' man, eh?'

'Enough, Mother!' shouted Mr King, then checked himself. 'Perhaps it is time for an afternoon nap.'

'I do not nap!' said Queenie, with disgust. Everybody knew she did have unofficial naps all the time, but never admitted it as she seemed to see it as a sign of weakness.

'Then perhaps you have consumed too much sugar and it has addled your brain. The things you come up with, I really don't know. Some might say they were the ramblings of an eccentric woman. You'll have to be careful, or others would say you need to be put away.'

Queenie turned her head sharply and narrowed her eyes at her son. 'Whatever you think of yourself, you will never do that to me. I control the money in this house. This house itself and everything in it belong to me, not you. And I have the controlling interest in the iron business, too. Never forget that. That was the meat of your father's will and well you know it. Despite being a weak and selfish man, he never liked you, and he trusted me. He knew I had a mind for business. So watch your step, my son. You and everything you think you own belong to me.'

Queenie's eyes were full of fire. But in a moment, she sighed and suddenly did look very tired. Lately she had that way, of being feisty and defiant, then losing interest in it all and changing her mind. Maybe she was a little touched after all, thought Margaret. But then she thought of this 'baby on the bridge'. Margaret had heard Queenie speak of this before in recent months, only ever a brief mention and a hint of something bad. Her father always reacted angrily, then twisted the subject. Margaret had once plucked up the courage to ask her grandmother, who was the baby on the bridge? But Queenie had just smiled, tapped her nose with one long, bony finger and said, 'That's for the squirrels to know.'

Margaret watched Queenie leave the room, accompanied by her lady's maid, Jenkins. Now was the time for her to slip out, too, but she knew her father would tell her off if she didn't formally ask permission. She noticed Cyril had already left a few minutes before, bored of his elders and free to come and go as he pleased.

'May I leave now, Papa? I am suffering from one of my headaches,' she said quietly.

'If you must, Margaret. You let me down again today. You did not even attempt to converse with our visitors. You really must improve yourself, or people will say you are indeed the weakling strain of the family.'

Her stepmother tittered.

'May I go?' Margaret whispered, desperate to escape.

'Yes, yes.' Her father dismissed her with a wave of his hand.

She left the room, crossed the hall and slipped outside into the courtyard. Her split lip was throbbing. Nobody had even noticed her injury, or at least no one had commented upon it. She was thankful for this, as she was not a confident liar and if she told the truth about Cyril, he would only make her pay for it later. But it left her feeling hollow, too, that nobody cared enough to ask after her. She tried to be a good girl, to do the things her father demanded of her. She did not defy him or anyone in the household for that matter. She was polite and helpful at all times. She tried not to get in anyone's way, even the servants. But she never received any credit for these virtues. They were silent graces, she supposed. Not so easy to hear as fawning and flattery. It was as if her true self were invisible, a ghost of a girl in her own home, her own life. Time for a walk. Anything to get away from that house, that family. To find a moment's peace.

She was permitted to take a turn about the gardens. She was not permitted to stray any further than that. Her father had expressly forbidden her from entering the woods 'where the common people go'. She had walked about the grounds so often these past years, she knew every bush, every flower, every blade of grass in the place. Beyond the boundaries lay the woods, the river below. How she longed to wander there, free of the pull of the house, of her family. But she never had.

What was stopping her, really? Would anyone notice if she strayed from the grounds for a half hour? She looked behind her at the windows of Southover, blank like blind eyes. Nobody was there. It wouldn't hurt, would it, just to have a quick look? There was no wall to climb over, no door to unlock. Just a quick step across the deep borders and around the boundary trees and she would be into the woods, deep, dark and unknown, as mysterious as an enchanted forest to Margaret. Many times she had thought of it, many times she had been too nervous to defy her father. But today, her hatred of her home and everyone in it was strong and the pull of the wilderness beyond equally so. Margaret decided to allow herself this small act of defiance. Today she would go into the forest. And explore.

Chapter 3

'Anny!'

She whipped round and looked up.

'Anny, get away from there!'

'Oh, Father!' she cried and threw herself at him, felt his strong arms wrap around her like they always had, ever since she was tiny and he could toss her into the air like straw. She was too big for that now – tall, lanky and a bit clumsy, as the other children often reminded her. But her father was tall, too, and he lifted her up off the ground and took her away from that place, that huddle of workers and the man with the ruined arm on the ground. He put her down away from the scene, nearer the river in a quieter place where they could talk.

'What're you doing here? You shouldna be seeing this, wench.'

'I thought it was you, Father. Oh, I'm so glad it inna you!'

She hugged him again, then added, 'That sounds wrong. That poor man. Is he . . . dead?'

Her father nodded, his eyes straying to the body on the ground. 'He was from Broseley. Three chillun at home. He was only young.'

Neither spoke. Anny thought about the children, who would never know their father. And what would happen to their mother now? *I'm still glad it inna my father,* she thought, then wondered if she were wicked, thinking like that.

'Here,' she said, and passed him the lunch she had brought, almost forgotten about in the drama. 'Open it.'

'I've lost my appetite,' he said, grimly.

'Just open it up, please?'

He did so and out slipped the note. He smiled, despite himself and the gravity of the scene.

'Oh, Anny, you silly wench. What does it say? You know I canna read a word of it.'

A man in a hat approached them. It was the foreman, Mr Pritchard. He was a nice man, despite being over her father. He never had airs and graces and he was fair with the men. Today he looked rather grim.

'Drodsome business,' said Father.

'Yes, bad business. We'll need to let the master know. He'll want an inquiry. But it's Mr King senior's funeral today. He won't want to be bothered with this. But he'll have to be. Oh, hell.' Pritchard drew his hand across his sweaty face, smudging the dirt, sighing all the while. Then he looked down at Anny and smiled. People always smiled at Anny. But then his face changed, when he remembered where he was and what he had to do.

'Hello there, Anny. You shouldn't be here, not now.'

'I just brought Father's bait. And a note.'

Pritchard looked to Woodvine's hands and saw the note there. 'A note, eh? You can read and write, can you, Anny?'

'Oh yes,' she beamed proudly. 'My mother taught me.'

'Well, no offence to your father, but it wouldn't be him that taught you, eh, Woodvine? Not the brightest! But, by God, the strongest and the hardest worker I ever saw. Strong in the arm, thick in the head, so they say.'

Anny was not pleased with the slight to her father's intellect. He wasn't stupid, not by a long chalk. But Father didn't seem to mind. The ironworkers always engaged in plenty of banter and never seemed to take themselves too seriously.

'We're mightily proud of her,' he said and squeezed his daughter's shoulder.

Pritchard said, 'You seem like a clever'un then, lass. Can you do a job for me?'

'Yes,' answered the girl, curious and willing, but she looked to her father for some reassurance, and he gave a little nod.

'I need someone to go straight up to the big house and give a message to the estate manager, tell him to tell the master about this poor man here. The estate manager's office is behind the big house in a little brick dwelling. He's called Mr Brotherton and his secretary is his wife, Mrs Brotherton. One or both of them is usually there this time of day. The name of the dead man is Lakelin. Can you remember all of that?'

'Course she can,' said Father.

'Of course I can,' she replied and again her father nodded, his eyes keen.

And off she went. A mission, a job for the foreman. She thought of the poor dead man and of his wife and children. But she was gladdened, too, that she could be of use and she was proud that the foreman had trusted her with such an important role. To carry a message to the estate manager, Mr Brotherton, that would be relayed to Mr King himself. She felt important. *If I'd never written that note to Father*, she thought, *Mr Pritchard wouldna have seen how clever I am and I wouldna be on my way to the big house.* Book learning does that, she realised. It was a ticket to the world of men.

Anny took the walk up the riverside towards the imposing King house – named Southover due to its aspect – situated high on the hillside frowning down upon the iron bridge. She thought of Mr King the iron-master, who had a reputation for being stern and cold. She thought of King's daughter Margaret, whom she glimpsed once from a carriage window; she looked beautiful and had ringlets in her golden hair. Anny felt a poke of envy for Margaret, remembering that she was born the same month as her. She wondered what might have happened if the babies had been swapped, and how different her life might have been. She'd have those ringlets now! But Anny knew that she'd rather have her poor old father than horrid Mr King any day of the week, for all his riches. The huge, dark King house loomed up before her, and as she went around the back to find the estate office, she swallowed her nerves and knocked confidently on the door.

Mr Brotherton looked confused to find a young village girl appearing at his door.

'I carry an important message from Mr Pritchard. A man called Lakelin has been injured at the furnace. Very seriously injured. In fact, he has passed away from the serious nature of his injuries.'

'Oh Lord,' said Brotherton, his gaze shifting to consider all the things that must be done.

Anny went on, 'He leaves his wife a widow and his children fatherless. They live in Broseley. He was only young. It is a drodsome business.'

Anny waited and eventually he recalled her presence and eyed her curiously.

'You're good with words,' he said.

'So my mother tells me,' said Anny. 'And father. He's Mr John Woodvine. He works at the furnace.'

'Good man, Woodvine,' he replied.

Anny replied, 'Would you like me to write a note down for you to take back to Mr Pritchard?'

'You can read and write, child?'

'I can. My mother taught me.'

'No need to write it down on this occasion. You clearly have a good memory. Go and tell Mr Pritchard that he must send a man into town to arrange a cart to be sent for the . . . for Lakelin. Tell him that I will inform the master, and I'll send Mrs Brotherton to Broseley to tell the family. Then I shall come down to the furnace directly. Are you sure you can you remember all of that?'

'I am certain,' she said firmly and looked him straight in the eye.

'I believe you, child.' He thought for a moment, then added, 'You can run for me again, if you wish. Come back here each morning, if your mother can spare you. I have plenty of errands for a reliable runner. Can you read a clock? Get here for eight every morning and I'll have jobs for you to do until lunchtime, shall we say till twelve?' He fished in his pocket and gave her a penny.

'Oh yes, Mr Brotherton! Thank you, Mr Brotherton!' beamed Anny, clutching the coin in her hot hand. She'd have to talk to Mother first, of course, but the time she'd miss helping her mother would be more than made up by the coins she'd earn. A real job! At the big house, no less!

As Anny crossed the courtyard, heading for the path to the woods, she caught sight of Master Cyril, standing near to the stable block, half hidden around the corner.

As she moved forward, she saw he was not alone. He was holding fast to the arm of a servant girl, his other hand raised, pointing viciously towards her face. She could not hear his words, but it looked as if the girl had committed some terrible crime, the way he was jabbing at her, his face distorted as he spat words at her. *No need to twist her arm like that*, thought Anny. The boy's face was ugly in its rage. Anny shuddered. Her new post at the big house felt tarnished already. *As long as I avoid him*, she thought, *it'll be all right.*

She raced off into the woods to take the path back down to the furnace. A few steps in and her eager ears picked up a sound. She glanced round, but saw nothing. She went on with less haste, her ears pricked. There it was again. She stopped and peered into the woods. She thought with a slight air of panic, *It inna that awful boy?* Then she saw the bounce of blonde curls as someone turned their head. It was a girl.

'Who's there?' called Anny. 'Come out, you sneaky beggar. I'm not frit of you.'

A figure stepped out from behind a tree. Anny was shocked to see it was the daughter of the big house, Miss Margaret King. Anny muttered under her breath, 'What's she doing here?' as she curtseyed awkwardly while the girl, also very awkward, attempted to step lightly through the woods towards her. Not an outdoor kind of a girl, Anny noted. What on earth could she want, out here in the woodland?

'Afternoon, miss,' said Anny, watching the girl, who looked pale and nervous. Anny was anxious to rush off and deliver her message, but didn't feel she could ignore the young miss. As she came closer, Anny saw that she had a split lip. She wondered how that had come about.

'Hello there,' said Miss King.

'I am very sorry for addressing you so, just now, Miss King. I heard a noise and didna know – I mean, I *did not* know it was the young lady of the house. Please accept my being sorry, for I did not mean any offence.' Anny knew she was rambling, but she was mindful of her new position with Mr Brotherton. She didn't want this getting back to him and for her to lose her position before she'd even started. *I'll have to start stopping my tongue*, she thought.

'Not . . .' began Miss King, but her voice cracked a little and she stopped. It was as if her voice wasn't used to talking and it came out wrong. She swallowed and tried again. 'Not at all. I didn't mean to startle you. It was my fault for being secretive.'

'That's true,' said Anny, without thinking.

'I'm not supposed to be out here,' said Miss King, wide-eyed.

'Out where?' said Anny.

'In the woods.'

'Why not?'

'My father says it's where the . . .' Miss King stopped and bit her lip again, then winced. That split lip must be bothering her.

'Where the what?'

'Nothing. But it's forbidden anyway. I decided to . . . to defy my father.'

Anny had no idea what to say to this, but Miss King seemed pleased with herself, so Anny replied, 'Good for you.'

'Thank you,' said Miss King, and smiled. She winced again, as it must have hurt her lip. What a nervy thing she was. She was very pale and looked a little poorly, but her hair was in lovely ringlets and she had a pretty face, but a sadness about the eyes. An awkward silence followed.

'Did you just come from Southover?' asked Miss King.

'Yes, miss. From today I work for Mr Brotherton. I'm a kind of messenger for him.'

'I'm . . . I'm a little afraid of Mr Brotherton.'

'Really?' said Anny, shocked that any King could be afraid of anything, with all their money to bolster them against the world. 'He's all right.'

'It's just his voice. It sort of booms. I don't like loud voices. My father's is loud and he shouts at me sometimes. Is your father like that?'

'No, not even a little bit. He's proper jam, me father. I mean, he's a good person, miss.'

Miss King looked disappointed. Or was it envious?

'That's nice. My name is Margaret. What's your name?'

'Anny, miss.'

'Please call me Margaret.'

Miss King's eyes were so big and wide. She looked a little lost.

'I dunna think I can do that, miss. Not with . . . you know. Me working for your father. And our . . . different stations in life.'

'How did you come by the post, Anny? I've never heard of a girl messenger before. It's always been boys. I was always jealous of them. Running here and there, out in the world, something useful to do.'

Anny felt proud to relate it. 'It's because me mother – *my* mother – taught me to read and write. And the foreman at the blast furnace saw I could, and he sent me with a message and Mr Brotherton liked me, so there you are.'

'You can read and write?' Miss King looked and sounded quite amazed. Anny bridled against it.

'Why, yes. Not all of us poor folk are daft, you know.'

But Anny immediately regretted her rash words, because the girl looked crestfallen. Anny felt bad.

'I am sorry,' said Anny, and took a step towards Miss King. 'That was hard of me. You didn't mean anything by it. It is strange, a lass like me learning her letters. I know that. Please forgive me, Miss King.'

'Margaret,' she replied, and smiled. It was a lovely smile and it made Anny smile too. 'I think it's marvellous you've learnt to read and write. I love reading . . .'

The quiet confession touched Anny. Then she remembered her errand, the crucial message for Mr Pritchard. She scolded herself inwardly, but then again, she was not used to being important.

'I am terribly sorry, but I must go. There has been a death at the furnace and I'm taking a message back from Mr Brotherton to Mr Pritchard.'

'A death?' said Margaret.

'Yes. A young man. With a wife and children.'

'Oh, how terrible!' cried Margaret and covered her mouth with her hand, her eyes shining with tears. It warmed Anny to see how it affected the young girl. Did the poor matter that much to the rich?

'It is, miss. But I really must go.'

'Can I see you again, Anny?'

'I'm sure you will, about the place.'

'No, I mean, can we arrange to meet, like this? In a quiet place? I'm not very good around other people. But I think I could talk to you. I would like to, I mean. Talk to you, that is.'

Anny felt quite pleased at the request. Truthfully, she was also curious to see what the young lady of the house might have to say to a village wench like herself.

'Mr Brotherton said I would be finished at twelve.'

'Then can we meet hereabouts, soon after twelve, tomorrow?'

'Yes, miss,' said Anny and turned to go. She had been delayed and was worried Mr Brotherton would get down there before her and then she would have failed in her duty.

'Please call me Margaret,' she heard the girl shout to her as she ran away.

'Yes, miss,' she called back and raced through the trees.

∽∾∽

Back at home that afternoon, her mother was thrilled at the news of her new post, and did not seem to mind at all that Anny would be absent from the washing work each morning.

'I shall come back home as soon as ever I can afterwards,' said Anny.

'Dunna fret,' said her mother. 'You stay as long as you're needed. Mr Brotherton might need you past twelve, and that's fine by me. This is a great chance for you, Anny. Working for the King family! You make yourself available to them at all times, whatever they're wanting. You wanna make a good impression.'

Anny almost mentioned her plans to meet Miss King, but somehow it didn't seem right to tell Mother.

The next morning she arrived early at Mr Brotherton's door. He had three errands for her that morning: a trip to the stationers in town to collect some ink; a message for the undertaker about arrangements for Lakelin and a note to be taken to the doctor's house on Tontine Hill about something, Anny didn't know what. None of her business, of course. She stood at the door to the office once she'd finished. It was quiet there at the office. The little brick building stood beside the woods and the big house loomed across the way. There was no hustle and bustle of people like in the town, and there was not the roar of industry her father had to work with every day. When Mr Brotherton came outside to give her direction, she took a peek past him into the office itself and saw Mrs Brotherton working with a pen at her desk. She looked up and gave Anny a small but friendly smile, which Anny returned. Mrs Brotherton's desk was busy yet tidy, furnished with all manner of stationery that Anny could only dream of. Oh, to have pens and bottles of ink and a blotter and fine paper, rather than a stubby pencil and scraps to write upon! To have a desk to work at, instead of her own lap. Anny had always enjoyed writing, adored it. But it always seemed a pointless extravagance, like wearing a lace apron. Now she had a glimpse of something a person could do with writing, a woman even.

When Mr Brotherton was done with her, she ran down the woodland path, racing to meet her new friend. She felt her legs weaken at the effort. She had not eaten since dawn and was ravenous. As she rounded a bend she spotted Miss King standing on the path and beside her on the ground a small wicker basket, its contents covered with a chequered cloth.

'I am sorry if the hour is late,' puffed Anny.

'It is not. I arrived early. I thought you would be hungry having worked all morning, and so I have brought us a picnic, if that is acceptable?'

'Oh, miss!' cried Anny, delighted, then checked herself. 'You did not have to do that. I can eat at home later.'

Miss King looked forlorn. 'But I asked Cook to pack all the things I liked, and I did so want to share them with you.' She knelt down and removed the cloth to reveal a dazzling selection of goodies. Anny spied a pie, sandwiches of some sort, boiled eggs, strawberries and slices of cake layered with purple jam.

Anny licked her lips. 'If you're sure, then if I may say so, I'd love to, miss!'

They sat down on the forest floor, Anny cross-legged and Miss King with her legs tucked neatly under her skirts. At first, they talked a bit about their families, then ate together in companionable silence. Anny was intent on the food. It was so good. Her mother cooked hearty dishes from the ingredients they could afford and what they could grow or find. Anny had never had cause to complain about her meals. But this was something else. The sandwiches were filled with roast beef, succulent and chewy. The pie was some sort of game bird – rich and spicy – encased in a savoury jelly and crisp pastry.

The cake was light and very sugary, the jam inside thick with juicy pieces of plum.

She looked up from her obsessive focus on the food to see Miss King watching her, nibbling on a strawberry and smiling. Anny smiled back.

'Thank you, miss. For all this.'

'Please don't thank me. It is my pleasure. I used to picnic with my governess from time to time. But she left us and I have not eaten out of doors for many months. I'm so glad you were kind enough to share it with me.'

'Dunna you have any friends?' said Anny and immediately regretted it. 'I am sorry, I didna mean . . .'

'No, it's fine. The answer to your question is no. I don't have a friend in the world. It's rather pathetic, isn't it?'

Anny looked away. 'Here,' she said and held out a piece of cake to Miss King. 'You need to eat more or I'll polish off the whole lot.'

Miss King's face lit up and she took a big mouthful of it, so big that Anny laughed, and she snorted and they giggled helplessly, morsels of cake spraying onto the forest floor. Once Miss King's mouth was clear, she had wiped her face on the chequered cloth and they had stopped laughing, she said again to Anny, 'Please will you call me Margaret?'

'I'll consider it,' said Anny with a cheeky smile and they laughed again. They began to talk then, Margaret querying Anny about her family and her village. The conversation was mostly one way, as Margaret was full of questions and Anny did not feel able to ask the same kinds of things, not after putting her foot in it about friends. It was also tricky because of Margaret's position; Anny did not feel it was her place to quiz the girl. And anyway, it was nice to gabble on about herself for once. Nobody else was interested in the everyday particulars of Anny Woodvine's life.

The food all gone and the sun long past midday, Anny knew it was time to go, though she could easily have curled up there and had a nap to digest this marvellous meal. They stood up and brushed themselves off. There was an awkward moment where neither knew quite what to say next.

'Ta-ta for now, Miss King.'

'Margaret?'

'No, I'm Anny.'

'Oh, Anny, you are a one! Will you meet me again tomorrow? And the day after that?'

Anny was tempted, especially if food like this was in the offing. But there was something about it that did not feel quite right. Her mother would not approve, she knew that, especially not of taking food without repaying the favour. She also knew she wouldn't be telling her mother about this, about any of it.

'It inna that easy for me, miss. I have to work for my mother at home in the afternoons. I ought to be back there now.'

'Yes, of course.'

Miss King's face was so sad, Anny felt a pang. 'But I could meet you here next week, same day, same time? That should be all right.'

'That would be lovely. I'll bring another picnic.'

'No, miss, it'll be my turn then. I'll bring something, dunna fret.' As she said the words, she felt her stomach twist into a knot at what she could possibly offer Miss King from her humble table. Well, she would just have to manage it. It was the right thing to do.

They were both true to their word and met the following week. They were easier with each other this time. It felt less like a curious encounter and more like companionship. It was the beginning of a friendship, one that grew as they met each week throughout the long, baking summer.

It was also the beginning of Anny lying to her mother, something that left a bad taste in her mouth. She'd told her white lies before, of course she had, like every child. But it was the first time she had set out deliberately to deceive her parents. She did not like it, but it excited her, too. It made her cheeks go hot. She kept telling herself that she was doing nothing wrong. And each time she saw Margaret she convinced herself further that there was nothing to feel bad about. They were just being sensible about it, that was all. After all, they both knew their families – and society itself – would disapprove heartily of the rich girl and the poor girl picnicking together in the woods. But families weren't right about everything, and society could be stupid. When the two girls met now, they did not feel that they were so very different anymore. They were not employer and employee; they were not even rich and poor. When they were together, chatting and laughing, they were simply Anny and Margaret.

But as the weeks went on, her work for Mr Brotherton increased and she was kept later each time. He always found so many things for her to do and tutted when she had to leave to go home to her mother. She had already had to miss one meeting with Margaret. She felt bad about it, but what could she do? Particularly as it looked as if Mr Brotherton was going to need her more and more at the office and she would not be able to meet Margaret so often. Even today she was running late, and her first words to Margaret had been an apology.

'Really, Anny, please do not apologise,' Margaret was quick to reply. 'It is not of your making. You are only doing your job. But it did give me an idea . . .'

'What's that, then?'

'Since you can read and write so well, I was wondering . . .' She bit her lip in thought. 'Maybe you and I . . . perhaps we could . . . write to each other?'

'I've heard that people do write letters to friends. But I never had a friend who could write.'

'And,' continued Margaret, 'whenever I leave a letter for you, I'll leave some paper and a pencil for you to write back. Then you don't have to worry about the ... well, the cost to yourself. If that's agreeable.' Anny did not like charity, not directed at herself or her family, anyway. But she could see that Margaret was being kind, not hoity-toity. Besides, she really could do with a more reliable source of writing materials.

'But how could we deliver them? They can't come to the house, then everyone'll know about us.'

Margaret considered this. 'Well, perhaps we could leave the letters somewhere safe, somewhere only we knew about. And then nobody would need to know.'

'I know the very place!' cried Anny. 'Not far from here, down by the riverside. There's an old lime tree with a hollow in the trunk. I used to hide flowers in there for the fairies. I'll show you.'

It wasn't far and was back towards the big house. Anny knew these woods like the back of her hand and she pointed out to Margaret a few natural landmarks on the way, so that Margaret could find the right tree again when she was alone. They were peering inside the hollow and laughing about Anny's flower fairy offerings, when they heard a shout nearby. Both girls turned, but Margaret's face was full of fear.

"That's Cyril's voice. That's my brother.'

Anny watched Margaret, who was now shaking, her hands and bottom lip trembling. Her friend so rarely talked about her family; sometimes it seemed they talked about everything else, but the mere mention of her family seemed to steal Margaret's voice.

'Is he calling you?' said Anny in a hoarse whisper.

They stood and listened, then heard more sounds, followed by movement through the undergrowth. They instinctively hid behind the tree with the hollow. Through the trees, they saw Cyril pass by. He was not alone. He was pulling behind him the servant girl Anny had seen him bullying once.

'It's Lucy,' whispered Margaret.

They both watched as the two passed by, the servant girl saying things quietly to Cyril. Anny caught the odd word, mostly 'please' and 'Master'. But his grip on her wrist was strong and she could not get away. Then he stopped. Anny and Margaret froze. He pulled Lucy towards him, then shoved her up against the nearest tree. His face was very close to hers and he was saying something in her ear. She was twisting away from him. He held her against the tree with his left arm, as his right hand went down, found the bottom of her hem and thrust up under her skirts. He was fumbling around for something. Margaret turned away and sobbed, then covered her mouth with terror that he might hear her.

Anny turned to Margaret. She whispered, 'We mun help her.'

'No!' replied Margaret, full of panic. 'We cannot. We must pretend we never saw a thing.'

'That inna right.'

'You don't know my brother like I do. He will find a way to punish us, you more than me. He has a hatred of . . . others less . . .'

'Poor folk,' said Anny.

'Yes. He will punish you. You'll lose your post. And he'll beat me.'

The two girls stared at each other, then turned back to gaze upon the scene unfolding before them. The boy's hand reaching up under the servant girl's dress, the sobs of the girl, his cruel sneer, his coarse whisperings of who knows what in her ear.

Anny said, 'This is wrong. All wrong.' She turned away and looked about on the forest floor.

'What are you doing?' whispered Margaret.

'Something. Something is better than nothing.' Anny found what she was looking for. A sizeable stone. She picked it up.

Margaret gasped. 'What on earth are you going to do with that?'

Anny aimed and threw it at a tree ten feet or so away from the struggling pair. It hit the trunk full square and bounced into the bracken. Cyril turned at the sound. The moment he was distracted, Lucy seemed to find a hidden strength and shoved Cyril hard. He stumbled back and cried out. Lucy dashed away through the woods towards the house.

'Anny, you are marvellous!' whispered Margaret.

'You'd have done the same, if you'd thought of it.'

'No, I would not. I'm not like you, Anny. I wish I were.'

They both turned and crouched lower as they heard Cyril swearing. Puffed and red-faced, he dusted himself down, then began to walk back in a leisurely way. Anny guessed he knew he could do this whenever he chose. There was no rush. It was all part of some horrible game. Once he was gone, the girls looked at each other nervously.

'I have to go,' said Margaret. 'I am so sorry about . . . all this.' Anny could sense shame in Margaret.

'It inna your fault. He inna your fault.' Anny thought, *He's a proper monster.* She looked at her friend Margaret, for that is what she had become. 'You're not like your family, you're good and kind . . .'

'Oh, Anny, there are times I wish I weren't a King. That I could be someone else, anybody else.'

'It'll be all right, Margaret. You inna just a King, you're my best friend. With me you can be just Margaret. Even better, you can be Peggy. Yes, that'd be perfect. To me you'll be Peggy, not Miss King or even Margaret.'

Margaret grinned from ear to ear. 'I've never had a pet name! Oh, yes please, Anny! Thank you!'

'Ta-ta for now, Peggy.'

'Good day, Anny.'

The two girls solemnly shook hands, then laughed. They turned in opposite directions and both went off, making their way home.

Dusk was approaching and an evening wind whistled through the forest. Anny pulled her shawl about her as she walked thoughtfully, thinking of her friend, her job and interesting times ahead. Yet slicing through the warm glow of a friendship with Peggy was the cold fact of Cyril. Above, the sky seemed to mirror her thoughts, as a rash of dark clouds swept in and the woodland ahead was cast in deep shadow as she moved through it, homewards.

Chapter 4

Dear Anny,

I am so heartened to have found a true friend such as yourself, and I find in writing that I can tell you things I somehow could never say aloud. My life to this point has been a struggle. My family are difficult people. My father is hard and unyielding. I believe he sees me as a disappointment because I find it difficult to talk to people in social situations such as balls and even tea parties and so forth. My stepmother is a silly woman who is only a few years older than I and adores her nasty little lapdog more than life itself. She thinks she is beautiful because she has big eyes and thick hair but her mouth is always in a turned-down position above a pointed chin, which gives her a most disagreeable and witching air always and, I believe, is the revelation of her true nature. My brother is a fiend. I do not need to explain more to you of this, as you have witnessed it yourself with your own eyes. I could not believe how brave you were when you threw that rock. I wish I were more like you!

My grandmother is the nicest of all my close family, in that I do not believe she hates me. She does talk to me at times. However, she does say odd things from time to time and I wonder if she is a little touched.

Thus, my home is not a place one might call particularly happy. I am fortunate that I have fine clothes, a warm bed and good food to eat. My family is rich, after all. But if my family were judged on its good company alone, I might well be the poorest girl in Shropshire.

Please tell me about your family, Anny, and how they are with you.

Fondest regards,
Margaret (Peggy)

Post Scriptum: please be aware that if my family ever saw these words I have written about them, or if this letter were ever to fall into public hands, I would be in the direst of straits. Perhaps I am foolish to write these thoughts down. However, this is the first time in my life I have had a true confidante, and I am emboldened by this to speak the truth. It is a great weight lifted from me that I can speak openly to a friend of my woes. Thank you for being that friend, Anny. I believe I can trust you, as you seem to have a kind, open nature. So please keep my letters very safe and secret. Thank you again.

Anny found Margaret's letter the very next day, in the hollow in the tree which they had agreed would be their postmaster. There were some parts of the letter she had to read again – despite being a good little reader – as she was not accustomed to reading such high-flown sentiments. It was a thrill to receive a letter, as this was Anny's very first. She decided she'd have to try her best to write in 'proper' English. She was delighted to have a confidante, but was ashamed that a worm of annoyance was wriggling inside her about some of the contents of Peggy's letter. This girl had everything a person could wish for, while so many people she knew had nothing, and still she was not happy. Anny had always thought if she had all the King's wealth, she'd never complain again. But even as she thought it, Anny knew she was wrong about that. She wouldn't trade her family for a room full of nice dresses, if it meant Mr King were her father and Cyril were her brother. She shuddered at the thought. *Who'd ha' thought that you could pity a rich girl?*

Dear Peggy,

Course I will keep your letters secret. I will keep all your secrets safe. That is what friends do. We should make a solemn pact never to tell our secrets to any living soul. What do you say to that? I think it is a sure way of friendship. Also I am thinking that we should make another pact and that is against boys. I know lots of boys round here where I live and I can tell you that they are not to trust. With secrets or any other important matters. It sounds to me that your brother is another like this. We should make a pact that boys never come between us. You have asked about my family and I could write all night about how good they are to me, as they surely, surely are. There is only one of me which is not usual as much of our neighbours have bundles of children but my mother had me and nearly died and something went wrong inside after and then she could not bring any more children into the world. I used to weep for this, as I wanted a sister for many years but now I am thinking it is a blessing as there are not many mouths to feed in our home and I can get some peace for my reading and writing which is my true joy. God is mysterious in his ways.

In your next letter, tell me what you eat for your meals. In every particular detail.

Yours sincerely,
Anny Woodvine

Post Scriptum: please explain what Post Scriptum means.

Also you are right about your brother. I do not like to speak ill of others but he is a nasty piece of work. I was at Mr Brotherton's office this morning and saw Master Cyril kick a dog. Only because it was there. And because he could. Mr Brotherton sighed and shook his

*head. The dog crawled away under a tree and Master
Cyril laughed his fill at this. I do wonder what makes a
person lungeous like this. If you do not know that word,
it is proper useful. It means spiteful.*

Anny read over her last paragraph and nearly struck
it out. Should she be more cautious? What if her letter were found and read by the Kings? She would lose
her new position at the estate office for certain. It might
even endanger her father's position at the furnace. But
something in Peggy's honesty was infectious and she
wanted to match it. She wanted a friend to have secrets
with, someone clever like herself, who she could share
her deep thoughts with in a way no local girl had ever
been able to match. And there was something thrilling
about being friends with Miss King, the daughter of the
big house, the daughter of not only her own boss but her
father's boss. It was lucky and golden, somehow. Maybe
it might even come in useful one day. As excited as she
was by the prospect, something told her that she must
continue to keep the whole fact of it secret. She mustn't
tell her mother or her father. She knew they would not
approve and they would warn her against it. She could
not clearly work out their reasons for it, but she just
knew they would. Something obscure stirred in her that
it could mean strife, somewhere along the twisting path
of time. But she was a girl, a child entering young adulthood, and whisperings of trouble served only to make

the whole thing more thrilling still. She folded up the letter and, evading her mother's keen eye, slipped out unnoticed to the woods and made her way to the fairy tree, whistling as she went.

∽

With nothing to do that day beyond terrorising dogs and servants, Cyril King decided to walk the circuit of his family's dominion. He wanted to see everything that the Kings owned. He strolled down through the woods towards the ironworks, his face beginning to prickle with heat. He wished he could remove his cap and so-called summer coat, though it was still infernally hot. He wished at times he had the life of a river waif, running about barefoot and shirtless. Only in the summer, though. He muttered to himself grumpily as he approached the furnace, great wafts of heat assaulting him the closer he came. Industry produced heat and heat transformed into money, he realised. He did not think of the manpower slaving away to create that heat in the first place. He thought only of his place astride it all.

All this will one day be mine, Cyril thought. This puffed his chest with pride, but he was also plagued with doubt. Was he up to the job? All these massive piles of matter to be dug from the ground, melted, moulded, refined, rolled, flattened, transported and sold. It was daunting, to say the least. And something he would never admit to his father, he hated industry. He hated the filth and the stink of it, the noise and intrusion of it. Luckily, an ironmaster could afford to hire help to deal with the worst of it and stay behind the scenes in a much more civilised situation of an office or up at Southover. Mr Brotherton came to see Papa daily in his study to speak of business matters. Other fellows – probably some sort of lowly manager – from the furnace, the forge and the mill would sometimes appear, cap in hand, at the estate office yet rarely, if ever, managed an audience with his father. It was the men that worried Cyril most. How did one talk to such rascals? Even Mr Brotherton unsettled him, with his twinkling eyes, something knowing behind them, as if he knew Cyril's secret doubts of his own worth. Mr Brotherton always spoke to him in that way too, that half-mocking way, overly polite but somehow undermined by wry humour. *You're not up to this*, his voice and those eyes seemed to say. *Neither is your father, just as your grandmother and grandfather knew. We run this place. You lot are not needed. Just your money. Run along.*

Cyril hawked up a good load of phlegm and spat on the ground in a fit of pique. The more he thought about it, the more he was determined to prove himself to these damned fellows. How dare Brotherton and the like mock him? A small part of him knew that there was no evidence whatsoever that any of his father's men mocked him, spoke of him or even registered his existence in their busy, difficult lives. But it was a small part, easily silenced. He marched down to the yard in front of the furnace and spotted a group of men drinking from large tankards, in what must have been a few minutes out of their back-breaking shift. But it riled him, these people guzzling his father's ale. He knew it was their daily ration, but at this moment Cyril did not care to acknowledge that fact.

'You there,' he called, waving his hand dismissively. Nobody turned. Nobody heard him. This annoyed him further. He stomped harder towards the men. 'I said, *you there*, damn you!'

This got their attention. The wall of backs broke and a row of black-smudged faces turned sharply, their white eyes alarmed, their red mouths open. Then their faces changed as they saw whose voice it was and yes, *there*, a smirk, he was sure of it. That blackguard was laughing at him, wasn't he?

'What do you think you are doing?' Cyril shouted and stood his ground, arms folded, as he'd seen his father do when telling him off for his own laziness or stupidity. But the men just stood there, gawping at him. 'What the devil is wrong with you? Answer me, damn you!'

Others had turned to watch, all frozen in place, yet one or two now were taking draughts from their beer again, which seemed the height of rudeness. One of the men stepped forward, a large man, built like a Shire horse, with arms as thick as thighs and hands like hams.

Cyril shuddered at the size of him and steeled himself. He wouldn't be intimidated by such a thundering idiot as this mountain of a man.

'Can I be of help to you, Master King?' said the man. This took Cyril aback, who was expecting some garbled labourer's nonsense to come from his wide mouth.

Cyril cleared his throat and squared up to him. 'I said, what do you think you are doing?'

The men shuffled awkwardly, one holding up his beer and looking at it, as if to answer. Why wouldn't they speak? They must be fools. He turned back to the big man.

'Will you not answer your betters?'

Some of the men shuffled and looked to the ground. One even shook his head, Cyril was sure of it.

'You there. How dare you shake your head at me! I am your superior.'

The big man took another step towards him and Cyril took a stumbling half-step backwards and someone sniggered.

'Master King, what can we do for you?' said the big man. 'We are supping our beer that your father provides for us. It is only for a short time, and then we mun be back at our work again, no danger.'

Cyril looked up at the man's eyes. The man's daughter and wife would have seen kindness and goodness there; the foreman Pritchard would have seen his hardest-working, strongest and most loyal man at the furnace.

But Cyril King saw only his own smallness and pathetic misplaced anger reflected back at him.

'How dare you speak to me,' he uttered low and guttural, clearing his throat.

'But you addressed us, young sir,' continued the man. The downright bloody cheek of these lower orders!

'How dare you presume to speak to me!' shouted Cyril, but it came out as a kind of squawk, like a parakeet he'd seen at the fairground once. 'What . . . what is your name?'

The man glanced sidelong, unwilling to respond.

'Answer me, damn you!'

Then another man came forward. He was less dirty than the rest, perhaps less of an idiot than the others.

'I'm the furnace clerk, Master King. My name's Pritchard. I'm the foreman and I'm in charge here. What can I do for you?'

'What is this man's name? He was insolent.'

The man and Pritchard looked at each other. Something passed between them in their look, something too adult for Cyril to grasp, which annoyed him further.

'Tell me your name, or you shall hang for it, by God!' shrieked Cyril. That shut them up. He knew he did not have such power, but it gave him the feel of it, just to say it. He realised he could say anything he liked to these people. Anything at all. It gave him a thrill.

Pritchard was about to speak but the big man interrupted him. 'My name is John Woodvine, sir. I have worked at your father's furnace these past score years, man and boy. If I have offended you, I am sorely sorry for it. Please accept my apology, most sincere like.'

Woodvine looked at the ground, Pritchard looked at him and the men stood with their chins up staring at Cyril.

Cyril had no idea what to say.

'Is our business concluded, Master King?' said Pritchard. 'I would like these men to get back to their duties now, if agreeable.'

Cyril turned and marched away, his face roasting hot from the furnace and his own self-hatred. But as much as he hated himself, he hated those working men more. Their sense of purpose, their camaraderie and loyalty. But most of all the swagger of having a useful job to do in this world. How he hated them all for that. Now he had a new name to add to his list of fools who had wronged him and must pay: John Woodvine.

Chapter 5

August passed in a haze of heat and letter-writing. Margaret sat in her room, her eye on the door, her pillow on her lap, propped up to hide the latest letter from Anny. She finished reading it and swiftly hid it away in a wooden music box she kept at the bottom of her handkerchief drawer. If Cyril found these letters ... well, it did not bear thinking about. He would have no cause to ever want a handkerchief – as a child he always was snot-nosed, but he had no interest in girlish items, so she hoped he'd never look in there. She had secured a pink ribbon around the growing stack of letters which she tied and untied fondly each time, smiling at her good fortune to have found such a correspondent and such a friend.

She had tried to explain to Anny that she had never had friends. No friends at all. The person she spent most time with was her maid, Royce, who did her hair every day and tended to her physical needs. But Royce was stiff, cold and quite old. Margaret could not talk to her. They barely spoke. Their relationship was purely functional. She'd asked her father if she could have the young, nice one, Lucy, as her maid, but she was informed that Lucy was only a tweenie maid and not at all the right class for a lady's maid for the daughter of a King. So, Margaret could not even make a friend in her own house.

But Anny, full of sunshine and fun, surrounded by close neighbours – sometimes too close for comfort, Anny once wrote – had had plenty of friends in her life, had never been without them. Margaret, educated at home – only in writing, embroidery, French and piano-playing from a half-hearted Parisian governess who had disappeared without warning the summer before – and never permitted to speak to local children, let alone play with them, had grown to the age of twelve a lonely girl. Tormented by her brother and bullied by her father, she had become accustomed to her own company. Now Anny had appeared in her life, she was beginning to understand the magic of friendship. It was new and exciting. It was easy to allow it to become an obsession.

She tried to stop herself from gushing too much in her letters. But she found it almost impossible to play-act nonchalance and instead poured out all her feelings to Anny. Her friend did not reciprocate in kind; Anny's letters rarely spoke of her feelings, instead they were always friendly and full of fascinating detail about her daily life. Reading about the lives of the working class was as exotic to Margaret as if she were reading about the wildlife of Africa. Anny seemed to enjoy similar details about Margaret's life, yet Margaret felt a little ashamed every time she described the ease with which she passed her days. She sometimes invented minor troubles to make her day sound more vexing than it was, but worried this would make her sound as if she were trying to make something out of nothing. So she filled her letters with her feelings, her loneliness and her overwhelming regard for Anny. She wondered if it would help if she gave Anny presents, but would Anny take this as an insult? Margaret agonised now over that possibility. She had never had a friend before – let alone one from a different social class – and did not know how to be a friend herself.

She was a worrier, and worried about this. Still seated on her bed, staring at the drawer in which her precious letters were hidden, she thought, *What if I drive her away?* The thought terrified her. She wanted help; she needed someone to tell her how to be a friend, before she did the wrong thing and lost this one through some dreadful *faux pas*. If only there was someone she could talk to about it. Only one person sprang to mind, as there was only one person other than Anny that Margaret would ever have a hope of confiding in. 'Grandmother,' she said aloud. Could she talk to her about such things? There was only one way to find out.

She found Queenie seated on a high-back wing chair in the drawing room, snoring noisily. It was Mr King's chair usually and Margaret smiled to see she'd used it to have a quick snooze, thinking herself hidden from prying servants' eyes, yet her lusty snoring gave the game away to all and sundry.

Since her grandfather's death three months ago, Margaret had noticed that Queenie had changed. She used to be up and about from dawn till dusk and beyond, involved in the business and socialising with local worthies and clients. Since her husband had gone, she had taken to her bed more and more. She had withdrawn from the family. And her odd comments had popped into everyday conversation. Margaret could see that her grandparents had not been particularly fond of one another, but perhaps her grandfather's death had upset her grandmother more than anyone realised. She felt sad for her grandmother and vowed to try to spend more time in her company from now on. Perhaps they could take up a pastime together, such as playing cards or something similar, where conversation was unnecessary. Anny might enjoy her conversation, but Margaret knew none in her family, not even Queenie, felt that way.

Luckily, Benjamina was taking her afternoon rest in her own room, her father was out on business and Cyril was off roaming who knows where. Margaret came in quietly, so as not to wake her grandmother, determined to sit and wait for her to awake and for herself to build up the courage to talk to her. She had to come up with a plausible story for the friendship.

The visiting cousin of some local dignitary's daughter, perhaps; they could have met at a tea party and become correspondents. Yes, that sounded all right. That might happen. But Queenie knew that Margaret never spoke to a soul. Maybe Margaret could convince her that she had developed some confidence recently, that the girl was shy. She began to invent more and more elaborate flights of fancy about this fictional friend until she thought to herself, *Why not tell her the truth? Why not try, at least?* Then Queenie awoke with a start and let out a piercing cry.

Margaret leapt to her feet and went to her.

'Are you well, Grandmother?'

'The baby!' cried Queenie.

Her hands rose up and were flapping about, her eyes still filmy with sleep.

'What baby?' asked Margaret, alarmed.

Queenie sat bolt upright and said in a low, knowing tone, 'The baby on the bridge. That poor girl died, right there.'

Then Queenie put her hands over her face. Margaret reached out to touch her grandmother's hands, so forlorn did she look. But Queenie awoke from her half-waking, half-dreaming moment and registered her granddaughter's presence.

'What's this?' she muttered. 'What are you about?'

Margaret withdrew her hands and looked down, to give Queenie a moment to recover herself.

'You were dreaming, Grandmother,' she said quietly.

'No, I was not,' asserted Queenie. 'I wasn't even asleep.'

Margaret looked up at Queenie and their eyes met; a flicker of a smile passed on their lips, a shared, rare moment of connection between them. Minutes ago, Margaret would have taken the opportunity to ask her grandmother's advice about her friendship with Anny. But now, something else had taken its place, something more compelling still.

'Won't you tell me who the baby on the bridge is, please, Grandmother?'

For a moment, Margaret thought she might answer, but all Queenie said was, 'It's a fortunate child that escapes the King family.'

Margaret's feelings about her family chimed with her grandmother's sentiment and this gave her a little courage to speak of it. 'I feel that way, too, Grandmother.'

'Feel?' Queenie snapped. Queenie never did seem to have much time for feelings or talk of such things.

'About the King family. I find it . . . difficult sometimes.'

'You have everything you need, child.'

'I do and I am grateful. But it's just that . . . I do feel very alone.'

'That is the woman's lot. We must suffer alone.'

Margaret swallowed nervously, but was determined to go on.

'But if I had a friend, it would help me.'

'Friend? What friend?'

'I've met someone, Grandmother. And she could be a great friend to me. But I've never . . .'

'Where? What? Who?' quizzed Queenie, leaning forward and scrutinising Margaret's face.

'It is a girl who . . .' Margaret hesitated. Whatever she said, however she dressed it up, she knew her grandmother's fierce gaze would reduce it to ashes. Perhaps this was a mistake. But she had started it now and may as well finish it. Maybe her grandmother would surprise her and understand. She wouldn't know if she didn't try. 'She is a local girl, a girl from the village along the river. She is employed by Mr Brotherton in the office. She can . . .'

'What's this? A worker? A friendship with a worker?'

'She can read and write, Grandmother.'

'Out of the question, child. How could you even consider such a thing? We do not mix with such people.'

'But if you could only meet her, you would see. She is so clever and bright and . . .'

Queenie held up her hand, her palm facing outwards, as steady and rigid as a stone wall. 'It is not so very long until you will come out into society and make acquaintances of your own class, after which you will make a good marriage and produce children. You will be too busy running a household to have time for friendship.'

Margaret saw her life stretching ahead of her into a desert of tedious yet fretful social events, ending with an arranged union of some approved male of her family's choosing. And it terrified her. Her fear made her bold and she spoke again to her grandmother.

'But if I could have one friend to see me through the years before that day. I am so lonely, Grandmother. Sometimes I fear I may die of loneliness.'

'Pish-tosh! Nobody ever died of unhap . . .' But something stopped Queenie and she did not finish her sentence. A moment of memory seemed to sweep over her features. She looked down, rearranged her hands in her lap and composed herself. 'We are the Kings. We did not attain our position today by fraternising with the lower orders. You are your father's daughter – a King – and you have our family name to uphold at all times. Let there be no more talk of friendships with the labouring class.'

∽

Queenie told the child to run along. *That little wallflower*, Queenie thought. Harmless enough and a heart full of secrets, no doubt. But the child was too young to be trusted with the truth as yet, if ever. One day, perhaps, if she proved herself a bit more spirited, showed she had a bit of backbone. Queenie despised weakness. She inwardly scolded herself. She really mustn't fall asleep during the day like that. It left her at a disadvantage. This never would have happened when her husband was alive. For all his faults, he was a marvel at organising their lives. Everything was arranged with military precision and fixed timings, every minute of the day accounted for. It gave her life a comforting structure, which she missed. The moment he died, she had watched the life rattle from his body and was surprised to find she had felt a tidal wave of relief. This man was gone from her life. Now she could begin again, regain her former self, her former life before marrying so young and disappearing into an existence for which nothing in her girlhood had prepared her. She did not have to brook his company for one moment more on this earth, and as the head of the King family she could marshal them in the right direction.

But in the days following, she began to feel inordinately tired. She could not stay awake or concentrate on things for long. She took to her bed most days, when before, a scheduled bed nap had been something she'd mocked, something that the elderly required and she did not consider herself elderly by any means, being only in her late fifties. The day after he passed away, she handed over the operations of the ironworks almost completely to her son, despite her fears that he was not up to the job. She hoped the responsibility would be the making of him. Ralph's death had aged her, overnight it seemed. She had taken to sleeping in the day and waking all night. Everything was out of kilter. She felt adrift in her life.

She'd hated Ralph King senior by the end, of that there was no doubt. But in some ways he was a useful husband. How she had desired him once! She scoffed to think of it. But she had been young and foolish, a pretty little flibbertigibbet; she'd danced with all the local young men, and could have snapped her fingers and they would all have come running. Ralph was older, less keen. Still waters run deep, she had thought of him. She wanted to break through that cool exterior and explore his depths. But it was all a facade. Once married, she soon realised there was nothing hidden beneath. Only a frozen emptiness. He made love like he was avenging something, cold, thrusting and heartless. Bed soon became a place to be dreaded. Her girlish days were long gone, too soon. Then came the babies.

Queenie thought of her twin daughters, both dead before six months had passed: tuberculosis. Her eyes filled and she brutally slapped away the tears. *No, one mustn't give in to grief.* It was forty-odd years ago, indeed. She had her son after that. And then, no more. Her husband did not visit her bed from then on. He had tired of her. He had developed a taste for virgins.

But her one child who survived, her son, had been her great hope and joy, at first. It was after his birth she'd found her strength and earned her nickname, Queenie. He was a bonny baby, plump and chuckling. But his true character soon revealed itself. Whatever differences she had with her husband, they certainly saw eye to eye on the failings of their son Ralph. *Look at him now*, she thought, with disgust. A great disappointment: lazy, proud and selfish. *Look at the grandson, the same.*

But the granddaughter ... she might prove interesting, one day. There was something behind those shy blue eyes that made one wonder what she was thinking. Those eyes, just like Queenie's sister, Selina. The very picture of her sister's face – same eyes, same nose, same mouth. But the girl had none of Selina's spirit. And there was another key difference: Margaret's eyes were clear and open, not a shade of oddness in them. *Not clouded by trouble*, she thought with relief. *Nothing like my dear sister.*

As grateful as she was for that difference, she couldn't help but be reminded of Selina each time she saw Margaret. She thought back to a time before she was Queenie, when she'd been just Alice and Selina had been with her every day. To have lived with her dear sister Selina forever, perhaps in a simple cottage, covered in wisteria and surrounded by pea plants, like the home of her old piano teacher. No husbands, no fathers, no children, no grandchildren – that would have been the best life she could imagine. Thinking of it now brought a tear to her eye – how happy they would have been! Alice and Selina, alone in perfect companionship. If only her life had been that way. But it had been Alice's duty to marry well. By the time Alice was sixteen Selina was already beginning to show signs of oddness, forcing her parents to expedite Alice's marriage. Selina had always been a curious child, creating a world filled with fairy tales, some read from delicately illustrated books but mostly weaved from her imagination. Their parents began to keep her away from visitors and the servants whispered about her below stairs. Everyone thought Selina was ill, but Alice alone knew how brilliant and bright her sister was. But difference threatens those who want to be normal and her sister was talked about in increasingly worried tones.

While Alice blossomed into an eligible young woman, her older sister retreated further into the nursery. Soon, Alice was married. It all seemed like a great adventure, until she realised that she would have to live with this man, share his bed and be subject to his every desire and whim. Alice's absence drove her sister to worse excesses and Ralph restricted her visits with Selina to once a month. He said they had an unnatural attachment. Each visit brought a further degradation. Selina would pluck at her cheeks, cry out as if a spectre or spider had appeared above Alice's head, talk in strings of words about people she'd never met. They took her away.

Some months later, news came that Selina had died. Years later, she discovered Selina had hanged herself from her door.

With Selina gone, Alice was alone in the world, and Ralph had the ammunition to keep her in line. What befell one sister could befall the other.

She did the only thing she could think of to survive: she made that life her own. She became the perfect wife, the perfect mother, the perfect hostess. She learnt the family business and drove it forward, making the King name the greatest in the neighbourhood, in the county and beyond. She felt she had truly earned the name of Queenie.

But at what cost? It was always the females who seemed to pay the price. It was a hard fact but it was true, and her granddaughter needed to learn that now, the sooner the better. Life was hard for everyone but hardest for the weak. The way through life was littered with the corpses of those who could not stay the journey. Only the strong survived.

She thought of the night before, when she had looked from her bedroom window, sleepless as ever, and watched the family tombstones glow whitely in the bright moonlight. How she wished she could have seen her sister's spirit there, flitting between the graves, her long, pale hair catching the moonbeams, silvery and spectral. She did not believe in ghosts. It was all stuff and nonsense the common people spoke of in their uneducated ignorance. But how good it would be to see her sister again, even as a spirit. And how curious it would be, that her spectre should appear in this graveyard, when her body was buried long ago, not here, but in that dreadful place, the place where strangers would pay pennies to view the inmates, a kind of zoo of human misery. *How cruel people are.* She thought of the ghosts of her dead daughters, how dearly she would love to see them playing amongst the gravestones. They would laugh and chase each other, their skirts and beribboned hair fluttering in some spectral breeze. They had died as babies, so they would not come to her as proper little girls, but she could dream, couldn't she? She would call to them and they would turn and smile at her, then continue their frolics. She thought then of the baby on the bridge, crying out in the night, its mother dead and cold in the grave. She recalled the day Jenkins had told her, that the maid she'd dismissed had been found dead on the bridge. But there was more: gossip had spread that the girl had been holding a baby, which someone had taken in. She thought of her husband's icy heart, dead too now. Queenie shuddered, then shook her head to rid it of all maudlin thoughts.

'Enough of this,' she said and made the great effort it took to raise herself from the chair. She needed a walk, to blow away the cobwebs. She would take a turn down by the lake and return past the pet cemetery. What fun it would be to see the ghosts of her old dogs frolicking there today! But no: she must stop with these foolish thoughts. She would be firm with herself. She should turn her attention to worldly matters and ensure that the King family continued to prosper.

Chapter 6

'You're doing a fine job there, Anny,' said Mrs Brotherton. She had kind, grey eyes that were always smiling, even when her mouth was set. 'One day, you might work in a bigger office somewhere. Maybe even Shrewsbury, who knows!' Anny looked up from her work and smiled back, then continued copying out the long list of ironworkers and their pay for that month. A job in Shrewsbury. Imagine that, actually living in the county town of Shrewsbury, looking out from your office window and seeing the town folk going to and fro, the coaches clattering over the cobbles, the bells of the churches chiming – that's how she pictured it, anyhow. How marvellous that would be! That could never happen, not to an ironworker's girl like her. Or could it?

Anny felt gratified. She was so glad that within only a few months she had moved up from a messenger and general runabout to a clerical assistant, and her pay had moved up too. She often thought of that first time she was invited in to the office itself. Mrs Brotherton had been ill and Mr Brotherton was huffing and puffing about the work that needed to be done. He had asked her to come in to the office so he could test her handwriting. She had never written with a pen before, so he gave her a pencil and asked her to copy out some lists of figures and names. She had sat at a small desk, focusing on forming her shapes beautifully on the page. Mr Brotherton had been delighted with her neat work and later that day had shown her how to use a pen. She took to it like a foal to standing, wobbly at first but determined and soon an expert. With Mrs Brotherton sick, Anny found herself buried in paper, ink and neatly copied-out ledgers, and within days Mr Brotherton wrote to her mother and requested that Anny be permitted to work for them full-time, and that her pay would increase to match her working hours, of course. Everyone was delighted with the arrangement.

Since then, Mr and Mrs Brotherton had taken Anny under their wing. They had no children of their own – 'It was God's manner of making us useful to other young'uns,' said Mrs Brotherton – and they had adopted Anny, in a way. They even let her call them Mr B and Mrs B; as Mr B said, their name was a bit of a mouthful. They were teaching her the skills needed to administer an office such as this one: the papers and ink and pens and pencils and blotters and bills that were required to keep it all running smoothly. She wrote out letters and lists and requests and so forth for them. Her parents were proud as punch, of course, and sorely glad of the extra money coming in. It saved Anny from the drudgery of washing at home and also from a life in service, or worse, which might have been coming.

Her other option had been pit girl, full of backbreaking hours of picking out the ironstone from the clay on a waste tip and carrying it in a basket on her head to pile onto another great heap. The tedium of it, the endless, mindless nothingness. Worse still were the jobs that girls did down the mines, where rats and goblins lived. Those girls rarely saw the light of day and so many died young. Plenty of her friends did these jobs, and Anny wanted nothing to do with that. She loved her friends; she had grown up with them. But there was a difference between them now. Anny's hands were softer and her face less ravaged by wind and weather and work, though her eyes and fingers often ached from the strain of too much writing in the dim light of the approaching winter. Her childhood playmates did not speak to her as much as they used to, sitting in huddles in their rare free moments and flirting with the local boys. That Peter Malone – her neighbour's son who worked at the forge – was always giving her the eye, but most of the other boys and girls ignored her. She found Peter's attention flattering and he was a nice-looking lad and easy to get along with. She liked the way he spoke, as he was quite clever with words sometimes, usually when he was teasing her. But she found that the things her local friends talked about did not interest her much these days and they seemed to sense it. She was still attached to them, for comfort mostly. Anny began to feel left out, even a little shunned.

She was contemplating this one cold night, warming herself by the hearth with her father, the room dimly lit by a single oil lamp.

'Ow bist, my wench?' he said.

'I'm thinking on the young'uns hereabouts. It's as if *they* think that *I* think that *I* am better than *them*, but I dunna think that at all.'

'It's the price you pay for being a clever'un,' he replied. 'It separates the wheat from the chaff. You just need to get used to it. You are better'an them now. Simple as that.'

'No, I'm not. I just do a different job, that's all. Folk who do finer jobs than me are no better than me, are they?'

John Woodvine gazed into the fire, a slight smile about his tired eyes, tapping his clay pipe on his bottom lip thoughtfully. 'You're too clever by half for me, my lass,' he said.

'No, Father,' she went on, a terrier with every argument. 'You must agree. The Kings are no better than us, are they? For all their money and learning, they are . . .' She thought of Margaret. 'They are our equals.' Then she thought of the brother. 'Or indeed our inferiors, if you count Master Cyril.'

Her father looked up, frowning.

'What do you know of him? Of Master Cyril?'

An image of Cyril's hand thrusting up that poor servant girl's skirts leapt into her mind. She felt queasy. She hated to think on it, but she did think on it often. It disturbed her and fascinated her in equal measure. Questions filled her mind: what was he doing up there? What did he want up there? She knew something of how babies came into the world, but didn't think hands and fingers had much to do with it. Or violence. Or throwing someone up against a tree and whispering nasty things in their ear. She didn't understand it, didn't understand him, that boy who kicks dogs. He was rather handsome, for sure, those pretty blond curls. But his mouth was cruel and his eyes were frightening. She did not like to think of him at all.

'Enough to know he is a bad'un.'

Her father sat upright and looked directly at her. 'You're right, my lass. You stay away from him. He is a bad'un, a rotten'un if truth be known. He made trouble for me at the furnace for no good reason.'

'What trouble?' asked Anny, worried.

'It's naught for you to worry about. It's just I think he took against me that day, Anny. And I wouldna want you to be caught up in that, not with your prize post at the King office. Just do your best to stay clear of him. There's a good wench.'

'Oh, I will, Father. Dunna you fret about that.' She stood up, stepped over to her father and put her arms around his neck, kissing his rough cheek. 'I can look after myself, no danger.'

It played on her mind though. Sometimes, from her desk in the office, she could hear Cyril shouting at the stable men or the yelp of dogs in his path. She would lift her head and listen intently, but he would always pass on, to some mischief or other. Luckily, he had no interest in the estate office or anything clerical, and never appeared there. She felt safe from him in its wood-panelled interior, cosseted and looked after by her kindly bosses.

Until one October morning. Anny was at her desk, copying out a letter to an iron merchant from Birmingham. It gave her much pleasure that her words would be transported far and away to such exotic places as these great cities of the Midlands and beyond. One day she wondered if a letter by her hand might reach as far as London. Mr B was going through a pile of receipts, while Mrs B was out on an errand. The office had an air of quiet industry, just the rustle of Mr B's papers and the scratch of her pen on paper, the tap of her nib on the glass rim of the inkpot. Outside, it was a blustery day where the wind swept up clouds of autumn leaves in the courtyard and threw them around like fiery confetti, some blowing in at the office door as it opened abruptly, and there stood Master Cyril.

Anny glanced at her boss, who lowered his eyebrows at the sight. Cyril looked both impatient and bored.

'Brotherton,' he said. 'My father tells me I must get to know the business. He's sent me here to start. You are to show me around, apprise me of certain particulars. It won't take long. It all looks dull and easy for any man of letters.'

Cyril glanced about the office with disdain, until he noticed Anny, who immediately fell to writing again, afraid to look up, afraid to meet those cruel eyes and be any sort of object of curiosity for them.

'Indeed, Master King. I'd be delighted to. Let me start with the accounts. We can go into my office and leave others to their business.' He opened out his arms, gesturing defferentially towards his room, where the safe and the accounts were kept, where Mr Brotherton did much of his wages work and Anny rarely entered.

But Cyril was not moving and instead stood quite still. Anny felt as if the top of her head were burning. But she would not look up. If she stared long enough at the nib of her pen, at the ink that issued in loops and lines from it, then perhaps this intruder would vanish into thin air and order would be restored.

'And who is this? Look at me, girl. You should get up when I enter and wish me good morning.'

She placed her pen in its stand, lifted her head and looked straight at him. She held his gaze while she stood up and performed a slow, slight dip of a curtsey.

Mr Brotherton cleared his throat and said, 'This is Anny Woodvine, our clerical assistant.'

Anny said, 'Good morning, sir.' Cyril's eyes had watched every movement, had peered about her body as if scrutinising an iron bar for flaws. Then he looked away. His cheeks were pink and he looked perturbed. Anny lowered her eyes and stared at the floor.

'Well, come on then, man. For heaven's sake, I can't stand around here all day waiting for the likes of you.' Cyril marched past Anny's desk and into Mr B's room. Anny wanted to glance at Mr B, see what he made of all this. But she kept her gaze low, not wanting to look at Cyril again. Mr B walked by her and said quietly, 'You may carry on, Anny.'

The door was shut behind them and she sat, picked up her pen and dipped it in the ink, blotted it carefully, then went to write. But she could not concentrate, listening to the barking voice next door and Mr B's conciliatory tone. She heard Cyril say, 'Show me the safe. I want to see all the money my father earns. I want to see it piled up.'

'Huh,' Anny quietly scoffed to herself. *It's not your father earns all that money*, she thought. *It's men like my father. And the Brothertons. And me!*

Then Cyril was shouting. 'How dare you! I am my father's heir and will be your master one day. Open the safe this instant. And don't forget to lock it afterwards. Any one of these workers on this estate would steal it as soon as look at it. That girl out there, for instance.'

What? The cheek of it! She heard Mr B say something about her, but his kind voice could not be clearly discerned through the door.

'I'm sure you do,' Cyril retorted. There was no problem hearing his strident tones. 'Because you are soft on the lower classes, Brotherton, being so close to that station yourself. The thought that an office girl like that is trusted to open and close the safe is outrageous.'

He really was such a nasty piece of work. And how dare he suggest she was not to be trusted! She remembered the first time Mr B had shown her how to unlock the safe. There were two keys, one kept in a hidden drawer in a bureau in his office and the other in a similar secret drawer in Mrs B's desk. She had felt a thrill, not because of the money, but because of the trust with which she felt imbued. She had experienced a true connection with the Messrs B that day and now Cyril King wanted to taint that. Mr B came out to fetch the other key from his wife's desk, letting out a long, vexed sigh.

He collected the key and went back into his office and shut the door. It went very quiet in there. She assumed they were looking at the money. She imagined Cyril fingering it, worshipping it. Herself, she knew its value, how it meant the difference between surviving and dying for her people. But she did not love it for its sake alone. It was only a means to an end for her. But these rich, they coveted it, hoarded it. How the upper classes disgusted her. Except Peggy, of course. Peggy was different. Somehow she had come through the mill of her revolting family and emerged untarnished, pure somehow. A kind and loving person. A true friend. Nothing would ever come between them. But her brother was barking orders again and a chill went down her back, as if Jack Frost ran his fingers down her spine.

Her nib hovered above the page, as if stuck in time. Then a drop of ink splashed onto her neat letter and ruined it. She scolded herself and screwed up the paper, shoving it into her pocket, afraid of admitting the waste of it to her employer. She wanted to get out of the office and away from Cyril. Luckily she recalled that Mrs B had asked her to pop down to the village to collect some green ink. Mrs B always wrote out the work rota in different colours for the different parts of the ironworks. At a glance, one could see exactly which part of the business the paperwork pertained to. Anny loved learning these little tricks of the trade, though Mrs B said it was not a cost-effective way of doing things, but it was how Mrs King senior always did things, and she'd insisted on it continuing. Anny jumped up and grabbed her shawl and bonnet, opening and closing the door as soundlessly as she could, to evade being heard. Only once she had a mile between her and Cyril King did she feel she could relax once more. She hoped against hope that his visit had been a singular event and that he'd soon tire of his father's directives. *If I never see him again*, she thought as she entered the stationer's – her favourite shop in the town, full of delights, better than a sweet shop to her – *it won't be a minute too soon.*

However, Anny was to hope in vain. Cyril made a point of attending the office regularly after that. Mostly, he would ignore her and bark a few things at Mr or Mrs B before disappearing again, but always she felt his eyes on her.

It wasn't until some weeks later, when Mrs B was out of the office and Mr B was shut in his room with Mr Pritchard, that Anny found herself facing Cyril. She was sitting quietly at her desk when the door opened and Anny looked up to see Cyril step in. He gave a quick glance to the empty desk to one side and the closed door opposite, then smiled smugly and shut the door slowly behind him.

He turned and said brusquely, 'Miss Woodvine.'

'Yes, sir,' she said and then remembered to stand up and curtsey. He motioned to her to sit down, then looked at his hands as if he had no idea what to do with them. He clasped them and said once more, softer this time, 'Miss Woodvine.'

Anny stared at him. Should she speak again?

He stepped over to her and hesitated, then awkwardly seated himself on the corner of her desk. Anny looked down from embarrassment, the sight of his thigh bulging towards her papers being just too much.

'Tell me about your work. What is it you do all day?'

'Clerical duties,' she answered, her eyes on her desk.

'I see, I see.' She glanced up to see him stroking his chin, as if she had spoken of some matter of great import. 'And you work with a pen and ink?'

She looked down again. 'Yes, sir.'

'Different coloured inks, I see.'

'Yes, sir.'

'And you assist Brotherton and his wife in . . . matters related to . . . clerical duties?'

'Yes, sir.'

'And you have worked here for some months, Miss Woodvine.'

'Yes, sir.'

'Woodvine. Are you related? To the Woodvine at the furnace?'

Anny had felt the heat of discomfort from the nearness of Cyril on her desk. Now, she felt his fingers prying into her life and it sickened her. What was he about?

'That is my father, sir.'

'Is he, indeed?'

Anny did not respond.

'Look at me when I'm addressing you, girl,' he snapped and she had to look up at those cruel blue eyes, hypnotic and revolting all at once. But he did not look at her with a mocking sneer, as she had seen him give others. When she looked up at him, his face softened and he seemed to be searching for something in hers. The intensity of that searching blue gaze was

82

deeply disturbing to her and she could not bear it. She looked down again.

'I did not mean . . .' began Cyril, but then he paused and stuttered as he continued, 'A pretty girl. You are. A very pretty girl. But you must, in your position, you see . . . You are . . . different from the other girls. I've never met a girl remotely like you. I am growing fond of you, Anny. Very fond.'

Anny could not believe her ears. The young master speaking so frankly to her, so softly. She had assumed he only wanted one thing from her, as with any other female subordinate he took a fancy to. But now? 'Anyway,' he went on swiftly, ignoring her lack of response to his declaration, 'perhaps you would come and sit with me one time and talk to me? Or we could go for a walk together? In the woods.'

At that moment, Mr B and Pritchard appeared from the inner office and both stopped nervously at the sight of Cyril. He hopped up from Anny's desk and bid good afternoon to all, swiftly leaving and slamming the door behind him. Mr B looked at Anny. She wanted to smile at him, but her eyes were wide with alarm. She'd not forgotten what happened to the last girl Cyril had taken into the woods. Whatever he said, Cyril King had a bad way with girls and it was always more force than fondness.

From that day forward, Anny did all she could to avoid the young master, but somehow he always contrived some way to be near her.

It was just a few days later when she saw Cyril hanging around outside the office at home time. Shaking at the thought of her long walk alone through the forest, she asked Mr B if she could stay behind to do some extra paperwork.

'But you've done more than your fair share today, my dear,' said Mr B. 'You run along home.'

She turned and eyed the courtyard nervously, hoping his figure had gone, but there he was, kicking about a stone, hands in pockets, waiting, waiting for something. Or someone. Mr B joined her at the door and then said, 'I see.'

He pulled the door to and said to Anny, 'Wait here for a moment, then you will see that you can go home soon, unmolested.'

'Thank you, sir,' said Anny, so grateful she wanted to cry.

Mr B smiled and a glance was exchanged between him and his wife, who came to Anny and asked after her mother and father. Anny answered politely, yet her attention was on Mr B, who had gone outside and was talking to Cyril. The boy looked annoyed as he looked in her direction. Anny flinched at the expression on his face, as if burned by it. But Cyril did leave, and soon he and Mr B were gone behind the line of trees that led up to the big house.

'Off you go now, Anny. Don't dilly-dally on the way. Quick march home,' said Mrs B, a knowing look in her eye.

'I will. Thank you, ma'am,' said Anny and Mrs B looked down at her kindly, yet her eyes were worried.

Anny ran home that evening, a stray twig scratching her face as she rushed through the woods to the safety of home. All the way, her mind twisted in knots. She must work out a way to escape this creature, this fly in the ointment. Her job at the office had been like a gift from heaven, so happy and fulfilled she felt. But then there was Cyril. She sensed he could ruin her happiness, every last drop of it. She wished he were an insect she could squash beneath the heel of her boot. If only. She knew there was no way to avoid him. He was a gate-keeper for the next stage of her life and she had to work out how to charm him, evade him or destroy him. Surely there must be a way.

She could not eat much that night, and felt sick all evening. She said she had a bad belly and went to bed early. She wanted to tell her mother and father about Cyril, about his strange looks and his declaration, but how could she frame it? She did not know how to explain it to them. It shamed her. And anyway, what could they do about it? What could anyone do?

She kept her candle alight to write a letter to Peggy. It always cheered her to write to her friend. Peggy, dear Peggy. So nice and caring, so interesting and interested. So different from her elder brother; how could they be siblings and turn out so opposing, like sun and moon? She knew Peggy hated Cyril. Perhaps she could write to her about Cyril's unwanted attentions, see if his sister could reason with him. But she knew it was hopeless. Peggy feared Cyril even more than she did. She put her pencil down, the letter unwritten.

But if Peggy knew her friend was in danger from Cyril, the kind of danger that the poor maid Lucy had suffered in the woods, surely she would do something? Anny decided that a letter was not the place to approach this. It must be explained to Peggy face to face. It needed to be somewhere away from the office, away from the big house or even the woods, in case Cyril found them on one of his roaming walks. She decided on a plan and began to write, new hope fuelling her tired fingers.

Chapter 7

Dearest Peggy,

I am considering that it is high time we meet up again as friends do. I also wish to speak to you of a private matter that would be best away from your home or even the woods. I cannot explain by letter but all will become clear when I see you. I am wondering if you would like to try a small adventure. If I meet you by our fairy tree, I could bring for you some clothing such as an ordinary working girl of my circle may wear, and you could use this to dress in. As you never come to the village, no one will recognise you. Then we could go to my house and I would introduce you to all as another girl who works at Mr B's office. They would not know the difference and would be accepting of it if I explained it right. I think this would be fun, and would allow us to talk freely away from the big house and my work, and away from other prying ears. It could be such fun, and I imagine it would amuse you to dress up and to see where I live and my neighbours. You are always so *nosy about such things in your letters, which I find most curious as I cannot imagine what a young lady like yourself could possibly find interesting in my way of life, but indeed your many questions on the subject convince me of this.*

What do you say to my plan, Peggy? Are you game for such a thing?

Yours sincerely and with great friendship always,
Anny

Margaret's delight could barely be contained. A 'small adventure', Anny had called it. Nothing could be further from the truth for Margaret. It was the greatest adventure of her life so far, bar none! To not only escape her home and environs, to dress up in the costume of another class, to meet new people and pretend to be another. Another name, another girl, another life. It was the most thrilling idea she could imagine. At breakfast on the Saturday morning, she almost gave herself away by laughing aloud when spooning out her eggs. She could barely eat, but knew she had to keep up appearances. Nobody cared where she was most of the time or what she was doing. Cyril was busy with their father and Queenie had a bad chest and was staying in bed, ringing her bell commandingly for Jenkins to bring warm compresses and hot lemon drinks at regular intervals. Everything was perfect. She passed the morning in a frenzy of anticipation. Margaret found her least fussy dress and smallest bonnet with the least number of ribbons to tie to keep it in place. At lunchtime she asked for lunch in her room, tied it up in a cloth and left the house by the back stairs.

It was November and unseasonably warm outside. She was glad of this, as the thought of shedding her coat and dress and putting on Anny's clothes – whatever on earth Anny had found for her to wear – would be a chilly business in the woods on a normal November day. In the shade it felt brisk, yet the sun was out and the feel of it on her face was good and warm. She loved the creaking of the tree boughs and the slow splash of heavy fish in the river beyond, the bird calls of alarm as she passed by and then the unmistakable sound of her friend, calling her name, the name only her dear friend reserved for her.

'Peggy! Over here!' Anny stood, a bundle in her arms, in the midst of a circle of trees just beyond their fairy oak. She had chosen her spot well, as it afforded a little cover from the elements and any passing strangers, though they rarely saw walkers here.

'Anny!' called Margaret, beside herself with excitement, breaking into a run and nearly tripping over some tree roots in her rush to see her friend.

Anny placed the bundle on the ground as Margaret approached, then the girls threw their arms around each other, laughing and laughing. It was so good to see each other!

'Those ringlets,' Anny said and tutted. 'They shall never pass for a working lass. What were you thinking, putting those in today?'

Margaret's hand went to feel one of her sausage curls defensively. 'Royce does this with my hair every day. One cannot arouse suspicion by changing one's routine for no good reason.'

'Who's Royce again?'

'My maid, of course.'

Anny laughed, a rich, throaty laugh like a boy. 'Well, of course, it was *my* maid's day off, hence *my* locks resemble a fox dragged through a hedge backwards! One canna get a reliable maid these days, can one?'

'You are mocking me!' cried Margaret, good-naturedly, though she was a little affronted.

'I am, I am. It is my job to laugh at the rich and your job to take it. It is the way of things. Now then, let's get those fine clothes off and here's my cousin's dress. She is away with family and I borrowed it from her closet. Here, let's dress your hair too. I'll pin it back up and hide those ringlets. Dunna fuss now. Dear to goodness, these ribbons take an age to undo.'

'Oh, you are a scold!' cried Margaret, laughing, poking Anny in the side to make her laugh, as they pulled off her clothes. The cousin's dress was of a rough brown checked material but was a decent enough fit. There was a shawl of beige and dark green, so soft to the touch that Margaret held it to her cheek. There were stout boots and a plain bonnet, Anny re-dressing Margaret's hair to take some of the lady out of it. Bonnet on, boots on and Anny stood looking her up and down.

'We'll have to hope nobody eyes your fine stockings. But other than that, you'll do. Oh, but we need a name for you. Something ordinary.'

'Mary?'

'Yes, Mary will do. Mary . . . Brown. That's the dullest name I ever heard.'

'Mary Brown it is,' said Margaret, thoughtfully. 'I wonder what Mary Brown's life is like.'

'Oh, awful,' said Anny. 'She's beaten every day at noon by her father, a terrible drinker. Her mother is on the streets of Shoosby and thrown in prison for doing terrible things with rich gentlemen. She has five younger sisters who all rely on her weekly pennies from Mr B's office to survive, and Mary Brown cooks them cabbage soup every night of the week so they all have stomach cramps and fart themselves to sleep.'

They fell about laughing at that, so much so that Margaret got a stitch.

They stashed Margaret's rich girl clothes beneath a bush in the little copse she'd changed in, then linked arms and walked on through the woods towards the tiny hamlet that Anny called home. All the way they talked and talked, a rushing river of words. As Margaret talked, she glanced at her friend and saw she was frowning at her.

'What is it, Anny?'

'That voice of yours, the words you use. Too much governess talk for this lot. You'll have to curb it. Use a bit of local talk. Now then, instead of *How are you?* you say *Ow bist?*'

'How be-ist?' attempted Margaret.

'Well, just say it quicker. And when you wanna say *going to* you wanna say *gunna,* and when you wanna say *want to,* you wanna say *wanna*. Like, you might say, *I'm gunna wanna do that after*. You try it.'

Margaret looked at her friend's eager face and wanted so very much to please her. 'I'm gur-ner wur-ner do that arrfter.'

Anny's face was a complete blank. 'I think it's best all round if you just keep your mouth shut!'

At that, Margaret laughed and agreed, 'You know best, Anny.'

They went on their way. Margaret did not want to let her friend down. She decided to play the shy card – she could do that. She knew it well.

'Here we are!' cried Anny, as they quickened their step down an incline. Ahead of them was a shambling collection of huts and small houses along the riverbank, mostly housing ironworkers and some miners, some brickmakers and a few random others. Anny's neighbours were hanging clothes out to dry, feeding pigs, collecting eggs, smoking pipes, talking, shouting at the children. A girl saw the two of them coming and shouted out to Anny, asking who the stranger was. Anny said simply, 'From the office.'

'Another'un who never uses her hands, is it?' shouted the girl.

Anny turned to Margaret and said, 'They think I reckon I'm big-sorted because I dunna do hard labour anymore.' Then Anny turned back to her friends and called out, 'Try writing a letter without using your hands!'

Margaret marvelled at Anny's bravery, shouting at her friends like that. There were a few retorts and shakings of the head and hand gestures. It was all good-natured banter but something that Margaret had never experienced. She may as well have been on the moon. This was a world where people shouted at each other for fun. The only shouting in her house was in anger and usually preceded violence: a slap across the mouth, a verbal insult. *You're a great disappointment. You're an embarrassment to this family. You killed your mother.* And so forth. She really would rather be Mary Brown, for all her flatulent sisters.

'Day off from pushing a pen, is it, Anny?' said a boy behind them. The girls turned to see a tall blond lad, hands in pockets, smiling at Anny. 'What terrible hard work it must be.'

'Oh, it is, Peter Malone. Those pens are awful heavy.'

'I'm sure. I warrant those hands are nice and soft, with no washing done or ironstone picking. I warrant they're soft as kitten ears.'

93

'You'll never know!' laughed Anny. 'I wouldn't touch you with a barge pole!'

Peter Malone glanced in Margaret's direction, then stepped closer to Anny and whispered to her, loud enough for Margaret to catch it, 'A kiss is out of the question, then?'

'Get off with you, hobbety-hoy!' cried a good-natured voice close by and Margaret turned to see a woman with flushed cheeks and broad, strong forearms, hands on her hips. Meanwhile, Peter Malone slunk off in response, grinning all the while. The cheek! The way these people spoke to one another! It was shocking. It was also thrilling.

Anny said, 'This is my mother. This is Mary Brown, who works at Mr B's office.'

Margaret was about to bob down in a curtsey when she remembered Mary Brown and said quietly, 'Pleased to meet you.' Is that something a lower-class girl would say?

'What's for tea, Mother?' said Anny. Margaret sensed she was changing the subject to distract her mother's curious gaze.

'Why, it's two jumps to the pantry door, Anny. Now run along, you lasses.'

Margaret felt she had evaded capture, thanking providence that Mr Woodvine was doing his Saturday shift at the furnace and was not due home until teatime. If anyone might recognise her as the young lady of the big house, it might be him, though she doubted it. How much attention was paid by everyone to her on her rare trips out of the house, she imagined it was little if any.

Anny chatted merrily to Margaret for a while about the different families who lived in her row of houses and what they were like, what jobs they did, tittle-tattle and gossip. Then they spent some time watching the little ones play a game of jacks that they'd fashioned from old animal bones found in the woods. Then, a man came from one of the little houses, an older man, dressed in plain clothes, the telltale flat-brimmed hat of a Quaker bobbing past them. Margaret saw that behind him toddled a very young child, maybe a year old, its arms outstretched, its hands opening and closing and its face upturned in delight towards the Quaker man. The child called out and he turned around, picked the child up and whispered in its ear, carrying it back to the cottage as it squirmed and giggled in his embrace. At the door stood a woman around the same advanced age. They were perhaps in their sixties, both white-haired. He gave the child to the woman and went on his way.

Margaret thought of Queenie and wondered if she'd ever carried her granddaughter in her arms. Again, that sense of deflation, that she would rather have Mary Brown's life any day of the week than her own. 'What nice grandparents,' she observed to Anny.

'Oh, not grandparents but parents,' said Anny.

'Indeed?' questioned Margaret, intrigued. 'But, their age?'

'Well, they adopted her. The baby came in recent months to live here. The Quaker family have taken it in. They have a grown-up son, a miner. Nobody knows who the baby belongs to and tongues do wag about it. But they are such good, caring people that nobody really minds, and so the villagers have taken the child to heart as one of us.'

Margaret thought, *It must be their son's child, surely, born out of wedlock and brought from the mother.* She watched the old woman take up the child. Ah, it was pretty, golden-haired with a laughing face.

'Anny, wonna you help with this a minute?' called Mrs Woodvine and Anny trotted off to her mother, who was doing something with a knife to a heap of turnips. Margaret had not the first clue how to deal with a turnip, and anyway, she did not want to engage in conversation with Mrs Woodvine too much, lest she give herself away. Also, she found herself drawn to the Quaker family and wanted to continue watching them. She wandered towards their house, listening to the child's sweet laughter. The woman was chucking her under the chin and talking gently to her.

'Come 'ere, little'un. Weer'st thee bin, eh? What's thee bin doin'? Me little ducky egg.'

Did anyone ever speak so lovingly to me? she wondered. The woman looked up as Margaret approached.

Margaret stopped, unaware that she had even walked over there, so lost in the reverie was she.

'Good day,' said the woman.

'Erm . . .' Margaret cleared her throat. 'Good afternoon.'

'A friend of the Woodvines, I see.'

'Yes, of Anny's. We work together.'

The toddler was staring at Margaret now, an uncertain hand grasping at her adoptive mother's apron for reassurance.

'What is her name?' asked Margaret.

'This be Martha,' said the woman. 'And I be Hannah Beddoes.'

'I'm Margaret,' said Margaret. 'No! I am not. I am Mary! Mary Brown.'

Hannah Beddoes looked amused, then replied, 'An easy error to make. The names are similar. Margaret and Mary. And Martha.'

'Yes,' muttered Margaret, keenly aware of her flaming-hot cheeks. What a terrible liar she was.

'Ma-ma-ma-ma-ma,' babbled the child, her eyes firmly fixed on Margaret, who crouched down and held out her hand to the child. One swift glance at Hannah gave her the courage she needed and she took some wobbly steps over to Margaret. Her speed increased, but the momentum was too much for her newly acquired walking and she tripped, falling into Margaret's arms. She was a brave little thing and did not cry. Up close,

Margaret stared at the girl's upturned face, now able to see what bright, large green eyes the child had. Extraordinary eyes.

'You are so pretty,' murmured Margaret, transfixed by the eyes. It was as if she had seen those eyes before somewhere, in another face, so familiar were they to her. 'Such a pretty one, she could be a fairy child. A changeling.'

Hannah Beddoes sniffed, and one look showed she did not approve of the comment.

'Oh, I am sorry, I did not mean . . . I mean . . .' Margaret stuttered, mortified.

'Think naught on it, my dear. She is a curious chicken, in her looks, indeed she is. And the babby did come from off, but not so very far away. She had a tragic story, you see. But it was God's will that my husband should be the one to find the babby and keep her safe.'

Margaret touched the little girl's face, who shrank from her and tottered back to Hannah. 'I cannot think of a luckier child, I really cannot,' said Margaret, looking about her at the ramshackle line of cottages and their disrepair, the poverty ingrained in the muddy boots and grimy faces of all who lived there. Yet she knew she'd trade her life with this green-eyed child in a moment.

'Time to go, Mary Brown!' called Anny as she approached.

Margaret wished the Quaker woman a good day and hurried to join Anny.

On their walk back to the fairy tree, Anny fell quiet. It seemed that her mind was heavy with something. Margaret suddenly recalled what Anny had said in her letter, that she had something to discuss with her. In all this excitement, she had forgotten it.

'You said in your letter that you wanted to talk to me about a private matter?'

'Yes,' said Anny and stopped walking. 'I do need to talk to you about summat.'

'Anything,' said Margaret, and meant it.

'It's about Cyril.'

'Cyril? What about him?'

'He's been bothering me at work.'

'Bothering? How?' A churning began in Margaret's stomach.

'He wants to talk with me, or sit with me, or go arm-in-crook with me. Mr B is very good and heads him off, distracting him and such, while I slip away. But I canna keep it up forever, and one day he will find me alone and . . .'

A flash of imagery jumped into Margaret's mind – Cyril pushing Lucy against a tree. Oh, the thought of it, the very idea of it for Anny.

'But Anny, didn't you know? He's going away.'

'Eh?'

'Yes, Father is sending him away to boarding school. He's always had a tutor, but I overheard Father say he was lazy and needed taking in hand, that going out into the world would be good for him. He's starting in the new year, when he turns fifteen. I've seen his uniform and kit, so I know it will surely happen. It was decided only recently and we have not written this week, seeing as we were about to meet up again. And I was so excited with the visit, it went completely out of my mind today to tell you.'

Anny fell to her knees. Margaret, shocked, crouched beside her friend, whose face was in her hands and she was sobbing, really sobbing.

'Oh Anny, oh Anny, my dear, dear friend. You should've told me. I wish you'd have told me sooner.'

Anny rested her head on her friend's shoulder as they hugged.

'Well, I am telling you now. And you dunna know how happy your news has made me. I could skip and dance and sing!'

The girls stood up and Anny wiped away her tears on her shawl.

'I do know how happy, as I am the same! It's as if a great stone were lifted from my chest. No more slaps for me, no more bullying. Until he returns in the holidays, that is.'

Anny's expression clouded. 'When will that be?'

'Well, not as often as all that. I heard Father and Queenie discussing it and they said that they were sending him away to make a man out of him and that meant no mollycoddling, and that he must not come home at weekends or half-terms. So he must stay until Christmas and thereafter only be allowed home three times a year, in April, August and December. And he's going there for three years, at least!'

'All my Christmases have come at once!' squealed Anny and, hitching her skirt up from her boots, did that little skip and dance of which she'd spoken. Then she stopped suddenly and said, 'Let us hope he inna expelled for bad behaviour.'

'Oh yes, let's pray to God to keep him good! He's a terrible coward though, Anny, so I think it's more likely that, never having been a regular schoolboy, he is the one who will be bullied and kept in line. I would like to see that happen with my own eyes. I would take great pleasure in it!'

'Me too,' said Anny. 'Though I'd rather never lay eyes on him again. No offence.'

'None taken!' laughed Margaret.

The friends linked arms and went on merrily to the fairy tree, gossiping about the locals Margaret had just met.

'You're so lucky to have so many friends, Anny. I do envy you.'

Anny sighed and said, 'I used to have lots of friends. Too many. All bothering me and making noise when I wanted to be peaceful. But now, since I started working at the office, they don't come to me so much anymore. I've changed, I suppose, and they can see it. Now they mostly just tease me about it. They dunna understand me.'

'I do,' said Margaret, squeezing her friend's arm. 'You are simply trying to make a better life for yourself. There is nothing wrong in that.'

'Exactly!' said Anny. 'You see that. But they only think I'm getting above myself. Especially that Peter Malone. He's always on at me about it. Laughing at me. Well, I dunna find it funny anymore.'

'Is Peter Malone in love with you?' Margaret asked.

'Oh, I dunna know and I dunna care! I'm not interested in him or any boys. I'm far too busy.'

'He seemed to like you very much.'

Seeming embarrassed at the turn of conversation, Anny became dismissive. 'He's nothing and nobody. Dunna waste any more of your thoughts on the likes of him.'

They walked on in silence, Margaret wondering what it was like to be wanted like the Malone boy obviously wanted Anny. It must be the most marvellous feeling. She envied Anny that. She envied Peter Malone, his easy way of talking. She envied Anny's neighbours, their simple, happy lives, as she pictured it.

'I have a question about your neighbours,' she said, as they reached the tree and she began to shed her working clothes. 'The Quaker baby. Where did it come from? Does anybody know?'

'Nobody really knows,' said Anny nonchalantly. 'But I heard my mother say they found the baby on the iron bridge.'

As Margaret changed back into her rich girl's clothes, a phrase echoed over and over in her mind. *The baby on the bridge, the baby on the bridge.* It must be the same one her grandmother mentioned, mustn't it? But what could Queenie have to do with this green-eyed foundling? Then she knew where she'd seen those eyes before. Her grandfather had those same large, bright green eyes.

∞

Once home, Margaret sought out Queenie in bed, surrounded by the clutter of illness: used handkerchiefs and hot compresses gone cold scattered amongst the sheets.

'How are you, Grandmother? Are you improving?'

'So, you've deigned to see me, child,' said Queenie testily. Then, more softly, seeming to recall that she was meant to be at death's door, 'Where can you have been all afternoon?'

'By the river, walking. That's all.'

'It does look a pleasant day, from what I can see from my sickbed.'

'It is. Quite warm. Grandmother, I wanted to ask you about something.'

'What is it now?'

Margaret had to frame it carefully. She must ensure it sounded casual, something overheard.

'Out walking, there were some local children playing in the woods. They were gossiping and one of them said about a baby that had been found on the bridge.'

Queenie looked at Margaret sharply, then turned away and closed her eyes.

'Leave me now, child.'

'But Grandmother, why is it that you talk of this baby, of it escaping the King family?' Margaret wanted to say it had green eyes, but she realised that would give her away, that she had seen the child itself. Questions would come thick and fast from Queenie about where she had really been that afternoon.

'I told you to leave. Your prattling on about nothing has exhausted me.'

'But it is not nothing, is it, Grandmother? Please tell me.'

'There is nothing to tell! Ridiculous child.'

'I will keep it secret. I am good at keeping secrets.'

'Oh, I am sure you are. Butter wouldn't melt. Those huge, innocent blue eyes of yours.'

'The baby on the bridge—'

Queenie pushed herself upright in bed and fixed her granddaughter with a harsh eye. 'Never ask me about that again. Never even mention it again in my hearing. Never, do you hear me?'

'But why?' cried Margaret.

'How dare you quiz me! You, a mere child. A mere girl! The King men act however they please. There was nothing I could ever do about it and nothing you can either. The men of this family are cruel.'

'I know this to be true,' said Margaret. She struggled to form the words, unaccustomed as she was to having anything other than small talk with her family. But she knew this was an important moment, that something crucial was hovering just beyond her reach. 'But I admire you, Grandmother, for the way you stand up to them and speak the truth.'

'Well, that is all very well, but it is sound and fury, signifying nothing. A woman can say what she likes, but the fact of her life remains. We can fashion a life from the scraps our men leave us, but that is all a woman's life is made of. The leavings of cruel men. You would do well to learn that now, before you are courted and wed. Now, where is Jenkins? I am ill and you have upset me. Fetch Jenkins this instant. And then, do go away.'

Chapter 8

Three years passed slowly for Cyril. The daily torture of boarding school: running and fighting, shouting and crying, writing and arithmetic, kings and queens, Latin and Greek, cricket and rowing, beatings and fear – the brutal camaraderie and casual violence of boys cooped up together in an upmarket prison paid for handsomely by their willing parents. Whatever little pockets of softness he had in him were gone by the age of eighteen. He had made some friends for life – fierce friendships forged in combat – and enemies, mostly amongst the masters for whom he dreamt up elaborate revenge fantasies he planned to carry out when he was older, a free man and out from under their dictatorship. The school had done its job admirably. The boy he had once been was gone; the man he was becoming had been hacked out of stone and stood proudly at the edge of adulthood, sturdy and jagged. His hunger to dominate females had matured into a cleverer, sneakier power play of sweet talk and mind games. He knew that some girls would not put up with violence, but wanted to hear and believe certain falsehoods in order to spread their legs. There were no girls in his environment to practise upon, but he made sure that trips into the local town were peppered with flirtations with local shop girls and other passing riff-raff of a certain class, higher than maids and lower than ladies. He sometimes found himself behind a bush in a park for a bout of sexual fumbling with one or other of these hussies. But all of them were simply passing through his affections, waiting for the day when he'd leave this cursed gaol of a school and go back home, ready to take up his position on his father's estate and declare his love to Anny. He loved her, or believed he did. What did he want from her? To bed her, every night and every morning too if possible, but also to be improved by her; he admired her. Mostly, he looked forward to the day when he would gloriously take her, the thought of her thick red hair flung across his face making him stiff with eager sexual anticipation.

Three years passed peacefully for Margaret, who had found her portion of contentment after a miserable childhood. Her daily round began with practising the piano, from which she derived huge pleasure, as she had a natural ability for it, a good ear and quick fingers. She played from the heart and found new pieces a welcome challenge that gave her the feeling of meeting new friends. She read many books from her father's largely untouched and undusted library. Her favourites were historical romances and any French literature. She spent much of her small allowance on ordering books written in French and tore open the deliveries when each arrived. How she loved to read aloud in French, in her bedroom, of course, as her father was as anti-French as the next roast beef Englishman. She wrote long letters to Anny. She spent her afternoons taking walks, sometimes 'happening by chance' on Anny at lunchtime to gossip on the path down from the office. The two houses knew that the girls were acquainted by now, though they acted in a restrained and civil manner to each other when others were about, and in private like the close, bosom friends they really were. At teatime every day, Margaret spent an hour with Queenie, not talking much, but playing Old Maid, their new obsession. They would gamble with dried peas, or seeds, or conkers, whatever the season provided. The only blot on her landscape were the thrice-yearly home visits from Cyril, where she mostly made herself very scarce or posted herself at the library window, which had a view across the courtyard to Mr Brotherton's office; if she saw Cyril heading in that direction, she would call to him and try to distract him – Queenie wanted him, Father wanted him, Cook wanted him – to give Anny time to escape from the office temporarily. Her only other problem was her father and his child-wife's continued efforts to match her up with the sons of landed gentry. She found she could not speak to any of them of anything that actually mattered to her. Indeed, she cultivated her reputation for shyness by appearing deliberately boring. Her friendship with Anny had taught her how to speak her true feelings, but with these ill-chosen suitors she clammed up, on purpose. Awkward walks were characterised by long silences, that these young men might have found appealing at first in the demure, pretty blonde, but soon became tiresome for a young man eager to make his way in the world. What a blessed release it was for her when each one fell by the wayside and stopped calling, and she could go back to her books and music. She secretly delighted in thwarting her parents' plans for her future. She was proud of her lovely hair and large eyes, her pale face and long limbs; she dreamt of a dashing romantic hero with flashing, French eyes that would come to her room at night, unannounced and undone by passion for her and her alone. She woke up damp and restless, yearning for something she did not understand yet could not resist. She wanted a different life than the one her father had planned for her.

Three years passed feverishly for Anny, a whirlwind of ambition and optimism. Her father was doing well and there was talk of promotion for him. For years he had been a furnace filler, tipping the charge relentlessly into the furnace mouth. Now he had a chance of becoming a founder, descending from the mouth of hell into the cast-house, where the molten metal ran into sand-sculpted troughs. The founders would guide the surge of iron into the channels and sub-channels, called the sow and pigs, as they resembled piglets feeding at their mother's belly. It was work that required more skill, and Pritchard had put her father's name forward. She was forming a deep conviction that hard work and belief in oneself led to success. All one needed was to do it and then good things would happen. Her work at the office went from strength to strength, learning side by side with the Brothertons, who grew as fond of her as kin. Her language changed, improved as far as she was concerned, as she moved further away from the local words and sayings of her family, friends and neighbours and grew more alike with her betters, as she saw them. It pleased her more and more to listen to herself talk. She excelled at problem-solving, her mind quick-thinking and logical. Her handwriting continued to develop beautifully, yet she tired of clerical work. She joined Mr B more in his office, discussing labour troubles and matters of commerce with him, learning from him always yet surprising him often with her insight into how to get the best out of people, whether workers or merchants; how to make them feel appreciated yet also get their best deal for the estate. Everyone winning was always her goal. She, too, wrote long letters to her friend, Peggy. She, too, did all she could to avoid Cyril when he visited three times a year. Sometimes she was not able to give him the slip and was forced to engage in conversation. He was not as arrogant, impatient and utterly objectionable as he had been in his earlier youth, but she did not like him or trust him. The hint of cruelty remained in his eyes and she did not like to look at them, as they made her insides twist and jerk, a most unpleasant and confusing sensation. Romance was a stranger to her, as the inept attempts of local lads to steal a kiss or more were always spurned forthrightly. They had no ambition, no get-up-and-go, no prospects. She stared at herself in the looking glass and hated her freckles, cursed her red hair. She had creamy skin and elegant narrow feet, which she admired, but wondered if anyone would ever notice such things, strapped up in her boots, or stuck in a dim, wood-panelled office. She longed for a young man like her, a good man, a moral man, with a burning ambition to change the world. Hand in hand, they would stride forward into the future. They would be masters of their own destinies. They would brush aside with ease any obstacles, which would disperse like wispy dandelion seeds on a warm breeze. She believed in this future utterly and saw no earthly reason why it would not all come to pass one day soon. All she needed was to find him.

⌒⌒

Anny was writing when she first saw Jake Ashford. People came in and out of the office all day, and with Cyril still away at school she did not flinch when the

111

office door opened. Mr B was in his room with the door closed, in conference with Pritchard. Mrs B was poorly and taking the day in bed. Anny was going to pop over to the cottage to see her and make her a little broth. She just wanted to get this letter finished. The door opened and she did not want to interrupt her work, so finished the sentence she was on, then looked up impatiently.

'Good morning,' said the young man standing before her. 'Or is it afternoon?'

Anny stared at him. He was an outsider to these parts. She had lived near Ironbridge all her life and worked at that office day in, day out for three years, and she knew everyone who was likely to come in. This one was new. He was far too well dressed for an ironworker, too fashionable for a merchant or salesman and not well dressed enough for a friend of the Kings. He fitted into no category she had experience of and was therefore a mystery. His enigmatic air was complemented by dark eyes and a tall, broad-shouldered frame curving into a narrow waist, clothed in a smart frock coat and he was holding a large leather wallet secured with a strap. He removed a tall hat to reveal a luxuriant mop of black hair, parted at the side and curly about the ears. *Who could this magnificent stranger be?*

Anny glanced downwards, struggling to contain her obvious curiosity and managed to utter, 'Can I be of assistance?'

'I do hope so. My name is Jake Ashford and I am an artist.'

'A what?' said Anny, before she could stop herself, then cursed her big mouth. Of course she knew what an artist was. Well, she had an inkling. But she had made herself look ignorant, she felt. 'I should say, an artist? How interesting.'

Jake Ashford's face broke into a smile and Anny could not help but smile too. Perhaps she had not made such a fool of herself. 'Thank you. I have come here to paint the wonders of industry.'

The what of what? she nearly blurted, but checked herself. *What could he want here?* 'I see,' she said, though she didn't.

'I wish to paint the developments happening here, in your area, to help show the world how extraordinary it is.'

'Is it? Extraordinary, I mean?' Anny couldn't see how her home town could be of interest to anyone. It's true she was proud of her father and his work, making iron that was shipped across the country, even abroad. But it was hard to see why anyone would want to come and see the processes by which it was made, let alone paint it. It was like painting the swan's feet and not the swan.

'Oh, yes!' he enthused. 'This is the centre of a revolution that is being felt all over the world. It must be recorded for posterity. Other artists have visited areas of industry to record the great rate of change taking place. Painters, poets and writers flock to them.'

'Do they?' she asked, amazed. *Here? Our little town?*

'Oh, indeed. The world's first iron bridge built here was a mighty advertisement to visitors to say, *Look, see what we have created here!* We come to marvel at the wonders of technology, improving year on year, the rate of change astonishing. And that is why I am here now. I wish to ask permission to visit the King ironworks and its workers and make sketches. I will then turn these into paintings, works of art for all to see the beauty and majesty of what is happening here.'

Anny was completely wrapped up in his words now. 'Beauty? What is beautiful about an ironworks? I've been around it all my days and never seen much beauty in it.'

Jake Ashford took a step closer, placed his hat on Anny's desk and raised his hands in the air. 'The night sky above the furnace here turns blood red and scarlet, fiery orange and burnt umber. It is spectacular! Have you not seen it?'

'Of course I've seen it!' she cried. 'I live here! My father works there.'

'He does?'

'Yes, he's worked at the furnace for years.'

'Can you not see its beauty? The hellish colours? The power of it?'

Anny pictured it in her mind's eye and thought about how impressive it was. He was right. She was simply accustomed to it.

'I suppose it is. I cannot, imagine a painting of it though. But I think you could make it beautiful.'

Her mouth moving faster than her thoughts, as usual. She was really thinking that *he* was beautiful, all fired up like that; she could almost see the flames reflected in those deep, dark eyes. She looked away and noted again the leather folder he held and wondered if his drawings were in there. She was about to ask to see them when the door behind her opened and out came Mr B and Pritchard, who were talking away until they saw the young man in their midst. Both stopped, and Mr B said, 'And who's this? May we help you, young sir?'

'This is Mr Ashford,' said Anny. 'He's here to paint.'

The older men's faces were as blank as her own at first. Once it had all been explained, Mr B was soon drawn into Jake's vision, too. He talked with Jake for some time and Anny listened intently, not able to add much to the conversation but watching Jake Ashford the whole time. Mr B agreed to take him up to the big house to speak with the master.

'I'll go and see Mrs B afterwards, Anny. You have your lunch in peace, go where you will. Don't forget to lock up.'

As Mr B left the office, he held the door open for the artist, who paused before he left. 'It was a pleasure to meet you, Miss . . . ?'

'Woodvine. But you can call me Anny.'

115

'And you must call me Jake,' he said with a smile, and bowed to her, flourishing his hat before him and walking out, the door shut firmly behind him by Mr B.

Anny did not eat her lunch that day. She had not the stomach for it. She did not even leave the office. She hoped Jake Ashford would return with Mr B. But he did not. She sat at her desk all afternoon, distracted from her beloved work for the first time since Cyril's unwanted visits. She wondered what Mr King would say to this young artist. Would he be flattered by the attention or see the young man as beneath him? Anny willed him to accept. If Jake were granted permission, he would be about quite a bit. He would paint her father's workplace and maybe even her father, who knew? Could she show him around? Could she be his guide? What would Father think of this? Her mind was filling with questions. But the uppermost one was this: when would she see Jake Ashford again?

∞

Whenever Margaret heard people in the house, it was usually either business associates of her father or fatuous friends of her stepmother, and neither were of any interest to her. She found both sets of people intimidating and usually slunk off to her room and stayed there. These days her parents had more or less given up on the idea of her being any sort of social animal and left her alone. She heard the door open that let in business visitors and heard Mr B's booming voice first. Well aware from Anny's accounts of how nice Mr B really was, she had no fear of him anymore, but anyone loud always set her on edge. She was seated in the library reading a French novel when she heard him and did not have time to get past him up the stairs to her room, so hoped that they would not come in here. Mr B was with someone, that was clear, as he was talking away and a voice was answering, quietly at first, so she had to strain to hear. What were they talking about? Something about the business, about the furnace? She went back to her book. But the other voice was louder now and talking about colour. Lots of colours. He was listing colours and applying them to the things he had seen. His voice was quick, eager and intelligent. She heard the maid say that her father had stepped out briefly and would they like to wait for him in the library? Before she had time to gather herself, the door was opening and the visitors were inside.

'Ah, Miss King!' cried Mr B, his voice as piercing as ever. Beside him stood a dark-eyed young man, but before she had time to fully register him, Mr B went on, 'Studious, as ever. Always a nose in a book. There never was such a child for quiet contemplation as Miss King. Never wants to talk, eh? Except to our Anny, the only one who ever was able to draw a conversation from you, Miss King.'

Margaret bowed her head, perceiving a slight criticism. She had no idea what to say to that; she never did in these moments of social chit-chat. It was always better for everyone if she just disappeared upstairs. Then, another voice spoke.

'But I see we are disturbing you, miss. My humblest apologies. I should wait outside, in the grounds perhaps.'

Margaret looked up. The young man was handsome, decidedly so. And his politeness to her made him seem even more so. Mr B was wittering on about her and her books and how her father wouldn't be long, yet she had lost all sense of what he was saying. Only those eyes held her. Intent, direct and as black as coals. She was compelled to do something she never did: she interrupted Mr B in full flight.

'Won't you introduce me?' she asked, never taking her gaze from the young man.

'Why, of course,' said Mr B. 'Mr Ashford, this is Miss King, the daughter of the household. Miss King, this is Mr Jake Ashford, an artist and painter who wishes to paint your father's ironworks and seeks his permission. A most interesting project, I must say.'

Margaret knew it was not etiquette to shake hands with a young man who was not of her acquaintance. She politely nodded her head and Jake Ashford did the same. Then, he spoke to her.

'I see you are reading in French, Miss King. When I was in Paris, the French shook hands with the left, as they deemed the left hand to be nearer the heart.'

Margaret stared at him. How she wished that when introduced she had extended her hand and felt his own. She was sure it would not be that worst of things – a clammy handshake – but instead imagined it warm and dry, firm and lingering. Her hands tingled at the thought. There was a moment of stillness between them, broken by the sound of her father returning in the hall beyond the library door.

'What?' she heard him say. 'There is a what in the library?' Margaret looked down at her lap. It was the instant effect her father had on her. She wished to look up again at Jake Ashford, but the heaviness of her head in her father's imminent presence prevented her from doing so.

The door opened and her father entered, saying curtly, 'What is this all about, Brotherton?'

Margaret listened to the introductions and explanations with her head still lowered, her eyes burning a hole in the French words on the page before her. Jake Ashford had been in Paris. What was he doing there? Painting, perhaps? How she longed to speak to him of it. She had never been given leave to visit France, her father being such a hater of the people, but she desired to utterly. A vision of walking in the gardens of the Palace of Versailles with Jake Ashford leapt to mind and she started at it, so ridiculous was it. But oh, what a lovely vision! She listened and willed her father to do the right thing, the best thing, for her, that is. Invite this young man to paint his stupid ironworks, but then to stay and become an acquaintance of the family. But her father was taking some convincing.

'But why on earth would an artist want to come here of all places? Shropshire is pretty enough, I suppose, but there are finer places to paint, surely.'

Jake held up his hands towards the window and made the shape of a frame in the air. All eyes turned to his hands and waited for his next pronouncement. 'Ironbridge and Coalbrookdale,' he declared. Names so familiar to Margaret were transformed into something epic in Jake Ashford's tones. 'Surrounded by thick forest yet smothered in coal dust, lit by the constant burning of the fires from the ironworks. Due to the complex geology of this area, a range of vital industries have sprung up along the majestic River Severn. The hills and banks are clustered with steam engines, limestone mines, brick kilns and tar ovens. Wagons loaded with ironstone and coal trundle on iron railways down the inclined plane from the pits to be delivered to the works that will transform them into vital products. Their fruits include pig iron, cast iron and wrought iron; chinaware and fine porcelain; pipes and ceramic tiles – these riches then sent out across the world. What finer subject could a modern artist find than this?'

Brotherton nodded proudly, as if he himself were solely responsible for the marvels the young man described.

Her father looked impressed, too, but was not quite won over as yet.

'Let us peruse your work, then,' he said. 'I cannot possibly agree until I have seen your calibre for myself. I assume you have some in that receptacle by your feet?'

Jake picked up the wallet and opened it on the table at which Margaret was sitting. She closed her book and pushed it to one side. Out came sketch after sketch of charcoal on creamy white paper. Beautiful buildings with elaborate architecture that she could only imagine might have been French or Italian or who knew what, as her education had been so limited and mostly self-administered. There were pictures of birds too and people, large crowd scenes or vignettes of individuals, great bridges that spanned mighty rivers and detailed studies of statues she imagined he must have seen in lofty museums. The beauty of the lines and curves that spilled across the table thrilled her, as if Jake Ashford's very mind had been poured forth before her. What a fascinating person he was, and very clearly talented. She thought the drawings were marvellous. She stole glimpses of him when she could and saw how he stared at her father, so keen was he to impress, it seemed. She wished the decision had been hers and that he had been looking at her so keenly.

Her father was quiet for some time, leafing through the sketches, his mouth tight and his expression giving nothing away. At long last, he spoke. 'These are good,

Ashford. You can draw, I'll give you that. But look here. These European flounces are all very well. But you must be aware that industry is a place of danger and you will be responsible for yourself at all times. I do not have the manpower to chaperone you when molten iron is about. You must be sensible and exhibit . . . . common sense.'

'I quite understand,' said Jake. 'I have travelled in Europe alone these past months, and believe I have developed a keen sense of self-preservation.'

'Well then, I cannot see any harm in it. You may become our resident artist. I will pay a small stipend to assist you in your endeavours, if you agree to paint my wife too. I desire a painting of her. Can you do that? Can you manage portraits?'

'I certainly can, sir. I would be honoured to paint anyone for you, sir. Anyone in your household.'

Margaret's heart leapt. Just imagine it, sitting for a painting for him, spending hours with him. Oh, it was too much to bear!

'Yes, well, we shall see about that. Now then, I am a busy man. Brotherton will attend to you and arrange suitable accommodation. See to it, Brotherton.' With that, Mr King left the room and Mr B instantly began to prattle on about the project.

Margaret carefully placed her chair back and stood. Jake was tidying away his sketches and Margaret wanted to help. She picked up one and passed it to him, which he took with a kind smile directed straight at her. She picked up another, a lovely sketch of a formal flower garden, perhaps in Paris, perhaps in Rome, somewhere beautiful. Her eyes lingered on it. The country around here was handsome, nobody could deny it; the Severn was banked by rich, dense woodland and rolling hills beyond. But that was wild and this was tamed nature, rows of hedging and swirls of what looked like tulips, making a stunning pattern of perfect symmetry.

'If you like it, you may keep that,' said Jake.

Margaret shook her head and went to hand it back – unable to agree to a gift from an unknown young man – but she wanted badly to keep it, and worried too that it would look ungrateful. She drew it to her, looked at it again and raised her eyes to his.

'Thank you,' she whispered, and clutched the picture tenderly.

'It is nothing, but you are welcome, Miss King. Most welcome.'

When he had gone, she stared and stared at his drawing. Her drawing, now. She looked up and out of the window, without thinking, clutching the picture tenderly against her chest. When she came to, she saw that the charcoal had imprinted itself onto her yellow dress, leaving a black mark across her breast. She ran her fingers over it, leaving a smudge of darkness on her hand.

Chapter 9

It was noon and Anny had escaped from the office, walked hurriedly down to Ironbridge and sought out a bench upon which to eat her lunch. She was just finishing off the Dawley doorstep spread with butter she had brought with her, when she saw Jake Ashford walking in a leisurely fashion up the street towards her. It was just as she had hoped. As she hurriedly brushed crumbs from her mouth and skirts, he saw her, smiled and increased his pace. They had spoken with each other several times now, either in the office or by chance, in town or near the ironworks. They had talked about his art and her work and more. She had never had such conversations in her life. She picked over the substance of their discussions after each one, rehearsing the arguments she would offer if the subject arose between them again. She was keen to impress him with her thinking, afraid that if she did not keep up with him, he would tire of their meetings. And these meetings had become the bright centre of her life. He seemed to have sought her out at the same bench she had been sitting on the last time they met – or was it merely a coincidence?

'I find you here again, Anny. A welcome escape from the rigours of work?'

'Ah, but I love my work. You know that.'

'True, true. Although, you are one of the few, perhaps. May I?' He motioned to the empty space beside her and she nodded keenly. He took his seat, placing his bag and wallet down on either side.

'Perhaps you're right,' said Anny. 'I know how lucky I am to find my work valuable and enjoyable, when to many it is a chore or a curse.'

'It is not luck in your case, though. Your mother taught you for a purpose and you made the most of that. There was design in it and you grasped it and let your ambition guide you.'

'But you are the same, Mr Ashford. You love your work and you are driven by it. Did you always know you wanted to be an artist?'

'Not until I travelled and saw the old masters. And please, call me Jake.'

Could she? They were friends now, she supposed. But who were these old masters he spoke of? She wondered if she should pretend to understand. But she knew that she'd never get anywhere in life by fakery. She knew nothing of art, and dearly longed for an education like his, even like Peggy's, as limited as that was. But she was not ashamed of this fact, particularly with Jake, who she felt understood that her lack of education was beyond her control, not a part of her but a fact of circumstance.

'What are the old masters?'

He gave her a potted history of Western art, which she tried to follow, but eventually gave up and contented herself with listening to his voice. Then he came to the point.

'These men painted scenes from the Bible, from ancient mythology. What relevance has that to me today? To you, or to any of us? It also seemed like the province of the rich, the classically educated. I knew this was not what I wanted to paint, definitely not. I want to get to the centre of things, to the core of mankind, not its luckiest, its richest, its most dominant. I want to answer the great unanswered questions. On my return, I determined that I would go out into the real world, into the everyday lives of the working people of our great country and discover for myself the substance of what really matters in this day and age.'

To listen to him speak of such things was a thrill like no other. She watched his mouth move with the passion of his thoughts, memorised the tiny details in the nuances of his face: the way he looked far ahead as he spoke, as if his inner eye had travelled forward in time and had already arrived in the future; the way his neck would flush pink when he spoke with fervour, and the way he would listen to her speak. She especially loved the way one eyebrow went up and the other down when she let slip something gushing about him or his ideas, as if to say, *I am not worthy of your fine words*. His modesty made him all the more attractive.

'I am quite sure I never heard a soul speak about the workers the way you do,' said Anny.

'I am not the only one who feels this way. There are writers all over Europe who see the world as I do, the artificial boundaries that exist between the wealthy and the poor. I want to change the way the rich see the working classes. I want my art to show them the dignity in a hard day's work, the wonder of the changes taking place in industry right here on your home ground – not from the scientist's or industrialist's point of view – but from the ordinary folk, how each man and woman is contributing towards this great movement. People like your father. I have sketched him at work, Anny. There is more honour in that man's muscle and sinew than in a thousand Greek heroes. For our modern times, your father is the hero!'

Anny laughed delightedly. If Father could hear himself called a hero, he would laugh his fill, too. But Jake's vision of him rang true for her and touched her heart.

'I am so very proud of my father and the job he does. His work has never been easy, even now he's been promoted. Not only the sweat of it, but the business side of it – the ironmasters and the way they treat the workers. It's not a new thing, been going on like this for years. Why, when he was a young man he stood witness to strikes and uprisings. He often tells us the story, at the fireside of an evening, of when his father's coal-mining friends gathered in protest at the cinder heaps, and the yeomanry were called and opened fire. Two colliers were killed. Others were arrested and one ringleader was hanged. They called it the Battle of Cinderloo. It sounds like a name heroes might choose. But it came to nothing, and still the workers are suffering at the whim of their masters. The working man is stamped on and crushed like an earywig.'

To say these things aloud, and to this handsome young man who listened intently to her every word, was like gulping down wine. Heady and dangerous.

'Seditious talk, Anny,' said Jake, with an approving smile. She did not know the meaning of this, but it sounded good to her.

'Truth, that's all.'

'I know it. I hope my art can help to bridge that gap between the classes. That is my aim. To create a clearer understanding between the masters and the workers. The honour would be mine, to attempt this necessary feat, to use my art for good purpose. It may be folly but I would rather try and fail than live a life of regret.'

Anny listened intently and marvelled at his resolve. Everything she felt was wrong with the world was found here in its polar opposite: this optimistic, heartfelt young man. He was talented, which was appealing enough, but he was also earnest – an irresistible mixture.

Jake went on. 'But I fear it may be a fool's errand. What bridge could ever span that gap, when the rich and the poor are separated as utterly as fish from birds? They live in different worlds. That the rich and poor could ever understand each other seems impossible.'

'Not impossible,' said Anny.

'How so?'

Anny glanced at him, his earnest face. Should she go on?

'I have a friend . . . a rich friend. We understand each other.'

'And how has this come about?'

Anny paused again. Surely he could be trusted. She believed it.

'My best friend is Miss King. Miss Margaret King, up at the big house. It's a secret we share. Most people know we are acquaintances, that we make polite talk with each other if we happen to meet. But what they do not know is that we have been friends for years, have written letters to each other for years.'

'Extraordinary!'

'And she is rich and I am poor, but we understand each other all right. Always have. Why, we are like sisters. Secret sisters.'

Jake clapped his hands and laughed. 'You are full of surprises!'

Anny grinned at this. It delighted her to delight him. The world went on behind them, around and beyond them, but her world consisted only of Jake's words and Jake's eyes.

He said, 'I have met Miss King. She is an intelligent, thoughtful young woman, I can see that. But other than that, she seemed entirely typical of her class. Accomplished, no doubt, yet uninspiring I'd thought, however pretty she may be.'

Pretty. The word sliced through her intimacy with Jake like a knife through butter. The day after both she and Margaret had first met Jake, they had contrived to find each other almost at the same moment, and had let the words tumble out simultaneously, talking under and over each other about all of his attributes. They giggled and blushed, enjoying the opportunity to talk to another who clearly felt the same way. There was a comradeship in it that nobody else but these two girls could understand, the complete wonderfulness of Jake Ashford. Yet, there was a moment, in that very first talk, when both girls had paused and were clearly, obviously, lost in their own private thoughts of him. Then they both glanced up and caught the other at it, a look passed between them, a knowledge of connection in their joint regard for him, yet it left an aftertaste of rivalry, of jealousy, of division. Anny tasted it again at this moment, at Jake's mention of Peggy.

Jake continued, oblivious to the upset he had caused, 'And to hear that you two are friends is quite delicious.

I am going up to the King house later, to fulfil my first appointment to paint Mrs King. I shall give your warm regards to Miss King, wink at her and see if she keeps your secret better than you have, Anny!'

Anny frowned and replied, 'Oh please, no! It was a confidence. I did not mean . . .'

Jake tipped his head back and laughed. 'Oh, but you are too easy to tease! Far too easy!'

Anny relaxed and found herself disarmed by a laugh, his own being infectious.

He lowered his voice and looked straight at her: 'I would never share your confidences, Anny. I wouldn't dream of it. After all, if you could not trust me, then I would lose my chance forever to . . . to become better acquainted with you. If that is something that you wish for also. Do you? Do you wish to see me again and talk this way, another time? Many more times? Do you, Anny?'

'I do,' Anny whispered, as if the words came from deep inside her and had lost their sound by the time they reached her lips. She said again, much more clearly, 'I do.'

⤜⤛⤜

'Now that you are home for good, Cyril my boy, you will take up your rightful place at my side. In your sojourns at home, you have accompanied me these past years in all aspects of the business and you have been educated to the correct . . . height – or is it depth? – to have developed your intellect and your sense of duty. I hope you realise how expensive your education was, and how grateful you ought to be for the opportunity?'

Cyril bowed his head suitably and replied, 'Yes, Father, of course. It has been the most enlightening education a boy could wish for.'

He thought of the way old Cadman would bring down his great leather shoe onto any boy's arse he was beating. He was an exceedingly tall man, so his shoes were enormous.

'A man, Cyril. You are a young man now.'

Then why do you call me 'my boy', you idiot? Cyril thought. He thought then of Bostock, the older boy who had also beaten him regularly, with even more viciousness than the masters. '*We shall beat the boy out of you yet, King,*' Bostock used to explain to him, as if each attack were doing him a favour, arming him for the journey into manhood. Oh yes, he had certainly become a man now. He had seen everything. He wondered if his father had been similarly treated in his own time. He supposed not, as if so, why would any father put his own son through that? He would never forgive his father for sending him to that place. Cyril was not the forgiving type. But Ralph King was useful to him – held his future in his hands – so he would play the game and continue to flatter the stupid old duffer.

'Yes, Father. I am ready and willing to serve. I was thinking that I would like to assist Brotherton in his office. There are some nuances of the selling part of the business that I feel I need somewhat more acquaintance with.'

And there is a flame-haired beauty I feel I need far more acquaintance with, thought Cyril. He was working his way up to proposing to Anny. But, as little as she seemed to care for him now, he put this down to her fear for her position. If he could persuade his father that he wanted this girl, then he could reassure Anny that his intentions were honourable – well, some of them – and that her life would be changed forever; she would become the lady of the house. After all, his father had married some jumped-up adolescent strumpet whose parentage was decidedly suspect. Why couldn't his son do the same? But deep down he knew his father would probably never agree to it, yet Anny didn't know that. And maybe he could keep her in a little house, a secret mistress. He was sure his grandfather used to bed the maids. Why couldn't he have his own little worker to bed? He thought, *Why can't I have what I want? I've always had what I want.*

'I cannot see there is much depth to what Brotherton and his ilk do. But if you feel it necessary, for a short time, you may. When you see Brotherton, ask him when this artist fellow is coming to the house. We made an arrangement for him to begin Benjamina's portrait, but I cannot recall when.'

'What artist fellow would that be, Father? What portrait?'

'Oh, some young fellow, a sketcher, who has been recording scenes around these parts. Quite talented, yes. Fired up with the enthusiasm of his craft. These artist types are all passion, you know. He has a Romany air. Ashford, his name. Well, he will do a good job of the portrait. I want him to get started on it.'

Cyril thanked his father. He didn't like the sound of this artist fellow, this Ashford or whatever he called himself, not one bit. You could never trust the artistic types; he knew this from school. There was always something queer about them. And smug, too. He would soon put him in his place, if he saw him about. This fellow was a servant, like any below-stairs washerwoman, and he must remember his place.

It was lunchtime when Cyril marched outside towards the office. *Oh, dash it*, he thought. Anny would probably be having her food somewhere. Margaret was not at home today, visiting some musical concert with Queenie, so Anny wouldn't be chatting with her. Those two were too chatty all round. He didn't like it. He wanted Anny to be his, not his sister's. Although, once he gathered enough courage to talk to his father about marrying Anny, perhaps Margaret could be a useful ally. Yes, that could work in his favour. Perhaps he should talk to the little wretch about it. He'd do that later. He opened the office door to find no Anny. On her lunch, Brotherton informed him. He knew he was supposed to be staying in the office to learn things, but he made his excuses and left. *Where would she be?* He walked down the lane towards Ironbridge. Perhaps she had gone into the town.

Ironbridge had only been in existence as a town these past few decades since the bridge itself was built. Now it was a bustling collection of a weekly market, coaching inns and boarding houses, a bank, post office, printers, grocers and drapers, lawyers and doctors, ironmongers and watchmakers, a meeting house, a school and a newly built church on the hill, and so on and so forth. All human life was here. Cyril thought of the ant nests he used to drown with buckets of water as a boy, only to find another spring up on a nearby patch of ground. Crawling things always found a space to crawl in, even under slimy rocks. You could never escape them. In his younger days, he had loved to bolt from the house and wander through town, jostling with people and looking for girls. These days, the locals mostly disgusted him. Their petty little lives. Each one of them thought they were useful and important. He hated them for that. He knew that many of them were truly necessary, to those around them. He felt he had more in common with the beggars than the workers or the merchants, the shopkeepers and the professionals. He had no place in life, no role. Anny had that. She worked hard and was valued. He wanted to take that away from her, make her his to own and mould in his arms, in his house. His value would be increased by subsuming everything Anny was.

Then, he saw her. It was her red hair he saw first. He could always spot it a mile away; a glorious beacon. She was not wearing her bonnet. She was seated on a bench looking down. Perhaps her lunch was in her lap. What good fortune, to find her away from the office, where they could talk properly. But what was this? A dark-haired man beside her was in conversation with her and she was smiling at him, smiling broadly, veritably beaming at him. The man took off his hat and ran his fingers through his black hair. He had the look of a gypsy about him. Was this the artist fellow? He had a bag on one side – to carry his damned brushes and paraphernalia, he supposed – and a wallet on the other, full of scribbles, no doubt. Cyril stood across the road and watched the two of them. The man opened up his wallet and produced some scraps of paper, in which Anny showed great interest, nodding and talking, looking up to this man, listening intently to every word he spoke.

What had this blasted artist fellow got that he hadn't? He had money and position, a safe future ahead of him. How dare this stranger fraternise with the local girls! The man cupped his hand over his mouth and leant towards Anny, whose head then fell back with laughter. Cyril's eyes narrowed. If this artist fellow was on the scene, well then, it was time to do something about it. In a moment, he would dodge the carts and horse dung on the road and go over there, tell this upstart a thing or two. Any moment now, he would do it. But the man was standing up, taking his leave of Anny with an affected flourish of his hat and a ridiculous bow. Anny watched him go, and Cyril watched Anny watching him. Cyril's blood was up. He straightened his cravat and prepared to cross the busy road. Into his mind came an image of Anny's laughing face tipped backwards in joy, but she was in bed and the man beneath her was not himself, but the damnable gypsy. *This will not be borne*, he told himself. *I will show her who her true master is.* But Anny was up and walking off towards the office at quite a pace. Cyril considered running after her. But what King had ever run after anybody for anything? No, he could wait. He would let his blood boil all afternoon and then, in a secluded place, he would find her, mark her and bag her.

Chapter 10

Margaret waited in the hall, listening to the silence behind the door in the sitting room. She imagined she could hear his brushes dabbing the canvas or the scrape of a knife on the palette mixing the correct hue of gold for Benjamina's silk dress. But in truth, he was most likely doing some preliminary sketches. She could hear nothing and had not the bravery to enter and see for herself Jake's progress with the portrait. She hovered uncertainly, picturing herself turning that brass door-knob and breezing in, asking him if he required any refreshment. She could do that. But she knew she never would. Instead she sat down on a chair in the hallway and waited. It was his first appointment painting her stepmother, so she didn't know how long they would be. If she retired upstairs, she might miss his exit, but if she stayed out here and he came upon her, sitting in her hallway alone, he would surely know she had been waiting for him. *Oh, what to do?*

Then, the door opened and there he was, her decision taken out of her hands. He smiled at her and closed the door gently behind him. He walked towards her with a confidential air, came quite close and – to her alarm and delight – bent his mouth to her ear and whispered, 'Your mother is fast asleep. With her mouth wide open!'

Margaret felt her cheeks burning. She felt quite faint at his nearness. 'She is not my mother,' was all she could think of to say.

Jake stood upright and smiled again, this time lowering his head in deference. 'Of course. Your stepmother. Please forgive me.'

Margaret stood and said, 'Not at all. Well, I must say it is time for her daily nap. Was her dog asleep too? It usually sleeps at this hour.'

'Yes, and it does exhibit a wide range of bodily functions when it sleeps,' he said with a wry smile, again bending closer to whisper, 'particularly of the windy variety.'

Margaret could not help but laugh. He went on, 'One wonders what exertions the lady of the house engages in to require a daily nap. She tells me she does not ride, walk or even leave home if she can help it. It's a wonder how such indolence can be so exhausting.'

Margaret was shocked by Jake's cheek but also rather thrilled by it. 'Mr Ashford, be careful. If my father were to hear you talk in such a way, you would be out on your ear in a trice!'

'But will you tell on me, Miss King?'

She said quietly, 'Of course not.' This confidence between them gave her a different kind of confidence to add, 'Shall we take a turn about the grounds, if you have the time?'

'I would be delighted,' he said and bowed slightly with his arm out, for her to lead the way.

As they crossed the hallway to the front door, she wondered what Anny would make of her asking Jake Ashford to walk with her. At once, she knew that she would not be telling Anny. She wished she could share this with her friend, but she knew she would not. She did not wish to analyse why this was, and instead pushed it to the back of her mind. She did not have time to consider that now, as Jake Ashford was asking her about botany. He wanted to know the names of certain shrubs they were passing and of the trees that circled the formal garden to the side of the house. She was pleased, as it was a subject about which she was quite knowledgeable, having read of them and spent much time in her childhood in the library or out of doors, both excellent for avoiding company. He revealed his ignorance of plants and flowers and the world of nature, having been brought up exclusively in a town house with no garden, front or back.

'I come from a middling sort of background that has recently moved up in the world. My father was a wine merchant in Birmingham, who then expanded into coffee houses, and thereby has made a pretty penny. I was given a good education and even a special tutor in art, which has always been my passion. My father kindly paid for me to take a trip to the near continent – a kind of truncated version of the grand tour – visiting Florence, Rome and Paris to see the great artworks there.'

'I would dearly love to visit Paris,' said Margaret.

'Ah, Paris. Such beauty all around you, everywhere one looks in that city. So unlike London. And certainly Birmingham. Yet there is beauty here in Ironbridge, true beauty, sometimes in the most unexpected of places.'

He smiled at her knowingly and she flushed hopelessly, unable to control her blushes. She changed the subject. 'Which was your favourite city that you visited?'

'Paris, indeed. The architecture and gardens are marvellous. I visited the Palace of Versailles. Have you heard of it?'

'Oh, yes! I have read of it.'

'Picture it. You walk into the central courtyard and you are surrounded by stone the colour of sun-baked sand, punctuated by row upon row of windows gazing glassily down upon you. The slate roof is topped with golden decoration. Indeed, there is gold everywhere to be seen. Particularly in the long gallery – they call it *La Galerie des Glaces* – the Hall of Mirrors – oh, but of course, you would know that, being a French speaker.'

As he spoke, the images he painted with his words flowered in her mind. 'Yes, the Hall of Mirrors. I cannot imagine anything so beautiful.'

'It is a stunning sight. The sun streams through the windows and is dazzled in return by its reflection in the mirrors that line the wall, surrounded by a profusion of fleur-de-lis and chubby, golden babies. One cannot help but be overwhelmed by such richness. But outside is where I felt most delight, in the formal gardens. I imagine that you might feel more at home there too, Miss King, with your knowledge of botany?'

'Perhaps,' she uttered. She loved to listen to him. She had never travelled further than Shrewsbury, and felt how provincial she was. She dearly wished she had something to say that would interest him but could think of nothing but more questions. 'How were the gardens?'

'They are extraordinary, constructed like a painting or even, one could say, like the finest, hand-painted wallpaper. Great swathes of patterned grass and path combine to produce a design best seen from the air, I'd imagine. Only the birds could truly appreciate the gardens at Versailles!'

'It sounds . . . wonderful,' she gasped.

'Oh, Miss King, you would be in heaven there, I am certain.'

A vision came to her for a second time, of Parisian walks with Jake. Just the thought of it made her blush again. She watched him as he walked, carefully, out of the corner of her eye. Then, he stopped.

'Miss King, may I speak freely?'

'Yes,' she said, alive with anticipation.

'I do hope I am not boring you. I worry that I am.'

'Oh, no, indeed. Quite the opposite, I assure you!'

'Ah, thank you, Miss King. I feel I am talking and talking away and you must be quite sick of me, because I have noticed that you do not speak very much.'

There came her blushes again, but this time, they signalled a flush of humiliation. Her old anxiety, her social awkwardness, was here again. And now it threatened to ruin this new delight, her relationship with this extraordinary young man.

'Mr Ashford,' she began, but faltered. She did not know how to explain herself to him. She felt that she had failed him, that it was in fact she who bored him. She was about to make her excuses and leave, when he stopped walking. She looked up at him.

'Miss King, I am afraid that I have insulted you, and that was strictly not my intention. It is so unusual in our class to find someone who does not prattle on in incessant and tedious small talk. It revolts me, this obsession the upper classes have with chattering about nothing, spending hours and days and weeks of their pointless lives on such mediocrity! That is one reason, of the many reasons, why I value talking to our mutual friend Miss Woodvine so much, as she seems to have no capacity for small talk whatsoever and always straightway cuts to the chase in all our conversations. Don't you find this is true of Anny Woodvine, Miss King? So easy to converse with, she is quite a joy.'

This sudden mention of Anny caught Margaret wholly by surprise. Of course, she knew they had met, but did not know they were on such good terms. *Quite a joy* . . . She looked down at her feet as they walked. She suddenly felt quite floored and had no idea what to say. But he was going on, filling the void for her.

'But also, how refreshing it is to find a person from the more refined classes such as yourself, who is careful and considered in her speech, who speaks only of those things that truly matter. It is like an oasis after a desert of trivialities. Please forgive me if you felt I was criticising your quietude. It is quite the opposite, I assure you. I admire it hugely.'

Now she found she could not speak, because she was quite overcome. But she wanted to speak, she wanted to say so much to him. She managed only a muffled 'thank you'.

'You are sure I have not upset you in any way?'

'Oh no, indeed. As you say, quite the opposite. Quite the opposite.'

'I am relieved. So, could I ask that, each time I come to paint your stepmother, we could walk like this and converse?'

'I would like that very much.' Margaret felt a sharp breathlessness building in her chest.

'To think that I have that time with you to look forward to . . . Well, it has cheered me so. My visits to you will be the high point of my week!'

'And mine! I will live for it!' she replied, before she had a chance to be shy. She was so unaccustomed to speaking her feelings to a man – indeed, she had never done so in her life.

Yet he smiled so kindly at her, that she relaxed and found herself smiling too. A little chuckle escaped his lips and she laughed too. How natural it was to be with him, how much easier than anyone in her family, those people who she was supposed to feel at ease with.

They fell silent for a while and walked on, past the vegetables growing lustily in the walled garden, strung round with twine and labels; past the beehive buzzing with life yet contained in their white, wooden home, their honey stolen at intervals; past the fuchsias and chrysanthemums beaming brilliantly in the afternoon sun, yet penned in by canes and perfect alignment in fixed patterns.

Jake broke their comfortable silence. 'It is a beautiful garden you have here. But so restrained, so trussed up and ordered. Nature is tamed here, I see,' he said and she looked at him. There was a look in his eye, something she could not place, but it made her feel weak at the knees. He went on, 'Wouldn't it be satisfying to see it run wild?'

She felt out of her depth and yet ready to dive deeper into a sea of impulsiveness. A wave of tingles ran over her whole body as she looked into his eyes. It was something she associated with certain passages in certain French novels she had read. It was something that alarmed her, and yet she wanted it more than anything. She could not put a name to it but it was the most powerful thing she had ever felt and it seemed to emanate from Jake Ashford's eyes.

Overcome by her feelings, she mumbled something about feeling unwell, unable to say a proper goodbye, mortified at her inability to speak. She rushed across the gardens, around the corner of the house, nearly colliding with Cyril, who was marching from the direction of the woods, a look of thunder on his face.

'Watch out, you bloody fool!' he spat at her, as he pushed her aside and leapt up the steps to the front door, taking them two at a time. She did not have time to wonder what had angered him in particular that day, as she was intent on her own escape from public view. She ran up to her room and shut the door. She curled up on her bed, closed her eyes and breathed deeply to calm herself. It was her first true experience of lust. It frightened her and it thrilled her. It was more exciting than any of her novels.

∽

That evening, Anny left the office after work with a head full of daydreams. She walked down the woodland path towards home with slow, languorous steps. Lately, she had been distracted at work and this was unlike her. Work was everything, closely followed by her family and her friendship with Peggy. But now there was Jake. She found herself often wanting to arrange time alone specifically to think about him. She looked for opportunities to be on her own so that she could devote the proper thinking time to the exclusive contemplation of Jake Ashford.

She marvelled how her life had been proceeding very nicely in one direction, more than a girl like her could have hoped for, with all its promise. And then this new element had suddenly dropped into her path, this young man, this artist. How strange life was, with its surprises and chance encounters, always when one least expected it! One could pray for things and they would never come, but then one day, when you were looking the other way, life served you up something delicious. Oh, and he was delicious! No, she mustn't characterise him that way. He was a serious person, a creative person, not a fancy piece of baggage. And his ambition, his artistic aims, all of this about him was so admirable. But those eyes. The way he looked at her, in a manner no local boy had ever done. When her eyes met with Jake's, there was a deep connection she had never experienced, like a series of small explosions happening in her mind. Surely the only name that she could give it was love.

But there was a stone in her path to true love. She tried not to think of it that way, but there it was, all the same: Peggy. Anny wondered if Peggy was sweet on Jake too. At first, it had been fun to share their impressions of the new arrival. After that, neither had mentioned Jake again; it became the elephant in the room. Anny did not tell her best friend of the meetings she'd had with him, of their long discussions, of her burgeoning feelings. And she did not ask Peggy if she had seen him either. The truth was that Anny did not want to hear about Jake from Peggy's mouth. She wanted to block out the wider world when it came to Jake; she wanted to pretend that he only spoke with her and that, along with his art, these were his only preoccupations.

Anny put it out of mind. She only wanted happy thoughts this day. Her dear friend Peggy, her true love Jake, her work with the Brothertons, her dear parents happy to see her so settled – and who knows what else the bright future held? She saw a simple white bind-weed flower on its vine encircling a tree and plucked it, to feel the soft petals in her hand, to hold it to her breast and sigh with languid pleasure at her thoughts. The warm summer breeze whispered through the woods and teased her hair, free from the bonnet she carried, too hot for this glorious July day, brimming with bird-song and the buzzing of bees and the scent of earth and bracken.

'Anny! Ahoy there, Anny!'

The voice assaulted her. It shattered her thoughts as surely as a brick through a hothouse roof. She whipped round, hoping against hope she had mistaken its owner. She had not.

'Why, fancy coming across you here. Are you not late leaving work?'

Cyril's face was red and puffed, as he lumbered up the incline beneath her. A quick survey of her surroundings showed her they were out of sight of both the road and the office, and she was still far from her home. She turned and quickened her step onwards, tying her bonnet back on as if for protection.

'Indeed not,' she said, avoiding looking at him.

'Ah, then,' he said, out of breath and reaching her side, struggling to keep pace with her now. 'You will have a little time to speak with me then.'

'I fear not. I must be getting on, as I have so much to do at home.'

'Ah, but I must insist, Anny. I simply must speak with you on a matter of great importance.'

Anny strode onwards, her breaths short and ragged. 'Perhaps in the office another day, sir,' she managed to say, despite the panic rising in her throat now. His hand was on her arm and she stiffened and stopped dead.

'How can you call me that, Anny? How can you call me "sir", after all these years?'

Anny would not look at him. She stared ahead, her eyes fixed on the path home, its safety well out of reach. 'It is the correct name for your position, sir. And my own, as your father's employee. Now if . . .'

His voice came closer. 'But I would like that to change. I would like us to form an alternative kind of relationship.'

'That will not be possible. Our stations in life are too different.'

'But you are friends with my sister. You have overcome the difference in your stations to become close friends, I see.'

She stared at the ground now, at her feet. Her mind raced; how to escape this, how to run without seeming to run. But it was impossible. The only thing to do was block his every verbal attempt and thereby shut down the conversation, as a handful of sand on a flame.

'We are not close friends, only acquaintances.'

Cyril laughed gently, a knowing laugh. 'But that is not true, is it, Anny? You are speaking falsehoods to me now. I know about the letters and the secret meetings. I'm not a fool, you know. But don't worry, I will keep your secret.'

She looked at him now. His expression was a sneer but it softened when their eyes met. 'Oh Anny,' he sighed, his hand still on her arm, squeezing it joltingly, no softness or rhythm in his touch. 'Let us not worry about such things, about who your father is, or my father. None of this matters, when two people are . . . when they could be . . . when we should be . . .'

He does not know how to speak of love, she thought, *he doesn't have it in him*. 'Oh Anny,' he said again. 'Such a lovely face, such red, red hair.' Without releasing his grip, his other hand reached up to touch her head and she jerked back suddenly, causing him to stumble.

'Now then!' he said, his face changing, annoyance and hurt pride in his eyes.

'I am promised to another,' she blurted out.

His eyes narrowed. 'What other?'

'Never you mind. That is my business.' Her fear made her bold.

'That blasted artist fellow?'

What did Cyril know of Jake? She instantly regretted her confession. It was not true, not by any understanding with Jake. But it was true in her heart and it was the only thing she could think of to fend him off.

Cyril's hands were on her again, grasping her upper arms. His face was transfiguring into anger. 'Is it? That Ashford? I saw you with him in town. I was watching you, the way you stare at him. It is not seemly.'

The thought of Cyril spying on them made bile rise in her throat. But her immediate danger was at hand and she must think straight.

'Release me,' she said steadily and looked directly at him. '*This* is not seemly.'

His face altered again, as changeable as spring weather. Now he implored her, still gripping her arms. 'Will you not satisfy me, Anny? A kiss? I have waited so long for a kiss from those rosy lips,' and he lurched towards her. With a great effort, she wrenched herself away from him and began to walk hurriedly away. He caught up with her and took hold of her again, saying her name over and over, trying to put his mouth to her neck. His embrace was incredibly strong, iron and solid against her resolve to escape.

Her mouth was close to his ear, so she used her voice, the only weapon she had left: 'Are you gunna shove yer hand up my skirts, like you do with the other servants? Is that what this is, eh? You gunna rape and ravish me, you forsaken bastard?'

It stopped him. It worked. He still held her tightly but he had stopped. He held her before him, so he could look in her eyes. Now his face was all hearts and flowers. 'How can you say such words to me, Anny? Don't you know how I adore you? How I've always, always adored you?'

She changed tack too. 'Well then, this is not the action of a man who adores me. Unhand me and give me my dignity again, if you truly do adore me.'

He did so. She thought briefly of running but he was too fast and too strong for her. She had the advantage now, and must build upon it.

'This is not the way to woo a girl,' she said gently. But it was the wrong thing to say. It angered him.

'And I suppose that silver-tongued counterfeit fop knows how to woo you, eh, with his ridiculous bowing and stupid drawings. Don't you see, he's not good enough for you. He will never earn enough money from his scribblings to provide for you.'

'We will save our money. We will earn it by honest labour and save it until we have enough. That's what our kind do. We don't have things handed to us on a silver platter. We earn our way through life, with dignity.' She was ranting now and had no idea why. Why argue with this monster? Why pretend that she and Jake had a plan? But perhaps saying it aloud would make it so.

'You are right. You do have dignity, Anny. It is in you. You were born for better things. And I can give you those things. Marry me, Anny. Become the lady of Southover, take your rightful place above your natural station. I don't care where you come from, how poor you are, who your family is. It is no matter to me that Woodvine is your father, that he is a low employee of my father's, that your mother takes in dirty clothes. You are not like them, Anny. You are a queen amongst them. Take my hand, and you can rise above all this mean ignorance. Oh, the fine things I could give you! You would be in heaven! Don't you want that? Don't you want to leave all that filthy squalor behind?'

Anny listened, incredulous. Her body was still primed for flight but a rage had risen in her now. 'We are not filthy. We do not live in squalor. We are not mean or ignorant. We are proud and hard-working people. Jake Ashford understands that, even your sister understands that. But you will never know it, because you are the one who is ignorant and mean. You strut and preen and stamp on small things beneath your feet. You pass through your pointless life blind to anything but getting what you want, when you want it. You will never be half the man my father is, if you laboured all your days, you would never. It is not in your nature. You are cruel and selfish, in love with yourself and your kind. You disgust me. I would not marry you if my freedom depended on it, if my very life depended on it. I would rather die!'

Her words had cut to the quick, she could see that. His face was white with shock. But his eyes were black with hate. He had no words left. She took the moment it gave her and ran. She ran down the woodland path, tripping over roots, her arms flailing, her throat rasping with dry fear. She could not hear him pursue her, but she did not dare stop. At last, she saw the edge of her village, there in all its dependability. Salvation. But everything seemed at sea, the ground rippling like water, her head swimming with confusion. She stopped and glanced behind her. Nothing there. She put her hands to her head to steady herself. She had escaped him. She was safe. But everything had changed. Somehow, she knew that. Something irreversible had happened, and she feared it.

Chapter 11

Anny did not tell her mother or father about Cyril. She was too ashamed, too disturbed. Also, she felt she did not need to tell her parents, despite her fear. She would handle it herself. She could handle Cyril King. But then, the fear crept back in. What would Cyril do next? She knew him well enough to know how damned proud he was, how he would detest any suggestion of humiliation. And what could her parents do, anyway? Nothing, precisely nothing. They would tell her to leave Mr King's employ, that's what they would do. They would say it wasn't safe. Well, damn that course of action. Why should Cyril King chase her out of her job? She had worked so hard for it, and it would lead on to wonderful things – a post in Shrewsbury, as Mrs B had once mentioned. Or beyond, if certain other circumstances developed, maybe in Birmingham, who knew? Yes, that was it. Jake was the answer. It was the perfect time. If she went to Jake now, confessed the horrible scene with Cyril, it would be sure to gain his sympathy. Then, to tell him of her true feelings. How could he refuse to love her? She was sure it was on the tip of his tongue anyway. Then, they could announce their engagement straightaway and stop Cyril in his tracks. He could have no designs, no revenge, once her relationship with Jake was above board and out in the world. Yes, the time was now. And what a relief it would be, to tell Jake how she really felt and to hear his feelings for her, to lock eyes, to kiss . . .

The day after Cyril's assault, she spoke to Mr B and managed to free up an extra hour that afternoon after lunch. She did not like lying to him – she said her mother was poorly – but needs must. She left the office in search of Jake. He had in the past sought her out at the office a couple of times at lunchtime, but she could not wait to see if he would today. She was on a mission. She asked Lucy if Mr Ashford were in the house today, but he was not. Perhaps he was in one of his other haunts, the furnace where he drew detailed line drawings of the men guiding molten iron into the moulds, the riverside sketching the curves and struts of the iron bridge; or perhaps he was further afield, and she would not find him. She was hungry and tired, rushing about from place to place, but she felt too nervous to eat. Then, with a wash of relief and excitement, she saw him, coming out of the baker's, cramming a pie into his mouth messily. It surprised her a little, as he always had perfect manners, but it amused her too and she thought of all his little ways she would get to know once they had an understanding between them and they could truly be themselves together.

She looked both ways at the busy lunchtime traffic on the High Street before crossing and calling to him. He turned, looking alarmed, then his face altered as he saw her. He smiled broadly and wiped his face and waistcoat down, the crumbs flying this way and that into the mud beneath his boots. She could not help but beam at him, as he held her happiness in his hands and each view of him released it from her face. But as she approached, her fears must have crept back into her eyes, for he looked concerned and frowned upon her as she reached him.

'What is it, Anny?'

She loved the way they were on first-name terms. She loved the way he said her name, the vowels clipped and precise, his accent speaking of city life and education.

'I must speak with you. Can we walk? I have much to tell you.'

'Of course. Let us cross the bridge, then go down the steps underneath it and walk along the path upstream, away from the furnace. We can find some peace there.'

The sound of the ironworks nearby receded as they descended to the path and walked onwards, past a coracle hut on stilts, where a man came out hoisting his circular boat onto his back to carry it down to the water's edge. They passed along the path bordered by woods of oak and birch, dotted here and there with pretty cottages, gardens and orchards. They could hear the roaring of the forge pools in the distance, emptying themselves into each other in cascades, a sound like remote thunder.

'What's wrong, Anny? Please tell me.'

'It is a shameful thing to tell. But not shaming of me, but of him. I've never done any small thing to encourage him or such behaviour.'

'Anny, do start at the beginning. You do have this habit of rambling so. You could take a leaf out of Miss King's book and cull your words a little, you know.'

The mention of Peggy caught her short. Why was he talking about her? 'Well, Margaret could talk a bit more, if you ask me. She is too shy for her own good.'

'I am only teasing you, Anny. Now, who are we talking of? Who is he? And what did he do?'

'Master King. Cyril King. He followed me in the woods. He accosted me. Took hold of me.'

Jake stopped walking and stared at her. 'Did he hurt you? Are you . . . intact? Are you well?'

The look in his eyes, of deep concern, was encouraging. She hesitated to speak, to hold onto his gaze for a moment longer and drink it in. 'I am quite well, thank you. He did not . . . interfere with me, except he manhandled me and tried to kiss me. But I fought him off.'

'But that is outrageous! How dare he! This is another example of the upper classes taking advantage of those they perceive as beneath them. I would guess he does this to all his father's employees.'

'No, it was more than that. He told me he loved me, that he wanted to marry me. Me! Become the lady at the big house!'

'And what did you say to him? I hope you said no. He's a pigeon-livered idiot, that one. Not right for you, not at all.'

'Well, I told him no, of course.'

'That must have been tricky, to turn down the master's son. What reason did you give?'

'I told him I was promised to another.'

'That was clever! Did he believe you?'

'Yes, and he guessed who it was.'

'And who is it, Anny? Someone from your father's ironworks? Or a handsome coal miner? You are too good for all of them, Anny. But you'll find someone in Shrewsbury, when you go to work there. You'll see. Someone worthy of you, of your intellect. You're wasted on the dolts around these parts.'

Every twist and turn of this conversation took her by surprise. She had to keep her wits about her to negotiate it and keep on track. 'No, Jake. He did not guess any of the local boys. You see, he was spying on *us*. He saw us talking on the bench and he followed me from there. He is jealous of *you*, Jake. You must watch yourself. He is vengeful, I feel it. You must protect yourself.'

'Me?' said Jake, incredulous. 'Why would he suspect me? How ridiculous!'

This was not the reaction Anny was hoping for. She stopped walking and yet Jake did not immediately notice, carrying on a few paces until he turned and frowned at her.

'It is not ridiculous, Jake. Not to me.'

He came closer. 'My dear girl . . .' He trailed off, seemed torn somehow, glanced across the river and frowned again. She held her breath. 'I like you very much indeed, you must know that.'

'I have hoped it,' she said.

'Yes, but it is not so simple as that. Life is not so simple.'

'It can be. Love is simple. We love or we do not love.'

He laughed, a gentle scoff. 'Love is perhaps the most complex part of life. But no, in this case – in *our* case – there are other complications at play. You see, I am not here to find love. I am here to pursue my art. Whatever else arises, this is my sole purpose. It is a stronger bond I have with my art than any other. It is hard for others to comprehend, those who do not have ambition. But I believe, of all people, you can understand it. You have that drive, too, that burning ambition, to change yourself, to change your environment, to change the world even. I saw this in you from the very first and knew we felt the same, that we were kindred spirits that way.'

'Yes!' she gasped. 'We are kindred spirits. And that is why . . .'

'No, Anny. I am sorry to rudely interrupt you, but no. I am guessing where you might be leading in your words, but I cannot follow. I am wedded to my art. It comes first for me in everything. Why, when I am painting, I do not eat, I do not sleep, I am obsessed. It means more to me than anything, more than the commonplace necessities of life that dull people worship. More than my health, more indeed than the fairer sex. I have no ambitions when it comes to love or marriage. I never have. I am a complete novice in the art of love. Only the art of drawing and painting has been my passion. Any woman in my life will find herself playing second fiddle, and that would be most unfair. Besides, even if I were to love another, I could not promise myself. I am not earning a living from my art. I am not established. Even if I wanted to . . . to marry . . . I could not.'

The weight of disappointment was too great to bear. But she had not given up yet. 'But I know all of this, Jake. I understand this about you. As you say, we are kindred that way. And I will wait. I will wait as long as it takes for you to become established in society.'

'I could not ask that of you, Anny. It might be years.'

'I don't care!' she cried. There was some hope rising in her now. 'I would wait a lifetime! Find your place in the art world, find your success, which I know in my heart will be coming for you, when your paintings of these scenes, this place, are seen. I feel it, Jake. I know it. I believe in you.'

'You are too kind, Anny.'

'No. No, it is not kindness.'

'It is, and you have too much of it to give. I cannot let you wait for me. It might be years. And I may never become successful. I do not have the blind faith in myself that you do.'

'It is not blind faith. It is knowledge. And it is love. I love you, Jake.'

She wanted to reach up and kiss him now, now as he looked into her eyes, listening to her passionate regard for him. But she was unsure of him, so unsure that she waited for him to be the one. She wanted a sign, a movement from him, that he wanted her. He was moving towards her; she closed her eyes. She felt his arms go about her; but his face moved to the left and went over her shoulder. He was patting her on the back.

'There, there,' he was saying. 'You're a good girl, Anny.'

This was not what she wanted to hear. The feel of his arms about her, even in this brotherly way, was overwhelming and she felt herself press into him. The heat of their closeness was heady and bitter, as she felt he was holding back from her. She had to make him feel what she felt. Surely he would, if she breathed on his neck like this, if she sighed like this, if she pushed her fingers into the hair at the nape of his neck, like this, like this.

She moved her mouth to his and pressed her lips to his. He did not resist. The kiss was chaste, lips to lips, gentle and tender.

She opened her eyes to see his closed.

'Anny,' he whispered, and they kissed again. 'You are so lovely.'

'You are everything to me,' she whispered back, then looked up at him.

'Should I ask you to wait for me, Anny? Is that wrong of me?'

Her heart leapt. 'How can it be wrong when we love each other?'

'Will you, then? Will you wait for me and come to me when I have made my fortune?'

'I will, I will!'

He kissed her again, and this time their mouths opened. She felt her whole body turn molten, fired by the burning heat in her heart.

❦

Good, heavy breasts, this one, thought Jake as he walked along the path. *Not skinny, like the other.* He'd left Anny by the riverside, sure in his love and full of foolish happiness.

Jake's past was something he had become adept at rewriting. He selected only the information to reveal to others which could be of use to him. Of course, neither Anny nor Margaret knew how many women he had bedded. Neither did Jake, as he had lost count of the females long ago. Neither Anny nor Margaret knew how heavily he was in debt. Neither did Jake, as he had lost count of the debtors, too, long ago. He had also never availed them of the fact that he had been disowned by his father.

As he strolled along, he replayed the circumstances in his life that had brought him to this moment. His parents had a disposable income and spoilt their two daughters and their youngest, a son. Jake's father was besotted with his son and yet at the same time hard on him. Having come from lowly parentage and worked himself up 'from nothing', as he termed it, Mr Ashford was determined his children would be swathed in as much luxury as he could afford. Yet his keen work ethic conflicted with this and he took it out on his only son, alternately fond and rough, chucking the boy under the chin one minute, then slapping him hard for insubordination the next. Rather than training his son up in the business, Ashford senior indulged the boy's one passion: art. However, on his return from the continent, he was called to his father's study and instructed to demonstrate what he had achieved on this expensive trip. Mr Ashford liked to indulge his son to a point, but beyond this he knew that only talent and skill would make any return in this world. He perused his son's work carefully, frowning. Then he had turned and said the words that still haunted Jake: 'It's not good enough, Jake. Not good enough by half. You're not a painter, and never will be. I've done my best for you, boy, and I have to admit that it was in error. You need to knock this idea of art on the head now and come into the business with me. No sense wasting any more time.'

Jake had been humiliated. He had compared his own skills with other artists he'd met on the continent. He knew he was not one of the best. But he was not one of the worst either. He had some skill, and surely this would improve with time. He told his father that nobody started off perfect, it'd take time to mature, like a good wine. He said how much his trip had changed him, how he wanted to change the world. He explained that he believed they were living through the most extraordinary era, one never before seen and never to be repeated, of such rapid and impressive change as to addle one's brain. Yet, at the age of twenty and full of energy, he felt ready for anything, eager to grasp this new era with both hands and let it speed him into the future. He had a great ambition to get to the heart of society and see what burned there. But his words had left his father cold.

'What a load of claptrap,' his father had scoffed. 'Fine words butter no parsnips. I'll not have a lazy, self-serving son. Put those ideas out of your head once and for all. Your talent is paltry and it will not serve those big ideas of yours.'

Jake had stomped out of the room, out of the house, and went off to get roaring drunk at a local tavern, after which he awoke with his face on the sagging breast of a much older prostitute, and he hoped he didn't have the clap. He'd slunk home to find his father raging, who, at the sight of him, grabbed him by the collar and pulled him close, spitting in his ear, 'You stink of booze and quim, lad. How dare you dirty my home and the home of your sisters and mother with your debauchery.' His father had thrown him to the floor, upon which Jake's head smashed into the hall table and broke his mother's china plate reserved for visiting cards from the great and the good. This was the final straw.

'Get out there in the world, boy, and don't come back until you've found yourself a living or a wealthy bride. Don't bother to darken my doorstep again until you've found one or the other. Be gone with you.'

One out of two will do, thought Jake, as he remembered Margaret's blue eyes sultry with desire every time she looked at him. In the meantime, he could amuse himself with this lovely redhead. And she was so very willing, he thought, she had allowed him to run his fingers up and down her back, her pelvis pressing against his in her need for him. Her passion for him would serve to make the rich one jealous. If he played his cards right, he could be married to a rich bride before the month's end and return home to his father in style. With his wife's money and his father's inheritance, he would never have to scrape a living again and could paint for his own gratification, not money. He could open a gallery in Ironbridge or Shrewsbury and display his industrial paintings for a fee, make a few more pennies and show his father who was the true artist around here, with paying customers eager to see his work.

'I will wait for you, until the end of time,' Anny had said, her voice hoarse with emotion.

Maybe he would bed the redhead on the sly after the wedding celebrations were done. He suspected the blonde was too prim to let him in as much as he needed. He had healthy, natural appetites, for sex and for money. These two would serve nicely to satisfy them.

Chapter 12

Cyril left the house by the back door and crossed the lawn. It was still wet with dew, his brown shoes were soaked black with it, and he shivered in the early chill. He was heading for a tall oak tree, one he had identified days before as being close enough to the office to watch the comings and goings, yet broad enough to hide behind and not be seen. He stood and waited. Anny appeared from the forest path, humming to herself, her work bag that held her lunch and other female sundries swinging to and fro. She was happy. He hesitated. He felt a surge of something for her, not only desire, but something else he did not understand. He felt it for no one else. Something like fondness. But the old knowledge crept in like a thief, that she did not care for him. She hated him. And what right had she to be so happy this day? He watched her retrieve the key from her skirts and open the door. He thought, *So, Anny has her own key to the office. That is most useful to know*. Now he waited further, but not for long, as minutes later, Brotherton was seen coming up the hill. No Mrs Brotherton today. That was fortunate.

Ill again, no doubt. A malingerer. He would deal with that later.

He turned and went around the house, skirting the gravel pathway his facile stepmother regularly minced down with her yappy little dog. He did not want anyone to hear his step. He reached the stable yard. The stink of horse dung and sweat emanated from the stables, while the fragrance of damp leaves and bracken drifted from the woodland that surrounded them. All of this was cut through with the tang of industry, of coal fire and metal, leaking from the works down the hill and upriver. He saw the stable lad gently brushing down a horse, which nickered and shook its head.

'You there,' he called and the boy looked up, startled. Everyone around here looked at him like that. A mixture of fear and . . . something else. Repulsion, was it? No, respect. Yes, that was it: respect. 'You. Come here. Take a message for me. Go and see Anny Woodvine in the estate office and tell her my father requires her attendance in the library immediately. And tell her that she must wait in the library until my father comes. Do you understand?'

The boy carefully placed his horse brushes upon their hangings on the stable wall. Cyril shouted, 'Hurry up, damn you!' at which the boy bolted from the stable like a colt, the horse whinnying with fright.

'Stop!' he called, and the boy skidded to a halt. 'I said, do you understand?'

'Yessir. I do. Go tell Anny to wait upon the master o'er in the library.'

'Not wait *upon*, you imbecile. Wait *for*. And she must be told to wait in the library until my father comes for her. Do you get it now?'

'Yessir.'

'And mind, do not mention my name at all. I am not in the habit of playing the part of messenger boy and do not wish to start a career as one. Do not say my name, do you hear? Well, hurry up, then.'

Cyril watched him go, then turned and walked back to the house the other way. He came round to the kitchen door. The smell of bacon wafted out and piqued his nose, causing his unfed stomach to grumble. He would eat once he had finished this business. The cook was in the pantry, shouting orders through at the help. Right by the door, he looked down upon an indeterminate maid on her knees, sweeping up a pile of grit with a small brush – he never could remember all their pointless names, especially the plain ones, like this one – and barked at her, 'Where is Lucy?'

That same look, except this one was tinged with horror. His reputation preceded him amongst the maids, he thought with some pride. 'Doin' the fireplace, sir, in the drawing room.'

'Fetch her immediately and bring her here.'

'Yessir,' muttered the ugly thing and clattered off, stupidly carrying her dustpan with her. He waited impatiently, thinking of the time it would take Anny to get to the library. His father was out all day, visiting friends in Oswestry, leaving at dawn. With a start, he realised that the stable boy would know this, would have attended or at least seen his father leave in the barouche. Well, what of it? The boy would follow orders, he would not speak out of turn. He would not question the young master of the house; would not, could not, as he did not have the wit for it.

Lucy arrived, her eyes wide and white. Cyril took some pleasure from the fear he generated in his past victim. This one was special – he liked her milky-white skin, the scent of soap in her hair. She kept herself very clean, this one. But she had been replaced in his affections by Anny and he had not bothered with her in a while. Still she would not meet his look and came to the door, staring down at her boots.

'Lucy, take a message to the estate office from my grandmother, Mrs King senior. Tell Mr Brotherton that she requires two bottles of green ink to be collected from the stationer's on Madeley Road. He must be the one to fetch it and he must take it back to the office and keep it on his desk to be collected later. Have you got that? Repeat it back to me.'

'I mun take . . .'

'Speak up, girl!'

She cleared her throat, never once looking up from her feet, then began again. She gave a good account of it and the most crucial part was there, that Mr B must not take the ink to the big house, but go back to the office.

Then he leant close to her and whispered in her ear, as he was wont to do in previous times, 'And I do not want my name mentioned to anyone regarding this. It was not me who passed this message on. If anyone ever asks, you are to say that Mrs King senior herself gave it to you. Do you comprehend me, girl?'

'Yessir,' she muttered, utterly still but breathing quickly.

'Get on with you then.'

He watched her go. He went into the house through the garden room and went into his father's study. He thought he knew which drawer the keys were kept in but he was wrong. He opened and shut all the drawers he could see until he finally found them in a single drawer in an occasional table by the door. He left the study and crossed the entrance hall. He thought he heard a door click – he'd been jangling the keys in his hand as he walked and abruptly stopped – but there was no one there. Back out across the garden room and through the glass door. Then he crossed the lawn again, this time in the direction of the woods. He went in deep, hearing the alarm calls of birds announcing his trespass. He needed to come from a place of cover to approach the office. He crept up to the window as quietly as he could and peered in. Anny's chair was unoccupied. He stepped around the neat brick building and looked in through Brotherton's window. Nobody there either. From his pocket, he retrieved the office key. He must remember to replace it later, or all might be lost. Looking behind him at the house, then at the path down to town, he satisfied himself that nobody was around and he turned the key in the lock. He knew Brotherton would lock up behind himself, good worker that he was. Once inside, he retrieved the two safe keys from the secret drawers. Then he approached the safe.

There was around a hundred pounds or so in there. He had to make a quick decision. How much should he take? How much would look correct? He decided upon thirty pounds. More would be too readily noticed, less would be a waste of the risk expended to take it.

He relocked the safe and replaced the keys, before going to Anny's desk. Where was her bag? She always had it with her, every morning. It was not hanging on the coat stand, or on the back of her chair. His eyes scoured the walls for pegs, but there was none. He started to sweat. He thought he heard the sound of feet approaching and rushed to the door, but there was no one. He thought feverishly, where could it be? She was a sensible girl and a neat one. Where would she put it? He eyed her desk and saw it had three drawers, two small and one large at the base. He pulled it open and there it was, stashed neatly in the bottom drawer. It had a clasp that was shaped like two halves of one heart. He paused. He was assaulted by a wave of nausea. His face was slick with sweat now. He did not have to do this. He could abort the whole scheme. But a memory came to him of her face, cursing him, hating him, and that artist rogue making her laugh. How dare such a girl spurn him! They were too proud by half, those Woodvines. The daughter must have learnt her pride from her insolent father, like that time at the furnace, all those years ago, when Woodvine had made a fool of him before the men. Well, now they would pay for their insolence. He forced open the clasp to Anny's bag and dropped in the cash, shoving it to the bottom of the bag, underneath the lunch wrapped carefully in a cloth. He clasped the bag and pushed the drawer shut.

But her lunch. She would get her lunch out of her bag long before counting up at the end of the day and she would see the money and know. He opened the drawer again and took out her bag, placing it on the desk. He nearly upset an inkpot and watched in a moment of horror as it tipped to one side a fraction, then fell back to its place, the red ink sloshing. His grandmother's damned stupid idea of all that coloured ink. It could have been the end of this, if blood-red ink had flooded across the desk. He opened the bag and looked inside. What he wanted was an inner pocket, something he could place the money inside that she would not necessarily look in between now and the end of the day. He took out her lunch, a handkerchief, a coin purse and a small notebook. These things of Anny's touched him and he paused. But his hand felt a button. He peered inside the bag's recesses and saw the pocket. He fumbled with the button and opened it, relieved to see there was nothing already inside; Anny clearly had no secrets. It was just large enough to stash the money inside. He put all her belongings back in just the way she had left them. He fastened the button, closed the bag and put it away in the drawer, then lurched to the door and slammed it shut, locking it clumsily, almost dropping the key. He rushed back to the garden room and went in through the glass door. Nobody about, thankfully. Straight to his father's study to replace the key, then across the hallway to the stairs. He threw a quick glance at the library, where Anny would be seated, waiting nervously for his father, who would never come. He turned from her and stumbled up the staircase and across the landing to his room. He shut the door, went straight to his wash bowl and vomited into it, retching for minutes after, the yellowish slime of his bile smeared across the back of his hand. There, it was done. Now he needed to deal with Anny.

⤎⤏

Anny stood stiffly by the library window. She did not dare sit down. She could not fathom why Mr King would want to see her, unless she was in some kind of bother. Heat prickled around her collar and her stomach churned. But she knew she had been working as well as usual, had met all of Mr B's requests, though they had had a little quarrel that morning. No, not a quarrel as such, but a disagreement. She had asked him if he would be so kind as to write her a reference if she were to start applying for jobs in Shrewsbury. They had talked about it in the past and the Brothertons had always been so supportive. But he had seemed flustered by the request and made excuses for her not leaving presently and giving it some time before making such a rash move, as he put it. She was frustrated with his negative response, but supposed it was to do with Mrs B being ill again and so much work to be done. He was being a bit unreasonable and the uncomfortable look on his face told her he knew that, but he insisted that she was needed far too much in the office to leave them at present. He had gone into his room and shut the door, which he rarely did when they were working alone in the office together and she felt shut out. She decided she would talk to his wife when she was back, see if she could soften her and then Mrs B might be able to work on her husband's resolve a little.

But why had she been summoned here, to talk to Mr King? Mr B had said only today how invaluable she was, and she had never arrived late or mislaid anything or given anyone any cheek or ... Could it possibly have anything to do with Cyril? Surely not. It couldn't be. She put her hands to her hot cheeks and felt a little faint. Then, the door opened.

'Anny!'

It was Peggy. To see her friend's open, smiling face here in this worrisome place was like a cooling breeze.

'Oh, Peggy! I'm that happy it's you.' Peggy came over to her, a look of concern clouding her features and her face looked pale. 'Are you well, Peggy? You look white as a sheet.'

'It is only I feel a little washed out. A good night's sleep will cure it. But what of you, my dear? I can see something is wrong, and I cannot imagine for the life of me why you are here in the library alone. Is there an emergency? Are you awaiting someone?'

'I was told to come and wait for your father, but I have no clue why.'

Peggy frowned. 'My father? But he is not at home.'

'He has stepped out?'

'No, he left very early this morning. I believe he is in Oswestry for the day and will return by teatime.'

'Oh, I am glad to hear that!' cried Anny. It must have been a mistake then. But what a strange one. Anny's relief swept across her face so clearly that Margaret smiled at her and reached out a hand to touch her shoulder.

'Is anything amiss, dear Anny? It is so long since we've spoken and I . . . I have missed you. I have missed . . . our confidences.'

Anny felt a brief flash of guilt. Things had moved so quickly with Jake, and then there was the trouble with Cyril . . . There had been no time to tell Peggy about either.

'Oh, Peggy, I have so much to share with you. Good news and bad news.'

'I have news, too!' Margaret's face lit up and Anny wondered what on earth it could be. 'But you first. What is your news? Bad first, to get it over with.'

The library door opened. Cyril strode in and turned his head in an exaggerated double take, whereupon he smirked at both of them. 'Now then, what have we here? Not so secret meetings anymore, eh? Flaunting your mismatched friendship before the whole household, is it now? I don't know. I come in to fetch a book and find the help seated in the library with the young lady of the house. Whatever next?'

Margaret stood up and faced her brother. 'As if you ever read a book, Cyril King. Are you spying on us?'

Anny nearly burst out laughing to hear Peggy stand up to her brother so. That was a first!

'Shut up, you little worm,' spat Cyril. 'And get back to the office, girl. How dare you sit here like an esteemed visitor.'

Anny stood and dusted non-existent dust from her skirt. 'I was told to wait in here for your father.'

Cyril scoffed. 'That's not possible. My father is out all day. Who on earth told you that?'

'The stable boy, Paddy. He said that I was to wait for Mr King in the library. No, he said, I must wait upon Mr King. And I said, Upon? And he said, No, I must wait *for* Mr King in the library.'

'That halfwit. He was dropped on his head as a baby. Everyone knows that. Now, get back to work. Hurry up, damn you.'

Anny quickly nodded to her friend as she walked past her. The conversation with Peggy would have to wait.

Anny left the room in a hurry and was worried to hear Cyril was walking right behind her. She did not turn. She did not give him that pleasure. She walked steadily and with dignity out of the servants' entrance and around the house to the office. All the while, Cyril's footsteps haunted hers. She stopped at the office door and turned the handle to discover it was locked. Now, where could Mr B be? She retrieved the key from her skirts and put it in the door. As she opened it, she turned to confront Cyril. She could not allow him to come into the office and be alone with her in there. As she turned, she was surprised to see he was walking away, down the lane towards the town. She shuddered. His whims were disturbing. Oh, for the day when she and Jake could escape this place! As she went in and shut the office door, she looked about her at the office that had housed her day in, day out for four years, had taught her so much, had raised her from washer girl to office junior. Despite Mr B's reluctance, she knew it was time to strike out now, to apply for jobs in Shrewsbury. Indeed, if she secured a better job, with a higher wage, then she and Jake would be one step closer to marriage. She pictured herself moving to Shrewsbury, her parents saying a fond goodbye as she climbed onto the coach, her trunk deposited on the top and the coach rattling along the roads to their grand county town, a place of dreams she had never been, where they said the jolly old river ran through topped by arching stone bridges, flanked by beautiful houses and churches full of history and pots overflowing with flowers on every street.

She sat at her desk and began her first task of the day. She worked alone for some time, over a half hour. Where could Mr B be? At least Cyril had not returned. That was something to be thankful for. Then she heard footsteps approaching and looked up. In came Mr B, puffed and looking annoyed.

'Well, I must say, what a to-do.'

'Can I help, sir?' said Anny.

'No, my dear. It is simply that I am so behind now. What with you being called away, I then received a message from Mrs King senior to fetch ink from town.'

'I could have done that for you.'

'Indeed! But you had to see Mr King. Is everything well?'

'Well, that is the curious thing. He is away from home all day. Went at dawn, apparently. I cannot think what got into Paddy, telling me that.'

But with no answers to be found they both got back to work.

The day passed slowly, with reams of figures to record, accounts to settle, sums to be done and papers to sort. Anny spent much of it thinking of Jake and their future, and worrying over the threat from Cyril. Near the end of the day, she heard the carriage arrive. Anny felt the same nerves from that morning, now that the master had returned. What if the message for her to see him had been correct, but delivered late, and he had wanted to see her? What if he still wanted to see her? What if he turned up now, at the door? She still could not imagine what on earth it could be about, if that did happen. She was distracted by the racing of her thoughts and did not notice Mr B come through and stand thoughtfully before her. She looked up.

'There is money missing from the safe.'

The statement shocked Anny. 'Shall we count it again?'

'I have counted it twice,' said Mr B, his face a picture of worry.

'Let us count it again together.'

They went through and she looked at the ledger on his desk, checked the amount that should be there and then set to counting the money with him, speaking the amounts aloud and jotting down each denomination on his blotter. Then she added up all of the amounts and wrote a total. It matched Mr B's twice-done calculations and was exactly thirty pounds off what the total should have been.

'But how can there be?' she said. 'It isn't possible. The count was all correct last night. Where could it have gone in the space of a day?'

Mr B was running his hand through his thinning hair and suddenly looked so much older than he had only minutes before.

'Oh, my word,' he breathed out raggedly, his hand on his forehead. 'Did I leave the office unlocked when I went to town?'

'No, you didn't,' said Anny. 'When I came back from the house, it was locked. I distinctly remember taking the key from my pocket and unlocking it. And the office was locked this morning too, when I arrived.'

'Oh, thank heavens,' said Mr B and slumped onto the corner of his wife's empty desk. He was thinking now; frowning. Then he looked up at her.

'When I returned from town, you were here alone, Anny. Did you leave the office for a moment during that time? Did you leave it unlocked? I'm sorry, my dear, but I have to ask.'

'No, I did not, sir. I assure you of that. I did not leave this office for a moment after I returned from the library. I came in. Master Cyril followed me from the house and saw me enter. Then I sat at my desk and worked until you came back. I was here the whole time.'

'Are you sure?'

'I am absolutely certain of it. I was here alone the whole time. And the door was locked when I came back from the house. No question about it.'

Mr B's eyes darkened, then he stood and went to the door, saying, 'There's nothing else for it. I have to inform Mr King.'

And out he went. She listened to his footsteps receding towards the house. Her mind was racing. How could this be? Where could the money be? She knew neither of them were to blame, but someone would have to be held responsible. Surely it could not be her, as Mr B was her senior. He was in the position of responsibility. She felt bad about wishing that on him, but if it came to it, better him than her. His years working for the Kings might stand him in good stead, whereas she was convinced that they would dismiss her in an instant if it was deemed to be her fault. There was that period of time when she was alone in the office. Would they hold her responsible, because of that? And what of the strange requests that morning, for both of them to leave the office? A creeping fear began to squeeze her lungs. There was something rotten hidden here and it was beginning to stink.

Footsteps approached. Mr King appeared first, stepping rather awkwardly into the office he had probably not set foot in for years. Mr B hovered behind him, wringing his hands like the very definition of anxiety. Then the door darkened again and in came Cyril. What was he doing there? Anny's chest tightened and she stood up and made a quick bob of a curtsey to Mr King.

'Your name again?' spoke Mr King, haughtily.

'Anny Woodvine, sir.'

'You comprehend the seriousness of this situation?'

'I do, sir.'

'Money has been found to have gone missing from this office. Mr Brotherton informs me that the office was not left unlocked at any time. Do you concur with this, Woodvine?'

'I do, sir.'

'Are you certain of it?'

'I am, sir. The office was locked last night when we left, it was locked this morning when I arrived. When I came back from the house, it was locked. It was not left open and unoccupied at any time.'

'From the house, you say? What do you mean, from the house?'

Anny looked at Mr B, expecting him to take over the explanation. But he said nothing.

'I was called to the house this morning, sir, to wait upon you, in the library. I mean to say, to wait for you in the library.'

'Me?' said Mr King, observing her incredulously. '*You* were called to wait for *me*?'

Anny looked at Mr B, who would not meet her eye. But he did at last speak up. 'Yes, it is the case that the stable boy came with a message, that Miss Woodvine should go to the house to wait for you in the library. That is the case.'

'What on earth could the boy be thinking?' scoffed Mr King.

'The boy is an imbecile,' interjected Cyril, staring at Anny yet speaking to his father. 'Or else easily led.'

'What do you mean by that, my boy?'

'Nothing. Just stating the facts as I see them.'

'But why would this stable boy say such a thing, when it was patently not true?'

Mr B cleared his throat, then said, 'May I just add that I did not actually hear him give the message to Miss Woodvine. I heard only the door open and Anny speaking with him. Then she popped her head into my room and told me what the boy had said. I did not hear it with my own ears.'

Anny turned to stare at him, but he avoided returning her gaze. Was he covering his own back and shoving the blame onto her? She couldn't believe he'd do such a thing. She expected more loyalty from Mr B.

Mr King frowned and looked back at Anny. 'Mr Brotherton tells me that he went to town to fetch some ink for my mother. And that when he returned, you were here in the office, alone. Is that the case?'

'Yes,' said Anny, her voice small. She did not like the way this conversation was proceeding. She did not like it at all. She knew she had done nothing wrong. But there were hints and suggestions buzzing in the thick air of that room and she feared them.

'How long were you alone in the office?' asked Mr King. A slight movement from Cyril, a leaning in, listening.

'A matter of . . . less than an hour?'

'As much as that?' said Cyril.

Mr King sighed and placed his hands into his pockets. Mr B was staring ahead, intensely. Anny did not know what Cyril's expression was, as she would not look at him.

'Woodvine, you were the only person alone in this office on a day that money has gone missing from the safe. You will have to be searched. Your person and your belongings.'

At last, Mr B spoke up, quietly. 'This girl is a very good worker, Mr King. I cannot see that she would have any shadow upon her in this case. Is this really necessary?'

Then, Cyril's voice: 'The girl knows how to open the safe. Brotherton told me himself.'

'Is this true?' Mr King asked Mr B, who looked exasperated but had to reply, 'Yes it is, but . . .'

'Then the girl must be searched. Stand here, girl. Do you have a bag? A cloak?'

Anny came out from beside her desk, where she had been standing, using it as a kind of protection.

'Brotherton, do it.'

Mr B came forward reluctantly and could not meet her eye. She raised her arms and stared straight ahead, inspecting the grain of the wood panelling on the office wall, every knot, every blemish. Mr B patted her hips, then withdrew again, his hands shaking. 'I can feel nothing untoward, sir.'

'Girl, pull out any pockets you have in your apparel.'

'I have none, sir.'

Cyril had fetched her cloak and held it up to the light. 'Nothing here, Father.'

'You have a bag, then?'

'I do, in the bottom drawer.'

She went to step towards the desk, but Mr King said, 'No, Brotherton will do it.'

Mr B approached and took the bag out. Anny thought, *What of it? They will find nothing and then they will leave me be.*

'On the desk,' said Mr King. 'Remove all of its contents.'

Mr B took everything out and placed Anny's things gingerly beside the bag.

'Too slowly, man,' said King impatiently. 'Here, hand it over.'

He took the empty bag and ferreted around inside it. Then, he stopped. He fiddled with something. Anny stared at him. He looked up at her, the first time Mr King had looked clearly at her and registered her as a human being. He looked inside the bag.

'A button,' he said. 'A pocket. Something is inside it.'

'There is nothing inside it,' said Anny. 'I keep nothing in there.'

But there was a rustling sound and Mr King withdrew his hand and in his fist were banknotes.

Mr B gasped. 'Oh, Anny,' he muttered.

'The rat is in the trap,' said King.

'I didn't do this!' cried Anny.

'Be quiet, girl,' said Mr King.

'I did not do this,' replied Anny, her voice lower, stronger and more powerful than she had ever heard herself speak before.

'Silence! How dare you deny the evidence before our very eyes! You have been caught in the act of robbery. Brotherton, go and fetch the constable from Ironbridge to secure this offender and take her into custody. If one is not available, we may need to send to Jackfield or Broseley and if so, we shall secure her here.'

Mr B did not even glance at Anny, but left quickly.

'But Mr King,' she began again. 'I had no reason to steal this money. I have always served you well. I have always valued this post. Why would I steal from my employer? Why would I bite the hand that feeds me?'

Cyril piped up, 'I know why she stole the money, Father. She is seeing that artist fellow, Ashford. Secret meetings. Kissing on the towpath. Everybody is talking of it. I've seen them. She is planning to run away with him. She stole the money to pay for their elopement.'

Oh, the tommy rotter! Such lies he had brewed up, but stirred in with a few facts to give the flavour of truth to it.

'Is this true?'

Anny hesitated. 'No, I mean, yes, it is about Jake . . . Mr Ashford . . . but not what you are saying or the way you are . . .'

Mr King interrupted. 'There is the motive, here is the evidence. You have been caught out in your crime. I shall immediately take this evidence to my friend, Mr Cribb, the magistrate. I have no doubt he will make the charge of theft and you will be committed to Shrewsbury Prison to await trial.'

'But Mr King!' cried Anny. 'Please listen to me!'

'How dare you speak to me thus! Do not make things worse for yourself. I will not listen to one more word from your dishonest mouth. And to think, we gave you a chance in life, a step up from the gutter. And this is how you repay us. Look on, my boy, look on at the result of kindness to the lower classes. This is how the scum answers it. With felony. With theft. With treachery.'

Anny looked now at Cyril, who was glaring at her and grinning in triumph. But his face was sliding away, melting and running into his neck, the walls tilting sideways at crazy angles, the room turning topsy-turvy and she was falling, falling. Her whole world was capsizing and she reached out for something to grab hold of, seeing her hands looming huge before her eyes. Then came darkness.

Chapter 13

John Woodvine was on his break, swilling beer, when he saw Brotherton coming down the path to the furnace. His first thought was trouble. It was always trouble when management came. But he did not think it was trouble for himself. He had done nothing to concern himself about, other than work like an ox, as usual. He turned away to put down his tankard and turned back to see Brotherton looking straight at him, his face wearing an expression that could only be described as shameful.

'What's this now?' he heard Pritchard say, who walked past him towards Brotherton.

Brotherton nodded at John and said something inaudible to Pritchard, who gestured for John to come. They walked away from the furnace to a quieter spot along the path, John's mind whirling like falling sycamore seeds. What had he done? What new trouble was this?

Brotherton cleared his throat and spoke to a spot on John's chest, just below his shoulder. He could not look him in the eye.

'Your daughter has been arrested for theft.'

John did not respond. The words made no sense to him. He stared at Brotherton, his mind like an old man considering the great effort of standing up from a chair. He was waiting for the words to mean something.

'What? Anny?' said Pritchard, similarly incredulous.

'Money was missing from the safe at the end of the day and it was found in her bag.'

'This is daft,' said Pritchard, shaking his head. John still could not speak. Why was the man speaking these lies, as stupid as saying the sky were green?

'I want you to know that I don't believe she could have done it,' Brotherton said.

'Of course she bloody didn't,' replied Pritchard.

But John only wanted to know one thing.

'Where is she?'

'She has been taken to the lock-up in town by the constable.'

With that John turned to Pritchard to tell him he was off to the lock-up. He was already walking away before Pritchard could respond.

When he got there, he banged on the door and the constable came out, a younger man he knew a little from the village, called Finch.

'Move along. No visitors.'

He heard a desperate sound from within.

'Father!' It was Anny.

He shouted back to her, 'I am here!'

'I said, move along.'

John eyed the man. He'd known his father, died of strong drink. He'd never liked this one. A sneak, everyone said. Nobody was surprised when he joined the law.

'Finch, it's me. You know me. It's John Woodvine. I knew your father.'

'I have my instructions,' said Finch and crossed his arms over his narrow chest.

'You know my Anny. You know she's a good'un. It's all rot this business. Let me in to see her.'

But Finch planted his feet firmly astride the doorway and stiffened his lip.

John stared at Finch's weaselly little face. He leant closer to it and was struck by the stink of bad breath. He spoke, low and slow. 'Let me in, Finch.'

'You threatening me, Woodvine? Is that what you're about?'

'I'm not threatenin', I'm tellin'. You dunna step aside, I shall make you, mon.'

Finch's eyes widened, but still he would not budge. It seemed the weasel was made of iron.

'Dunna hit him, Father!' shouted Anny.

John stared at Finch.

'It'll make things worse for me a hundredfold if you do,' she added. She was right. Always the clever one. John unclenched his fists and took a step backwards.

Finch cleared his throat and said, 'The magistrate has already been seen at his home to peruse the evidence and he immediately charged the felon with theft. The felon will thus be taken to Shrewsbury Prison on the morrow. And I'll do you the kindness of informing you that visiting day's the day after, on Saturday. Not that you deserve such kindness, with your idle threats.'

'Come see me on Saturday, then, Father,' called Anny. Her voice was clear and strong, but he knew her so well; only he could discern the quavering note in it. When she was a little one, she had the same tone after she'd fall and scrape a knee, hopping right up, brushing herself off, trying to be brave. Any fuss would set her off weeping. He knew now that she was about to cry and he didn't want to upset her further.

'I will be there.'

'All right, Father!'

'Dunna you worry, Anny. We'll get this sorted out.'

'I know you will, Father.'

He glared again at Finch. He had called Anny a 'felon'. The word had sickened him. How he wanted to douse him in the chops. Instead, he kicked the wall of the lock-up. Finch leant in and sneered at John, adding, 'Like fadder, like darter,' and shut the door in his face.

He could have beaten it down with his bare hands. But it would not have helped her. The vision of her in there, friendless and afraid, tore at his heart as he stared at the walls that stood between them. He marched off, not giving the door the satisfaction of seeing him loiter there, impotent.

On the walk home from the lock-up, he knew he should rush to give his wife the news, but instead his legs felt like lead. He dreaded telling Rachel. She never took bad news well. She worked so hard without tiring, but a hint of bad luck could send her into a swoon. She was sensitive that way, and superstitious, always fearing the worst. He was generally the cheerful one, willing to see the goodness in the world. And the world had treated him quite well, thus far. But how quickly a man's life can turn. He had been at work that afternoon, struggling on against exhaustion, thinking his biggest problem was how to get enough sleep before his next shift. Work had filled his life for more years than he cared to remember. It had seemed to have a purpose, to support his parents' family, then to provide for his own, to give his wife and daughter a home, food on the table and a future for Anny. All that work, all that sweat, all the noise and the heat and the danger. What was it all for? A man works himself nearly to death and then, out of the blue, comes this, landing in his path with no way past it, no way round it or over it or through it. He did not often have poetic thoughts, but he thought then, *You walk through your life and the way is long, the way is hard. But you keep on going. Then summat happens and the land slips down upon you – all the rubble and the trees and the rocks and the earth – all slides down and buries you. You couldna see it coming and you couldna run in time.*

Rachel called him her rock. Well, now he had to prove it. He had to protect Anny from this, he had to protect Rachel from this. He had to solve it. Brotherton said the money had been found in her bag. Then, someone must have put it there. Who would put it there? Why? It made no sense. He knew in his bones that Anny would never steal, would never lie, would never cheat. She did not have it in her. She had no secrets from him or from Rachel, he was sure of that. And if it was money she needed, she would have known to just come to them, tell them. They'd help her, whatever it was. And anyway, she was earning it herself, earning it very well and she was saving. She had cash in a box under the floorboards in her room. She'd been saving it for months, to set her up when she got to Shrewsbury. They'd discussed it all. Why would she need to steal? Questions, questions and no answers.

He'd have to talk to someone educated, someone in the know, who would tell him what he could do. Would he have to hire counsel? They'd have no money to pay it. He could use Anny's savings. But that was her money, for her new life. Well, she'd have no life if she was found guilty of this crime, so her savings it would be. How would he find reliable counsel? He knew no one in Shrewsbury, knew nothing of the city at all. He'd lived his whole life in Ironbridge and never travelled further up than Oakengates, further down than Bridgnorth. He'd had no need to. His father had worked for the ironmasters and so had he. Their world was work and home. There was no need of anything further afield. His trips away had been family events, nothing more: weddings and funerals, the bookends of life. Some people did a good deal of toing and froing about the place and what was it all for? People were the same everywhere, he was sure of that. It might be interesting to some to see other places. But the woodland and the river running through it around his home was all he needed, all he wanted. The walk to Shrewsbury would be the furthest he'd ever been from home. And it was for the most terrible reason he could imagine, other than the death of a loved one; yes, that was the only thing that would be worse than this, if Anny was gravely ill or gone forever.

He thought back to the night Anny came into the world. Rachel had bled and bled and they all said she'd die, but she didn't. No more babies after that, and just as well. In the hours he thought he'd lose his wife, he blamed himself for bringing her to this pass, for giving her a baby to bear and that bearing would kill her. When she recovered and the baby thrived, he thanked God for saving them both and wished to never have another child. They did not have relations for a year or more after. He missed it, he mourned it, but he was determined that she wouldn't be put in danger again, ever again, his beloved Rachel. He thanked God again, for giving him Anny, for keeping Rachel alive. He would have liked a big brood, as he loved little children, babies most of all, their absolute innocence and complete reliance on him. He liked nothing more than to be relied upon. It was his lifeblood. He'd see an old man who lived alone in the town or a widower or a bachelor and shudder; to be alone, to be unwanted, unnecessary, unloved. He'd rather die. But one child it was to be and he was content. More than content! His girl, his Anny, was the sun and moon to him. He loved to watch her sleep when she was a baby, not that she slept much as she was always up and about wanting to learn the next new thing. These days he would sit by the fire of an evening and watch her writing away at the table, see the pencil she held moving in mysterious shapes across the paper, shapes that were beyond his mind and always would be. He liked nothing more than to listen to her talk, the way he could sense her mind racing and see her trip over her words to catch up with it. Rachel was much brighter than him, he'd always known that, but to think that they had created this little wonder, this clever girl with her words and her thoughts. And that hair, that deep red hair like leaves on the turn. His own had been pale and orangey when he was younger, deepening to a reddish-brown scored with grey nowadays, while his wife's hair was the colour of tree bark. Together they had made this miracle, this beautiful, sparky girl, this child of his heart. His one child. He had only this one, singular vessel to pour all his fatherly affection into and it brimmed over with his love.

Now his one child was in danger, mortal danger. His wife would be floored by it, he was certain of that. It was his job to protect them both. What other point was there in a husband and father than that? His walk was coming to an end and his cottage was just along the way from here. How he wished he could slow down time and never reach it, never step over its threshold, never stand before his wife and tell her this darksome thing.

Chapter 14

Anny had dreamt of this. She had dreamt of entering the city of Shrewsbury, drinking it all in for the first time, seeing the pale stone of the walls and the coloured windows of the churches. She had imagined herself coming into the city by coach, gazing at the majestic buildings. The wheels of the coach barrelling along the streets, she would arrive at a busy square and the archway to the yard of a coaching inn, where she would alight and find her way to her lodgings; and recently, she had pictured an addition; later that day, after she had received her trunk and unpacked, there would come someone knocking upon the outer door and her landlady would call her down to greet her gentleman caller and there would be Jake, come to take her out to supper. She had pictured this, all of it, many times.

Now, she really was entering Shrewsbury for the first time, not in her imagination, but in full wakefulness, and nothing could have been further from her dreams. She was sitting on the back of a farmer's cart pulled by a leisurely old nag, shoved up beside three other women, reeking of the lock-up they'd all been in for the night, where the walls seeped with mildew and the room stank of damp and piss and the odour of unwashed, desperate bodies. The constable sat opposite them on the cart, silent and stoic but watchful, not speaking a word to any of them. The other women had not spoken to her either. Two of these were very poor, filthy and dishevelled. One had been drunk in the lock-up the night before and was now moaning and groaning at every bump in the road. The other had been rouged like a Frenchwoman and slept almost the whole time, seeming unsurprised by the whole business. The third was a nursing mother, dressed more respectably, who cooed at her baby and nursed it or else wept silently, tears running down her face and snot pouring from her nose, which she wiped away from time to time, but who never talked, except whisperings to her child. Anny could not bring herself to speak to them either. She had existed in a state of pure terror since the moment she had awoken at the lock-up in Ironbridge the day before. She had fainted in the office and had not come round until she was incarcerated. She knew nothing of what had occurred in between. The thought of being out cold, her body not her own, was horrible.

She had not slept at all that night and rued it now, as sleeping had proven impossible on the bumpy cart that had taken the best part of a day to travel the fifteen or so miles from Ironbridge to Shrewsbury. At least it was summer and at least it was not raining, though at some points on the road the sun had beaten down upon her face so harshly, she felt as if her skin was beginning to sizzle like bacon. She had pulled her cloak over her face but then felt suffocated by it. Walkers on the road and others in carts passing by had stared at her, some laughing, shaking their heads. One child threw a couple of stones in her direction and some men shouted at her and her fellow female felons, calling them hedge-creepers, then laughed raucously.

She watched all of this occur in a kind of stupefied horror, unable to process the nightmare that was truly happening to her. Her life of only a day before was gone, replaced by an existence in places and in company she had never considered, let alone imagined herself inhabiting. It was as if her tongue had seized up at the shock, that her brain had no frame of reference to compare this madness to and so had simply given up trying to respond to it. She was in shock, and could not fathom what had happened to ruin her life so quickly, so completely.

The cart passed over the sparkling Severn on a stately stone bridge, the river high, with here and there a tree emerging from it, the lower trunk submerged. They meandered on through a maze of streets, then climbed a long, slow hill past ancient, timber-framed buildings on each side. Anny looked up and saw the castle walls looming above them, rough-hewn and reddish, topped by grey battlements stark against the blue skies. The cart turned off the main roadway and took a track upwards further, the castle on her right, her constant stony companion until the cart came to a sudden halt. There before them was a gatehouse, a large, imposing structure of sandy-coloured stone, two bulging circular buildings on each side and an archway in the middle. The constable motioned at them to get down, still not deigning to speak actual words to them. The cart driver lit up a pipe and ignored them too. Anny looked around at him, unspeakably jealous that this man would be returning along the road to her home town, a place she wondered if she would ever set eyes on again. The constable was arguing with him about the fee, so many pence a mile from Ironbridge to bring the felons.

Then he grunted at the women to follow him. After no food or drink since a cup of water and a hunk of old bread in the lock-up that morning, Anny was unsteady on her feet and feared she might pass out. They were led towards the archway. The constable had words with the gatekeeper, who used two keys to unlock the tall, iron gates. She wondered if the gates had been produced with local iron. Had her grandfather's hands fashioned the iron rails that would soon stand between her and the freedom of the streets? Above the gates sat an alcove inside which had been placed a bodiless statue, the grey face of a stern man looking downwards upon them as they passed under it. Despite the heat, the stone eyes frowning at her gave her a chill and she drew her cloak around her. The woman's baby had awoken and was starting to fuss. Its small sobs soon reached a crescendo of wailing. This desperate sound accompanied them as they passed into the courtyard of Shrewsbury Prison. The gates were locked behind them.

The constable said to the gatekeeper, 'This'un a vagrant. This'un assisting a murder. This'un theft. This'un with the nipper is debt. Here y'are.'

He handed over some papers from inside his coat and continued conversing gruffly with the gatekeeper. Anny stared at the woman who had been wearing rouge the night before, which had since rubbed off. She was accused of assisting a murder. A murder! Anny had spent all night in a cell and all day on a cart with a woman who had assisted a murderer. Her mind raced with scenarios of who this woman might have helped in murdering and the murderer she had helped. She did not look like a violent woman. She just looked very tired and very bored.

Her attention was drawn away by the rising voice of the gatekeeper, 'Nay, she canna and you had no business bringing it here,' the gatekeeper was saying, pointing at the mother. 'It needs taking back to its own parish.'

'She's nursing it, you fool. If you think I'm taking a starving waif back on a day's journey by cart, you're half-soaked,' said the constable, and with that, he demanded the gate be opened and he be allowed to leave.

Two men approached them and the gatekeeper said, 'Go with the turnkeys, then,' and motioned them to walk through another archway into a courtyard. It was surrounded by two high walls on either side and before them the frontispiece to a long building, with arched windows along the breadth of it, all barred. She could hear shouts and calls from people behind the bars, the deeper voices of men coming from the left, the higher voices of women from the right. One turnkey took the murderer's assistant, while the rest of them, including Anny, followed the other turnkey through a door, past an office with a brass plaque screwed to the closed door entitled 'Keeper'.

'You've missed supper,' said the turnkey, not looking round at them. 'Straight to the cell.'

They followed him round to the right, walking on through a maze of corridors, alive with the stink of many bodies and the grumblings, mutterings, chatter and yelling of women. Some shouted at them as they went past: 'What did you bring us?' and suchlike. One bright spark with a throaty voice called out, 'Abandon hope all ye who enter here!' They walked on past small groups of cells arranged around a central area. Each group also had an open room that the guard pointed at and said, 'Cells there, court there and that's the day room.' He hacked up a good load of phlegm and spat it out in a grey, jellied lump onto the ground and then said, 'In the morning, follow the others. Wash outside, then breakfast. Surgeon'll see you, give you the once-o'er. Matron'll see you and give you your uniform. Set you to work. Your court is yours to keep tidy.'

They stopped at one of the courts and the turnkey said, 'Debtors. You with young'un. You're in there. Visitors you can have daily except Sundays. Regular visitors in the Visitor's Room or your husband, if you have'un, in your cell. You'll get a half-pint of wine. Not now. Tomorrow.'

The woman bowed her head onto her baby's and went into her cell alone. The turnkey locked the door. Some cells were single, like that; others had three beds in. Anny prayed for a single. They walked on and stopped again. The turnkey said, 'Here we are. Female Felons for Trial.' He opened a cell door and inside were three beds and two women, who looked around. 'You. Theft. In there.'

Anny walked in and the door clanked shut behind her. The sound of the key turning screwed her insides. She stood awkwardly on a grubby rag rug in the centre of the small space between the beds. The women were seated together on one bed, knees close together as if caught sharing secrets. They stared at her and Anny took a quick look around. There was a chamber pot in the corner filled to overflowing. Apart from that, the cell held only its beds and its inhabitants. And a high, small window, its view out of sight and reach; barred, of course.

'Now then, Theft. What's your real name?'

Anny looked at the women. Both wore the plain grey shapeless dress of the prison uniform. This one looked to be the same age as her mother, the other much younger, more like her age.

'Anny.'

'I'm Ellen, this is Jane. First time inside? You look like it is. You look as frightened as a mouse in cat country.'

Jane tittered at this.

'Yes, first time.'

'Sit down then. That's your bed over there.'

Anny stepped over to the spare cot. It had a thin mattress on it, which as she sat down made the rustling sound of straw stuffing. She could feel the bedstead through it, hard and bony against her behind. Where had these iron bedframes been forged? She thought of her father and wanted to weep. Folded up at the end of the bed were two sheets and two blankets.

'You look like a good wench,' said Ellen. 'But you're mucky. You'll need to scrub yourself right in the morning, or you won't get your breakfast, mind.'

'She has purty hair,' said Jane in a small, high voice. Jane's hand was resting on Ellen's knee, like fond sisters. 'Bonny colour.'

'Thank you,' said Anny. Jane smiled at her, a crooked, unsettling smile. Her hair was such a light yellow, it was almost white. Her pale eyes wandered a bit. Perhaps her thoughts, too.

'Not married, lass?' said Ellen. Her brown hair had grey streaks in it and there were dark pouches under her eyes and her cheeks and chin sagged. She looked directly at Anny without blinking. Anny was afraid of her but couldn't explain why, as Ellen was talking kindly to her.

Anny shook her head. 'I live with my parents in Iron-bridge.' She could not stop thinking of her father. Her mother too. What would they be thinking? They would be beside themselves. 'They'll likely visit tomorrow. See how I'm faring.' Somehow she wanted to prove that she had support, she had others outside this hell who cared about her. That she was not alone in this place. But even one night's wait here sickened her with fear. She thought she might start sobbing again, so bit her lip. She would not cry in front of these two.

'What did you steal?' said Ellen, those blank eyes unblinking.

'I didn't. I didn't do it.'

Jane tittered again.

'Of course you didna, lass. I didna write any threatening letters either, did I, Janey, eh?'

'No, Nelly. No, you never did,' said Jane, shaking her head violently from side to side, whereupon they both laughed and held onto each other, rocking back and forth. *If they touch me*, thought Anny, *I shall scream*.

Ellen stopped laughing and peered at Anny, looked her up and down. 'Give me your hands.'

Anny did not want to. She hesitated.

'Give me your hands, for God's sake, girl. I dunna bite.'

'Not hands, anyway,' said Jane, mysteriously.

Anny could see no way round it. She held out her hands slowly, watching Ellen warily. Ellen took them roughly and rubbed them, turned them this way and that, then dropped them.

'Office worker,' she said, triumphantly.

'Yes,' said Anny.

'I knew it. Not rough enough for hard work. Ink under your nails. We've got an educated miss here, not unlike myself, Jane. You mun mind your manners round this'un. I suppose you'll be wanting a glass of wine, my lady.'

Anny remembered what the turnkey had said to the nursing mother. 'Will we get ours tomorrow?'

'Your what?' said Ellen.

'Our wine?'

Ellen and Jane looked round at each other and fell about laughing again. 'Ooh, Lady Ann of Ironbridge is wanting her wine!'

Anny waited for the mockery to subside. 'But the woman with the baby, he said to her . . .'

'That's just for debtors,' snapped Ellen. 'You're a felon. You dunna get the same privileges.'

Jane piped up, 'She's a fine'un, like the last. They'll make her monitor, now the other'un's been sent yonder.'

Anny frowned and Ellen said, 'Yes, they will, no doubt. She looks like the type who'd suck up to the turnkeys, this'un. Just like the last'un. Well, it did her no good, let me tell you, Lady Ann. She was Theft like you and she herself got transported for seven years, she did. Being the keeper's pet did her no good at all, wunna do her no good either, out in Australia.'

Anny felt her head would explode. The effort was enormous, of remaining vigilant of these two, of keeping her mouth closed on a scream, of stopping herself from running to the door and pounding upon it. Her head felt so heavy, so heavy. She let it drop into her hands and screwed her eyes shut. She would not cry, must not cry.

She heard Ellen sigh heavily. 'Lie down and sleep,' she said in a kinder voice.

Anny did so. Too exhausted to make the bed up with the sheets and blankets, she rested her head upon them and was out in less than a minute.

She woke in full darkness. It was a hot night, stifling in the tiny cell. She felt suffocated by the heat and the stench of the chamber pot and her two companions' bodily emissions. Her mouth was so dry she thought she would gag. Oh, for a cup of cool water. She would give her life for it. She could not think of any other thing for several minutes, just water, water, water, a drink, a drink, a drink. To think of how busy her mind had been only a day and a half before, filled with girlish notions of love and kissing and a happy future. And now she would die for a sip of water. She listened to the other women breathing. The tears came then. She could not stop them. They flowed out of her eyes like the gush from a waterwheel, unstoppable, unending. She let them run into her mouth. At least they moistened her tongue a little, despite their saltiness. She pursed her lips to stop a sound escaping, but that betrayed her too and let out one small sob.

Jane suddenly sat bolt upright. She stared over at Anny, who stopped whimpering immediately. Jane stood and stepped over to her. Anny looked up and Jane brought her hand down very fast, whacking her hard on the ear. Anny cried out, then bit her lip and cupped her hands over her poor ear. Her ear throbbed with sharp pain. Jane bent down very close and delivered her words in a breathy yet vicious whisper: 'Hush your noise! I'm in here for assault, see? I know how to handle meself with a chit like you. You wake me up again and I shall thrash you. I shall murder you.'

Chapter 15

Margaret had found out that morning. She had gone to sleep early the night before with bad pains from the monthly curse. She had slept late and was breakfasting in bed when the news came. It was the maid, Lucy, that had gently knocked on her door, come in and told her: 'I thought you'd want to know, miss. Your friend, Miss Woodvine. They say she took money from the safe. They found it in her bag.'

The news had almost shocked Margaret into silence. It was so preposterous. 'Lucy, what are you talking about?'

'Anny, miss. They're saying she stole from the master.'

'It is a mistake,' said Margaret. 'Anny would never do that.'

'Yes, miss,' said Lucy.

'But, what is happening? Where is she now?'

'The constable Finch came and they locked her up last night. It's said she'll go to the Dana today to wait for trial.'

'The what?'

'The prison in Shrewsbury. They call it the Dana there.'

'What do her parents say? They must be distraught.'

'Her father goes to visit her tomorrow, I heard. At the prison.'

'Forgive me, Lucy, but I must go and speak with my father.'

Margaret had not known what to do. She was frightened of her father, more so of Cyril. But she had to do something. She called for her maid Royce, who dressed her. Then she gathered her nerve and went straight to her father's study, knocking meekly on the door. But he was not at home. He had gone out for the day. Cyril too. Queenie was in bed and not to be disturbed. Her father did not return all day. She sat in her room and thought it all through. It filled her with fear, the thought of acting beyond the narrow confines of her existence, but her friend's peril spurred her on.

She swallowed her nerves and walked to the stables. She spoke quietly with the coach driver and instructed him to take her to Shrewsbury first thing in the morning. The driver looked askance, momentarily seeming to doubt her authority. She had cleared her throat and spoken louder, telling him to be ready at dawn. She knew that all of her family were slugabeds, unless a trip out beckoned them from their abandoned sleep. She could leave early and face her father's wrath when she returned. Then, once she understood the situation better, having heard the details from Anny herself, she would speak to her father. She would insist, she would make him listen. Seeing Anny would give her the strength to do it, to face him and tell him: this simply must be wrong. This was not possible. Anny would never do this. Her father must believe her.

The ride to Shrewsbury the next morning was long, hot and uncomfortable. She tried to imagine the inside of a prison, tried to picture her friend there, but all that came were scenes from French novels of convicts chained in dungeons with long white beards. She scolded herself for being so unworldly, so sheltered and foolish. When she arrived, she must face it with fortitude, for her friend, for Anny.

The coach wound its way through the city that she had visited before, for trips to the theatre and to buy clothes with Benjamina. She had seen the castle on the hill and glimpsed the prison beyond it, but had never given it a second thought. The coach jolted to a stop and the driver opened the door for her. She gathered her embroidered purse and hitched up her stiff skirts as she descended the step onto the street. Then, someone said her name.

She looked up. Before her stood a very tall, very broad man, dishevelled, his boots grey with dust, his hair thick with it, his face grimed by it. She had not heard what he'd said and was about to ask what on earth he wanted, when she recognised something in his face. He spoke again: 'I am Anny's father, come to see her. Are you come to see her too, miss?'

'Indeed, Mr Woodvine,' she said kindly. 'One moment, please.' She turned to the driver and told him to wait for her there, for as long as it took. The driver nodded and prepared to move along to find a more permanent spot to rest in. She looked back at Anny's father and glanced behind him. 'Is your wife here with you?'

'She is at home. She . . . took it badly. She collapsed.'

Margaret thought of the strong-armed, vital woman she had met and could not imagine her fainting. Only news as bad as this could fell such a woman.

'Oh, I am so sorry to hear of it. Is she being looked after?'

'She is. We have good neighbours. She is not strong enough to travel, so I have come alone, bringing things for Anny that her mother packed for her last night.'

'Mr Woodvine, how did you travel here today?'

'Walked through the night,' he said, fingering his hat nervously.

'Please forgive me,' she said. 'I have been so thoughtless. I should have arranged to take you myself.'

'Very kind of you, miss. But I think we both know, that wouldna do.'

Perhaps he is right, she thought. But she felt it was the right thing to say. 'Yes, I have come to see Anny.

You may not know, sir, that your daughter and I are dear friends. I'm sorry to say we have hidden this fact for some years now. We felt it would be better to be . . . discreet about such a close friendship. But I assure you, that Anny is the best friend I have in the whole world.'

Woodvine seemed abashed by this. He looked down, sidelong, up. Then he said, 'I didna know of that. But I'm hoping now it'll be something that'll help my girl. Can you help her, miss? Can you?'

'I will do anything in my power,' she said earnestly. 'Anything a friend can do, I shall do.' But she had nothing for him, no plans and no information. She saw his expectant face and wanted to answer it, to give him the hope he clearly wanted, but she had only her position, her money, her friendship to offer. What good it would do, she knew not. She smiled at him wanly, pityingly, and his face changed. It fell and hardened. He shoved his hat back on his head.

'You'd better not go in there, miss,' he said gruffly. 'Not a place for young ladies.'

'Oh, but Mr Woodvine, I am determined. I must see Anny. Shall we not go in together? It would be my honour if you accompanied me.' Something in his face and manner made him comfortable to talk to. She had not been this at ease talking to someone since Jake. She saw Anny's features in this man's face and it made her feel at home.

'Mr Woodvine, I assure you that once I have heard Anny's side of the story, I will be going directly to talk to my father. I am convinced that this must surely be a miscarriage of justice.'

'That's what I think,' said Woodvine, his face lit with possibility now. 'My lass would never do this.'

'I know that, sir. I do. Anny is the most honest, upright person I know. Your family are well respected in my father's works and in the neighbourhood. I am sure we can settle this, once we have the facts.'

She had no idea where this resolve had come from, never in her life being sure of herself in any single thing. But there was a first time for everything, and this was hers. How would she persuade her father? What could ever move a weak-minded, selfish fool such as Ralph King to help a girl like Anny? Now, standing with Anny's father, she saw he was everything that Mr King was not. In his shabby working clothes he had more dignity in his fingernail than her father would ever have in his whole person. She felt that envy again, that pang of wanting to have another family, another life. The wish to be a changeling. But then she caught herself, her stupid self, wishing her lucky life away while her poor friend sat in the hellish place before them. And Anny's father stood and looked to her, the rich friend, for some crumb of help.

'Come,' she went on. 'Let us go and see her now.'

Woodvine nodded and they approached the gate. Once inside, the gatekeeper searched through Woodvine's package, scattering the contents. Three bread rolls fell onto the filthy floor and Margaret cried out as they were soiled. The silly man, ruining Anny's precious food like that. She helped Woodvine pick them up.

'Should we throw these away?' she said quietly to Woodvine.

'No, miss. She'll be in need of them.'

She noted that the gatekeeper did not ask to see inside her purse. They waited in silence for some time, the gate-keeper having taken Anny's name and told them some-one would come soon. She glanced at Woodvine, who stood as solid as oak, patient, unreadable. Then a man in uniform approached and gestured at them to follow. What came next was as a nightmare, the kind of dream that wakes you in dreaded wonder at how your mind could dream up such a thing, yet this was real. The sounds that came from the women, the screams and yelps and sobs. The stink that flowed through the fetid air, so thick and rank that Margaret feared she would faint. Woodvine kept an eye on her, at one stage putting a hesitant arm about her shoulder to steer her away from arms reaching out from bars, streaked with filth and what looked like dried blood and their owner screeching at the rich girl passing, calling her words that Margaret had never heard but sounded like the names that demons would dream up in hell for the torture of its inhabitants.

Not soon enough, they arrived at a room set out with tables and chairs at which sat women in grey dresses and opposite them an assortment of people, mostly poor, one or two more well-to-do. There was a woman nursing her baby, and the thought of babies existing in this dreadful place sickened Margaret more than anything. And then she saw Anny.

Woodvine was already there. He had stridden across the room before Margaret had had a chance to register her friend, so different did she look at first glance, an impression that increased with every step towards her. It had only been three days, but already Anny looked like a shadow of the feisty young woman she knew and loved. Her face was pasty, marked only with dark shadows beneath her eyes. Her glorious copper tresses were mostly hidden under an off-white cap, the strands that escaped messily were lank and greasy, the hair dirty-red, as if the colour had leaked out of it. She sat upright though, her back straight, her face uplifted. They had not broken her yet. She stood as her father approached, her face crumpling into distress and joy intermixed, an expression Margaret had never seen in a person until that moment and it broke her heart. Margaret's eyes filled with tears and she caught a sob in her handkerchief, raised to her nose to try in vain to block out the smell. She watched as Anny's father threw his arms about her, his huge frame enveloping her utterly so that she temporarily disappeared, but a guard by the wall shouted at them 'No touching!' and they pulled apart reluctantly, Woodvine shooting a look of hatred at the man, as if he would kill him with a flick of his hand. Anny was whispering to him, beckoning him to sit down, her eyes wary of trouble. Then she looked over and spotted Margaret. Her face changed again, this time showing surprise, then a smile and a frown at once, her hand raised towards her. Margaret came quickly, grasping it, and then remembering the guard's order, letting go quickly and taking the seat that Woodvine held ready for her, trying to dust it off. Margaret had worn her plainest, dullest gown but still felt a perfect idiot in that place, like a peacock in a coal mine.

'Ow bist, my wench? How be it here?' Woodvine was gabbling. 'I brought things from home. Here, food, clothes. Your mother packed them. She's ill or she woulda come. No, dunna fret. Dunna fret, little'un. Dunna cry. She'll be right. Just upset with all this business. I'm here. I'm here, now. Dunna cry, my sweet lass.'

Woodvine's commentary ran on desperately as Anny wept and wept. She had not spoken properly yet; neither had Margaret. She was crying too; her eyes blurred, she wiped them with her lace handkerchief which soon crumpled into a useless wet rag. She had another one in her sleeve and passed it instead to Anny, who did not see it, blinded by tears as she was. Woodvine took it and used it to wipe his daughter's face tenderly, so tenderly, the huge hands capable of such sensitivity.

After a time, Anny calmed down and composed herself. She looked up at her father, then at Peggy, and forced a feeble smile.

'Thank you for coming,' she said in a small voice.

'Anny,' said Margaret, determined to be of some use now. 'I intend to speak to my father about this tonight. I need to know everything you can tell me of what happened. I need all of the facts, so that we can try to fathom what happened here. So we can solve it.'

Anny nodded solemnly, then began to tell it all: how Paddy had come and called her away to the library, which of course Margaret remembered, how strange that was; how she'd gone back, followed by Cyril, and unlocked the office, found it empty, Brotherton away somewhere; how she'd worked for a while then he'd come back, complaining of an errand to town for Mrs King senior, to fetch some ink, usually Anny's job, so that was strange, too; then they'd worked all day and only discovered the money missing at the end of the day; how Mr King had found it in her bag.

Margaret had listened keenly to each turn of events. 'So, the office was left locked and unoccupied for a time, between Mr B being sent to town and you returning from the house.'

'Yes, that's right.'

'That's when it happened,' said Margaret.

'Yes, that's what I think,' said Anny, her tired eyes brightening.

'Think what?' said Woodvine, slow to catch on.

Margaret answered, 'Someone went into the office when it was unoccupied, took the money from the safe and put it in Anny's bag.'

'Yes!' cried Anny.

Woodvine said, 'But who? Who would do such a thing? Why wouldna they just take it for themselves? And how would they get in? It was locked. Who could do that and how? Why?'

So many questions. But Margaret knew. She looked at Anny and saw that Anny knew too. She wondered if Anny did not want to speak of this before her father, but saw also that they must be allies now, the three of them, if they were to save her.

'Anny,' she said and leant forward, speaking low. 'That day, in the library, you were going to tell me something but we were interrupted. What was it?'

Anny glanced at her father.

'What is it, lass?' he said gently.

'Cyril – Master King – he found me in the woods the day before and he asked me to be his wife.'

'What?' gasped Woodvine, turning to Margaret for some enlightenment, but did not wait for further explanation, his mind clearly running onwards. 'Well, if he's sweet on you then this problem is solved. He can vouch for you. He will speak to his father, surely.'

'No,' said Margaret firmly. 'Anny, what did you say to Cyril when he asked you?'

Anny looked down at her lap, pain flitting across her eyes. 'I refused him.'

'Well, I'm not surprised,' began Woodvine, then, remembering the company they kept, gave a sidelong look at Margaret and muttered, 'No offence to you, miss.'

'None taken,' said Margaret. 'How did it proceed, Anny? How did Cyril take it?'

'Not well,' said Anny, grimly. 'He . . .' Another glance at her father.

'Please, Anny,' said Margaret. 'We must know it all.'

'He attacked me, tried to kiss me. I fought him off. I told him I hated him. I ran away.'

'I'll get him,' said Woodvine, in a guttural tone. 'I'll get him and I'll lamp him.'

'No, you won't!' said Anny. 'Mother needs you. Don't get yourself in here, for assault.'

'It's more serious than that,' said Margaret, and they both looked at her. 'From what you've told me, Anny, I am convinced of it. Cyril put that money in your bag, as revenge for turning him down.'

'Yes,' said Anny. 'I'm certain of it.'

Woodvine erupted, standing up, his puny chair careering backwards as if made of matchsticks. 'I'll murder 'im!' He stood, puffing like a bull, clenching his fists. Two guards hopped to it and were beside him in a second, shouting at him to clear out. There was a scuffle and Anny called out to her father to calm down, and to

223

the guards to leave him be. Thus, Woodvine was manhandled from the room, calling behind him to Anny, saying sorry, how sorry he was. Margaret called to him, told him to wait for her outside, that she would come presently. One of the guards stayed and told her she'd have to go too.

'If I may, a further few minutes is all I require to speak to Miss Woodvine here. I would be most grateful.' She smiled at the sour-faced oik who stank of spirits and sweat. He grinned as she raised her purse a notch, catching his eye. She removed a couple of coins from it and handed them to him.

'Long as you want, miss! Well, until visiting time is up, anyhow,' he said, taking the coins and performing a twisted kind of bow, taking his place again in the corner, watching her closely as she sat down once more with Anny.

'Dear Anny,' said Margaret, risking the guard's wrath by taking her friend's hand and enfolding it.

'I'm so glad you came. I'm so glad you're here,' said Anny. It was the kind of thing someone would say and smile, but there was no smile. It was as if her face had been newly made, only for sadness.

'I will talk to my father tonight. But it will have to be handled carefully. I will have to think on it, how it is to be done best. He adores my brother and will not hear him badly spoken of by others, so I need to be clever in the way I do it, the way I say it to him.'

'Thank you,' said Anny, staring desperately at her now, squeezing her hand. 'And I hope to God it works. I cannot stand it here much longer.'

'Visiting time is nearly up,' called the guard and people began to busy themselves to leave. Anny said, 'There's no time, Peggy. Listen, does Jake Ashford know I'm here? Does he know about this?'

The mention of Jake's name was a shock to Margaret. What was this? She frowned at it.

'Well, I don't know, Anny. I've not seen Mr Ashford these past few days.'

'Will you take him a message for me, Peggy? Please? I know he comes to the big house. Will you please tell him something from me?'

Margaret fought to control her expression. 'Of course I will. What is it?'

'Tell him I didn't do it. Tell him you're going to help me. Tell him . . . to wait.'

'Wait . . . for what?' said Margaret.

'Visiting time is over now. Out you go. Out you all go,' called the guard, who was joined by a turnkey, ready to take the prisoners back.

'And Peggy,' said Anny, standing, grasping her friend's hand now so tightly, so desperately it crushed her fingers, 'tell him to visit me. Please! Tell him to come to me, as soon as he can, Peggy. Please!'

The visitors were leaving and the guard was approaching. Anny released her friend's hand and turned from her, a turnkey standing between them, ushering the prisoners out.

'I will speak to my father,' called Margaret, as Anny gathered up her package and left the room by a back door. Anny looked back once, eyes pleading, then disappeared into a gloomy corridor beyond. Despite the weight of this terrible place upon her, Anny's bearing was ramrod straight. So, was there an understanding between Anny and Jake Ashford? Margaret's heart twisted with it. It couldn't be. Jake had asked to spend more time with her. There must be some mistake. How she wanted her friend to possess this happiness, and yet at the same time how she smarted with envy. Could it be true? Whatever the case was, she had to drive it from her mind. The only thing that mattered now was helping Anny to get out of this hellish place. Margaret inhaled deeply, breathing in the stink of the prison, which only minutes before had sent her coughing into her lace handkerchief. But she was determined to overcome her previous sensibilities. As she left the room and followed the turnkey out into the corridors and beyond, she felt she was changing inside. For the first time in her sheltered life, she had been shaken to the core by the reality of what other people had to endure in this world. How stupid she'd been, how pathetic and scared and shy – and of what? These were real problems, solid, unavoidable problems as heavy as iron, and as immovable. And now her dear friend was in mortal danger and she was the only one on earth who could do anything about it. She felt herself grown an inch by the time she reached the prison gates, and as she left the prison behind and entered into the sunshiny afternoon, she emerged as a new creature.

Chapter 16

Ralph King sat at his study desk, looking down gloomily at his mound of a belly that pushed up against the drawer handle. Where did it all come from, this flesh? As a younger man, he had been able to eat like a pig and never put on an ounce. He hunted, walked, rode and even swam without a second thought. Nowadays he broke into a sweat climbing the stairs. He thought about going up there to look at himself in the mirror, to turn sideways and see if his profile was worse than the last time he looked. But Benjamina was up there, taking her customary nap. What on earth did she do to warrant a sleep every afternoon? Weakness, that was it. Women were weak. But she ate bonbons and cake and other delicacies and all of it disappeared without blemish into her slim frame. Her breasts and hips and buttocks were womanly and ample, he thought with a minor jolt, but everywhere else was lean and firm. How did she do it? How he envied her that. It must be born in her. Or perhaps it was age. She was so very young, at twenty-three. And he felt so very old, though surely forty-three was not ancient. He felt somehow he was ageing more quickly than her. She was receding from him, growing distant. With a looming sense of doom, he wondered why his pretty wife did not want to bed him anymore. She had been voracious when they first married and now had cooled off considerably, always complaining of headaches and so forth. Even when they did, she would just lie there and stare off into the distance, waiting for it to be over. And why did she always ask him to leave her alone straight afterward? She said she didn't want a child yet, as she was too young. He could understand that. He didn't want one either in particular, but surely this was unnatural for a woman. His first wife had had two, long before she was twenty-three. But look what happened to her. Celia, lovely, loving Celia. She had been so innocent, so giving, so sweet. Benjamina's lasciviousness had been stimulating to begin with, but it didn't last and now it seemed tarnished, when he thought of Celia. It nearly broke him, when she bled and died like that in their bed. How he hated Margaret after that; couldn't hold his baby daughter in his arms without cursing her. That was wrong, he knew that. But can a man help how he feels, really feels? No, he cannot. And no man loved a woman more than he had loved Celia. His love for Benjamina – well, that was lust. And necessity. Mostly lust. Her body, soft here, tight there, open to him. Or had been, once upon a time. Maybe he should tell her he wanted a child and then she'd be duty bound to perform. Yes, he'd try that. And stop eating so much.

He realised that he was lonely. Yes, the great Ralph King. Did his wife love him? His daughter? His mother, even? Anyone? Cyril. His beloved son. Did the boy love him, though? Could he love anyone, that boy? The doubts came thick and fast, like flies to fresh manure. The boy had that cruelty in him, just like Ralph King senior, his own father. He knew they'd both had their way violently with maids about the place. He'd heard his father grunting away with them at night, seen his son manhandling them. He'd had words with Cyril, only one time, when he was caught almost in the act, ravishing that pretty one, Lucy. It would cause such a scandal if word got out. Didn't the boy know to keep his activities private? He'd never had the urge, himself. He never wanted to touch the lower classes, if he could help it. Couldn't understand it.

And then there was Margaret. Only today she had taken the barouche without asking and kept it out all day and was still not back. He was furious with her. So out of character and so damnably selfish. Cyril had wanted to take it out this morning, and he himself had required it this afternoon. They had to make do with the curricle. What in heaven's name was the girl thinking, sneaking off like that at first light? How dare she! He'd have a word or two to say about that when she returned.

And Benjamina. He'd have a word or two with her as well, this evening.

A knock on the door dragged him from his musing and he called whoever it was to enter. It was Brunt, his faithful butler of over thirty years, around when he was a boy and his father was young and vital. That should be the way of things, servants committing themselves to one family. So many of these younger ones hopped from job to job, never sticking at anything. Times were changing and he did not like it. He did not like it at all. Brunt was waiting for him.

'What is it, Brunt?'

'Messrs Brotherton and Pritchard are here, with their daily report. Shall I show them in, sir?'

'Indeed, indeed,' said King, forcing himself to appear businesslike. Oh hell, these meetings were tedious. And, if he admitted it fully to himself, they were confusing. They often tried to explain things to him of the nature of the business, and he so often failed to grasp the gist of what they were banging on about and ended up bluffing his way through it and hoping nobody noticed. He was sure, actually, that nobody did notice. He was very good at bluffing.

The two men came in, caps in hand. Ralph would usually stand up and address them from in front of the fireplace but today he was weary and quite comfortable in his position at his desk. He remained seated and said, 'Proceed, gentlemen.'

Brotherton began with some figures about labour and materials, then something about breakage in the machinery at the rolling mill that would need fixing – something about the screws of the pillars of the rolls that would need re-cutting – and Ralph just said affirmative things on occasion and hoped Brotherton would shut up soon, which he did. Then Pritchard started up about the illness of some key workman which delayed production, and then about working hours and Ralph lost interest. Why did they bother him with such things? So far, no questions had been asked, so he felt unencumbered by having to do anything more than nod sagely and agree with all of their conclusions, unless it involved the spending of more money, in which case his ears always pricked up and he weeded out such revolutionary ideas and crushed them.

Just then, the sound of a coach and horses coming up the drive alerted him to the return of his daughter. He must get rid of these fools and take her to task for her behaviour. Surely they had finished by now. He attuned his mind to the string of words that came from Brotherton's mouth and nodded twice. But then Pritchard piped up and was talking about materials, and how the cost would be increased but that it would surely be a worthy investment, and so forth.

'What's this?' said Ralph, and the two men stopped and stared in embarrassed silence. 'Pritchard, do go over what you just said, as I can hardly believe my ears.'

'Uh . . . well, sir, the problem is occurring with the raw materials. The coke and the limestone we are supplied with needs a more uniform preparation, if slips are to be avoided.'

What were slips again? Oh, the processes that went on in these blast furnaces were so complicated, one needed to concentrate damnably hard to understand them.

'Slips?'

More staring. 'Yes, sir, slips,' said Pritchard.

'And your argument again is . . . what? About slipping?'

'Slips, not slipping, sir. You see, at times the materials stick to the inside wall of the furnace and cause a blockage. That's your slip. If it builds all the way across, that's a scaffold. That's very dangerous, sir, and could cause an explosion. The coke and limestone we're presently receiving are of a poorer quality. The pieces are so uneven as to cause blockages, as they burn at different rates. We need to increase the checks on the production of our materials to ensure a more uniform size and . . .'

'It sounds expensive, Pritchard.'

Brotherton piped up. 'Not really, sir. It might be only further instructions needed to the bridgestocker in the proper preparation of the materials and may only require a small increase in expenditure, due to the . . .'

'No,' said Ralph and decided to clench his fist and place it commandingly on his desk for effect. 'No, no, no. This business is already spending far too much money on labour and materials. We will not be adopting anything that drives the cost up further.'

Pritchard started up again: 'But, sir, the safety of the furnace and therefore the men themselves . . .'

'Are well taken care of,' Ralph interrupted.

'With respect, sir,' Pritchard began. Well, he didn't like the sound of that. If he had respect, he wouldn't need to declare it in such a presumptuous manner.

'Now then, Pritchard, this won't do. This really will not do. You come in here and make these demands like a common highwayman. Yes, it needed saying. My furnace runs very well and has done these past years. I trust in the ability of you and your workers to keep an eye on these things and do your best with the materials you are given. Why, if we spent all the money in the world on perfect materials and perfect labourers, I dare say we'd have a perfect ironworks. But we would not make a profit, would we now, hmm? And you would not earn a wage and neither would any of your men and I would be a beggar on the streets alongside you.'

He would have liked to add, *And what do you say to that, eh, Pritchard?* But he restrained himself. He had made his point, brilliantly. He didn't need to rub their noses in it, though it was tempting. But he had had quite enough of these two for now and was itching to launch his wrath at his daughter.

He rang the bell for Brunt and when he came, told him to escort them out and bring Margaret to him forthwith. When Brotherton and Pritchard had finally gone, he breathed a sigh of relief. Another problem dealt with in an excellent manner, and any possible humiliations due to muddles had been swiftly sidestepped. He got up from his chair, which took more effort than he'd like and took up his favourite spot by the fireplace, sucked in his stomach and waited. There was a knock on the door.

'Enter.'

In came his daughter, and her appearance surprised him. Somehow, she looked older than she had only the day before. Her bearing was more upright and her gaze more direct. She suddenly seemed the very image of her dead mother, the same large mouth, swan-like neck and graceful hands. He really must remember to be nicer to her in general terms, but not at this moment. Now what was needed was a hard lesson.

Chapter 17

At the sight of her father, Margaret quailed. She had never willingly approached him to converse about anything. But she knew that the moment had come to steel herself and act, for justice, but most of all, for her friend.

'Father, I must speak with you,' she said and approached quickly, placing her purse on his desk with a confident gesture that seemed to unsettle him.

'Indeed you must. What is the meaning of this, Margaret? How dare you take the barouche today without my permission! What makes you think that a girl of your tender years can go gallivanting about the countryside without a chaperone, without ... my permission, as I have just said. I demand an explanation.'

'Never mind about that, Father. It is something else I need to discuss with you.'

Her hands were trembling and she clasped them together to steady herself.

'What in God's name is this? What has happened to my shy, retiring daughter of only yesterday? Who is this arch young woman accosting me with demands? I say again, Margaret . . .'

'No, Father, really. We don't have time for that now. We must discuss Anny Woodvine.'

'What is this, now? Woodvine? What the devil . . .'

'I've been to see her in Shrewsbury. She's innocent, Father.' Margaret walked over to the fireplace and stood at the other end of it, directly opposite him.

'You've been *where*? To *Shrewsbury*?'

'Yes, I visited her in prison. I saw her father there. We spoke to her. She told us everything that happened. And I must say . . . it is my duty to inform you . . .'

'You? You went to Shrewsbury Prison? With an iron-worker? A *prison*?'

She took a step towards him. She was within striking distance now. She felt her knees weakening but she forced herself to stay upright. She would not allow him to win this one. Everything was at stake now.

'Yes, Father, but that is of no consequence. You really must listen to me, Father. I have to . . .'

He hit her very hard across her right cheek. She did not fall to the ground. Instead, she bent right over, but her knees did not give way. She cradled her cheek in one hand, but stood her ground and looked up at him.

'I will be heard,' she said, quietly but firmly.

'Must I strike you again?' he said, his voice low.

'Cyril put that money in Anny Woodvine's bag. He did it out of revenge.'

'What witchcraft is this? What lies are you cooking up? This is madness!'

He went to hit her again, but she was wise to it now and dodged out of the way, causing him to stumble forward. He caught his balance with one hand on the mantelpiece. She hopped behind his leather armchair, the bulk of it between them.

'It's the truth, Father, and you must hear it. Cyril is no good. He's rotten to the core.'

Margaret was still stationed behind the chair, her eyes alert, her stance ready to flit away again. He was looking at her with narrowed eyes, as if trying to fathom her. Perhaps he was realising that his old ways were not working now. She would not be cowed by the back of his hand. She could see him changing tack. What would he say next?

'I am sorry I struck you, Margaret,' he said carefully. 'I lost my temper there for a moment and it is regrettable. It won't happen again. Let us discuss this like civilised people. Here, come sit beside me and we shall reason this out, together.'

He put his hand out to her. She hesitated. She did not take his hand but she did come out from behind the chair. He sat in his leather chair and motioned to her to sit on the matching footstool, but she declined and stood on the hearthrug. She did not trust him. She knew at that moment that she truly hated him. But she needed him to save Anny. And so she must listen and deal with him. It was heartening to see him acting more reasonably.

She began, 'You may well be unaware of this, but Cyril has been after Anny Woodvine for years.'

'It is his way with the servant girls. An unfortunate weakness, but one I am preparing to take in hand.'

'No, Father. It is more than that with Anny. He asked her to marry him.'

'He did *what*?'

Margaret thought her father might explode. 'He told her he wanted her to be his wife. But she refused him.'

'Has he told you of this himself?'

'No, but Anny told me. And I trust Anny with my life. I never knew a more honest person than Anny Woodvine. Mr Brotherton would concur with this, I am sure. And he can confirm that Cyril was always bothering Anny at the office and trying to get her alone. Just ask him.'

Her father was pinching at his lower lip, staring at the floor.

Margaret went on, 'Father, you know what Cyril is like, how proud he is. It would have humiliated him, to be refused by a girl like Anny. He would have wanted revenge. He must have come up with this plan to ruin her. But she is innocent of this crime. Cyril orchestrated the whole thing. We must force Cyril to admit it and you must tell the court to let her go.'

She was standing over him, her arms crossed in an unfeminine stance which would probably infuriate him.

Speaking the truth had given her courage. Also, he had not shouted at her again and he had not tried to deny what she said. This gave her hope that, finally, her father might just take her side, for the first time in her life. It felt extraordinary to talk to him in such an open, direct way. To be on equal terms, almost. She felt a great shift in power was occurring. Her father took a breath and she prepared herself for his next pronouncement.

'My dear, I have listened to your accusations. There is no question of your brother being involved in any such plot. And there is no question of doubt in Woodvine's guilt of theft, as charged. If you choose to speak your ridiculous theories about this elaborate plot that my son is supposed to have been involved in, I will disown you as my daughter. Not only that, I will personally see to it that our family doctor pronounces that you are feeble of mind, just as your grandmother is, and just as her sister was, who, as you know, though we never speak of it, killed herself in a lunatic asylum, the family shame. So, you see there is in the female side of this family a weakness, a propensity to madness . . . of invention and imaginings. Any such story bandied about by you concerning any male member of this family will be met with your own incarceration. You will be as surely locked up as your friend Woodvine. But there is one difference. In her case, she will go to trial and may be fortunate; she may be transported to Australia for seven years and not serve her time in a prison here. You, on the other hand, would be sent to an institution for the rest of your life. Mark my words, my girl, for I will make sure of it. So, the choice is yours. It will be your freedom or hers.'

❦

The child came into the room, her face white with shock, a scalding red mark on her cheek and a bluish bloom beside her eye. Queenie glanced at Jenkins, who shot her a knowing look back. Queenie nodded and Jenkins went to the girl, made a bit of a fuss about her and steered her to sit down on the end of the bed.

'Oh, Grandmother!' cried Margaret and sobbed, covering her face, which made the girl flinch at the touch.

'Stop that now!' Queenie heard herself cry. She did not intend it to sound so harsh, but she could not abide tears, she really could not. 'Crying never did a person one shred of good,' she continued in a softer voice. It seemed to do the trick as Margaret calmed a little and wiped her face, wincing from the tenderness around her left eye. 'I am not one to condone your father's violence, but you must admit that it is your own doing on this occasion, disappearing like that without permission.'

Margaret looked up at her. Those blue eyes, just like Selina's, her poor lost sister. 'It wasn't that, Grandmother. It was about Anny.'

'Who on earth is Anny?'

'Anny is my friend. Anny Woodvine. She works at the office with Mr Brotherton.'

'The thief?'

Margaret shuffled closer along the bed, her tears gone now, a look of activated energy in her eyes. Queenie felt alarmed. What could the girl have to do with this person? She had heard of it from Jenkins, the shame of it, the degradation of having a thief in their midst, a cuckoo in the nest, whose sex and lowly station in life had been overlooked and who had been given a chance at a plum job, only to betray them all and take their cash, like a common pickpocket.

'Grandmother, I must tell you the truth. I tried to tell Father but he would not listen. Anny is not a thief. She is innocent. Cyril wanted to marry her and she said no, so he put the money in her bag. It's all a lie. She is in prison now and we must help her. We simply must help her, Grandmother.'

The words of the girl had tumbled out at such a pace that Queenie's sense of it was muddled. There was something about this thief and her grandson and marriage and prison. It all sounded like a romance novel and not at all what Margaret ought to be reading. She would have a word with Ralph about that, about curbing his daughter's reading habits, which were tending to the dangerous by the sounds of it. But then she remembered they were talking of something real, that Margaret had been struck by her father and that something bad had occurred. Could it be real? Cyril and a common office girl?

'I do not believe a word of it,' said Queenie, finally, and looked at Jenkins, who nodded her head, her mouth set in a hard, straight line. If Jenkins agreed, it was sure to be right. She took comfort from that. But Margaret was standing up, taking a step closer to her, looking down upon her and talking again. What could the child be thinking?

'It is the truth, Grandmother. Cyril is rotten, through and through. He attacked Anny in the woods. He has been doing it to the maids for years. Surely you're aware of this.'

A quick glance at Jenkins, who raised her eyebrows and looked askance. So Cyril was about the same business as his grandfather, was he? As her husband? Yes, she could believe that.

Margaret went on. 'Anny is a good person, Grandmother. A wonderful person. She works hard and has ambition. She has no reason to lie or steal. She was planning to apply for better jobs in Shrewsbury.'

Queenie was now focused on what the child was saying. Sometimes her mind fogged over, like the stealthy arrival of the mist that hung about the river in autumn. It would linger a while and her thoughts would be confused and lost. But then a meaningful word, a look, a deed by others about her could bring her back instantly to herself; the mist of her mind would be burned away and she would find herself as clear and sharp as she ever was in her youth. She sat up straighter in her bed and said, 'Perhaps she stole the money to help set herself up in Shrewsbury. Have you thought of that, hmm?'

'Why would she risk it, though? She would ruin her chances. She is intelligent, far cleverer than I. She had no necessity to steal, with her good job and the promise of a career to come.'

'You are young and do not know people. People are stupid. People act in a stupid manner, a nonsensical manner. If you try to fathom every act that people do and why they have done it, why, that would be a futile exercise.'

'This one is not stupid. I *know* her.'

'Sit down, child, will you? You are hurting my neck, making me gawp up at you like this.' Margaret seated herself and continued to stare unsettlingly at her, her back straight and her hands folded in her lap. *She is blossoming*, thought Queenie. 'Now, how could you possibly know an office girl like that well enough to make these pronouncements about her character?'

'She and I have been friends for years, secret friends and correspondents. We began writing to each other as children and have met up many times since. She is the person I know best in the world. She is my dearest friend.'

'How did I not know of this?' said Queenie. How could such shenanigans have been occurring in her household without her knowledge?

244

'I did tell you, Grandmother. When I first met Anny years ago, I told you I wanted to be friends with her.'

'And I advised you then that it was a preposterous idea. But you defied me! How can this have come to pass, in our family? Friendships with servants?'

The child was protesting about it, saying something about an office, but Queenie was not listening. She was scolding herself inwardly. It was because she spent too much time in bed these days. Yes, that was it. Well, this would not do. She would have to insist that Jenkins got her up and about more. She had become indolent and this was the outcome. The child needed taking in hand. 'Well, I must say, any such friendship is wholly ill-advised and should never have been allowed to prosper in the first place. The poor are an unknown quantity, my dear. We can as little understand the workings of their minds as that of Benjamina's dog. They are simply another species.'

'You would say that of Jenkins, would you?' said Margaret, not looking round at the subject of her sentence.

The very thought! Queenie saw Jenkins puff up with consternation. Jenkins, her mainstay, her friend, her everything! 'What a ridiculous notion!' she spluttered at Margaret. 'Jenkins is not poor. She has a job for good here. Well, until I pass on, but I have ensured she will be looked after when I am gone. The idea that Jenkins is poor or could ever be poor is insulting and you must apologise immediately, girl.'

Jenkins had folded her arms and was looking pointedly above Margaret's head, with an air of disgruntled forbearance that Queenie loved about her.

'Please, Grandmother, we digress. I am merely saying that Anny is not poor and is not another species. She is a wholly dependable, intelligent person who has been cruelly wronged. Cyril – your grandson – has committed a crime. He is the one who has stolen money and has then tried to blame it on an innocent person. He is the criminal.'

Another moment of lucidity came to Queenie. Her grandson, a criminal? Whatever the boy had done, this must never be permitted to come to pass. The family name would be in tatters. She alone knew what she had suffered and sacrificed all these years to bolster the King family name. Her dear sister had died for it. Selina, her darling Selina . . .

To think of all that had been lost to make the King name what it was, all that Queenie had suffered to build this family into the tower of strength it was today. And now this girl, this office girl, was going to bring it all crashing down? With nasty accusations of attacks and theft and whatnot? An ironworker's daughter at that? A nobody? Never!

'Grandmother!' cried the girl and Queenie was snapped back into the present moment. What was it they were doing again? Margaret's voice was shrill and harsh. 'What do you have to say about Cyril? What are we to do?'

'Why,' said Queenie, recovering her senses and sitting up straighter, 'nothing. Absolutely nothing. It is out of the family's hands and there is nothing to be done. If the girl is innocent, then the truth will out in court. The family cannot be seen to bring disgrace upon itself. As the elder of this clan, I will never allow the King name to be brought into disrepute by accusations against any member of this family. Now, go away, child. Never let me hear you speak of it again.'

There. Another crisis averted. The girl was still wittering on, something about her father threatening her but Queenie had stopped listening and waved her hands to shoo the noise and fuss away, which Jenkins did with swift economy. When the girl had gone, she said to Jenkins, 'I'm still queen of this castle.'

Jenkins winked at her and plumped her pillows. Queenie soon drifted into a dreamless sleep. When she awoke, it was dark. Jenkins must be next door, asleep. She turned her head towards the drawn curtains and saw a slit of light emanating from outside. Not daylight, but a shifting, curious sort of a light that was bright then dimmer, bright again. She stared at it for some time, her eyes adjusting to the pulse of it. She felt compelled to leave her bed and seek it out. She drew back the curtain and looked down upon her family graveyard.

An apparition stood before the grave of Ralph senior, pulsing with light. Queenie blinked and looked again. It was still there, gazing across the graveyard into the distance. Its hair and skin were the hue of moonshine. Its eyes emanated the bluish flare of a city street gas lamp. Queenie pinched herself, hard, and cried out. But still the vision was there and had not moved. Could it be real? Was she losing her mind? She had hoped to see spirits before, those of the ones she had loved the most and lost. But this was not her sister and it was not her daughters. It was some other entity and it stood below her, as real as herself. And it was beautiful.

Queenie gazed at its splendour, then shuddered when she recognised that exquisite face. It was Blaize. The servant girl, Betsy Blaize. It was the maid she and her husband had dismissed five years before. It looked up, directly at her. It stretched out its arms and opened out its palms, showing her how empty its embrace was with no baby to fill it. It spoke to her, though not with its mouth. She heard the voice of Betsy Blaize in her mind. It said four words only, but those four little words terrified Queenie so greatly, she turned abruptly from the window and cried out, losing her footing and falling to the floor. Jenkins arrived from the next room, in a flurry of white nightdress and unpinned hair, rescued her from her collapse and got her back into bed. Jenkins scolded her for being out of bed at the witching hour. Queenie grasped Jenkins's arm and glared at her. 'Yes, it is the hour of the witch. She visited me. She told me. She cursed us.'

Jenkins tried to soothe her and lay her down but Queenie was having none of it. She must tell Jenkins what the ghost had said.

'This house will fall.'

Chapter 18

The following morning, Margaret arose early. She breakfasted alone, glad to be by herself. She felt so lost and
powerless. Her family was beyond redemption, even
Queenie. She wondered what rock they had found to
crawl under and hoped they were hiding in shame. She
knew Queenie and Benjamina usually breakfasted in
bed but the absence of her father and brother was odd.
They did not materialise for church either, which was
highly irregular. When she, her grandmother and stepmother returned from church, she made her excuses and
went upstairs. Her every movement felt mechanical, like
a repetitive steam hammer along the river that marked
time. But all the while she was screaming on the inside.
Desperate for some way to save Anny, she changed into
walking boots and a warmer cloak. It was a drizzly day,
misty and muggy after the yellow heat of the day before.
She left the house, unnoticed, made her way down to
the riverside and walked through the woodland fringe
towards the Woodvines' cottage, her tread slow and a little clumsy.

She was tired. She had wept a lot the night before. Her eye ached where her father had walloped her. Memories of Anny's imprisonment and visions of her own possible incarceration haunted her through the night, whether her eyes were open or closed. She feared for Anny, feared her father's threat. She did not know much of what had happened to her grandmother's sister, Selina, as it was a tale that had been silenced long ago. There were whisperings in the family and Cyril had mentioned it once or twice, about their lunatic great-aunt. As bad as Anny's prison was, she could only imagine that a madhouse was worse. It was too terrifying to contemplate. She tried not to think of it, but then her mind filled with the anguish of not being able to help her friend, of the promises she'd made to Anny and Mr Woodvine. Stupid, reckless promises. But she had been so sure of herself yesterday. So sure that truth would win the day, that all one had to do was state the facts and the world would listen, and change.

Too soon, she arrived at the cosy gathering of houses where the Woodvines lived. She dreaded this visit, of what she had to report to Anny's parents. She had not seen John Woodvine again the day before. He had not waited for her outside the prison and she had instructed her driver to look out for him on the road home, but he hadn't been seen. She hoped he had found his way home all right. As she approached the house, the neighbourhood children looked up from their games as she passed.

Mr Woodvine appeared at the door as she neared it, his face lit up with expectation. Oh, how cruel it was to bring bad news to these good people! His wife could be seen behind him and they both came outside and nodded to Margaret, smiling uncertainly and both of them wiping their hands, as if she deserved it. But she did not deserve it, any of their politeness or kindness. She had failed.

'Miss King,' said John Woodvine. 'Please come in. We are glad to see you.'

She stepped over the threshold into Anny's house. She had glimpsed it before, during her fancy dress ruse as Anny's workmate, all those years ago. But she hadn't seen much of it, as she'd been too shy to speak to Mrs Woodvine and had stayed outside, so sure was she that her hopeless attempts at blending in would be scuppered if she opened her mouth. What she wouldn't do to turn back the clock to that day.

Once inside, there came to her a delicious aroma of dough. She saw it placed on the windowsill in earthenware pans to rise. It was small inside the house, very small. It was a one-storey dwelling, the front room a neat square with three chairs arranged about a fireplace. One took a few steps and reached the kitchen area, a large table and every other surface and piece of furniture swathed in the products of Mrs Woodvine's washing work. Beyond the kitchen were two doors, to each of the bedrooms. All of the walls lacked plaster and thus the lumps and bumps of the stone that built the cottage jutted out into the room on all sides. But instead of feeling hemmed in by this, it gave the rooms a cosy, comforting appearance, as if the walls themselves were part of the family, gathering it in and keeping it safe. Such a tiny dwelling, so little room. But so filled with love all these years, replete with happiness. Until now.

'May I fetch you any ... refreshments, Miss King?' asked Mrs Woodvine, her eyes ringed by deep shadows. How little she must have slept these past few nights.

'No, please. I require nothing. Thank you. I must speak with you both.' Margaret faltered here, as she had no idea how to continue, how to explain what had occurred. There was much she could not say to them, to anyone, so that anything she said would only be a fraction of the truth. With that in mind, it was so difficult to know how to convey her sympathy for them, how to explain how hard she had tried. If they only knew how much she had wept for Anny. But there she went again, feeling sorry for herself. She wanted to slap her own face.

'Please sit,' said Mr Woodvine. She glanced at him and his face was dark. He had such an expressive face, as if one could read the weather of it changing moment to moment. Then, it was overcast. He knew it was not good news. Margaret sat down on a chair and the others did so too. There was no more putting it off. Now she must speak.

'I am sorry to say . . .'

Immediately Mrs Woodvine began weeping. Oh heavens, oh God. What could she say to make this better? Nothing. Nothing. Mr Woodvine was shushing his wife gently and patting her shoulder, staring into the bare grate of an empty fireplace as he did so. The muggy day had turned it stuffy in that little house, almost unbearably so, and Margaret could feel wet patches blooming under her arms and behind her knees. She forced herself to go on. 'I have spoken to both my father and my grandmother. They were both . . . unwilling to change their positions on the matter. My father will not withdraw the charges against Anny.'

At the mention of her daughter's name, Mrs Woodvine sobbed loudly and hid her face. Mr Woodvine turned his towards Margaret – he was not able to look at her directly – and said, 'It might be best if you go now, miss.'

Margaret stood up quickly, the speed of it and the heat in there making her unsteady. There was so much more she wanted to say but she knew she was no longer welcome. Yesterday, she had been a friend. Now she was just another King. She made it to the door without speaking and out into the day, the heavy air cooler out here and most welcome. She breathed deeply and was about to flee the scene when Mr Woodvine appeared beside her.

'I ought to say . . .' he began, wiping a hand over his eyes, 'I mean . . . I mean to say that I am grateful . . . that we are grateful to you, miss. For trying. For visiting Anny. There's many that wouldna done that, that would've done naught for her, for our kind. It was good of you.'

Now Margaret wanted to sob. But she was so impressed by Mr Woodvine's dignity, she forced herself to keep her emotions at bay. 'I wish I could do more. I do have one last attempt, and that is to speak with my brother. He is a . . . difficult person. But I am determined to confront him at least. I will be doing this upon my return to the house. I will be honest and say that I doubt anything will come of it. But I must try. For Anny.'

Mr Woodvine listened to her speak with such intensity, she almost looked away. Then she saw he was looking at the side of her face where she had been struck. Even in this moment of desolation, his expression showed he still reserved some pity for her. She put her hand up without thinking, to shield it. She had forgotten the bruise since arriving. There were more important things to consider.

'I'd better . . .' Woodvine trailed off, a gesture towards the cottage sufficed.

'Yes, of course. Thank you. And, I'm sorry.'

He shook his head and looked about, as if searching for the right words. But there were no right words.

Margaret turned and started the trudge homewards. She saw the Quaker cottage and out in front of it were the old couple and the child. She had not seen them for years. The child must now be – how old? Four or five? – and was more lovely than ever. The girl had such a healthful bloom about her cheeks, she seemed formed from milk and red roses, like an enchanted child from a fairy tale. Margaret watched her as she slowly passed by. *The baby on the bridge.* She thought of Queenie's mysterious words, that this was a lucky child to have escaped the King family. She recalled how the child had the same green eyes as her dead grandfather. It all pointed to the old story, the rich master and the poor maid. But Margaret could not prove it. And she didn't care to. Queenie had been right: for all their wealth, it was still the lucky child that escaped the King family. Her dear friend's life was about to be ruined by the very same family, her family. It sickened her. Her own family was like poison in her veins.

At the very least, she would confront Cyril and attempt to force him to admit his guilt. When she arrived home, she went to look for him. She knocked on his door to no answer, but this was not unusual. Cyril rarely followed convention when it came to basic manners. She could hear him moving around in there, though, so she opened the door and stepped inside.

'What the devil do you want?' he scowled at her. He was standing at his wardrobe, choosing cravats, several draped over his arm already. Behind him stood a trunk, the lid open to show it had been fully packed by his manservant already, and Cyril was finishing off with his own crucial choices of which neckwear he most desired.

'Where are you going?' said Margaret.

'To Germany, if you must know.'

'What for?'

He finished with the cravats and threw them onto the trunk, knowing his servant would sort them out later.

'Cyril, what for? Why are you going to Germany?'

'To an ironworks there. To learn the business, from the continental perspective.'

Margaret recognised her father's words in Cyril's mocking tone. To spirit him away, she realised. Across the sea and out of reach. He would have no part in the trial and no case to answer. She had always thought of her father as a bit dim. Now she saw he could be rather clever, when it served him, or was it Queenie's hand in this? Cyril was getting away with it, scot-free and out of harm's way, while Anny would languish in prison. The world protected men like that, she realised. The world was unfair.

'I must speak with you before you go.'

'I am about to leave, so there is no time,' he said with finality.

'This is important, Cyril. It is about Anny.'

He shot a glance at her, his eyes widened with – what was it? Worry? Concern? Guilt? Then he looked away to hide it and went to stand at the window, looking out. 'I have nothing to say on that matter. Some office girl caught thieving is far beneath my notice.'

'But I know differently.' Margaret never knew what tack to take with her brother, but she decided that a bullying approach would never work on him, as he could out-bully just about anyone, except their father. But perhaps she could appeal to something else in him. 'I know you had feelings for Anny.'

For once, Cyril did not speak. Margaret used the moment to go on.

'She is in a terrible place. A terrible state.'

'What has that to do with us?' he said, strangely quiet for him. Was she getting through to him?

'Could we not help her, Cyril?'

'She has made her own bed.'

She knew this utterance was fraught with meaning. She could hear Cyril's jealousy in it. He must have found out something about Anny's feelings for Jake. Margaret had tasted that bitter disappointment, as much as she hated herself for it. The thought of Anny and Jake was torture to her. Perhaps she and her brother had some-thing in common, at long last.

'This is true,' she said, choosing her words with the utmost care. 'It is hard to see others make choices that . . . we do not like, that hurt us.'

Cyril made a scoffing sound and turned to her. 'What do you know about such things?'

She almost told him. She heard the words in her mind: *I am in love with Jake Ashford.* But she could not speak it, not to this viper – she did not trust him an inch with that precious cargo – but also these were words she did not wish to reveal to anyone. Anyone but Jake. It shamed her that she still hoped for a future with Jake when it was becoming clear to her that Anny still hoped for the same.

She must do whatever it took to help Anny. That was her role now, to save her friend. 'All I know is that Anny Woodvine is innocent. She did not steal that money. She does not deserve this fate.'

'You know nothing of the sort,' Cyril spat and strode back to his trunk, fiddling with the cravats, looking busy.

'I do and so do you. Because you are the one who took the money, Cyril.'

He glared at her. 'Say that again,' he said in a low, threatening voice. 'I dare you.'

'I am not afraid of you, Cyril King. Not anymore.'

'You should be.' She saw his right fist clench slowly, deliberately.

'But I have the truth on my side. I know you loved Anny once. I think you still do. Come with me to Father and tell him what happened, explain about Jake Ashford. Father might even understand. He has loved and lost our mother, after all. All it would take is a word from you and Father could withdraw the charges and Anny would be free.'

'Lies! Lies, all of it. I had nothing to do with it!' Cyril's voice broke, his face contorted.

'And who knows,' she went on, fired up with momentum now. 'If Anny knew you had set her free, perhaps she might forgive you. Perhaps she would come to you to thank you. Perhaps . . .' A horrible thought came to her and her mind was racing so fast she had no time to stop and look at it closely, so she blurted it aloud: 'Perhaps she would drop Jake Ashford in favour of you, and he would be . . .'

Cyril's face changed. His eyes lit with a cruel sneer. 'He would be *what*? What would he be, sister? Yours?'

'No, I meant he would be spurned and you . . . that you . . . you could turn Anny to love you.'

Cyril laughed and stared at her, nodding. 'Dear sister. We are more alike than I ever thought possible. So, you want the artist?'

'I never . . .'

'Oh no, it is too late for that. You have revealed yourself. It does you credit that you fight for your friend when it would suit you far better if she rotted in prison forever or was sent across the world never to be seen again. Yet if she is to be free, you argue that she might come to me, that she would be grateful, that she would

260

forsake her jumped-up little scribbler for me. How convenient that would be for you!'

'No, you have twisted everything! This is not . . .'

Cyril was shaking his head and smiling smugly. 'The fact is that you have nothing to taint me. There is no evidence against me, no proof I had anything to do with it. I will go to Germany today and think no more on this trifling little drama. You, I suspect, will go to your room and twist your sheets about you in passionate contemplation of Jake Ashford and his lead-smudged fingers . . .'

Margaret clenched and unclenched her own fists, furious at herself yet also wanting very much to smash that smug look from Cyril's face. How could she have let this conversation veer so far off track? It was all her fault.

'I am busy now, preparing for my journey. Leave me. And if you ever find proof of my crime, be sure to march straight to Father with it, won't you?'

And he lifted his hands and gestured her away, as if shooing a fly. She knew she was beaten. But she had found her voice. She would not go silently.

'You think you have won. But you are the one who will be alone for all of your days and nights. For you do not have the capacity to love. And so you are cursed, Cyril King, to live alone and die alone.'

With that, she turned and left. He did not shout after her. She heard the door slam behind her. She felt some satisfaction at this, at least. But beneath it was the dull ache of having failed, again.

How could she help Anny now? She thought she might offer to testify in court to Anny's good character, even tell them of her suspicions of her brother, but Cyril was quite right – she had no evidence, no proof. Who would believe her? It all seemed hopeless. Nobody would support her in this endeavour and her father would send her away to a fate worse than death. Suddenly, she felt utterly alone in the world. Her family were against her and she had lost her only friend. She had no one, not a soul that cared for her, no one she could talk to.

But there was someone. Jake. Oh, Jake! Of course – she must take Anny's message to him. This comforting thought was spiked with conflicted feelings as she found she was jealous of the message, which appalled her. She would deliver the message. At the very least, it meant it was some small thing she could do for Anny and now she had a reason to see him, to talk to him alone. Another feeling assaulted her: remorse. How could she feel excitement at seeing him, at this time of all times? What a terrible person she was. But she reminded herself that she had no one, and that the small grain of hope at seeing someone who seemed to like her was not so unforgivable, was it?

An idea rose in her mind, as innocently as thistledown on a breeze. She would go to his lodgings and see him. She might be seen; there might be a scandal. She realised that she did not give a damn. She had kept on her boots and cloak and took up her purse from the bed. She quietly descended the stairs, keeping a lookout for her father bustling about, and managed to get to the front door without being seen.

Jake had mentioned once where he was lodging, or at least, the house he was in, to the left of the Tontine Hotel, immediately opposite the iron bridge. She wasn't used to walking the streets without a chaperone. But now, here she was. Alone, walking along the road to town. No family, no restraints. There was a marvellous kind of freedom in it, walking along a path on your own. The air around her body and head gave her a giddiness. Imagine it, to walk away from this family and never go back. This thought gave her a jolt.

She was coming down Lincoln Hill, past the rows of low, neat brick houses with cellar windows peeping out below street level. She glanced back up the hill and could see the King house from here, her family home. It was perched above the town, looking down upon it, literally and figuratively. The people surrounding her, busy in their own lives, all believed themselves to be the masters of their own existences, the protagonists of their own stories. None of them cared a hoot about the Kings, about her father or her brother or herself. Quite rightly. What was it about class that set one above another? The thought of never returning to that house felt like the longest, coolest draught of water after a hot day. As she rounded the bottom of the hill and turned into the High Street, where the Tontine Hotel was situated, it occurred to her that, more than anything she had ever wanted, she would sell her soul to escape from her own story and walk right out of it.

She thought of the baby on the bridge she had seen that morning, frolicking in front of its humble home. She felt inspired by the baby's example: how happy its life was, how simple and sweet. Of course, there would be hardships, living the life they did, down there amongst the struggling poor. Look what happened to a family like the Woodvines, when the forces of the rich were drawn against them. But the Quaker child was raised by kind and loving people and no amount of money can buy you that kind of comfort and love. Margaret knew that more than most.

As she passed the Tontine and looked for the building beside it, she thought of Jake Ashford. Whatever her mission was that day, whatever her love for Anny, her need to support her friend, she knew that underneath all of this beat her heart and it beat for him alone. She loved him. And amidst the ruin of her family life, her love rose like a phoenix and gave her a burning strength within her. Everything in her life had been thrown into question, and now she felt sure that Jake Ashford was the answer.

The house had only one door. She knocked upon it and waited. The door opened and there stood a middle-aged woman with a pinched face bordered by greasy ringlets. Margaret was given a quick look up and down and then the woman put on a simpering smile.

'How may I help you, miss?' said the woman.

'I am Miss King, from the big house.'

'Of course y'are, of course y'are!' said the woman delightedly. 'What assistance or service can I be of to you, Miss King?'

'I have a message for a Mr Ashford. He has been painting a portrait up at the house and I need to convey a message to him from my father.' The woman was starting to frown a little. 'Would it be at all possible to discover if Mr Ashford were at home? So that I could deliver the message to him? In person?'

She knew it was unorthodox. Why had the family not sent a messenger? But she braved it out and smiled at the woman, who seemed eager to please. Perhaps a coin would be in order, if she was veering towards being unhelpful.

'I can deliver the message for you, miss, unless . . .'

The woman eyed the purse that Margaret was clutching.

'Is Mr Ashford at home?'

'He is, miss. I believe he is sleeping.'

'At lunchtime?' queried Margaret.

'Oh yes, miss. He often does that. He's been home late every night this week. Out . . . painting, I should think. Such a dedicated artist.'

'Indeed,' said Margaret, uncertainly. She looked down at her purse, snapped it open and reached inside. One coin, two . . . how many would it take? She wanted to glance behind her, to see who was looking at the King girl bargaining with a landlady of a gentleman's residence, in full view of the whole town. The scandal was unthinkable. But she felt as if the ropes that had tethered her to the ground had been freed and she was floating up, up above her class, her reputation and all the weights and restrictions it brought with it. She was beyond the pale and she did not care one jot for it anymore. Even pretence seemed pointless.

'I will give you this, if you will take me to him,' she said, looking the woman straight in the eye.

'Come in then,' said the woman throatily and shut the door. She pocketed the money swiftly and pointed up the stairs. 'Top floor. The attic room.' And with that, she went off down the corridor to her own rooms, not giving Miss King a second look. Their business was concluded.

Margaret looked up the stairs and felt light-headed. They seemed incredibly steep and her head was swimming. Her stomach lurched. She began to climb, her breath quickening. The top room had a tiny landing and she stood on it, before the door, the only thing that stood between her and him. She listened at it, to see if she could hear him inside. She felt dizzy and steadied herself with a hand upon his door. She gathered her courage and made a fist, then knocked. No reply, no movement. She knocked again. Had the woman lied, to get her money for nothing? But then there was a shuffling inside. She held her breath. Footsteps. The door opened.

There he stood, black glossy hair on end, squinting at her through his sleep-addled eyes, which soon snapped open when he saw who it was. He was dressed, that is, he had on his trousers and a shirt, untucked. No waistcoat or socks, she noticed, glancing at his naked feet with a shock.

'My dear Miss King!' he cried. 'Is there an emergency?'

'No, Mr Ashford. I am sorry . . . to awaken you from your slumber.'

'Not at all,' he said, running his fingers through his hair in a vain attempt to control it. It delighted her to see him so ruffled, so normal, so unprepared. His real self, beyond all pretence and manners. 'Please tell me how I can assist you. I am worried for you, Miss King.'

'I came to bring you a message of the utmost importance and I could not wait upon . . . the more . . . accustomed channels. I simply had to come. Can you forgive me?'

Jake listened to this with a serious face, but now he smiled. 'There is nothing to forgive. I am only apologetic to receive you in a state of such dishevelment. But please, I am unforgivable, allowing you to stand there and not invite you in. It is very humble, if you will forgive me.' He began hurriedly tucking in his shirt and stepping back.

'Not at all,' she said and entered. It had a smell of things new to her, a heady mixture of maleness she had perceived emanating from her brother's room at times, and perhaps wine and pipe smoke, or something similar. It made her head spin. Luckily, the windows were open and a breeze came in and brought with it a breath of fresh air badly needed and she felt a little recovered.

'I have water, if you would like a glass.'

'Yes, please,' she said and sat upon a wooden chair that stood beside a table covered in papers and pencils. An easel was beside the window, surrounded on the wooden floorboards by a mess of paints, brushes and a palette. Against the other wall was a narrow bed, its covers awry. Beside it were a pair of shoes, kicked off, one on its side on top of a fallen pile of books, some splayed open, others shut. Suits and shirts hung on the picture rail and hats hung on nails on the wall. A cabinet held other secrets, topped with a basin and jug. His whole existence in one room. It was the most wonderful room she had ever visited in her life.

He fetched her a glass from a cupboard and poured out water from another jug that stood on a little table beside his bed. He drew up another mismatched chair and sat opposite her. He looked down at his feet and saw he had no socks. There was a moment of awkwardness where he seemed to consider whether or not to fetch his socks, and then he glanced up at her.

'Your feet do not offend me, Mr Ashford,' she said. She smiled and he smiled. Then they laughed. It broke the ice, and now they could sit more comfortably together.

'Please, Miss King, I am quite alarmed by the news that you bring. What can it be?'

'It is about Miss Woodvine. Anny. I do not know if you are aware of what has befallen her.'

'I am not. I have been busy with my paintings these past few days. I have been inspired. I have barely left my room.'

That is not what his landlady said, Margaret thought. But perhaps she was a liar. She dismissed this thought and proceeded to tell him all about Anny. She left no detail out. She trusted Jake. She knew implicitly that he would understand. He listened attentively, shaking his head at each new awful turn of events. But he did not comment on anything she said, not even a 'How terrible!' or 'Poor Anny!' Perhaps it was a characteristic of male speech, that men said only what was necessary. Now she came to the difficult part.

'When I saw her in that place, she asked something of me. Well, it was something she asked of you, Mr Ashford.'

'Please, please call me Jake. I believe, sitting here together in my shabby lodgings, we may be permitted to use our Christian names, may we not?'

'Of course,' she said, but was a little perturbed at him smiling at this, at a moment when she had told him the most dreadful news. Perhaps he was nervous. 'Anny asked something of you, Jake. She said to tell you that she didn't do it. I tried to help her . . . You've heard that part of the tale at least, including my own failure.'

'You are too hard on yourself, Margaret,' he said and leant forward, his elbows on his knees, his hands clasped beneath his chin, his eyes dark and full of sympathy.

'Not hard enough, I fear,' she said quietly, as she looked down, away from his captivating gaze. 'There is more. She asked that you wait.'

'Wait?'

'Yes. She said, "Tell him to wait". And also that you must come to visit her, as soon as you are able.'

Jake stood up quite suddenly. He stepped over to the window and looked out of it. She could not see his face. She turned in her chair and watched the back of his head as he talked.

'I do not think that I am able to do that.'

'I could send our carriage to transport you, if that is what you require to travel to Shrewsbury.'

'No, it is not that. I do not think it is a good idea for me to visit Anny.'

'Why ever not?'

'Anny and I spoke of . . . a future. A possible future. She wanted me to promise. But I could not.'

Margaret had guessed at this, of course, as Anny had asked her to tell Jake to come to her in prison. But to hear it from Jake's mouth was hard. It felt like a slap in the face, yet she cursed herself for wanting to help her friend and yet at the same time . . . at the same time, she wanted something else entirely.

'I had to explain to her that it was not that simple. I could not promise her. I tried to let her down gently. But you see, I am an artist. I am wedded to my art.'

'Of course,' said Margaret. 'I quite understand,' though indeed she did not really understand. What a complicated person he was, how deeply his feelings ran. It was the artist in him that made him so profound.

'I knew you would,' he said and turned to her, looking down at her.

Margaret heard herself ask him a question, before she had time to regret it. 'Do you love Anny?'

'I am fond of her. But I find myself caught between two mistresses.'

She held her breath. She stared at him. 'Which two?' she said and it came out as a whisper.

'My art and my fondness for Anny.'

'Indeed,' she said and looked away.

'She would make a good wife and she does love me, I'm sure of that. But there is a further obstacle.'

'What is that?'

'There is another.'

'Another what?'

'I love another.'

Margaret felt she might be sick. She could not speak a word.

He went on, 'But I believe the match is impossible. I am unworthy of her. I am so very glad I can confide in you of this. You are such a very good listener.'

He smiled at her and she forced her mouth to turn upwards just a touch. 'Who is it, this other match?' she managed to say, though she wished to rush from the room.

'Why, it is you, of course.'

'Me?'

'Yes, dear Margaret. But I suspect your father would never allow it, and so I have repressed my feelings for you and instead have allowed Anny's feelings to rule my own. It may be wrong of me, but I do not know how I must act for the best.'

'You have feelings for me?'

'I do, I do, my dear. How could I not? You are divine.'

He looked searchingly at her, then he fell to his knees and took her hands.

'Could it be,' he began and kissed her hand so gently, 'that you feel the same for me? Can you tell me your feelings for me, dear Margaret?'

'Why, I love you, Jake.'

'You do? Oh, my dear!'

He leant in and kissed her lightly on the lips. She leant in further and kissed him again, softer, longer. But suddenly he withdrew and stood up. She stood up too, not wanting to be further apart than the breadth of their kisses. But Jake had let go of her hands and was running his fingers madly through his hair.

'But what of Anny? And your father? Oh, I am over-wrought. I cannot think straight with you here, so close to me. I am intoxicated by your presence. I need time to think it all through. There must be some way we can be together. Can I come to see you tomorrow? Not here. Let us meet in the woods, away from prying eyes.'

'Of course. Do you know the place where the two paths meet in the woods, just beyond the coracle sheds?'

'I do, I have passed it on my walks.'

'Shall we meet there at noon, tomorrow?'

'At noon.'

They stood and watched each other.

They kissed again. This time his tongue was in her mouth. It was so wet, such a queer taste of tobacco and sleep, a sour taste that startled her, but her desire for it was so overwhelming that she welcomed the bitterness and fed from it. Kissing this way was a kind of devouring and she had a hunger for it.

Desire in her rose like a wave and she pressed herself against him with such force, their teeth clashed. She felt mortified with her own clumsiness but he was kind about it and stroked her cheek, held her and shushed her. Then, he let go and took a step back.

'My dear girl, please. There is nothing I would like more than to kiss you again, a hundred times. A thousand times more! But we must be sensible. There is much to consider. I will meet you tomorrow, as planned. And we shall talk it all through. Do not fret. Sleep well tonight, my love, and I will see you on the morrow.'

It was hard to leave him, so hard. It was only when she came down the stairs and saw the landlady standing in the hall, smirking at her, that she recalled the shame of what she had done. And as she stepped outside into the street and looked up at the iron bridge, she recognised the forlorn figure of Mrs Woodvine crossing over it, laden down with linen, delivering her work to the households of the town. Margaret turned in an instant and rushed away up the street, fairly breaking into a run to get up onto the hill and away from that woman, that kind, sweet woman. Anny's mother. She had started the day with a visit to Anny's parents and ended it by smashing the fragile hopes of their daughter because of her own selfish desires. But he loved her. *Jake Ashford loves me*, she told herself. And Anny loved him, waited for him, in that hellish place. Oh God in heaven, what had she done? Was there ever a betrayal lower and more cowardly than this? Anny's pale face in the prison floated before her in her mind's eye. *How could you, Peggy? How could you?*

Chapter 19

'Ow bist thee faring, Anny?'

'Fair to middling, Mother.'

There was so much that Anny could not tell her mother. It was her first visit, and when Mother came into the room and gave her the seed cake, bread, ham and apples she'd brought from home, Anny fell to eating it like something feral. Ham first. Meat! The smell of it drove her mad, and she saw the other prisoners in there waiting for their visitors sniffing the air like dogs. She had not said much yet, only one word that she mouthed as she came in, 'Mother!' But then the smell of food took her and she could think of nothing more until she had it in her hands. Her mother watched her devour the meat, then move on to the bread, but put a firm hand on Anny's and said, 'Slow down. You'll make yourself heave. Save it for later.'

She shook her head hurriedly. 'They'll take it from me.'

'Who? The guards?'

She shook her head again, now working on the cake. 'The others.' She had no time to explain. She had to eat all of this before they sent her back. Her mother waited for her to eat, wiping her eyes with the tips of her fingers from time to time. Her mother couldn't stop the tears coming, but was doing her best to hide them.

When she'd finished eating, she came back to herself and remembered that her dear mother was there. She wanted ever so much to feel her mother's arms around her, but she didn't want to risk a beating from that one over there. He was one of the worst turnkeys, mean and petty. Her cellmate Jane had gone off with him three times these past days and come back sore and achy, but also with crumbs and wine stains down her front, so it was worth it, Jane said. Was it worth it? Anny had been considering it. She'd had some offers but never spoke to the turnkeys if she could help it, and always avoided their gazes and whisperings. But the hunger had been getting to her, gnawing at her and she'd nearly succumbed yesterday when they gave her no breakfast gruel, saying she was not tidy and clean enough. But now she'd had her mother's food, she'd be able to hold out for a while longer.

'What do they feed you, lass?'

'Gruel for breakfast. Potatoes or soup for dinner. Gruel or soup for supper. Some bread each day. Not enough of it. Never enough.'

It was good to talk, to hear her own voice. She spoke to nobody here. It was banned in her cell. Ellen had banned it. 'I dunna wanna hear a peep out of you again.

Not a sound. If you cry, we'll leather you. If you snore, we'll leather you. And no talking, not ever.'

She went on, getting a feel for it now, remembering how she'd loved to talk in her other life, in the time before this. That time seemed to have never happened. Everything was this now. 'Soup sounds good, doesn't it? You would think it was good. Nourishing.' That was a nice word. 'But it's not. It's lukewarm, greasy water with bits of who-knows-what floating in it.'

'Anny, I wanna say I'm that sorry I couldna come sooner. It took me very bad like, all this. And you know how weak I get when I hear bad news. It is a terrible failing of mine and I curse myself for it and I am sorry for it. I shoulda been there with your father that first time he came but the shock had me laid up for days. I wish I were stronger for you.'

'Please don't fret,' said Anny and reached out to touch her mother's cheek, withdrawing her hand quickly as she glanced at the guards, knowing they would shout at her for touching. Mother followed her gaze and frowned at the man who lolled against the wall.

'Do they treat you well, the guards?'

What could she say to that? Mother did not need to know the truth. If she had a bruise here or there her mother might notice. There was a big one on her arm, yet luckily her sleeve covered it. Everyone knew the turnkeys would beat you as soon as look at you, but they showed a little care to keep it off the face.

'I don't speak to them,' she said, eyeing the one at the door.

'Do you have to work? You look tired.'

She was exhausted. But mostly that was because she could not sleep at night. There were comings and goings from the cells, sad women crying, mad women screaming and her own cellmates plotting and whispering before they fell into a deep, guttural sleep. She would rather listen to the cacophony of the blast furnace all night, every night instead of the random, terrifying sounds that emitted from these cells, all cloaked in a heavy silence between them that smothered you and mocked you, an emptiness that reminded you of everything you had lost. Sometimes she wondered if she were going mad herself.

'Anny, do you have to work? Do they make you work?'

'I'm the monitor of our court. Our group of rooms. Every morning, I have to make sure the rooms and arcades are swept and washed down. That windows and doors are opened on dry days and all the beds are turned down to air. If I do that right, I'm supposed to get fourpence a week. In credit, like. Not in my hand. On Mondays, they put a table out in the courtyard and you can buy things, like cheese or stockings. But only if you've done your job as monitor. But the others don't do as I say, so I've not received anything yet. During the day, I work in the wash house. Just like back at home with you, Mother.'

They both smiled grimly. Simpler days. Happy days. She never thought she'd miss it. Now she believed she'd give her right arm to be a washerwoman with her mother again at home. If she had, none of this would ever have happened.

'This is what happens when you get above your station,' she said, thinking aloud. She hadn't intended to actually say it.

'What can you mean, Anny? This inna your fault. Never your fault. Dunna tell yourself that ever.'

'If I'd never worked for the Kings, this would never have happened. I should've stayed with you. Why didn't I stay with you?'

This was the kind of thing that tortured her in those silences at night. That, and why she didn't simply lie back and let Cyril King do what he wanted with her. If he'd bedded her, he'd have probably grown tired of her and not even pursued the marriage. She could've played that smarter.

Her mother was weeping openly now. She couldn't keep it in anymore.

'Hush now, Mother.'

'I'm sorry, lass. Look at you. I'm the one who should be comforting you. Oh, dear heart. You're so strong.'

Anny scoffed then checked herself. She did not want to upset her mother further. 'Yes, I am coping. Is there any news of when the hearing shall be?'

'No news to us.'

'To me neither. They tell us nothing here.' She had lain awake at night obsessing over the possibilities of her punishment, if found guilty, which she would surely be. It could be imprisonment, probably with hard labour, which would mean years of breaking stones. At least you'd get more food each day. It could be transportation to Australia. Never to see your family again and banished to a foreign isle, if the ship journey didn't kill you first. Then, there was hanging. It was unusual, for a woman to be hanged for theft. But it could happen. She imagined the rope around her neck, the moments before. Would she scream? Would she weep? Would she face it with dignity?

'Tell me more about your days. Is there no one you can talk to? What's the keeper like? Is he a good man? Can you talk to him about more food?'

Some of this she could speak about. It was generally a safe topic for her mother to hear. 'He seems a good enough man. He visits the cells once a day but just gives us a quick look, nothing more than that. It is said we are allowed to make complaint to him but he never gives us the time to do so and all the women are afraid of him.'

'I've heard there are male prisoners here too,' said Mother, looking worried. 'Do you ever see them?'

'No, we are separate at all times,' said Anny, glad of this, yet knowing that the turnkeys were worse than any prisoner she could imagine.

'What else do you do here? Do they give you time to stretch your legs?'

'We have time in the exercise yard daily.' A place of bullying, taunts and being thrust up against the brick wall by a turnkey, maybe clouted on your body some-where for looking at them the wrong way. But yes, you could stretch your legs. She did not say any of this to her mother, of course.

'And do they let you read and write at all? I know how you must miss it.'

'We have Bible class every morning. We listen to the chaplain read. And as monitor, I am responsible for the prayer book in our day room.' She did not go on to say that, as monitor, she was also responsible for telling tales on other prisoners. She would never do it, under threat of various methods of subtle torture from her cellmates, but then she incurred the wrath of the turnkeys, who would grab her and twist her arm to make her say some-thing about the others and the tricks they got up to, but she never did. A quick whack on the leg or back with a turnkey stick would be her reward for that. 'There is a schoolmaster, but when they heard I could already read and write, they said I had no need of lessons.'

'Could you ask to be his assistant?'

'I have already asked. They said no.'

'It would get you away from all that washing. I worry about your soft hands going hard again.' Her mother took Anny's hands and began to inspect them. Anny knew she could get a clout from the guard for it, but the feel of her mother's beloved hands around her own was so overwhelmingly comforting, she had to force herself not to sob with relief. She knew the shape and texture of her mother's hands better than almost any other thing she could think of and they meant home, they meant safety and love. 'No ink stains anymore. I miss those,' Mother said, sadly. Tears ran silently from Anny and dripped onto her arms. Her mother squeezed her hands and muttered, 'I meant to be more help. And I've been no help at all.'

'No touching,' called out the guard and Anny snatched her hands away. She did not wish to get on that one's bad side. She leant a little closer and whispered, 'Just by coming you have helped. Just to see a friendly face makes such a difference here in this . . . place.'

Her mother looked up at her, fearful. 'How bad is it? Are you suffering badly? I mun know, Anny. I need to know.'

Oh, the things she wished she could tell her. More than anything, she longed to describe the horrible scene only the day before, where she stood in the yard and listened to the sound of death. The yard was usually filled with the mutterings of inmates and the harsh shouts of guards. But that day, all the inhabitants were silenced by the sound of a great crowd of people arriving all morning outside the gates, their hubbub floating over the walls, bringing the flavour of freedom. The crowd was silenced by a stern voice that read out a long list of information, too indistinct to hear the details, with only the pious tone discernible from beyond the high yard walls. Then, two other male voices spoke their turn but again, no words could be heard clearly. After this, there were some shouts from the crowd, replied to with some unkind laughter, some heckling and more laughter. Then, there was a long silence. A snapping sound of rope pulled taut and a cheer went up. So ended the lives of two Irish thieves, she heard later. Two men hanged atop the prison gates, for theft. The sound of the laughing crowd haunted her, that so many should come to witness death and that they should find it worthy of amusement. The world was cruel and full of bad'uns. The good people were as tear-drops in an ocean. The ones who cared a jot for you were fewer still and the ones who loved you, numbered on the fingers of one hand. Love. What was it good for now? It could bring only temporary comfort but it could not fetch her out of here, and it could not save her from this hell or from the gallows. But the comfort of it was better than nothing.

'Mother, before you go, and it will be that time soon, I must tell you that I have a sweetheart. I have an understanding with the artist Jake Ashford. I asked Margaret to tell him to please come and visit me. Will you find him and tell him too? Please?'

'A young mon? An understanding?'

The turnkey called time and everyone stood up sharp-ish. She never kept them waiting. Her mother's face was confused and frightened. She wished she'd asked this earlier, so she'd have time to explain the understanding between Jake and herself and how much she desired to see him. But there, it was done now and she was leaving the room, looking back at her mother, whose hands were over her face now, her tears freely flowing. Anny called back to her, 'Tell him?' and Mother nodded quickly and lifted a hand, calling her name and saying farewell, till next time.

In the corridor, the turnkey shoved her hard, so that she fell against the wall and felt the cold stone bite into her soft cheek. She wouldn't give him the satisfaction of a look, let alone a complaint. Now that her mother had gone, she would speak to nobody until another visitor came. She missed talking so much; she spoke to herself in her mind often, great long monologues commenting on all the madness surrounding her and telling herself stories of her past, of the people she loved. It was a kind of prayer, it was offered up to the god of her mind to keep her from losing it. She prayed for deliverance, for help to come from Margaret, for her mother to stay well and her father to be safe at the ironworks and, most of all, for Jake to visit her.

Chapter 20

John Woodvine listened obsessively to every detail Rachel gave of her visit to their daughter. As she spoke, the rage that built up inside him, fit to blow, every time he thought of Anny in that place, was like nothing he had ever experienced. To be fifteen miles from his beloved girl, to be able to walk there, to be able to see her even, in a room across a table, and speak to her; to be able to do all these things and yet not scoop her up in his arms and take her from that place. These were the things that could drive a man to madness.

'There was one more thing she told me, John,' said Rachel. 'She said she has a young mon. She wants him to visit her. Did you know? I didna know she had someone sweet on her.'

'What young mon?' said John. He had heard nothing about this. He'd been relieved, actually, that Anny had never seemed interested in that sort of thing. She'd always given the boys round their house short shrift. She was devoted to her work and her family and long may that continue, he used to tell himself. Now this, a sweetheart? It made him feel a bit queasy but at the same time, a seed of expectancy was planted in him and he wondered for a moment if something helpful might come of it.

'She said he was an artist called Jake Ashford. You know him?'

That scribbler? Could him and Anny . . . really? 'Yes, I've seen him. He comes to the furnace sometimes and sketches what's occurring around and about. He keeps himself to himself, mostly. Some of the men ribbed him a bit when he first came, but they soon got bored of it and left him to his own devices after that.'

'Is he a good man?' said Rachel, looking at him hopefully.

'He's no great shakes, is my impression. I dunna know. But I'm gunna find out. He's certainly better off than us. Good clothes. Not wealthy, like the Kings. But good clothes, you know. Smart.' John thought more about him and an uneasy memory of his general impression that the lad was a bit of a fop, maybe even one who liked boys rather than girls, was the sort of whisperings that went round. And what kind of living could be made from scribbling?

'Well,' said Rachel, 'if he has a well-to-do family and if he's promised to our Anny, perhaps his family could help her. Perhaps they could go to the Kings and speak for her.'

287

'Are they promised?'

'She didna say. She only said something about an understanding.'

'Well, why didna you ask her? Why didna you get more out of her, for God's sake?' John's voice grew much louder. He was on edge all the time these days and found it increasingly hard to control his temper. But the hurt look in his wife's eyes toned him down and he dropped his head, ashamed of raising his voice to her.

'She only mentioned it in the last moments, before they took her away,' said Rachel, and put her hand on his arm. She understood. She never held it against him. Oh, this woman. What a fine wife she was. What a lucky man he'd been, in this at least.

'I will certainly look him out. If he inna at work today, I'll ask around and find out where he's lodging. I'll find him, dunna worry, dear.'

He reached over and put his arms around his wife, drew her to him and kissed her tenderly. After all these years, the feel of her was home and all things good. She had always been too good for him, a good wench like she was with her book learning. But she chose him. The warm roundness of her woman's body was everything he ever wanted. It was obvious to think it, that a man loved his wife, but then so many men he knew didn't seem to feel it, not anymore. They complained bitterly about theirs, and some of them sought comfort else-where. Not him. Not ever. But these days, the sadness that he and Rachel both bore like a cross on their backs tainted all comfort he felt with her. He felt he had let her down, by allowing this terrible thing to happen to their child. He would fight till the end of his days to get her out of there. He kissed Rachel again, this time a peck on the cheek and a big squeeze, before he pulled back and looked at her.

'I'm thinking of leaving a bit early for my shift. I'm thinking of going up to the big house and asking to talk to Mr King.'

'Oh, my dear, are you sure? If his own daughter . . .'

'I know, I know what we said. I know he hit her, and why would he listen to me if he didna listen to her? But I'm thinking we mighta got all this around the wrong way. Think on it. She's his daughter and he might have a hundred reasons we're ignorant of to give his daughter a slap. Maybe she's been playing away from home, maybe she's a real handful, who knows? Nobody knows what goes on inside a family, behind closed doors, except them people themselves. Maybe he wouldna listen to her because he still thinks of her as a nipper. Dunna take her serious, like. I know I'm the same sometimes with Anny, despite all her learning. Maybe if I presented the case to him very civil, very serious, very polite like, he might listen. It's worth a try, inna it? I know it is. And I'm gunna do it.'

It was Rachel's turn to put her arms around him now and kiss her husband. 'You're a good man, John

Woodvine. How would I manage without you? Like a frog without a pond.'

'Like a mole without a hole.'

They both laughed. It was a small laugh but the only one they'd shared in days. He was beginning to feel something like hope kindling inside him. He took up his lunch and his work gloves and stashed them in the ragged bag he stowed across his chest. He left, striding with new purpose along the river then up the path to the big house. He went to the servants' entrance. He knew he couldn't march up to the front door. There was a girl there, cleaning the step. He told her his business and she said she'd ask the butler. The butler came – a wizened old'un with a mistrustful eye – and said the master wasn't available. John told the man who he was and told him something of his tale of woe. He asked only for a minute of the master's time. The butler went away for quite a bit – John began to wonder if he'd be late for his shift – but then the old bloke came back.

'One minute,' he said. 'But you're too dirty for the house. You'll be seen outside the estate office. Go and wait there.'

John went over to Anny's old workplace and scowled at it. It brought back bitter memories and he wished he'd not had to see it. The rage was rising in him again and he had to swallow it. He must be respectful and respectable for Mr King. His stomach lurched and he cleared his throat several times, a bile rising there that he could not cough out. Then, footsteps were coming along the gravel and there was King, his stomach preceding him and John felt he might stride right up to the bastard and give him a bunch of fives in his face. He clenched his fists and stood up straighter. King was not looking at him and stopped near to the door of the office, as if he were about to go in but instead turned, folded his arms sedately across his chest, his elbows resting on his girth. He said, 'You have your minute, Woodvine.' King looked pompously into the air to the left of John's shoulder. John tried not to let this put him off. He cleared his throat one last time and began.

'Mr King, you may know I am Anny Woodvine's father.'

'Obviously, obviously. Don't waste your one minute on pleasantries, man. Time is ticking.'

John rushed on, rattled now. 'I mean to say that she is my daughter and I would do anything to help her. I am sorry for calling on you unannounced but I canna stand to see her suffer anymore in that prison, and so here I am. I wish to tell you, sir, that I heartily believe in my daughter's innocence. She never had no reason before to steal and has never been that kind of a girl or person. She had been saving money for her advancement and was proud of her job here. She had no reason to steal and no need to. She knew we would help her too, as much as we were able. She has never lied to me, never hidden things from us. To think of her as a thief is very much not in her way, not in the way of what she is, in her character, in her . . . well, the good girl and person that she finds herself . . . that we find herself to be. To be of.'

'Good God, man, don't tie yourself in knots.'

John took a breath. He wanted to throttle this pig. But he must control his feelings, to help Anny.

'I am not a well-spoken man, I know that, sir.'

'Indeed not.'

Another breath, deeper this time. 'But I am honest and true, sir. And I beg of you to reconsider this case and this charge.'

Now King focused his eyes on John, his head tipped back as he wasn't a tall man and John was huge. King now deigned to speak directly to him. 'Woodvine, I agreed to see you today as I could not fathom what would possess you to approach my house with such impudence, and so I came out of mere curiosity. I thought you must have some compelling new evidence to put before me of your daughter's innocence. Was there a mysterious man in black cape and mask who tiptoed up the driveway and planted the money in your daughter's bag? Or was it a fairy queen who stole through the window glass by magic and put it there?'

Jesus Christ, the mon is mocking me, thought John. How he wanted to kill him, actually murder him, right there and then, watch the life pour out of him onto the gravel. 'No, sir,' he said, his blood as cold as ice now.

'I dunna believe it was a mysterious man or the fairies that did it. I believe it was someone else, sir. But not my daughter, sir. Someone else.'

King narrowed his eyes. 'And who did you think it might be, Woodvine? Do tell.'

'Someone with a grudge against her.'

'Do you have the name of such a person?'

John looked at King. The master actually looked interested. Maybe he knew it was his son that did it, maybe he knew and didn't care. Or maybe he genuinely didn't know and maybe he was genuinely asking.

'I dunna have a name, but . . .'

'Well, then,' said King, with a dismissive wave of his hand.

'No, sir, please, sir. I mean to say, there are many who are envious of my daughter, sir. That may seem strange to one like . . . to one of your . . .' The struggle to be eloquent was hard, but he knew this was his chance and he must dredge up every word he could to fight this battle. '. . . *station* in life, sir. But my daughter is clever and pretty and hard-working. She has all the boys after her and all the girls jealous of her and her success. She is never proud, though. I meant to say, she has pride in her post and her work. But she never acts proud or . . . in *conceited* ways. She is very humble about herself. But there are those in this world that when they see such a person as her . . . as *she* . . . they dunna like it. They wanna smash it. They might even want to take it and make it . . . make her their own. And if that person canna have it, they might . . . do bad things, sir. In their revengeful thoughts, they might do a bad thing. But any man can understand that. Show me a man who's never had a revengeful thought. It can be . . . forgiven. If . . . things are put right . . . by a person.'

Halfway through that speech, John had begun to feel as if King were turning. His narrow gaze had gone and he was listening, really listening to his words. But by the end, John had begun to realise that King knew only too well what his son had done, that he understood only too well what John's meaning was. Now was the crucial moment. Which way would King turn?

'You seem to lean towards some hidden meaning, Woodvine. Is that so?'

'I only wish to save my daughter. My innocent daughter. I swear that she is innocent, on my very life.'

'Life is cheap,' muttered King.

'If it were my death that could save her from this, I would gladly give it.'

'Nobody is asking for that, Woodvine. Please resist melodrama.'

John was lost now. What was the man saying? What else could he say himself? 'Please, sir. Will you give me your verdict? What say you, sir?'

'What say I? Who do you think you are talking to, man?'

John clenched his fists and screwed his eyes shut. *God, give me strength with this bastard!* his mind shouted, but he managed to contain it and instead opened his eyes and said, 'Please, sir, I humbly beg of you, show my daughter mercy and leastways, please, investigate this further. Please, I beg you. I am begging you, sir.' He had run out of words. He thought about getting down upon his knees on the gravel.

'Woodvine, you have had more than your minute. You have presented no new evidence, no compelling arguments and no facts to back up your position. You have verged on harassment, a most inadvisable position to take with your master. And I am your master, Woodvine, do not forget that. If you continue with these claims against me and against my son—'

John gasped. King stopped, his mouth open. He actually said it. He actually came out and said it. John leapt on it. 'I never said a word about your son, sir.'

'Yes, well. No. You did not and neither . . .' King was blustering now, waving his hands about, his face colouring into the hue of a ripe Victoria plum. 'Well, God save us, what on earth am I doing conferring with a giant dolt in my back yard about legal matters? I cannot imagine what possessed me. I am too kind, that is it. I am too kind for my own good. Now, listen here. You've had your hearing and that's the end of it. If you continue with this, I'll have no choice but to dismiss you. I've half a mind to in any case. The cheek of it! But I am not a cruel man. So you will escape with your wages docked for a month. You will work at half pay for four weeks and be glad you have kept your job. Now, get off my land and get back to work.'

King stomped off, the gravel flicking from his heels and tip-tapping his retreat.

It was over. John stood with his shoulders hunched, all of his fight draining out of him. There was nothing to do but go. He walked straight into the woods and forged on through the bracken, his legs whipped by low branches and spikily caressed by banks of nettles. He did not look where he was going, just knew it was downhill, down to the furnace, along the river here somewhere. He had not the heart to stop walking, for if he did, he thought he would surely scream or tear his hair out or dash his head against a tree trunk.

If he'd been a cleverer man, he might have used words better. He might have outwitted that fat idiot and made him admit it was his son that did it. Well, he almost did. But it was not enough. King would never give up his own or at the very least, would never allow his son to be called into question. And even if King did admit it to him, it would only be a working man's word against the ironmaster. Everybody knew how that one would work out: in the master's favour, of course. The way of the world. John felt it was a fool's errand, and he'd only made things worse. Now his pay was docked and they'd struggle with the loss of money. He was lucky he hadn't been demoted from his new position in the cast-house or even dismissed.

He walked on, hurriedly, worried that Pritchard might dock his pay further if he turned up very late. He began to jog through the trees, getting faster, the speed taking away his breath and his memories, the ground rushing at him as he leapt forward down the incline. He tripped over a tree root and fell forward heavily, his huge frame crashing into ferns and jolting every bone as he skidded to a halt. He turned onto his back and groaned, staring up into the meeting of the treetops that sheltered him overhead. He did not move, could not move. He despised King, but he hated himself more. He had failed Anny.

Then, he heard voices. A high one, a low one. He lay very still and listened. They were close by, the sound of the undergrowth signalling they were walking away from the path, as he had been. They were talking as they walked, in serious tones, question and answer, sounding earnest and concerned. If he stood up now, they'd probably see him and be shocked by a man looming out at them. If they stumbled across him, they'd be more shocked still. He'd have a hard time explaining why he was hidden away in the woods, and the last thing he needed was to draw further notice. The voices were close enough to hear now. They had stopped.

'Here?' said the female. She sounded young. 'Is it here you wish us to stop? The wood is thick here, that is certain. Thick and full of secrets.'

'To think, you were the quiet one,' said the male. 'Now you're full of poetry.'

'It is love that has done it. It gives me the words to sing.'

'Enough of that now. I will have to stop that mouth of yours.'

Next came silence, then as John strained his ears to listen beyond the birdsong and the breeze that ruffled the thousands of leaves about him, he heard the girl moaning, high and reedy. They must be kissing. He listened on, miserable, frozen. They were quiet for a long while. Then she spoke again.

'Will you give me your promise?'

'I will, I will. Oh, my sweet, sweet girl. I want to be with you. But I fear your father will never approve the match. What are we to do? Oh, Margaret.'

John sat bolt upright. He looked around, in the direction of the voices. They were a little downhill and were up against a tree, not turned in his direction. It was Margaret King all right. Who was the man? They were kissing again and John could not see his face. Then the man came up for air. It was him. The scribbler. It was Anny's sweetheart, Jake Ashford.

'I don't care, I don't care!' cried Margaret, as she ran her fingers ardently through Ashford's hair. 'I will be with you come hell or high water! Kiss me again!'

John could not look away. He moved slowly. He did not have the vitality left in him to murder these two, as his hands might have wished any other time. He barely had the vigour to stand. He got to his feet stealthily and managed to reach the broad trunk of a nearby oak and stand behind it for a moment, hidden from their view. They were talking again, then kissing. In their passion, they did not seem to notice a giant of a man sidling through the trees away from them.

The sounds of industry were soon upon him. How many more shocks can a person stand? How much disappointment? He felt like a man in the stocks, humiliated and pummelled with the mockery of life and circumstance. Nothing he did came right. And those Kings. Those Kings were all alike. That girl who had simpered and smiled and looked the part of pity and kindness and was now whoring herself in the woods with Anny's sweetheart. Those Kings. They were poison, every last one of them.

When he arrived at the furnace, he glanced at Pritchard, who must have seen the look of thunder on his face and did not say a word, not a word about his lateness or his dishevelled appearance. John realised there were bits of bracken stuck to his clothes and his face was aching where he must have struck his head in the fall. He went straight to the cast-house, where the metal had just been declared fit to run and so the men were rushing to action. He worked in a rage, throwing things down and whacking things about. One of his workmates shouted at him, 'What the bloody 'ell's up with you, mon?'

'Bloody well leave me be,' he shouted in return and looked up with a slaying expression that made his mate slink away. John stopped for a moment to catch his breath, going over to the door of the cast-house to calm down. Looking outside, he saw at the edge of the river, leaning on a trunk and watching the scene, the figure of a young man. He was holding a pencil and sketching energetically across a page clipped to a board. John's eyesight was not good, he had to squint to make out the face, but there was no mistaking the action. It was Ashford. The little bastard had left off kissing the King girl and come down here to practise his wretched hobby, while Anny festered in prison desperately awaiting his visit that would never come. And it would be him who had to tell his girl of Jake and Margaret. How much more could she take?

'There will be blood today,' said John, and threw down his gloves and made a beeline for Ashford. He cared for nothing anymore, only that someone would pay. Someone had to pay for all this.

There came shouting from nearby. Men around him pointed up at the top of the furnace. Clouds of dust were issuing from the top. Pritchard was running past him, waving his arms and shouting, 'More burden! More burden!'

As an ex-furnace filler, John knew what was happening. He had seen it before. Blockages in the furnace built up and had to be cleared by a swift increase in the amount of materials tipped into the opening at the top. He turned and ran up the incline to help shift the loads. Another great cloud of dust spewed forth from the furnace's blazing mouth, filled with fiery embers. Men at the very top fell backwards and twisted away, trying to escape from it, stumbling and tripping over each other in their haste. All in a moment, there was a great roaring sound from deep within the furnace, like the din of a thousand cattle stampeding down a hill. Seconds later, the top of the furnace exploded in a riot of fire, stone, brick, lime, coke, liquefied iron and luminescent dust. There were no more sounds, no more sights to see. He had no time to think of his daughter, of his wife or of his life upon this cruel earth.

Chapter 21

Margaret was in her room when the blast came. Her shelves rattled and a troop of prancing porcelain ponies wobbled violently and fell, smashing into shards on the floor. Margaret had been lying on her bed, replaying every moment with Jake. She thought the world was coming to an end. She had read once of an earthquake in a novel and wondered for a second if these ever occurred in Shropshire. When the sound and the vibrations passed, she came to and ran out of the room. Her father was downstairs shouting at Brunt, as if all this were his doing.

'From the direction of the works,' Brunt was saying.

'Good God,' said her father and issued instructions about collecting his coat and hat.

Benjamina came out onto the landing, sleepy-eyed and squinting at the harsh light of day interrupting her afternoon nap. Queenie was calling from her room: 'Jenkins! Jenkins!' Margaret heard the lady's maid's footsteps running from the adjoining room, then her voice soothing her grandmother. It was as if time had slowed almost to a halt, and yet Margaret's perceptions were screwed up to the highest notch. She ignored her stepmother's sleepy questioning and went down the stairs quickly. She could hear running on the gravel outside. She went out of the sitting room garden door to see Cook telling the maids not to go, but Lucy – Margaret's favourite maid – was running ahead of the others and not stopping for Cook or anyone. For a moment, she wondered why they were all running down there. What could maids and a stable boy do? But then she scolded herself as she realised that, of course, all of these local girls and lads had family that were ironworkers – uncles and cousins, brothers and fathers. Fathers. Anny. John Woodvine!

'Lucy!' she called out and ran to the woodland path that everyone was heading down. 'Lucy, stop!' She saw the girl turn, about to run on, so she called again. 'Lucy, please, it's Miss Margaret. Please!'

Lucy spotted her from the edge of the wood and hesitated. Margaret could see she wanted to run on with the others. She went towards Lucy and called to her. 'I'm sorry, Lucy. Do you have family down there?'

'Course, miss. My uncles. Four of 'em.'

Margaret caught up with her. 'I'm sorry. You must go. But please, will you find out if John Woodvine is well? Anny's father?'

'I surely will, miss,' said Lucy and did not wait to be dismissed, tearing down the hill, fleetly winding her way through the trees till Margaret lost sight of her.

She turned to see her father and Brotherton coming from the office and running down the path. She had never seen her father run. Mrs Brotherton was standing at the door to the office, wringing her hands. Margaret rushed over to her.

'What do you think it is, Mrs Brotherton?' She saw that the woman was already crying.

'Oh, my dear. You should not be here. You must go back to your room. Your father will be angry if he sees you are not safe.'

'Please, do tell me what has happened exactly.'

'There was an explosion at the blast furnace. Sounds like the whole thing blew. It'll be a miracle if there aren't a dozen or more dead. Oh my, it is a terrible day for all of us. Terrible. I must go and fetch the surgeon.'

'I do hope you don't have family there, do you?'

'Oh, miss, do go back in the house, do,' said Mrs Brotherton peevishly. 'This is no place for you.' With that, she pulled the office door to behind her and locked it with a key she kept on a cord around her waist. She bustled off down the path and Margaret felt herself well and truly discharged. She wandered back to the house and went up the stairs. No sign of Benjamina. She'd probably gone straight back to her nap. She knocked on Queenie's door. Jenkins answered it, looking harassed.

'Not now, miss,' she said and shut the door in her face.

Margaret waited in her room for a while. She sat by the window that gave out on to the driveway, looking out for her father returning. Then, she went downstairs and sat in the library, watching the opening to the woodland path and the edge of the office for any comings and goings. But there were none. She wanted to leave the house, sneak down through the woods and see for herself. She nearly did it once or twice, nearly got up the courage. But she was afraid. She was too afraid, of what she might see, of the horrors that awaited an observer at the aftermath of an explosion. She had once seen a painting in a book that depicted hell and it was full of tiny people in various stages of torment in dark caves, fire blooming all around. That was the image in her mind now. She knew she was not strong enough to bear it. So she prayed instead, that there were not too many dead, that most had escaped miraculously with their lives, perhaps just some injuries. And most of all, that Anny's father, that good, good man John Woodvine, had not been by the furnace when it blew, that he had been at home, or by the riverside, or anywhere else but there. Was there a chance? Of course there was. And she was sure he'd be all right, she had a good feeling. Surely, two appalling things could not happen to one family?

But, of course, they could. Life could be cruel. Woodvine could have been miles away or inches. He could be alive or dead. Dead. Jake! Suddenly, she remembered that Jake said he was going to do some sketching. He had his bag with him. He had walked away from her, leaving her panting from his kisses, in the direction of the furnace. He had not said where he was going precisely, but it could have been there. Would he have been close enough to be hurt? Killed even? She ran from the room. She crossed the lawn and headed for the woods. Then she heard someone running up the path and turned to see her father approaching the house, in a state of exertion, puffed out and grubby-faced. She went to him and saw that all of his clothes were smeared with dirt. He was pulling off his cravat.

'Father, please, tell me. How many hurt?'

'Not now, Margaret,' he said and stormed past her, calling, 'Get back in the house, for God's sake!'

'Father, please!' she cried and followed him. 'I must know. Is Jake Ashford killed? And John Woodvine?'

'We don't know names. Nobody knows names. It's just butchery everywhere. Lord knows what effect it'll have on profits. The break in production will cost us a fortune. Now, get away with you, girl!'

He took the stairs two at a time and disappeared into his room. Margaret felt faint. She went back out into the garden. She could not bear to face it, the scene of carnage that must be down there. But she could not wait either. She went to her room and took her purse, collected her cloak and bonnet and walked away down the path to town. She would go to Jake's lodgings, see if he were there. That was something she could do. As she walked down the hill, she realised that everyone she passed was rushing past her, all heading towards the river or the woods, all in the direction of the blast. The town was emptying and she was in the course of the flood. She fought her way through it, hearing all manner of voices concerned, worried, shocked, shouting and some sobbing.

She reached Jake's lodgings and banged on the door. No answer. She tried again, and still no answer. Nobody at home. Now, she felt nauseous. She decided she would not go home again and wait. She grimly set her mind to follow the crowd. Jostling along with so many others, her progress was slow. She began to feel queasy, the smell and heat, the clamour of horrified voices. Then she heard her name, her surname. King this and King that. People were talking about her father. She managed to catch a snippet here and there and all of it was bad. There were curse words, followed by her family name. There was such anger and disgust. They blamed her father for this. She felt her cheeks glow hot with shame and pulled her bonnet forwards to shield her face. Yet why would they blame him? Surely it was an accident. But there were whispers of delayed repairs, faulty equipment, inferior materials . . . Should she turn round and go back? She was not far from the furnace site now, and the crowd was so thick here. She kept her head down and her feet shuffling forward.

The crowd slowed and she could hear cries, women weeping and being comforted. She looked up and was surrounded by heads, shaking and gasping. As she came past the last clump of riverside trees and the furnace loomed into view, the sight froze her.

The brick structure of the furnace was gone, only the rubble of its foundations remaining, jagged like broken teeth. Broad grey puddles of solidified iron splattered the scene, as if a giant's paint pot had been kicked over. There were huge lumps of wall punctuating the churned ground down to the riverside, some still glowing with embers. Everything was veiled in dust, patches of white, brown, reddish and black dust cloaked the ruins, the earth and the surrounding vegetation. There were men everywhere, standing in groups, walking amongst the ruins, muttering to each other. There were a couple of blankets on the ground, here and there, lumpy, unmoving forms beneath them, feet stuck out of the end, some with boots on, some bootless, naked feet. Elsewhere, there were bodies with only a coat thrown over to cover the faces. A large cart was arriving along the riverside road from downstream, trundling along the rutty way, drawn by oxen. Some of the men moved towards the bodies and began to lift them into the cart. The crowd's noise changed, its voices slowing and deepening into moans of sympathy and thence to a kind of shuffling silence, as if nobody wanted to utter a sound in the presence of the moving of the dead. Margaret looked away, unable to bear the sight of the bodies, having been cradled by the firm ground, now hanging limp and loose between the men who carried them. She turned her gaze towards the furnace itself, her father's moneymaker, now just wreckage. She saw a man fish for something in the piles of scattered bricks and lift it up. It was a boot, with half a leg attached to it, blown off at the knee, its stump bloody and glistening through the lime dust. But there was no sign of Jake or of John Woodvine.

'Miss,' said a voice to her left.

Margaret flinched as if slapped. Had someone recognised her? She turned her head away, terrified to show her face. A hand touched her arm.

'Miss, you shouldna be here.'

Margaret had to turn and look. It was her maid, Lucy. To see her face there in that ghastly place was like balm.

'Oh, Lucy,' she said and felt her face crumpling.

'You shouldna be seeing all this, miss.'

'Please,' Margaret whispered and glanced about, hoping that Lucy would cotton on that nobody must know who she was.

Lucy nodded and said, 'I shall walk back with you.'

'But your family . . .'

'No sign of them yet.'

She fought to calm herself and fall into step with the sad, slow gait of the returning crowd, aware of Lucy's presence beside her. After what felt like hours yet was just a matter of minutes, she found herself ascending the steps to the road by the iron bridge. They were met with a logjam of people, some coming, some going, in a melee of confusion, like a gathering of boiling wreckage in the path of a flood.

She felt Lucy's hand on her arm, steering her onto the bridge, away from the worst of the throng.

'We can wait here a moment,' said Lucy. 'Catch your breath. Then you ought to get yourself home.'

'Thank you,' said Margaret in a small voice. 'You are so kind.'

'I am that surprised to see you here, miss.'

'I felt I should come,' said Margaret, 'Mr Woodvine, Jake Ashford. Have you seen them?'

'No, miss.'

'Oh, Lucy. This is beyond bearing . . . and all the fault of the Kings. What must you think of us? What must everyone here think? I know what they are saying, about . . . my father, the family. I know they say it is his fault. He should be there, he should be down there, helping. Instead he came home. I saw him retreat to his room. He ran upstairs, I tell you.'

Lucy did not speak. Her face betrayed no opinion. But she was listening and this gave Margaret the confidence to go on. 'But I want you to know that I am not like him, or my brother. I am not one of them. I never have been. I know my family is rotten and I cannot imagine why anyone would want to work for them, especially a kind and good person like you, Lucy. I cannot understand it.'

Lucy looked down, a grim smile played about her lips and she answered, 'We must work, miss. We have no choice as to our masters. And all masters are the same.'

Margaret was shamed by her forgetting of this hard truth.

'You are right. I am sorry, Lucy.'

'Dunna fret yourself, miss. It is the way of the world.'

'But it doesn't have to be so, does it? Cannot we strive for change?'

'Change is for the rich, not for the likes of me and mine.'

Margaret stared at Lucy's face. She was an attractive girl, pale skin and pink cheeks, black hair tucked neatly under her cap and pretty dark eyes. It was the first time Margaret had observed her closely, the first time she had ever looked carefully at one of the servants' faces, looked into their eyes to see the person they were, not simply the role they played in her father's house.

'I am powerless, too, in my own way,' Margaret said to Lucy, whose eyebrows rose just a touch, enough to show her derision of such a statement, yet sufficient to remain respectful. 'I know you don't believe that, but it is true. Yet, there are ways. There are ways we can break free of our bonds. One of them is friendship. It can break down the barriers between us.'

She expected another world-weary retort from Lucy, but the girl was quiet, regarding her steadily for a moment with those small, intelligent eyes. Then she glanced about her. 'I should get back now, miss. But, in all this muddle, I still have no word on my uncles. I've been down there and back and all over town looking for word, and none yet. Will you give me leave to keep looking, leave from my post at the house?'

'Of course, Lucy. Will you bring me news of John Woodvine and Jake Ashford?'

'I will if I can, miss,' she said and turned away, slotting into the crowd and moving as one with them, her drab servant's clothes mingling her into obscurity amongst her people.

Margaret stood on the bridge and looked through the iron rails, the river flowing peacefully beneath her, oblivious to the human drama enacted upon its banks. She watched those coming from the direction of the blast, shaking their heads, some of the women crying, others covering their eyes with their hands.

She wanted to run, run home and never leave it. She raised her head to catch a glimpse of her house on the hill, presiding over the town. Despite the rot that she knew grew daily within that house, it was the only home she knew. She turned her eyes to the road, summoning the courage to enter the fray.

Then, she saw him.

'Jake!' she screamed. 'Jake Ashford!' Some looked around but she was not alone in calling out, as here at the bridge there was a loud hubbub of voices, of similar reunions and shouts and cries. Jake had not heard her and was pushing his way through the throng to get across the road to his lodgings. She rushed to him and reached him at his door.

'Jake!' she cried again and grasped his arm. He turned to her.

'Oh, Margaret!' he gasped and let her throw her arms about him.

'Are you hurt?' she said.

'I am well, quite well. I was there. I was there, Margaret!' His eyes were lit up and his face was grubby.

'You are not hurt? Are you sure?'

'Quite sure. I was along the river a way and was sketching a scene of the workers framed by trees when it went off. I was thrown to the ground by the blast, but I was not injured. I was very lucky.'

'Oh, thank heavens!' she cried and began to sob, resting her head on this chest. He patted her on the back then stood her upright.

'There, there, dear girl. I am well. But many others are not. It is the most incredible scene down there.

I simply cannot describe it. But I must not, for you will never sleep again if I do.'

'I was just there myself, Jake. It was terrible. The worst thing I have seen in my life.'

'What on earth possessed you to go down there?'

'I came to find you and Anny's father. I did not see you there. A maid of ours took me away from it.'

'Well, she did right. These are not sights for eyes as beautiful as yours. Now then, I lost my bag in the blast. I must go upstairs and fetch more materials. I must record it.'

'You are going back there? To *sketch*?'

'I must! This is an extraordinary event. I must record it for posterity.'

Margaret stared at him. 'Please do not go back there. Please stay with me.'

'Ah, my little mouse,' he said and took her hands, squeezing them. 'There is no danger now. I am fine. You must go home and stay safe. I will come to you soon. Then, we will talk. We will make plans. But for now, I must go. You do understand, don't you?'

She thought of what he'd said about his mistress, art, who now had put fire in his belly; he would not be turned.

'Of course. Please be careful there, Jake. And if you can, please can you ask about Mr Woodvine, Anny's father? And come to the house to tell me if you hear news of him? Will you do that for me, Jake?'

'I will do what I can.'

'And you will send me word, of when and where we can meet next?'

'Of course I will, my sweet. Now, go. Go home. I will see you anon.'

With that, he turned and went into his lodging house and shut the door in her face.

She walked home and waited in her room for hours. Cook prepared a plate of cold meats and had them sent up to her in her room. In the late evening, she heard sounds downstairs of doors closing and the voices of servants. She went out onto the landing and made her way across to the servants' staircase. She heard weary feet coming up them, and there was Lucy.

'Lucy, I am glad to see you,' she said. Lucy stopped on the stairs and lifted her face. It was grimy like the others who'd come from the site, but Lucy's eyes were ghostly, haunted by what they had seen, no doubt. 'Is your family safe?'

'Yes, miss. All my uncles are safe.'

'What good fortune, Lucy. I am so glad to hear that. How did they escape it?'

'They was in a different part of the works. Luckily none of them near the blast.'

'Lucy, did you hear any news of the Woodvines? Of Anny's father?'

Lucy did not speak. She looked down at her feet. She shook her head.

'Do you mean, you have no news? Or that it is bad news?'

'It is bad news, miss. The worst. John Woodvine is dead.'

Chapter 22

Anny did not open her eyes. She knew she was awake, she knew that the touch of Jake's hand on her face had been a dream, she knew she was in the worst room she had ever been in her life. She had thought the cell must be the worst, until she fell ill with fever and they brought her here, to the prison infirmary. After days of fever, of a boiling heat in her body that left her wordless and limp, she had begun to cool down and slowly crawl back to the land of the living. At her lowest moments, she did not know if she wished to recover or not. She wanted to escape the infirmary but the cell was nowhere she ever wanted to be again. The only thing that kept her going was the thought of what her death would do to those who loved her. Her father and mother mostly, but also, Peggy. And Jake? How she longed for him. Her dreams were plagued by soft, sweet memories of his touch. But she was haunted by doubt. Did he love her? Why had he not come to her? There was something about him that made her doubt herself, her own judgement. She wanted him, indeed she did, but his love was not for her alone – she had to share it with his art. It was not how she pictured love would be: simple, warm and good. Jake's love was like fire, but cold too, like a mirror on a winter's morning.

On waking in the infirmary, the smell hit her first. The only thing close to it was the butcher's stall in Ironbridge mixed with the stench of the stale sweat of the men coming back from the furnace, including her father. Bless him, but he did stink after a shift. There was another smell in there, something sickly and sweet she couldn't place. Something to do with death.

She lay listening to the sounds of the sick. Some were coughing, others moaning, one snored. She could hear her heart beating, as it echoed dully deep inside her ears. She thought about how nobody else in the world could hear that sound but her. She was the only person allowed inside her own mind. This thought had comforted her these past weeks in prison. Whatever was happening outside of her body, or to her body, nobody could get inside her head. It was her refuge.

She heard voices in the corridor beyond the infirmary. Her eyes opened and she looked towards the door but could not see anyone. She scanned the room, to see if anyone else had passed in the night. Two had perished since she'd been in there, carted away, staring, dead eyes still open, no sheet to cover them, taken with no ceremony. She wondered where they were buried, if anyone informed their families. It was a gloomy room lit only by candles, with eight beds arranged in two rows along each opposite wall, three of them occupied with sleeping prisoners, two men and one other woman. It was very hot and airless in there. She craved water but they were only given a small cup once a day. This was not a place where the sick were tended. This was a place where most came to die.

There were those voices again. She saw a silhouette appear in the doorway, joined by another. She couldn't make out the faces. But then she heard her surname and she saw the matron turn and look at her. She pulled herself upright. Was it Jake? Oh, let it be Jake! She squinted at the figures in the doorway, one of whom stepped into the room, where the candlelight caught her face.

'Peggy!' said Anny, her voice cracking as her throat was so dry.

Peggy looked at her and smiled, then turned to the figure behind her, who Anny saw was Brotherton. Mr B! Come to see her with Peggy? She still held his disloyalty against him but maybe he was making amends now. Could it be . . . good news? Why else would both of them come? Was she to be released? Oh, happy day, if it were true!

'I fear this was a mistake,' said Brotherton and looked about to turn around and leave.

'Wait outside if you must,' said Margaret. 'I am going to talk to Anny.'

Margaret walked over to Anny's bed and sat down at the end of it, smiling wanly. Anny saw Mr B wait at the door, then he stepped outside into the corridor. Anny thought, *Why is he not coming to me?* Anny looked back at Peggy, whose face showed the shock she knew came from her own pale and drawn appearance. She guessed she must look so much worse than the last time Margaret had seen her. She imagined she must look years older.

'It's me, Anny. It's Peggy. I am here. I came to tell you—'

'Is Jake with you? Is he here?' she asked weakly.

'Jake is not here, no. I am sorry, Anny. I do not think he will be coming. But I am here.'

'Why? Did you talk to him? What did he say?'

'Only that he must serve his art. I think he is too committed to his vocation. He isn't deserving of you, Anny. You need a man who will devote himself to you.'

Anny's head dropped and she covered her face with her hands. *I knew it*, she thought. *I knew he was not a good man. Deep down, I knew it. He is selfish and untrustworthy.*

'Oh, Anny, please don't take it so. *Please.*'

Anny looked up and set her face straight. 'I am glad you told me the truth and that I won't have to waste my time thinking of him any longer.'

Oh, but it sustained me, she thought. *It kept me going in this awful place. How I have missed him. How I will miss the thought of him.*

She could not keep up the brave face. She broke down and sobbed. Peggy handed her a clean handkerchief, pure white, embroidered fancily with the letters M and K. Then Peggy reached over and put her arms about her and held her as she cried.

'He's not the one for you,' Peggy went on. 'Not this one, not him. Forget him. Better to cry for him now and forget him. Better for everyone,' said Peggy.

Through her tears, Anny wondered, *What does she mean, better for everyone?*

'I am so sorry, Anny,' said a voice behind them. It was Mr B. Anny looked up.

'Mr B,' she managed, wiping her eyes and composing herself.

'Yes, Anny. Oh, I don't know what to say. I doubt I can add anything to what Miss King must have said so eloquently.'

'No, Mr Brotherton! Not yet!' said Margaret urgently.

'We will all miss your father,' Brotherton went on. 'A good man. The best. Such a worker he was, like no other.'

Anny looked at Peggy. 'What's this?'

'Oh, Anny,' said Margaret and brought her fist to her mouth.

Nausea rose in Anny's throat. Her head felt like it was draining of blood. 'What is this about my father?'

'But Miss King, have you not . . . ?' began Mr B incredulously.

'Your father . . .' said Peggy, looking at her with wide, fearful eyes. 'There was an accident. At the furnace. There was an explosion. Your father, Anny . . .' She reached over and took Anny's hands in her own.

'No.' Anny's voice was low at first. 'No,' she said again, louder and higher.

'It was an accident,' said Brotherton. 'Fifteen dead, Anny. Your father was one of them.'

'No, no, no.' Anny was shaking her head now, her eyes moving erratically with each phrase, each new thought. Not Father, not dear old Father. Not him, never him. He was in the cast-house these days, much safer than the furnace top.

'There is a mistake. It cannot be Father.'

Mr B shook his head. 'There is no error, Anny. It is definitely your father. They say he ran towards the furnace top just before it was about to blow, to help the others, but got caught in the blast himself. He died a hero, Anny.'

'And my mother?'

'She's taken the news badly and isn't well enough to come, but she will recover.'

Anny's mind had been racing, but now it stopped dead, as if hit by a heavy object and trapped beneath it. There was no point in struggling. That would only cause more pain.

'No,' she whispered, the truth dawning on her now. 'No.'

'It is a tragedy,' said Mr B in a soothing tone. 'A terrible, awful tragedy. A terrible, awful accident.'

'No,' said Anny again and looked up at Mr B. Something new was brewing in her now. It was not grief or pity. It was not misery. It was anger, pure, white-hot rage. 'This was not an accident. Father used to tell me about the furnace. About the danger. There were blockages, poor materials. King could have stopped this. It's his fault. Not an accident. It's King's doing.'

Peggy was staring at her, shaking her head. 'You,' said Anny and looked upon her, as if seeing her clearly for the first time. 'You are a King. It's your fault. It's all your fault.'

'No, Anny!' said Mr B, attempting to soothe her. 'Miss King is here to . . .'

'No!' It came out as a screech. Anny thrust Peggy's hands away. 'The Kings are behind this. They are behind everything. How could I have trusted you? You, just another King!'

'Anny, please!' Peggy was sobbing now.

'You're the worst of the lot! You pretend to be good, but you're just like them. What have you ever done for me? You desperate . . . little *bitch*! You had no friends of your own, so you picked on me. Made me think I could aspire to something, a better life. But look at you. Why should I want anything that you have, anything that you are? You're pathetic. You disgust me. You're all the same. We were never friends.'

323

'We were, Anny, please! I've always loved you. If you only knew how I've tried to help you.'

'Oh, poor you! Poor little rich girl!' Anny spat out the words like poison on her tongue. 'Do you want me to pity you now? We were always different. You'll always have a pillow to lay your pretty little head on. Below the poor, there is no pillow. There is only a hole, a bloody great hole with the workhouse, poverty, disease and death at the bottom of it. Rich and poor can never be friends.'

Mr B tried to intervene. 'Oh, Anny, you don't know what you're saying.'

'Shut up, you snivelling bastard!' Anny cried. 'You're as bad as the Kings. When did you ever speak up for me? When did you ever risk a moment of your comfortable little life to speak for me? You knew I'd never steal, you knew that and so did your wife. But here I am. And where is Cyril? Off scot-free, no doubt. And you knew about the furnace, too, about the danger. And yet here you are. And where is my father? Dead. Dead! Murdered by the likes of you – and you!'

Mr B patted Peggy on the shoulder and muttered, 'She's not herself. We must go.' Peggy stood up reluctantly and followed Mr B to the door. The other prisoners in their sickbeds were all wide awake and upright now, enjoying the show, one man grinning at Peggy as she passed. They could do that, Peggy and Mr B, they could walk out of here and never come back. But she was left here, in this hell, with the knowledge of her lost father haunting her forever. *Oh, Father! There could never be a daughter who loved a father more than me. My lovely father, my dear father. Gone. Ruined. Dead.* The rage boiled in her like the furnace that killed her father. Now, it was about to blow.

Anny shouted after them: 'That's it. Run away, you bloody cowards. That's right. Canna stand the truth? Run away, back to your wife who I tended when she was sick I dunna know how many times. Where is she, eh? And you, run back to Jake Ashford. Oh yes, dunna think I dunna know what your game is. *He's not the one for you, Anny.* Oh yes, we all know why that is. Because you're after him for yourself!'

At this, Peggy turned to Anny, her face betraying her. 'I knew it!' cried Anny, with bitter triumph. She guessed it the moment Peggy had said 'Better for everyone'. But she did not know if it were true, not until this moment, when Peggy's guilt-ridden eyes gave it all away. She looked at the face of this young woman who had been her closest friend, her ally in a difficult world. She felt ice water run through her veins. Hate had replaced love in every fibre of her being. She spoke again to Peggy, in a low, unearthly voice, 'You traitorous whore.'

Peggy flinched. A stab in the heart. Good! Anny felt she could kill her just by looking at her. Anny was panting with exertion, her skin shining with sweat, her eyes bright with hate.

Peggy muttered, 'I shall come again soon, when you are better.'

'No, you will not!' shouted Anny, mustering energy for one last blow. 'I never want to see you again. I curse you, Peggy, and I curse Jake Ashford. I curse you to lose everything you have and to a miserable life and a lonely death. I curse you, Margaret King!'

Chapter 23

Margaret sat on her bed and stared at the walls of her room. She knew she was tired but were her eyes deceiving her? She could swear that the walls were closing in on all sides, all four slowly but steadily moving towards her, to crush her. She closed her eyes to escape it and pictured instead her best friend's face, twisted with hate, screaming at her. She jumped up from the bed and left the room. She had only been back from Shrewsbury for a quarter hour or so, yet she was rushing out of the door again. She could not bear to stay in that house. She could not bear her own memories. She walked hurriedly along the path to town, the summer sun beating down on her like a judgement and making her sweat. She wanted to rip off her bonnet and cloak and throw them down, feel the sun on her bare skin and the breeze in her hair. But not only was it unseemly, it would be drawing attention to herself and she could not risk that. It was several days since the blast, yet the town would not forget the accident so quickly, would never forget it, she guessed. She must remain incognito and calm herself down. She slowed her pace and caught her breath, trying to regulate her step with her breathing, two long steps for every breath: one, two, one, two.

I am behaving like a mad person, she thought. *Is it in our family, this madness, as Father said?* She thought of the walls closing in, of Queenie's oddness, of what happened to her great-aunt Selina. Perhaps it was. Perhaps all the women of the family had this feebleness of mind. But then it occurred to her that whatever weakness ran in their female blood, it was corroded further by the acid of the King males. They destroyed things, by design or by carelessness. As she walked she decided that they would not destroy her. There was only one way to escape them and that was by leaving that place, for good. She knew where she was heading now, to Jake.

The very thought of him twisted her insides, not merely from her desire for him, but from the remembrance of Anny. She shook her head to clear her thoughts. Yes, she could crucify herself for the rest of her life about Anny or she could buck up and realise she had done all she could. She had begged her father and her grandmother to withdraw the charges, she had confronted her brother to force him to confess and she had not stolen Jake from Anny: he had made that choice himself.

In the aftermath of the blast, Margaret had tracked down Mrs Woodvine, hired her a doctor. She'd gone to Mr Brotherton to ensure Anny was told, and when no family could be found to take Anny the news, she had gone herself. True, she'd made a mess of it, and it seemed little enough in the face of Anny's pain, but it was all that was within Margaret's power. Even if she sacrificed everything and walked away from Jake, what would that win Anny?

She thought of Jake. He had not contacted her since the day of the blast and she did not want to bother him, but she was restless and ached to see him. She wanted to make their plans, to escape before further tragedy could strike.

There was no escape for her friend. Anny's father was dead, her mother ill and her imprisonment seemed certain, with nobody to speak for her and no other comfort for her. She did not blame her friend for her anger. But because Anny's life was over, did Margaret's need to end? Anny's curse . . . Margaret's eyes welled up and blurred her path ahead, the bridge on her left, the Tontine Hotel to her right. And then she was there, standing before the door to Jake's lodgings. He was everything to her now, he was all she had left.

She knocked on the door. After a wait and the sound of heavy footsteps, it opened. There was his landlady, an obsequious smile on her face, which vanished.

'What do you want?' she said in a hard-edged tone.

Margaret's shock made her pause. They had spoken before. Could the landlady not remember her? 'Uh, good afternoon. I would like . . . is Mr Ashford at home?'

'The cheek of yer! Showing yer face round here.'

Then it dawned on her. The landlady had recollected her very well. She knew exactly who she was.

'I would be most obliged if you could tell me if Mr Ashford is at home. I have an important communication for him.' Margaret lifted up her purse and snapped it open, just as she had done the previous occasion she was here.

The woman snarled, 'You Kings think your money can solve everything. I've got friends round here lost family because of you and yours. It's blood money now.'

Margaret felt as if she had been slapped in the face. But she also believed she could not be blamed for her father's mismanagement. That was simply unfair and, quite frankly, bullying. And she had had enough of being bullied. She jutted out her chin and said, 'If you will not tell me if he is here, then I shall go and look for myself.'

'Oh, will you now, missy?' began the landlady, squaring up to Margaret, yet they were distracted by the sound of footsteps coming down the stairs. Then Jake appeared and saw Margaret, his face showing surprise.

'Miss King!' he said and smiled. 'Do come in.'

The landlady said, 'Not in here. I run a respectable house, me.'

Jake glanced at Margaret, then replied, 'I was just about to go out in any case. Will you take a walk with me, Miss King?'

She nodded and Jake came out onto the pavement. His landlady slammed the door behind him. At the nearness of Jake and the horrid treatment of that woman, Margaret wanted to burst out crying but she controlled herself. Jake's expression showed concern for her. 'We shall find a quiet place to talk,' he said and she nodded. Taking her arm, he led her over the street. Jake paid the toll for them both to cross the bridge. They went down onto the river path, walking away from town until they reached a secluded spot, then stopped. Margaret glanced about to see if anyone was around and then threw her arms round him and began to weep.

'There, there. My darling, sweet girl.'

'Oh Jake, I cannot bear it any longer.'

'Surely not, my darling. You have so much to be happy about. You have me, for one.'

'I know, but everything else is hopeless. The accident. The town blames my family. And rightly so! I saw Anny, and she too blames me. She also knows about you and me. She guessed it. Oh, she screamed at me, cursed me. She hates me. She was my only friend.'

He kissed her tenderly and it stopped her tears. Her desire for him was greater than her grief, in that moment.

'We must leave,' she said. 'We must get away, before it's too late.'

'I wish I could make it all better,' he whispered to her.

'You could. You can, Jake. Let us run away together.'

'Run away? Where?'

'Paris. We could be together, walk the gardens, read poetry . . . and be far from the curse of the King family.'

Jake took her hands in his own and said, 'Do you mean . . . could you mean, to elope, my love?'

'Are you asking me to marry you?' she whispered and held her breath.

Jake sighed and squeezed her hands. 'There is nothing I want more. But I have few funds and my father would not sanction us running away together. He would expect a dowry from your father. I cannot rely on him to fund this trip for the sake of elopement. He would never agree. I do not have enough money, my love, and I know of no way to put my hands on such an amount as we would need for the journey.'

'I do.'

'Do what, my love?'

'I know a way of finding the money. I can do it tonight. I can take it from my father's office.'

'That sounds like a terrible risk,' he said, looking worried.

'I would do it, for us. I know exactly how. Cyril's crime and Anny's descriptions have taught me where my father's keys are and how to open the safe. I will do it for us.'

Jake smiled widely and kissed her again, this time with passion. 'Then we shall go! Tonight, my love?'

She hesitated a moment. This night? Could she do it? Could she turn her life on its head this very night? What had she to stay for? 'Tonight!' she said.

'Will it give you enough time? To pack a bag? To take the money?'

'Yes. I intend to travel light.'

'I shall meet you on the bridge then, by moonlight. What time?'

'Midnight,' she said and he kissed her again, so long and so slow, she thought she would melt.

It was the most romantic moment of her life. Nobody could feel this way and be wrong. It must be right.

They collected themselves and walked back, he to his lodgings to pack and she to Southover.

Margaret rushed up the stairs to her room and began packing feverishly. She looked around at all her precious possessions. She was surprised at how easy it was to leave much of it behind. She quietly selected the most valuable items from her collection. Anything small, easy to carry and valuable. They would need as much as she could take to start their new life. With each step she felt empowered and trembled with excitement. Taking one last look at the room that had been home all her life, Margaret said goodbye to it and found she had never felt so free. Lifting her bag she turned to leave, only to find herself facing Lucy. Her heart stuttered as she realised how quickly her new life could end.

'Lucy!'

'Miss . . . What . . . ?'

Margaret lunged forward and gripped Lucy's hand and pleaded with her, 'Oh, Lucy, you must not say a word. I'm eloping, escaping this cursed family and starting a new life.'

'But, miss, I—'

'Lucy, I'm begging you. I cannot stay here. It is this family, this house. I believe it is rotten to the core. This family is poison.'

Lucy stared at her again, that unblinking, direct stare.

'I believe you understand what I mean by that, Lucy. Is that true?'

Lucy continued to look and say nothing. Then, almost imperceptibly, she nodded.

'I thought you would. I know you have had some . . . trouble from my brother. Anny Woodvine and I were in the woods once, years ago. We saw him with you. We threw a rock to distract him. You got away.'

'You did that, miss?'

Margaret considered embroidering the truth, to show herself in a better light. But she said, 'No. It was not I. It was Anny. She was always like that. Always thinking of others . . . Oh, Lucy. Anny is in a terrible state. In that hellish place, the prison. And she has been so ill. When I went to her, to tell her about her father, she screamed at me. She cursed me.'

Margaret wanted to sob, but knew it was self-indulgence. It was Anny who had the right to weep, not her.

'It inna your fault, miss. What your father did. What your brother did. None of it is your fault.'

'That's kind of you, Lucy. But, you see, that's why I must go, before I end up like Anny, or worse, like my family. My only regret in leaving is that I cannot save Anny. Anny Woodvine never did a bad thing in her life. She is goodness itself. So brave and honest and true.'

'She is, right enough. Good people, the Woodvines.'

'Yes, good people. The opposite of my people. Mine are heartless. And cruel. I am sorry that I did not help you more. With Cyril. I am so sorry for that.'

Lucy looked at her feet. 'There was nothing you coulda done, miss. I know he hits you. We all live in fear of him.'

'But what he was doing to you that day, in the forest. It was unforgivable.'

Lucy still stared at her feet. She let out a long, heart-felt sigh, so affecting was it, that Margaret felt she must ask her, 'What is it, Lucy? Is there something you wish to tell me?'

'Oh, miss,' whispered Lucy.

'What is it, Lucy?'

'It was worse, much worse than that.'

'What is it?'

'My shame and my disgrace.'

Margaret felt a chill run up her spine. 'I am sure that is not true. Please, Lucy, sit beside me on the bed. Please, tell me.'

Lucy looked at the bed, as if considering the idea of sitting beside her mistress. But she did not. She did not lift her head but began to speak.

'When I was a young'un, I decided I was going to save myself for marriage, not even kiss a boy till I met the right one at church. And then I pictured he'd treat me right and we'd step out together. One day, he'd ask me very polite like and very respectful, if I'd be his wife. That was my dream. But that will never happen now. Not now Master Cyril has stuck his filthy thing in me all those times and then one time, he gave me a life growing inside of me.'

Margaret covered her mouth and shook her head.

Lucy went on. 'But the child died inside me. I lay in my attic room that winter night and it bled out all over the bed. Jenkins dealt with it and nobody was told. I had to wash out my own sheets. I could hardly stand up from the loss of it. The pain was summat terrible, both in my insides and in my heart. For I hated the child that grew inside me, put there without my saying so, without me wanting it. By that ... that *monster* Cyril King.'

'Oh, Lucy,' Margaret whispered, tears coming now. 'I am ...' But Lucy interrupted her. Lucy's story, that had started as a trickle of words, gushed out like a flood.

'But I loved it too, that child, for it was mine and part of me, and it was innocent, surely, as are all babes. And I would have loved it, if it had grown and come naturally, instead of weeping through like a bad

336

monthly. Jenkins fished it out from the mess and took it away. I've always wanted to ask Jenkins what she did with the little thing. It would have been very tiny, as it was only a few weeks in. It might've been the size of a plum. Would it have had fingers and toes yet? Would it have had feelings or thinkings or memories? I sang to it as it bled out of me. I sang it the songs my mother had crooned to me when I was little, after we'd lost my father and the dark days began. The job here at the King house had come as a blessing, to help us survive in those difficult times. But I hadna been here long before I caught the whiff of evil in this house. I was only eleven when Cyril first grabbed me, sticking his tongue in my mouth on the servants' staircase. I didna know what was happening to me. I never told a soul. I had to keep this job. How I hated him, how I hated all of you, I'm sorry to say, miss. But I had to keep this job, for my mother. I had no choice.'

Lucy fell silent. Margaret tried to think of the right words to say next. But what could she possibly say, to this girl who had been so cruelly used by Margaret's own family? Nothing could make it better. Nothing could make it right. She could only stare at her own hands, wringing uselessly in her lap. Guilt-ridden hands, King hands, with the stain of Lucy's sacrifice all over them.

'I am so, so sorry, Lucy. I don't know how to ... I don't know what ...'

'Dunna fret, miss,' said Lucy, and though she still stared at the floor, she moved her hand and put it over Margaret's own. 'It never were your doing. It's that Master Cyril. It is his crime.'

'And not his only one.'

'That's right. Not his only one.'

Margaret looked at Lucy. 'I know something else he did, Lucy. Another crime. I told my father and my grandmother, but they have done nothing about it. I confronted him, but he did not care. My father threatened to send me to the asylum if I ever told a soul.' But she wanted to tell Lucy, very much. What harm would it do now, now she was running away to Paris?

'I know what it is, miss.'

'I don't think you do, Lucy. This is about Anny.'

'I know all about it. Everyone knew he was after Anny. When I found out, I was grateful at first, that he'd moved on from me to another girl. But I liked Anny, we all did. I thought she would escape him, though. She was cleverer than me. Then, that morning he came to the kitchen door, and he gave these orders to me and to Paddy, about her waiting in the library and suchlike. It was all very queer. I knew that look in his eye, when he was up to mischief. Like he enjoys cruel thoughts and cruel deeds. So I fetched Paddy and we followed him. Very quiet like. We followed him to the office and we hid in the woods. Then we saw him go in. So we crept up to the window of Mr B's room and we watched him.

He took the money out of the safe. We crept around the office, ever so light-footed. We looked in the other window. We saw him messing about in Anny's drawer. He took her bag out. He put the money in.'

Margaret's eyes fairly popped. 'You saw the whole thing? Why did you not come forward?'

Lucy glared at Margaret. 'Do you think I am a fool because I am not your equal?'

Margaret hurriedly shook her head. 'Oh no, no. I would never think that.'

'Then you mun know, miss, that it would do no good. Who would believe us, a maid and a stable boy? Who would even listen? And we would lose our jobs.'

'Yes, of course. You are right. I am sorry, Lucy.'

'It was awful, though. To see Anny taken away and locked up. And then her father gone. I know what it is like to lose a father and I feel sorrowful for Anny in a heartfelt way for that. I admired her, too. To come from that low place in life and work her way up like that. I feel dreadful about it all. Anny dunna deserve that, nobody good does. Master Cyril mun pay for what he did. But he never will. And Anny will be sent away across the ocean. Or hanged. It is the way of things. When my baby perished, I knew it was his fault, but I felt bad for it too, that it was *my* fault it died, by letting it slip out of me. It's like being careless, to lose hold of a child so easy, though I fought to save it, praying all the night through, that terrible night. Did it go to Heaven, my tiny babby's soul?

Surely it would, surely the Lord could not turn away such a small, innocent thing, despite the sins of the father and even those of the mother, myself. I felt a part of the fault, by working for this family, by staying on after Cyril's ruin of me, for swallowing up my guilt and pretending nothing had happened. But I told you afore, miss, these are the hard choices of the poor. I did my best to save my babby but it died anyway. I did my best for it. That will have to be enough on Judgement Day.'

Oh, the courage of this young woman. She was looking at Margaret that way again, that clear-eyed, honest stare. No tears now. They had all been shed many moons ago, she guessed. Lucy Arnett's fortitude shamed Margaret. Listening to her story, hearing those words of pain and survival changed Margaret forever. Something clicked in her head, a cog slotting into place, set in motion. 'No,' she said. 'No. We will not allow this.'

'We dunna have no choice.'

'Yes, yes, we do.' Her mind was moving fast now, possibility rushing like water over the wheel. 'Lucy, listen to me. You've said this to me before, that there is no chance for change, that this is the way the world works. Well, what if it didn't have to be that way? What if we could try, just one time, to change things? To make things better for everyone who counts? For Anny and for you. What would you say to that?'

'I would say they'd have me guts for garters.'

'Have faith, Lucy. If it fails, I shall give you money anyway. I shall leave it for you here, secretly, hidden in my room.'

'If what fails? What money? Are you mad, miss?'

Margaret lifted her head up. 'No. I am not. Now, listen carefully. For we are going to fix this. I have nothing to lose, as I am away this very night. And whatever happens, I promise that you will be free of this place. We are going to make that change and make things right. Do you believe me, Lucy? Do you trust me?'

Lucy narrowed her eyes at Margaret. 'Dunna go all round the Wrekin. Stop blethering and tell me. What's yer plan?'

Chapter 24

Queenie sat in her favourite chair in the drawing room. Her son Ralph sat opposite her, reading an illustrated paper of some sort, something cheap and thrilling, no doubt. He had not the wit to read books. Every so often, he would snort with amusement. Queenie watched him with her usual distaste. What a lonely thing it was to dislike your own child. Nobody understood, nobody except Jenkins. Ah, Jenkins. Her only confidante. If Jenkins ever left her . . . The thought was too much to bear! But Queenie was worried. There was talk in the house, gossip amongst the servants of how the Kings were responsible for the explosion. Queenie felt the danger of a great scandal unfolding and she smarted at this. She knew there would be plenty around these parts who would love to see the Kings in disarray. It was satisfying to the envious poor. The poor around these parts had suffered, indeed they had. But didn't the poor always suffer? Now the rich were getting some of it too. And nobody deserved to suffer more than this family, some may be saying. She knew her useless son would mismanage it, as always. She needed to keep her wits about her and step in. Something needed to be done, and soon. Reparation must be made, swiftly, to the affected families, the ones with dead and injured men and boys. There must be some sort of grand gathering, a service to honour the lives lost. She should meet with Brotherton and Pritchard on the morrow, to arrange these things and to talk about the future of the iron-works, now production at the furnace had been halted. The accounts must be scrutinised, money rerouted to other parts of the operation, new revenues of cash flow must be sought out. She had seen her son running about like a headless chicken, trying to solve the mess, but nothing had been decided, nothing achieved. It was her turn now. This could bring them down, destroy not only their reputation but the business itself.

The stark, bright image of Blaize's ghost appeared in her mind and gave her a chill. The curse would come true, if they weren't careful. This was just the kind of thing that destroyed good families. Well, not on her watch. Nothing must be allowed to threaten the King family reputation. Everything from then on must be about the limitation of the damage, stemming the flow and rebuilding their defences. The fortress of the Kings must not fall.

The drawing room door opened. Queenie did not look round, as she assumed it was Benjamina joining them – that indolent, lazy strumpet. But there was not the whiff of Benjamina's sickly perfume. Instead, two sets of footsteps came across the hard floor and onto the rug before her. There stood Margaret and another figure, one of the maids. Queenie had heard that Margaret had been to Shrewsbury again that day. The last time she took the barouche without asking, all hell broke loose, but her son was so preoccupied with his own troubles these days, he barely noticed what the girl was up to. Queenie had noticed, though, and had made her mind up to call her granddaughter in the following day and discuss these reckless trips to Shrewsbury to see the Woodvine girl. All right, the girl's father had been killed and that couldn't be helped. But it was not seemly for the King daughter to be involved any more than was necessary. That was something else on her list: take Margaret in hand. The child needed a husband, and soon.

Ralph looked up, peeved to be interrupted. 'What is this?'

Margaret spoke first, the servant girl standing with her hands clasped behind her back, eyes down. Queenie felt unsettled. Something was not right here.

'Grandmother, Father, I must speak with you both.'

'Arnett, is it?' said Queenie, fixing her eye on the servant girl. She was always good with servants' names, prided herself on it.

The girl looked up, not wide-eyed and fearful as Queenie expected, but she looked straight at her, direct and steady. 'Yes, ma'am.'

'What is the meaning of this?' spluttered Ralph.

'It concerns Cyril,' said Margaret. 'I have approached you both before to voice my concerns about my brother's behaviour. I have told you both that I was convinced of Cyril's guilt in the matter of the theft of money from the safe. But my concerns were dismissed and Anny Woodvine remains imprisoned for a crime she did not commit.'

'This again,' said Ralph in a low, threatening voice. Queenie saw her son's hackles rise. Would he strike the girl? Possibly not in front of a servant. This was something the King men liked to imagine was done in private, though word always got around. But whatever Margaret had suffered from her father in the past, it did not stop her now. Queenie saw her turn her gaze on her father, unintimidated and determined.

'Yes, this again, Father. But now we have a witness. Lucy Arnett, a maidservant of this household who has served us faithfully for many years. She has something to impart to you both. And I urge you to listen to what she has to say.'

'Get out,' said Ralph simply, placing his reading material on the settee beside him, looking about ready to leap up and box both their ears.

'No,' said Queenie. Ralph glared at her. 'Let them speak. I am curious.'

'The very idea . . .' began Ralph.

'They will be heard. In these trying times, the whole community in mourning, never let it be said that the

Kings do not listen to reason, that we are too far above the common fray to at least let them be heard. Proceed, Arnett. Tell us what you wish to say.'

Ralph puffed and shuffled in his seat, his anger barely contained. But Queenie could see that he was caught in the trap of having to appease the neighbourhood, and this servant girl was one of theirs, so he had to resist, for appearances' sake. 'Arnett, go on. Say your piece.'

The girl had her wary eye on Ralph, her body stiff with tension. She turned to Queenie, and there came that clear look again. She began to speak, no hint of a wobble in her voice. Queenie was convinced in that moment that anything this girl had to say was the truth, no doubt whatsoever.

'On the day that Anny Woodvine was arrested, Master Cyril sent for me. This was first thing in the morning. He told me to take a message to Mr Brotherton, that he should go to town for ink. He said the message had come from Mrs King senior. From yourself, ma'am.'

'Did he now?' said Queenie. What a fool Cyril was, involving her. Anyone in the household would know she would never send Cyril to do such a thing. Why would she need that idiot boy, when she had Jenkins?

'Yes, he did, ma'am. He surely did. He said to make sure that Mr Brotherton himself was sent to town to fetch the ink, green ink, for you, ma'am. Then he said, very certain like, that I was not to tell anyone that it was

346

him that gave me the message. That if I was ever asked about it, I shouldna mention his name and I should say that Mrs – that is, you, ma'am – were the one that gave me the message for Mr Brotherton. Well, I did as I was asked and delivered the message. Then, the stable boy, Paddy, came to see me soon after. He was worried about summat. He said Master Cyril had been to see him earlier, had told him to take a message to the office, that Anny Woodvine must go to the library and wait on you, sir.'

Queenie was even more impressed with Arnett, now that she had had the nerve to address Ralph directly, despite his barely contained rage. She liked this girl. She liked any girl with spirit.

Arnett continued, 'Paddy was worried because he knew you were out all that day, sir, because he'd seen you go himself, up before the larks. He liked Anny, did Paddy, and he didna want to think of her alone in the library waiting for you, sir, when you were never going to come. Well, not till hours away, leastways. I told him not to interfere with family business and get on with his job. But after, I went back into the house and I saw Master Cyril go into your study, sir, and he came out holding your keys, sir, and he went off towards the office. Why would Master Cyril do all this? Why did he send those messages from you, ma'am, and from you, sir, that were not true? And why would he take the keys to the office from your room, sir? Why would he do all that?'

'You were spying on my grandson, then?' said Queenie.

'Servants dunna need to spy, when things are done before their very eyes. Servants are invisible to gentlefolk sometimes, so they say. But we do see things, ma'am, sir. We see things and we know things.'

This last statement hung heavy in the air like cigar smoke. Arnett waited. King, red-faced, looked at Queenie.

Margaret said, 'Go on, Lucy. Tell them what happened next.'

'So, Paddy and I, we were worried about what it all meant. We were suspicious. You must forgive us our cheek but we thought we should follow him, follow Master Cyril and see what he was about. So we did. We crept behind and saw him. He went into the office. We peeked through the windows. He took the money from the safe and he put it in Anny Woodvine's bag. Paddy and I saw him do it, clear as day.'

Queenie said, 'And why did you not speak up before now? If this were true, you should have said something before the Woodvine girl was taken away. Why have you waited so long for the truth to be shared, if it is indeed the truth and not some tale of your own devising?'

Queenie was bluffing. She had not one shred of doubt that the girl was speaking plainly. Margaret answered for her: 'I have encouraged her to speak out now but I'm sure we all know that, without my support in this matter, it is a universal truth that servants are not listened to. That they fear being dismissed over any hint of disloyalty to their masters. Lucy did not say anything about this before as she feared losing her job. She cannot afford to do so, as she has a widowed mother to support.'

Ralph spluttered, 'The perfect excuse for blackmail then, this sob story about her poor mother! Throwing false accusations of theft at my son!'

'It is not false. And he has done worse than theft,' said Arnett. The courage of the girl! Queenie was eager to hear more from her, but a creeping sense of unease caused her to shiver. What more was there? What else had she to tell of Cyril King?

Margaret placed her hand tenderly on Arnett's arm. 'Shall I . . . ?' Margaret began. For the first time, Arnett appeared to falter. She blinked rapidly and looked down at her shoes. She nodded.

Margaret said bluntly, 'Cyril raped Lucy. Many times. He gave her a child. The child died . . . before birth . . . and the whole thing was covered up by Jenkins.'

Jenkins? What had Jenkins to do with this? Queenie was certain Jenkins would have told her of such a thing. But now she regarded this girl, who had raised her head and was looking now at Margaret, her eyes steady again, her back straight. She knew it was true. She knew that Jenkins had hidden it from her to protect her. Queenie felt sickened. Another girl's life ruined. Another hateful crime perpetrated by the King men.

'This is slander of the worst . . .'

'Shut up, Ralph.'

'There is no proof of this!' he cried. 'Just the word of a common slut below stairs!'

Margaret stepped forward towards her father and pointed at him. 'You are wrong. There are many in this house that know this to be true. Paddy the stable boy saw Cyril take the money. And Jenkins, Grandmother's own trusted lady's maid cleared up the bloody remains of this girl's dead child, of your son's dead child. When will you stop protecting him, when you know him to be rotten to the core?'

Ralph cried, 'Never! I will never stop protecting my only son!'

Queenie saw the situation getting out of hand. 'Now then, we must remain calm.' But Margaret was not listening.

'And that is your greatest failing. Cyril is rotten through and through. But even if you cannot see that, know this: if word of this gets out, this family's name will be mud. The explosion at the furnace already has our reputation in tatters. The careless death of our men is already a disaster for investors and clients. And I know you were responsible. You knowingly used materials that were inferior and were sure to lead to an accident. It was only a matter of time. And if the truth comes out of Cyril as a thief, a liar and a rapist, our name will be destroyed. Cyril King is this family's heir. He must make a good marriage and produce his own heir. What decent family in their right mind would willingly offer a large dowry and wed their daughter to Cyril King, with stories like this on everyone's lips? Bad blood, they will say. Those Kings have bad blood. We all know this family has a history of abusing young women, and it is only a matter of time before more secrets come out. And the name of King will always be spat out, like a bitter taste on the tongue. If you do nothing to remedy this, you, Father and you, Grandmother, then you leave us with no choice. We will speak the truth, far and wide. And make no mistake. This house will fall!'

Those four words shocked Queenie rigid. She felt her body seize up, pinning her to her seat. How did Margaret know of this? Had the ghost visited her too? But she could see that the child was not looking knowingly at her. She was incensed with a hatred of her father, her brother, of all the Kings. Margaret had turned. She would not care if her name were ruined, if indeed the house and everything in it fell to the ground. She would never give up on this and her determination alone would ruin their name, if the truth did not do it by itself. If Queenie dismissed these children and their threats, the curse of Betsy Blaize would come to pass.

'I never thought I'd . . .' began Ralph, too stupid even now to see how close they all were to ruin.

'Silence!' Queenie cried, her strength mustered and returning admirably, now, when she needed it. Her son

351

stopped. He might make a noise about being the master, but everyone knew it was Queenie who ruled this roost. 'There will be no more argument. It is clear now how things proceeded. You, Arnett. I suspect you do not want to stay in this house, but of course you will be in need of employment. I will write you an excellent reference, but it will be best for all if you leave our employ as soon as you are able. I will give you three months' wages and a bonus, if you will leave tonight and never mention any detail of this again.'

The maid looked her in the eye and nodded. 'Agreed.'

'Good,' said Queenie and turned away.

'On one condition,' said Arnett.

'You are in no position . . .' began Queenie.

But the maid interrupted her. 'That they let Anny Woodvine go. You can do that, sir, ma'am. I know if you drop those charges against her, they'll set her free. That's my condition.'

'And mine, too,' added Margaret. 'Anny must be released. If you drop the charges, Father, and Anny is freed, with no stain about her name, and if Lucy is given a good reference and the wages you suggest, Grandmother, then and only then will we keep our silence about these crimes of Cyril. We shall never speak of them more.'

Queenie smiled at Margaret with begrudging admiration. Despite her distasteful threats, Queenie was pleased her granddaughter was coming into her own, at last. She wondered what the girl would do with this new-found confidence. Ralph clearly did not feel the same way about his daughter. He huffed, threw his hands up in the air, then folded his arms tightly. He had lost his voice all of a sudden, but let out a kind of frustrated whine. What a wretched man he was. But no matter. It was the old sow who would make this decision, not the squealing piglet.

'It shall be done,' said Queenie. 'You are dismissed, both of you.'

Her granddaughter was grinning at Arnett. Was this all a game to her? True, she was proud of Margaret for finding her backbone, but the girl had turned traitor to her own family. God knows Queenie had hated the Kings at times over the years, but never had she been a turncoat. There were rules about such things. These young ones these days had no sense of duty or honour. But these two had the Kings in a pickle and a deal had to be done. Margaret and Arnett left the room. She heard them talk excitedly outside. She never thought she'd live to see the day when servants and family plotted together and crowed about it. All except her and Jenkins, of course. They had their own rules.

'Mother, this is a travesty. How can you support such lies?'

'So, now you speak. Once the children are gone.'

'I would not deign to argue like fishwives before them. But now you and I will have this out. What can you be thinking, giving in to their demands? It's a disgrace! Never in all his years would Father have accepted such a thing.'

Queenie looked at her son and heard his wheedling voice, as she might watch a fly buzzing against a window, aware of its struggle but having no pity for it, just annoyance at its noise.

She said simply, 'We will agree to it. They are not lies, as well you know.'

'We do not know that.'

Queenie sighed. She had no time for nonsense. 'Cyril is capable of all this and far worse. Let us not pretend, not to each other. And the girl is right. The scandal of it all coming out would ruin us, coming after the monumental mess you made at the furnace.'

'That was an accident! How many times do I . . .'

'Do not pretend with me, my son. It is your mother who listens to your pathetic protestations. All of this is your fault. Penny-pinching and lack of forethought. Spoiling that wretched boy and not attending to his rotten behaviour earlier. Yet the fault lies not only at your door. I blame myself, too. I should have been more vigilant. I have not been myself these past years. But all that will change now. I am taking control again.'

Ralph stood up and loomed over her. But even this physical show of strength had no impact on her. She saw him only as he once was, red-faced in short trousers, throwing himself on the floor in a tantrum. 'You are not yourself!' he spat at her. 'You are quite right. You have lost your mind. And if you insist on allowing those two little sluts to blackmail us, I'll send you away. I will denounce you, you and your traitorous granddaughter. You're all the same. Just like your crazy sister.'

Queenie had heard such threats before. But she had her own plan now for how to waylay that one. 'Oh, you could try, Ralph King. You could try. But first, consider this. Not only would your mother and daughter be denouncing your lying, thieving, raping son. They would then be tainted with the poison of madness. Who would marry into the King family then?'

'I don't need you or them, any of you! I have a new, young wife who adores me!'

'Ha!' crowed Queenie. 'Your weakest strike yet. Everyone knows Benjamina does not allow you to bed her these days. Even if you did manage to breed, it would still have tainted blood if this all comes out.'

Queenie thought her son might strike her then. His cheeks, always a little purplish due to his debauched state of health, seemed to darken further, as did his hateful eyes. But he said nothing. He had nothing to say. Everything she said was true.

'And furthermore, if you threaten me again with the asylum, never forget that I have the controlling interest in the business and of this house. And I will sell. I will sell my percentage of the ironworks and I will even sell Southover if I have to. I will do so and go to live abroad, alone.'

Ralph's chin actually dropped. He hadn't seen that one coming. 'And you know how useless you are at managing this business. You would never manage with a new partner, who would see through your incompetence in a flash. And the thought of you trailing behind me and coming to live abroad is ridiculous. You are not an adventurous man, Ralph. You never have been. Always lazy, always useless. A life of indolence and luxury is all you are fit for.'

He was staring at the floor now, his eyes dazed. He muttered, 'Because of you. If I am a useless son, then it is your fault. You are the mother. You should have loved me more.'

Was there a tear in his eye? This gave Queenie pause, but only momentarily. Ralph King senior had taught her the value of a heart of stone. 'Love did not make us rich. Love did not raise the Kings above all others in Ironbridge and its environs. Your father knew that. I know it. And so do you. Look at your children. They hate you. Everyone does. But it is no matter. The business remains, the money remains and the name of King remains. You cannot manage without me. You never have. This latest disaster is proof of it. You can't pass it on to your son either, as he is as bad as you – worse, if that's possible.

No, you need me to run this for you, or you will drive this business into the ground. My mourning period for your father is done. I am coming back to take over the business. I am stronger than ever. I will not require anything of you other than to behave yourself and spend our money, when I give it to you. Cyril must be left in Germany until all whispers of this scandal have passed. Margaret must be taken in hand and married off as soon as we are able. Now, all you need to do is inform the magistrate that you wish to withdraw the charge of theft against Anny Woodvine. Do it immediately and insist it be acted upon with haste. Now go.'

Ralph had nothing left to fight with, no words to use as weapons. He was a fool at times, but he knew when he was beaten. He summoned as much dignity as he could to stand and then said pompously, 'I shall inform the magistrate that I wish to withdraw the charge of theft against Anny Woodvine,' as if it were his own idea, all along. With that, he walked sedately from the room.

Queenie's head fell forward. She felt utterly shattered. She would call for dear Jenkins in a minute, but not yet. She did not want her son to see her in need. She had to appear fearless now. But she was not fearless. She looked at her hands to see them trembling. She thought, *Is it enough?* Would paying off Cyril's victim and saving this poor girl from prison be enough? From now on, every act must serve to save the name of King and to atone for their past sins. She congratulated herself for taking control of this latest drama. Every decision she made must serve the aim to prevent the fall of the house of King. But still Queenie wondered. The image of the white-haired spirit beside her husband's grave sprang up in her weary mind. *Would it be enough to appease the ghost of Betsy Blaize?*

Chapter 25

Margaret and Jake were married a day after they had
arrived in Paris, in a shabby little church with strangers
for witnesses. Their honeymoon was a stay in a mangy
hotel for a few nights. He quickly found them an apart-
ment owned by a musician friend of his who was off
travelling: two rooms, above a butcher's. They had so
little, but Margaret had never been happier. And Paris,
beautiful Paris, its thronging streets alive with liberty,
did not disappoint. Their early days were spent together,
in and out of cafés and bistros, sipping bowls of coffee
and chocolate, feasting on sweet, sticky pastries and
crusty bread spread thickly with apricot jam or honey.
They ate tiny sardines in oil mashed onto toasted bread,
chicken in a rich red sauce or beef with tiny onions and
whole cloves of the stinking yet succulent garlic. The
Kings kept a good table, but the food of Paris was a riot
of taste and colour like nothing she'd ever consumed
before. Her days were spent walking and kissing and
eating, her evenings spent in more feasting and drinking with his artist friends, she sipping the local wine,

careful with the quantity, as she was not used to it. But Jake and his friends guzzled it down nightly, until they could barely walk. To trip along a dark Paris street long after midnight and giggle herself hoarse at the antics of Jake and his drunken friends – what larks! Never had she laughed so much in her life!

Those who were still not too far gone would come back to their little room, or they would go to friends' apartments and chat and read till the dawn chorus brought her to the window to see the pink light of day seeping into the dark skies. One of Jake's friends loved to read and Margaret scoured his bookshelves, taking down favourite French novels she had read and discussing them with him. Sometimes she spoke in French, soon realising her language was a little bookish and rusty. They laughed at her, but good-naturedly, as at least she tried. Jake's French was hopeless and they appreciated her making the effort. She quickly learnt some of the new street lingo and felt more at home in the language as the days and nights passed. Another friend had a piano in his room and Margaret delighted them with Mozart and Beethoven, as much as her fingers could remember through the fog of memory and wine. She was a good player and many said so, that she should perform, that she should teach them, or their sisters, or their children, or the children of friends and family. It occurred to her that this could be a way for her to support Jake, to give lessons and charge for it. To earn her own money would be quite something – utter freedom! As she played, she became lost in the music and delighted with her talent, now properly appreciated. They applauded her and asked for more; they laughed with her and talked to her. For the first time in her life, she felt at home in society. There was no small talk, only discussions of literature, art and music. She was a small-town girl come to the big city, yet still she held her own in these talks, citing books she had read and music she loved. She listened to their knowledge of painting and sculpture, drinking it all in, learning new ideas from them as a child gulps milk. At Southover, she had grown up in an icy, loveless existence consisting of confinement and bullying. Now she was bathing in the warmth of Paris, her whims indulged and satisfied, her voice heard and answered, her thoughts echoed and delighted in. She had found a place where she belonged.

Jake and Margaret were quite the couple, celebrated as the romantic duo who had escaped their families' old-fashioned expectations and eloped to Paris. They were welcomed everywhere and kissed on both cheeks, hugged and sang to, spoken about and spoken to, every day and night. The Margaret of her childhood would have run in horror from such extremes of companionship, but she revelled in it. And then there was Jake. Kissing had seemed the height of glory, until she had felt him inside her, truly inside her and the feeling of completeness was so overwhelming, she often cried real tears during their lovemaking. She felt life would be like this forever, an endless whirl of bed and parties, wine and laughter. It was intoxicating, unsettling and sometimes scarily out of control, but it was so utterly different from her previous life as to be as addictive as opium.

But the months passed, and sex, parties and wine couldn't make up for the increasing hollowness in the rest of their life together. There was no purpose or direction to their existence. Only chaos prevailed. And she felt Jake was drawing away from her. He began to go out alone much of the time, armed with his sketching book and pencils. She found herself walking the streets looking for greenery, a park or a stream, or even a tree, but there was precious little of it in this part of the city. He would come back hours later, often drunk, often denying it, saying how the muse had left him, shouting about it and throwing himself down in despair. She tried to comfort him, but he was inconsolable. He said the muse had abandoned him, ever since . . . but he wouldn't finish those sentences and she knew he meant ever since the elopement. It racked her with remorse, that through her desire to possess him, she was robbing him of his gift. To assuage her guilt, she would give him money from the roll of cash she had in a stocking hidden in a drawer, and he would disappear again for hours. The night she ran away from Ironbridge, she had stolen the money from her father's safe. It seemed a vast amount – and appeared to double in size when it was changed into French currency – and she was certain it would last them for years, that they would live the high life until Jake's undoubted talent would catch the eye of a Parisian gallery owner and his artistic career would be made. But he seemed to be spending most of it on drink. And the money was running out so quickly, too quickly. She knew he was taking from it when she wasn't looking. She knew he was spending it on drinking, and who knew what else.

In the long evenings she spent alone, when he had not come home at all since lunchtime, she would think of the library back home – why had she not brought any English books with her? She missed the sight of her own language on the page. She would think of the woods and the River Severn – why did the city feel like death to her, when home had been so full of life, of living things all around her? She even missed the sound of the steam hammer, booming through the trees, marking out time, to be replaced here by the clattering of coaches and hooves, the shouts of street sellers and arguing couples – exotic and exciting at first, harsh and jangling now.

When he did take her out with his friends, she tired of the constant drinking and began to stop after a glass. But Jake showed no signs of abatement and, if anything, drank more than before. And Jake was not a jovial drunk. His artist friends – who she now began to see in a new light, a ramshackle lot, all come to France to waste away their talent through strong drink and carousing – began to warn her about him. Night after night, one or other would come to her laughing, saying colourful and unsettling things about him, such as, 'You've bagged yourself a blackguard there, Miss Margaret', and 'Don't try to cage him like an animal. He'll tear your throat out.'

Then, only three months after their arrival, she had stopped bleeding. She was vomiting each morning and felt drained all day. It was Jake who explained it to her. She was with child. She felt so woefully uneducated and unprepared. She stopped drinking wine as it made her feel worse. Suddenly, without the drink to fog her mind, she saw her life for what it was. And she did not like it.

Chapter 26

Anny's father had walked these miles between Shrewsbury and Ironbridge in one morning. But he had been strong as an ox and tall as a tree. Anny was weakened by her months inside and the minimal rations. The gaol fever that had floored her for weeks was gone, but that had taken a lot out of her too. She used to bound up the forest paths with an innate knowledge of how strong her young legs were, how far they'd take her. She remembered feeling invincible, that she would never tire, never falter, never die even. The folly of youth, that they think they shall live forever. One bad turn of circumstance and the body crumbles. It was frightening how quickly that could happen. She had been a little plump once, a curve to her hips and limbs that was pleasing to the male eye, though she'd sometimes wished to be more svelte and slim like some girls. Now the flesh had dropped from her body and she was skin and bone. It was November, and it was cold. Her body gave her no comfort and she shivered as she walked.

Leaving the prison had been nothing like Anny had imagined. No family to greet her, no friends to ferry her home. The prison warden hadn't let her leave till the afternoon and her progress on the road to Ironbridge was slow. She had little natural sense of direction and had to wait around for passers-by to ask at various junctions of roads if she were on the right path. She had a vision of wandering around in circles for the rest of her life, until she dropped in exhaustion. It was good to be outside, though. She'd rather die on the road than in that vermin-infested hospital. A man died in there one night and the surgeon didn't come till morning and the rats were already on him by the time they came to take the body away. The smell was still in her nostrils, the rich and heady variety of prison stench. She wondered if she'd ever lose it. As she walked, slowly, she breathed deeply, taking in the scents of fresh, new air, winter greenery and earth.

People used to delight her. She had once loved to be in crowded places, like the fair at Christmastime or the May Day dancing, surrounded by the excitement of new faces and the buzz of humanity. Now, people disgusted her. She had seen bodies and minds at their most degraded. Peggy had told her once of a book about a man who travelled to foreign lands and met giants and midgets and also intelligent horses who had people as beasts roaming around on all fours. That writer must have been inside a gaol. Thoughts of Peggy. Yes, well, she did not wish to think of Peggy.

She'd had no word from home since that day. She'd not heard from Peggy or Brotherton – not surprising, but still. Nothing from Jake, of course. Most worryingly, nothing from Mother. It had been four months since her father's death. Two months since she had been called into the warden's office and informed that the charges had been dropped and she would soon leave. She had told no one. She'd heard of prisoners bragging about release and then being beaten or even murdered by inmates or guards, as a kind of revenge and punishment, as if to say, *You're not getting away that lightly; you must suffer, as we do*. She kept it quiet. Instead she lived as much inside her own head as she could, in a time before all pain, where she washed clothes with her mother and ran to take her father's lunch. That was when it all started, with Mr Lakelin's death. If she'd not written a note to her father, Pritchard would not have noticed how clever she was. She should have refused Pritchard's request, should have said no to Brotherton, should have stayed at home with Mother. Everything would have been different, everything would have been better, if she hadn't got ideas above her station. It was all her fault. Well, she'd learnt her lesson. As she trudged along the road home, she knew her life would not aspire to be anything more than it was. That way pain and madness lay.

She had to sleep on the roadside that night. She had no food, no money. She asked the guard at the gate about her earnings while she'd been in prison, her promised earnings of a penny a week for this or that duty, more for her washing work and her role as monitor. He laughed at her. She was packed off in someone else's shabby dress, too short, halfway up the leg and too tight under the arms. No bonnet. A tatty shawl with holes in it. She looked like a ragamuffin. Her smart work clothes she'd been brought in wearing had gone, probably sold on by the guards. Her boots pinched and by nightfall she had red raw skin where her heels should have been. She found a quiet road with woodland running along it on one side, fields on the other. She went behind a little copse of trees, so that she could not be seen from the road. She didn't want any unwelcome attention from travellers. It was a bitter night. She did not sleep. Her body was racked with quaking.

When dawn came thinly, she pulled her boots back on and cried out at the blisters. The sky above was luminous, a bright yellow-grey that promised snow. The wind whipped up. There were few people on the roads. All sensible folk were inside. Carriages rumbled past and she barely looked up. She had to keep going, keep going, keep going. She had to get home. Snow began falling; bright flecks of ice lashed by the wind into her face, hair, eyelashes, sticky and wet. She was afraid, very afraid her body would not hold out and she would collapse there, in the deepening snow and simply die, a few miles from home. To come so far, to be so near. No, no, that would not be her fate. She willed herself onwards and banished all thought but the movement forward, onwards, home. One foot before the other. Her whole existence was reduced to her feet.

It was the afternoon of the second day when she saw the iron bridge. She did not turn and look up at the King house. She went down the slippery steps to the riverside and stumbled, nearly falling into the high, broad river. It had not frozen over yet, though it might if this cold grew and lasted the winter through. The water was churning beneath the roiling blizzard, confusing her eye with its complex movement. She felt she might faint, but she closed her eyes and recovered herself. Then she forced herself onwards. So close now, so close. Her collection of houses came into view and she saw her parents' cottage and cried out with relief, sobbing and muttering as she approached. The door was shut against the cold and she fell against it, banging with her fist.

'Mother,' she cried. 'Mother, Mother!'

Anny had slumped to the ground and fell inwards as the door opened.

'Mother,' she whispered, but when she looked up, there was a man with a big black moustache staring at her.

'Get away with yer!' he said.

'Mother,' she whispered again. She heard voices from inside the house. They were asking who it was.

'Some vagabond. There's nothing for you here. Get away with yer, I say,' said the man and began to shove her from the door.

'Anny?' A different voice came from behind her, away from the house. 'Is that you, Anny?'

Her name. She had not heard her name spoken in so long. At the prison, they called her Woodvine or Theft or worse, much worse. The door to her parents' house was shoved shut against her and she turned deliriously in the direction of the voice.

'Bless my soul, it's Anny Woodvine,' it said. It was a woman's voice. 'Peter, Peter! Come quickly! It's Rachel's daughter.'

There were arms about her, strong male arms and the whiff of coal dust. She was lifted from the ground and felt her head falling backwards over an arm, the snowflakes rushing into her face, into her mouth and landing on her tongue. The rest was a blur that melted into sleep, a restless sleep filled with nightmares of falling through ice into the river, being swept along by the current and banging her fists in vain upon its frozen ceiling, watching the white sky looking down upon her as she drowned.

She awoke in a bed, tucked up in sheets and blankets. Her eyes were crusted with the sleep of many days. Her feet were bound with bandages. Her filthy dress was gone and she was clothed in a cosy, long-sleeved

370

nightdress of soft material. Her hair was clean and smelled of soap. Was this heaven? It felt like heaven. Warmth and comfort. It was evening or night-time, the room flickering with candlelight. She had a dim memory of being sat up and liquid being spooned into her mouth. Was that a dream?

'Anny,' came a voice, the same voice she'd heard at her mother's door.

'Where is my mother?' she said, her voice croaky through disuse.

A face came into view, an older face, about the same age as her mother, but not her mother.

'Dunna fret, lass,' said the woman and smiled. She sat down on the bed and passed her cool, dry hand over Anny's forehead.

'Is my mother dead?' said Anny. The moment she said it, she realised that had been her greatest fear, lying beneath the surface as she slept.

'No, lass! No, she's all right. But she dunna live here no more.'

Anny focused her eyes on the woman's face. 'I know you,' she said.

'I know you do, lass. I'm your neighbour. You remember my son, dunna you?'

Another face appeared, standing tall above the bed. It was a local lad who'd tried to woo her once, many moons ago. He smiled at her. It was a kind face. Two kind faces.

'Mrs Mary Malone,' said Anny. 'And Peter Malone.'

Anny did not have the strength to say more. Seeing the faces of their old neighbours had the most peculiar effect on her; she felt as if she were tumbling down a hole, a dark, earthy descent into her childhood. When she landed, she curled up in a hollow, snug and warm and content. Her eyes glazed over and closed. She drifted into a deep sleep. Safe, at last.

Chapter 27

They called it the quickening, that odd fluttering sensation when the unborn child could first be felt inside the mother. Margaret had read that in a novel once and loved the term. The idea that the woman was quick with child, that it was making its presence known. It began for her on a quiet Sunday morning. She was lying on the hard, rough cot they slept in below the small, high window, the only window in the room. If she stood up on the bed and peeked out of the window, she could look out across the grey roofs, chimneys, skylights and domes of Paris, stretching out as a jumbled vista that seemed romantic at first, oppressive now. Jake was sprawled out on the floor, not having made it to the bed the night before. She looked across at him. Even snoring open-mouthed, his hair greasy with sweat and plastered across his face, she still felt the old desire lift in her. But something else was there, deep down inside and it wasn't calling for him. It was the quickening.

'Oh, my life!' she said aloud, then checked herself, as she did not wish to wake her husband.

They'd had a fearful row the night before. It wasn't the first.

Looking back on the past few months, she realised the cracks had begun to show from the earliest days, though she had chosen to ignore them. On the journey across the channel he thought of his own comfort before hers in every regard and she allowed him to, feeling comfort in comforting him. She overlooked his selfishness in a hundred tiny ways every day, but once she was with child, her feelings on this changed. Jake was still her world, but there was a newcomer there. And as the life grew inside her, her thoughts were filled with her baby and not with her husband. He was annoyed that she was not obsessing over him anymore. He would pout and say she did not love him. She would throw her arms about him and kiss him and kiss him, asking how could he say such things, when she waited for him every day impatient for his company. This he would take offence at, saying she was trying to trap him and must he stay there every day to hear her nonsense and not be off living life, painting life, as he ought to be? She would caress his hair and try to calm him, tell him how talented and clever he was, and he would be assuaged, sometimes. But there was truly no pleasing him.

So it went on, these endless squabbles about how hard his life was, how little she understood him, how selfish she was. He began to shrink in stature before her very eyes. The morning she felt the quickening, she lay and watched him sleep for hours. The night before had been their worst row yet. Some horrible home truths had come out. She had accused him of taking her money too much, too often and what were they to do when it ran out? What about things for the baby, and what about their future?

The conversation was still fresh in her mind, the wounds it inflicted still felt in her heart.

'Our future is taken care of,' said Jake dismissively, taking another gulp of wine.

Did he mean his art? She had not seen him do a painting since they'd arrived, and his sketches were few and far between these days. He had never sold a picture, in all the time she'd known him.

'In what way?' she asked, carefully, not wishing to anger him.

'We will return to your father's house, of course. With a child in your belly, all will be forgiven and we shall live in style in Shropshire. I have in mind a little gallery in the town. I met a fellow in Ironbridge who loved the idea. We'll need your father's capital to set it up. I'm just waiting for you to get a bit fatter and then we'll go.'

'But . . . I stole from my father. All that money. He'll never forgive me.'

'Oh, yes he will. He just needs to see with his own eyes the condition you're in. What with the marriage certificate and my gift of the gab and your poor little victim act, that'll sway him. Then once your family are in the bag, I shall present you – ripe belly and King fortune – to my father and he shall welcome me as the prodigal son. We shall have his blessing and money, too. It'll all work out, you'll see.'

Margaret was horrified. 'But I do not wish to return to my family. I hate my family. I thought you understood that.'

'Oh, what rot! Did you think we'd live in this hole forever, little mouse? This is a holiday for us. But we must go back. We have to get what's rightly ours.'

'I would welcome the idea of visiting your family. But I never want to see mine again. Can we not do that, and just avoid my old life altogether?'

It seemed perfectly reasonable to her and she quite liked the idea of meeting his parents and seeing his family home in Birmingham, enjoying a hot drink in one of his father's coffee houses. It must be better than this miserable life, at any rate.

'Don't be a bloody fool,' he said. 'I can't go home empty-handed.'

'But you won't be. You shall have me. And our child.'

'That's not enough! I can't go back without a rich wife, he told me so, in no uncertain terms. A rich wife or to make my fortune by my art. Well, the latter will never happen, that's clear to me now. So, a rich wife it must be. And you are rich. You just need to bend the knee to your dear papa and grandmamma and all will be well. And all manner of things will be well!'

He was swigging back the wine now, his speech slurring, his cheeks red and his forehead shining with sweat.

'I won't do it,' she said quietly.

He turned a cold eye on her. 'Oh, yes, you will, mouse.'

'You can't make me,' she said, feeling she sounded like a recalcitrant child. But she meant it all the same.

He stood up swiftly and staggered, the speed making him dizzy. Margaret didn't know what he would do next. She eyed the door and thought of how she could get to it and evade his reach. He recovered himself and lurched towards her. She made a break for it, but he grabbed her and fell on her, his dead weight pinning her to the wooden floorboards.

'The child!' she cried.

'Shut up! Shut up!' he was spitting in her ear. 'I never wanted you, you simpering little bitch. I wanted the redhead more. She had something about her. By God, I wanted the local whores more than I ever wanted you. Even your stepmother, that brainless slut, was better in bed than you.'

He heaved himself up and slapped her hard across the face, the effort of it making him fall sideways and bang his head on the floor with an almighty crack. All was quiet. As she struggled away, sobbing and holding her belly protectively, she heard him moaning. Not dead, then. He muttered a few incomprehensible sounds then turned on his side and slept like an infant. Heartsick, she put her hand to her cheek. Whores? Anny? Benjamina? What a fool she'd been. She thought of all the times a man had hit her: her brother, her father and now her husband. And she decided, enough was enough. She made herself a promise: never again would a man strike her.

That was last night. Now, she felt her baby's fluttering movements inside her and it seemed like a clarion call. She looked again at her husband. So, he had bedded Benjamina. He had wanted to bed Anny. He had been with prostitutes. He had never wanted her, never loved her. He was a drunk and a failure. Despite everything, she could not hate him. He was her first love. Or rather, she could not hate the man she had fallen in love with. But the man lying down there was not that man. He had never existed and was a fiction of her own making. It was astonishing, how completely one could invent a life and believe it to be true.

This life was over, she knew that now. As quiet as the mouse he named her, she stood. She dressed. She found her money and packed a few essentials into a carpet bag. She left her husband sleeping on the floor. Descending the spiral staircase, the smell of dead animals growing stronger with every step, she marvelled at how stupid she had been, how naive and reckless. She thought, *A bigger fool there never was upon this earth*. She resigned herself to making the best of her disappointing and difficult life ahead, her growing babe inside her at least being a source of joy.

But as she thought of her unborn child, she recalled how her father and brother had always called her the weakling strain of the family. She wanted at that moment to prove them wrong, to never live down to the King family's low expectations of poor little Margaret, the poor little mouse. She thought for a moment of her pointless education, how she could play the piano well and could speak French. Perhaps it wasn't so pointless after all. She could try teaching English and piano to French children, just as their artist friends had suggested. It was a tall order, for an Englishwoman on her own to make her way in a foreign country. Margaret felt her baby quickening inside her again and it spurred her on, out into the street. She was encouraged too by her memories of Anny's strength and bravery. She still blamed herself for Anny's ruin. And she realised that their friendship might have been Anny's downfall, but it was the very making of herself. Fuelled by her determination to prove her family wrong and her admiration for the strength of her lost friend, she walked away from her husband and into the Paris morning, full of hope and the resolve to make a life for herself, without the Kings, without Jake, without anyone but herself and her child. She would do it; she would be strong and she would survive. Anny had taught her how.

Chapter 28

In the time after her salvation, Anny was feverish. She was aware only of sips of water and the gentle touch of a cool cloth about her face. Days or weeks passed; she had no way of telling. A day came when she felt brighter and wanted to say something. She watched her saviours pottering about their tiny house and she said, 'Thank you.'

They turned round to look at her and came to her, smiling at each other.

'Do you know your own name?' said the woman.

'Anny.'

'And mine?' said the young man.

'Dunna fuss the wench, son!'

'Peter,' said Anny. 'And Mary.'

'That's right,' said Mary.

'Malone. Mary and Peter Malone,' added Anny.

'Nothing wrong with your memory then,' said Mary. 'Glad to see it. You were in a terrible state when we found you. But I'm glad to see you're still all there. I'll get you some soup and Peter will sit and talk with you, wonna you, Peter?'

She went off to the kitchen table. Peter drew up a stool and sat down beside the bed. He looked awkward but willing. His arms were ingrained with coal dust. A miner, then.

'You used to work at the forge,' said Anny.

'I did, but I didna wanna stay there after . . .' He trailed off.

'After what?'

Peter looked round at his mother. He was tall and strapping, his arms muscular, his neck thick and his face well formed with high cheekbones. They were around the same age, him and herself, yet she'd not mixed much with the neighbours since she'd started working at the big house. What a fool she'd been. What fine friendships she could have had. He'd grown into a man since the last time she'd seen him, kicking about with the other kids. But he looked like a child again when he turned his worried face to Mary.

'The blast?' said Anny. 'Do you mean the blast?'

'Yes, the accident at the furnace.'

'That was no accident,' said Anny. 'That was King's fault.'

'Well, no. I mean, yes. That's what they say. That's what I say. That's why I left King's employ.'

'Really?'

'I couldna stand to line the man's pockets after that. I'm a collier now. Different master.'

'What's it like, down the mine?'

'Oh, you dunna wanna know about that,' said Peter.

'I do,' said Anny.

Mary appeared, carrying over a tray with a steaming bowl. 'Here's your soup. Come now, Peter. You'll tire Anny out with all this chit-chat. Let me feed her now. Fetch that extra pillow, will you, lad?'

Mary helped her sit up a little and spooned the soup into her mouth. It was good to taste good food. Life came down to simple things like this. Simple, good things.

'Thank you,' she said to Mary, when they were done.

'You're very welcome,' she replied, standing up to return the bowl to the table. Peter was sitting by the fire, reading a book. Mary pottered around the table. Anny closed her eyes and listened to the comforting sound of a mother's tasks at day's end.

'Mrs Malone,' she said and opened her eyes. 'Where is my mother?'

Rachel was sent for and came the next day, a Sunday. There were many tears and kisses and hugs and hand-holding, much of which had been banned by the prison, of course. Anny noticed Peter watching them with shining eyes, an emotional young man. Mother looked like an angel to Anny, but after talking with her for a while, she could see that her mother's face was drawn and she had black shadows of exhaustion beneath her eyes.

'I shall come home with you today, Mother. I shall help you at home. I'm never leaving you again. I want to stay with you always, just the two of us.'

'Oh, my dear lass. Dunna say such things. You have had a bad time. But you will rally and then you will make your own life.'

'No,' said Anny strongly, hauling herself to sit up. 'No, I won't. I don't want any part of it. Any of it. I just want to be with you.'

'Dunna upset yourself, Anny, please,' said her mother and soothed her, stroking her hand and easing her back down on the pillows. 'You mun rest. You mun get well. Mary wants to nurse you back to health and I will visit when I can.'

Anny glanced over at Mary, who was whipping up cake batter with a wooden spoon, wafts of sweetness filling the little house. Anny whispered, 'They are very kind and I am so grateful. But I should come home with you, to my own home.'

Mother looked down and shook her head. 'It is not what you think, Anny. It is a bad place, in a bad part of town. I lost our home after Father died, as I couldna pay the rent. They say King will pay compensation to the families but it's not come yet and it was too late for me. I had to find any place I could afford on my earnings and it inna good. I'm working all hours, washing at home and I do a bit of picking at the pit too. I canna look after you, lass. You are much better off here, until you are strong.'

Anny saw the shame in her mother's eyes. The old rage swelled in her at the mention of King. But she had not the strength or appetite for railing against her foe. She only wanted to comfort her mother. 'If that's what you think is best, then that's what we shall do. I shall be strong again, you'll see. And then there'll be two wages coming in and we'll get you out of there and into a good home again. Don't you fret, Mother. We shall do it together, you and I.'

Her mother left. She wouldn't stay for cake, as she had to get back to work. Anny was despondent after. She turned on her side and stared at the wall for a long time. Peter brought her a slice of seed cake, warm from baking. He sat with her and they ate their cake in silence. She felt comfortable sitting there, not talking. It was curious how awkward that felt with some people. But Mary and Peter were comfortable people and they didn't seem to expect anything from her.

'Could you tell me about the mine?' she asked him.

'If it would entertain you,' he said with a small smile. 'Though heaven knows why it should.'

'It would.' She wanted to hear about something completely different, something that was not about iron, or prison, or family, or love. Something safe to listen to.

'The pay is all right. There are worser jobs. I like the work very well. There are old lads and young chappers and plenty of chunnering on about life.'

'Tell me what it's like, underground. So I can picture it.'

'It's a rum old world down there,' he began. She watched him stare into space as he conjured it in his mind. 'When we descend the shaft, we're lowered down on chains and each hold a candle, a bunch of us like a catch of fish. The chain has broken in many a pit and sometimes a man can fall down the shaft and be killed. We strip off to work and put our clothes back on before we come up. The shadows flicker across the black walls and can haunt you a little at first. You think of all the weight of the world above you and what if it comes crashing down upon your head? But you have to have faith that it wonna or you'd lose your mind down there. Once you get used to it, there is a peace to be had in the dark, a kind of understanding between you and the deep earth.'

He's a born storyteller, Anny thought. It must come from the books he read by the fire or maybe it was just him, a natural talent. 'You're wasted down there,' she said.

He looked up and stared at her, his cheeks colouring. 'Oh, I dunna think so. I'm strong and I work hard for them.'

'I mean, you speak so well. You ought to be ...' She trailed off and thought of all the things that Peter Malone could do in the world, with his gift for speaking, his turn of phrase, his reading. Another reader, like her. His mother must have had hopes for him, to teach him that. But Anny realised she was doing it again, aspiring. And she knew what came of that.

'Ought to be what?' he said and leant forward, his eyes intense with interest.

'Exactly what you are,' said Anny, and smiled at him. He beamed at her. She liked him very much already. How had she not noticed what a nice lad he was, when he was living on her very doorstep all those years? He was everything that Jake Ashford was not – honest, hard-working and humble. And a poet too, in his way.

'Anny, I'd like to say that your father . . . well, he was a good mon, a rare mon, decent through and through. Everybody thought it, everybody said it. It was a terrible day when he left the earth, when all of them did. But he was the best of them, the best of men.'

Anny looked at Peter, moved and grateful. She had been so alone in her grieving, so alone. She let her tears come and he waited for her to cry it out. He didn't try to stop her and he didn't try to comfort her. His quiet, patient presence there was comfort enough and some- how he knew that.

They talked into the evening, Mary scolding her son for not letting Anny rest. And in the days that followed, when he came back from the mine, Anny would insist on wrapping her shawl about her and going outside to throw scraps for the pig, to give him the privacy to have his tin bath by the fire. She thought of him there, scrub- bing the black dust from his skin, only to suffer it all again the following day. She was getting stronger by the day and it wouldn't be long before she could join her mother. Yet Mary and Peter seemed in no hurry to shift her and told her to stay as long as she needed. It was company for Mary during the day and Peter said earnestly that she should stay as long as she ever wanted. Anny believed them. They were truly good people and they were fond of her, very fond. And she felt the same for them, increasingly so. But Mother needed her, and one day she would need to leave this comfortable house and go back out into the world, face whatever it might throw at her and begin again.

She carried inside her the shame of gaol, despite her innocence of the crime. It had tainted her through and through; like contagion seeping into a lake, it spread through her and reached every part of her. From a practical viewpoint, it had ruined her chance of a clerical job and a better life.

She thought of the day Peggy came to her house, dressed up in her cousin's clothes. She realised she had done the same all those years working at the office. None of it had been real, though she had heartily believed in it at the time. The forces of society did not want the poor girl to rise above her origins – it smashed that nonsense down with an iron fist. She thought of her father, his years of toil. And for what? To line King's pockets? No, it was more than that. It was for her and her mother. That's what it was for. And it was worth it, to provide a home and put food on the table. It was noble, it was good and it was enough.

As her health returned and her hair shone red again, she could feel the life coursing through her. She was luminous with it; she knew that as Peter Malone could not take his eyes from her, or she from him. When Mother visited, she looked as tired as ever, but her spirit was buoyed by her daughter's rejuvenation and she always left smiling. She told Anny, 'Each new day is a gift.' Anny thought about this, about her darkest days these past months. She told Peter all about it, when Mary was asleep, in their long winter evenings by the fire, discussing books and thoughts and their lives to this point. Things about prison that she knew she would never tell her mother; but she felt she could tell him anything. They even spoke of the future, of what it might hold for them. They began to talk of a shared future, hinting at it, knowing yet shy looks across the dancing light of the hearth.

Her shame of her prison time was receding with each footstep she took towards her recovery, replaced by a growing pride that she had survived it. She hated the Kings, to be sure, and that would never leave her. But the best revenge was to survive, to live and to love. To stay with her people and work hard with them and for them. Her people were the best in the world, hands down. The upper classes could keep their fancy clothes and their silly lives. Never again would she aspire to be like them. Never again would she try to play their game. There was release to be had when you let go of those tethers, of aspiration, of wanting and of envy. She had been bound by it, and worse: she had known true imprisonment. Now, she had been handed her freedom, the raw material out of which a life could be crafted. What would she make of it? Despite everything that had been lost, her future was in her own hands and that was good enough for Anny Woodvine.

Epilogue

Queenie sat alone in the library. She placed her hands on the table and brushed her fingers across the cover of a French novel that Margaret had left there months before and nobody had thought to tidy away. *She will miss her books*, thought Queenie. She wondered how her granddaughter was faring. There had been no word. For such a quiet girl, it was curious how empty the house seemed without her presence. The house felt haunted by too much absence now. Cyril was still away in Germany. Some of the younger servants had left the King employ after the explosion. With no young people around, the house felt empty. It was like Hamelin, after the piper had exacted his revenge.

Queenie shuddered. The curse on the house. It was coming true, she was sure of it. First the blast, and now Margaret gone. But these things were not random occurrences, unlucky events. These things had reasons, they had fault. The men of this house were to blame. Her grandson interfered with that Woodvine girl, which set off a chain reaction of events that led to Margaret running away and ruining her life. Her son scrimped on the furnace expenses and caused an appalling tragedy, that left a seething hostility towards the King name in the town and far beyond. Son and grandson acted entirely through their own stupid selfishness. These men carelessly smashed their way through people's lives like a beater on a pheasant shoot. They'd destroyed the lives of these two women, and who knew how many more? Her husband had been their model, his own vicious nature leaving victims strewn in its wake. How many more vengeful spirits like Betsy Blaize would turn up at the graveyard seeking recompense? This time, the Woodvines had paid the dearest price, but the Kings would pay too. She feared now a feud would grow from this, a hatred that could last years, generations even. She would not blame them. The men of this house were like a canker that would one day fell the family tree.

But not if she could help it. She sat upright and steeled herself. She'd said she would take back the reins, yet Margaret's loss had taken the wind from her sails. But, no more. This simply would not do, sitting here feeling sorry for herself, feeling powerless. Yes, it was the King men that had brought things to this pass, but she herself had allowed them to happen, through her own weakness and lack of vigilance. She stood up and resolved to walk that day, to walk every day. She vowed to regain her strength through vigorous daily exercise and to regain her mind through clarity of purpose and thought. She left the library and passed across the hall. If Jenkins had seen her, she would have instructed her to put on her fur-lined cloak, hat and leather gloves. But she did not wish to cosset herself. She wished to feel the cold sharpen up her bones and wake her from this years-long stupor she had allowed herself to fall into like an enchantment, like a drug. Well, now she was awake and no handsome prince's tender kiss had been needed. She'd kicked herself awake, and now she was going to kick this forsaken family into shape. She ignored the closet with her outdoor garb in it and crossed the garden room, leaving the house through the glass door. She would take a turn about the grounds and work out a plan of action.

The February air was bitter. The hour was later than she had realised and a grey gloaming was falling, the sky darkening. Queenie watched her breath blow puffs like a chilly steam engine and walked onwards, skirting the house and heading for the herb garden, her favourite part of the grounds. The beds were largely bare, the twiggy remnants of summer lushness stark and dead around her. She marched onwards and with each ten steps forward she listed her recent triumphs to warm herself. The day after Margaret had left, she had met with Brotherton and Pritchard. They agreed to write off the furnace part of the ironworks for good. There had been talk of rebuilding, but it was hopeless. The furnace was already inefficient before it blew and the town would not send its men to work at a King furnace again. The forge, however, was doing well and so were the rolling mill and the foundry. Yet there was talk that iron in this area was on its way out. So she would diversify – buy up other businesses, perhaps a brickworks or shares in a mine. That was where the future lay. She made Brotherton and Pritchard into partners and met with them daily to secure the recovery of the King fortunes. Soon, they would pay some reparation to the families of the dead and injured, but only a small amount, enough not to be insulting and not too much to damage the ironworks' profits. In the spring, once the business was back on its feet, she would send for Cyril and instruct the partners to train him up properly in the business. This would circumvent her useless son completely. There, that was that sorted.

As to Margaret, she thought about ways to find her and bring her back into the fold. She thought of hiring men who could follow her trail and track her down, a constable or suchlike who could do with the extra cash. But the more she plotted this, the more she disliked the idea. Yes, her granddaughter should be here to take up her rightful place in the King family. But what if she were happy? Did happiness matter? She realised that the first emotion she'd felt when told of her granddaughter's elopement was envy. Actually, she was glad that Margaret has escaped. She wished she'd had the nerve to do the same all those years ago when they married her off so young. Margaret had escaped the King family. Others had, too. The Woodvine girl, despite her terrible losses along the way, had been lucky to escape its grip and was free now. That servant Arnett had escaped, with a good settlement and reference and no more interference from the Kings. Even that innocent child – the baby on the bridge – she imagined had been blessed by escaping from the Kings. Yes, it was a lucky child that escaped the King family.

She stopped walking. She had walked right through the herb garden and, without noticing, had turned back towards the graveyard, so caught up in her plans she had been. She was penetratingly cold now, her teeth chattering, her bones aching. It was nearly dark and the fog of confusion began to descend in her mind. She fought to clear it.

'No,' she said aloud. 'No, I will not allow it. I am Alice King and I am the queen of this castle.'

'Your castle walls will fall,' said a voice.

Queenie gasped and looked up. There, beside her husband's grave, stood again the ghost of Betsy Blaize, the maid her husband had raped from the age of twelve till she fell pregnant with his baseborn child at fifteen and who had died on the iron bridge at the tender age of sixteen. Her eyes burned bluer than ever and her long, luxurious white hair flowed over her shoulders like an avalanche.

'Blaize!' she gasped, her hands shaking from fear and the cold. 'I am sorry. I should have stopped it. I should have done more. Forgive me, Betsy. Oh, I beg you to forgive me.'

The spirit spoke again. 'Dark times are ahead. The crucible will purify. The house will fall.'

Queenie dropped to her knees and sobbed. She could not feel her fingers now or the skin on her face, so numbed were they with nightfall and haunting.

'I have done good deeds. I have helped others more lowly than ourselves. I have made reparation. Is this not enough? What can I do? Tell me what I can do to save ourselves.'

Then, she felt a curious sensation in that frigid place: a hot waft of air enveloped her. She looked up and the ghost was leaning down towards her, breathing warmth across her face and hands, which tingled now with life. The ghost was smiling curiously at her, then spoke once more.

'After the fire, I will come again. A baby will bridge the divide.'

Queenie hid her face in her hands to escape the spirit's gaze. She felt the cold deep in her bones and wondered how long she had been sitting by the graveside. Time seemed to have lost its meaning, as frozen as the hard ground beneath her. At the crunching sound of footsteps, she slowly turned her head to see Jenkins approaching. The ghost was nowhere to be seen.

Jenkins helped her to her feet and they began the slow trudge back to the house.

'The baby, the baby on the bridge,' Queenie was muttering.

'What are you doing, you mad old bat?' said Jenkins. 'It's black as your grandfather's hat out here.'

Queenie peered at her maid, right in the eye. 'Jenkins, where have you been? I could have died for all you care!'

'Hush your noise, woman. You'll outlive us all.'

Then there came a sound, a breathy whisper behind that made Queenie turn and look back. The ghost was still there, watching her with accusing eyes. Then it turned, took one long look at the resting place of Ralph King senior and faded from the night, leaving Queenie shivering in the gathering gloom.

Acknowledgements

The Royal Literary Fund, whose award of a grant and fellowship has saved me and means I can write these books in peace. I will be forever grateful. A particular thanks to Eileen Gunn and Steve Cook of the RLF, for coming to see me and supporting my applications throughout.

Shroppiemon, founder and administrator of the hugely popular Facebook group Memories of Shropshire, dialect master and number one research support of this book during its writing. He has always been on hand for questions concerning dialect and local history, as well as reading in detail the final draft and offering reams of helpful advice. Couldn't have done it without you, mon.

Stephen Dewhirst, of the Broseley Local History Society, for essential information on ironworks in the 1830s. Also, huge thanks for reading the final draft and offering such useful advice on a range of issues.

Pete Jackson, for all things pertaining to Cinderloo.

Geoff Fletcher, for detailed and fascinating help on a range of Shropshire issues, such as providing photos, information on an 1801 walking tour of the area, family history and dialect.

All the members and administrators of the various Shropshire Facebook groups who kindly let me join, for generously giving great advice on dialect and local history, as well as recommending resources:

- Memories of Shropshire
- Shropshire Tales, History and Memories
- Telford Memories
- Ironbridge and Coalbrookdale pictures
- Ironbridge ♥ through the Dale Yesteryear

Nicholas Feeney, for information on local history.

Sarah Davis of the Shropshire archives, for particular help about Shrewsbury Prison rules.

Toby Neal of the Shropshire Star, for dialect help.

Rita Rich-Mulcahy, for helpful advice on the local accent and dialect for the audiobook.

Staff at the range of Ironbridge Gorge Museums, for invaluable information on the area and its history, who do a fantastic job of keeping that history alive.

Joanne Smith, Museum Registrar at the Ironbridge Gorge Museum Trust, for book recommendations and useful contacts.

Kerry Hadley, for advice on Black Country matters and a variety of other matters, professional and personal, including making me snort with laughter on a regular basis.

Early readers – Lucy Adams, Lynn Downing, Kathy Kendall, Pauline Lancaster, Louisa Treger and Sue White – for reading with such speed and enthusiasm, giving me confidence to carry on with my first foray into saga.

My dear brother Jon Chadwick and his lovely wife Pauline, for hosting and looking after Poppy and me during our many research visits to the Ironbridge area.

My agent Laura Macdougall, for the brilliant idea of suggesting saga in the first place and for always being there for me; the best agent this novelist can imagine. Also gratitude to all at United Agents for support and help.

My editor Tara Loder, for believing in this story from day one, for coming all the way to my kitchen table to discuss character arcs and for superlative editing, honing this tale into the novel it is today.

Everyone at Bonnier – special mentions to Sarah Bauer, Katie Lumsden, Eleanor Dryden, Sahina Bibi, Imogen Sebba, Felice McKeown, Ellen Turner and Kate Parkin – for making me so welcome and providing brilliant support throughout the writing, editing and publicity process.

Book bloggers, readers, reviewers and booksellers, for continued support in my writing career, sticking with me through the transition from Mascull to Walton and championing anything I write. I am so grateful to you all.

Tim Marchant, web designer, for creating wonderful Mollie Walton and Rebecca Mascull websites, which are even more gorgeous than I envisioned.

Sasha Drennan and Gill Hart at Lindum Books in Lincoln, for supporting this writer in everything she writes – whatever my name or genre! – and providing friendship and chats. And always stocking my books on your lovely shelves.

My author friends, those in and out of various collectives, such as my dear and original Prime Writers, and newer groups to me like the Savvies, the Loungers, the Romantic Novelists' Association and the Saga Girls – you have kept me sane, educated me and kept me smiling. Special thanks to Kerry Drewery, as ever.

All my Facebook mates, for indulging my penchant for cat videos and edgy humour.

My friends and family, for keeping me going with advice, hugs, childcare and other invaluable resources during the writing of this book.

Vanessa Lafaye, who cheered with me when I got this book contract, yet left us too soon to read it. You were my beta reader extraordinaire and my beloved friend. I miss you, darling.

Colin Miles, for loitering, laughs and love.

Poppy, my darling daughter, for making it so easy, every day, in every way, to be your mother.

Dear Readers,

In the summer of 2016, I took my daughter to visit my brother and his wife in Shropshire. I'd never been to the county and knew nothing about it. All I remembered was an old friend of mine from university days saying she'd been to Ironbridge, how it was the first iron bridge ever built and that the area was the cradle of the industrial revolution. She also said it was beautiful there. I recalled thinking, how can something be industrial *and* beautiful? We arrived in Ironbridge and took a walk up to its main attraction, the glorious iron bridge itself, spanning the River Severn. We walked to the centre of the bridge and I looked down through the iron bars at the slow-moving river below. And then it happened.

It's what I like to call the 'history shivers'. This isn't a phrase I created; I've heard writers and history enthusiasts use it when you experience something that really takes you back to a past age. I felt it when I saw the Brontë sisters' writing table at their home in Haworth. And I felt it that day, standing on the iron bridge. I suddenly had a vision of how the river must have looked two hundred years before, flanked by all manner of burning, smoking industry, fed by the workers and masters who fuelled it, sending goods out into the rest of the world along the river and roads, the canals and railways. All that was gone now, but the remnants remained, overgrown by the beauty of nature. My friend had been right.

Just weeks before, my literary agent Laura had brilliantly suggested a brand new idea to me: writing a saga trilogy. She wanted me to come up with an idea for a story – families, industry, a beautiful yet industrial setting, conflict and drama. Standing on the bridge, I knew this was the place. Looking at both sides of the river, I realised I had my two families: one of poor workers, the other of rich masters. I had my setting, my characters, my conflict and drama all built in, just by gazing down from the bridge. I was itching to start writing! We visited some of the many museums of the area and everything I looked at took on a new meaning: this was where my two families lived and worked; this is what they ate and how they dressed and where they travelled to and so on. I took dozens of photos, bought a lot of books and postcards and started filling a notebook with ideas. The two families sprang almost fully formed into my head: the masters lived in a house on the top of the hill, looking down on everybody below. The workers lived in the ramshackle cottages that grew along the river when industry took hold.

When I got home, I sketched out a family tree, then, by researching common names of Shropshire, I was able to fill in the blanks. I had my Woodvines and my Kings, my two daughters, their secret friendship and the troubles that awaited them. I planned out their lives over forty years, over three generations and three books, all mysteriously linked by a baby found on the bridge . . .

I went back to the area several times, visiting other important sites, such as the ruins of the Bedlam Furnaces, the Coalbrookdale Museum of Iron and the Dana, otherwise known as Shrewsbury Prison. I fell in love with the area and with my characters, Anny and Margaret. My agent was delighted with the whole project too. When my publisher took on the saga trilogy, I found my editor Tara, who loved these girls and their story as much as I did. We talked about them always as if they were real people! We cared deeply what happened to them; we felt bad when we put them through hard times and cheered them on when they battled against adversity. Such is the stuff of saga! I hope you love them as much as we do.

Best wishes,
Mollie

Glossary of Shropshire Dialect Terms

Definitions have been collated from experts in dialect, such as Shroppiemon (see Acknowledgements) and also the Shropshire Word Book by Georgina Frederica Jackson, published 1879.

All round the Wrekin: taking too long to get to the point
Anna: haven't
Babby: baby
Bait: food, a meal
Big-sorted: proud, stuck-up
Blethering: talking too much
Canna: can't
Chappers: lads
Chillun: children
Chunnering: chatting
Clemmed: hungry, famished
Darksome: gloomy, melancholy, sad
Darter: daughter
Didna: did not
Drodsome: dreadful, alarming
Dunna: don't
Earywig: earwig
Fadder: father
Frit: frightened

From off: from outside the local area

Gunna: going to

Hadna: had not

Hobbety-hoy: a youth or adolescent

Inna: isn't

Lungeous: spiteful

Mon: man, often used as a term of address to males

Mun: must

Ow bist?: How are you?

Ow bist thee fairing?: How are you doing? How are you managing?

Proper jam: lovely; really good.

Shoosby: Shrewsbury

Shoulda: should have

Shouldna: should not/should not have

Summat: something

Trow: a cargo boat used to transport goods

Wanna: want to

Wench: used for a young woman in a similar way to 'lass' and is in no way derogatory to females. See the *Shropshire Word Book* definition: 'a young girl, or young woman, of peasant rank, to whom it is applied in no unworthy sense – the good old word maintaining its respectability.'

Wonna: won't

Wouldna: would not have

Rachel Woodvine's Fidget Pie

This recipe makes a traditional Shropshire fidget pie, just like Rachel Woodvine makes for her husband John and her daughter Anny to take to work for their lunch. A slice of a fidget pie is delicious and filling.

You will need

For the pastry:
500g plain flour
1tbsp salt
140g lard, diced
200ml water
2 tbsp butter, for greasing
1 egg, beaten

For the filling:
300g ham or gammon, diced
2 onions, peeled and diced
3 large apples, peeled and diced
3 large potatoes, peeled and diced
100ml cider
50ml milk
2 tbsp plain flour
2–3 tbsp soft brown sugar
1 tsp black pepper
1 tsp dried sage
1 tsp salt

Method:

1. Pre-heat the oven to 200°C/180°C fan/gas mark 6.
2. Mix together the flour and salt in a large bowl.
3. Heat the lard and water in a saucepan, until the water is simmering and the lard melted. Pour the hot liquid into the bowl with the flour.
4. Stir with a wooden spoon, then turn out onto a floured surface and knead to form a soft dough. Cover and set aside.
5. In a separate bowl, mix the ham, onions, apples and potatoes together. Add the cider, milk and flour, then the salt, pepper, sugar and sage. Mix together well.
6. Grease a cake tin (approximately 22cm) with butter.
7. Roll out two thirds of the pastry dough made earlier onto a floured surface, in a large circle. Line the cake tin with the pastry, letting it overlap the rim a little.
8. Roll out the remaining third of the pastry to make a lid large enough to cover the pie. Set this to one side.
9. Put the filling into the pie case, packing it tightly down.
10. Brush the pastry's edges with beaten egg, then cover with the lid. Crimp the edges together, then brush the whole lid with beaten egg.
11. Bake in the oven for an hour, then turn off the heat and leave in the oven for another half hour before removing.
12. Enjoy!

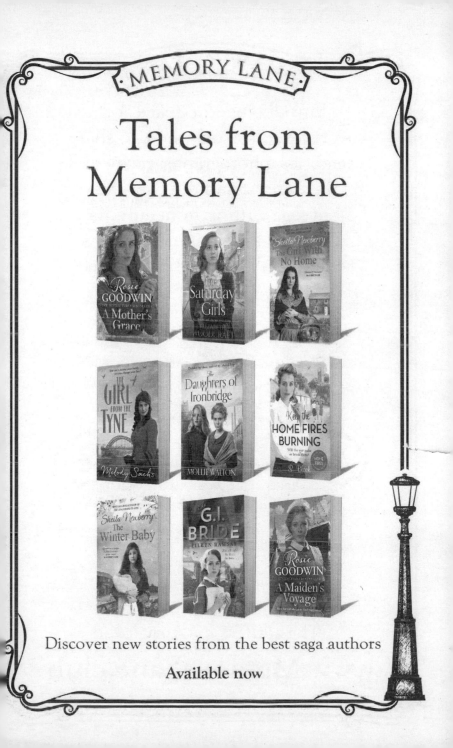

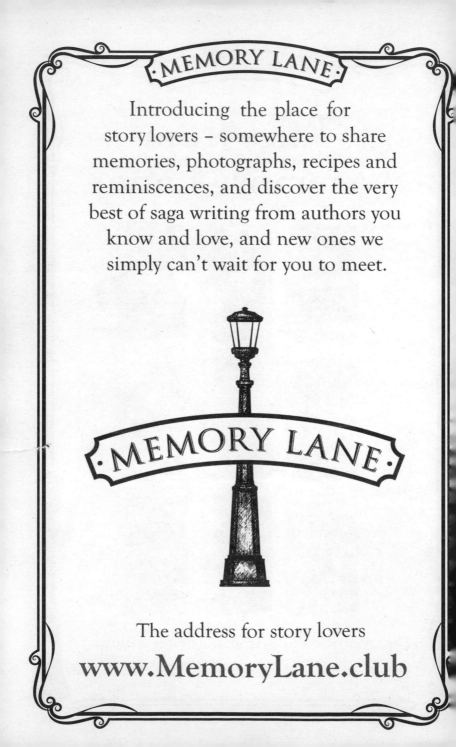